FEAR OF THE DARK

The Doctor Who *50th Anniversary Collection*

Ten Little Aliens
Stephen Cole

Dreams of Empire
Justin Richards

Last of the Gaderene
Mark Gatiss

Festival of Death
Jonathan Morris

Fear of the Dark
Trevor Baxendale

Players
Terrance Dicks

Remembrance of the Daleks
Ben Aaronovitch

EarthWorld
Jacqueline Rayner

Only Human
Gareth Roberts

Beautiful Chaos
Gary Russell

The Silent Stars Go By
Dan Abnett

DOCTOR WHO

FEAR OF THE DARK

TREVOR BAXENDALE

BBC
BOOKS

3 5 7 9 10 8 6 4 2

First published in 2003 by BBC Worldwide Ltd.
This edition published in 2013 by BBC Books, an imprint of Ebury Publishing.
A Random House Group Company

Doctor Who is a BBC Wales production for BBC One.
Executive producers: Steven Moffat and Caroline Skinner

The Random House Group Limited Reg. No. 954009
Addresses for companies within the Random House Group can be found at
www.randomhouse.co.uk

A CIP catalogue record for this book is available from the British Library.

ISBN 978 1 849 90522 0

The Random House Group Limited supports The Forest Stewardship
Council® (FSC®), the leading international forest-certification organisation.
Our books carrying the FSC label are printed on FSC®-certified paper. FSC is
the only forest-certification scheme supported by the leading environmental
organisations, including Greenpeace. Our paper procurement policy can be
found at www.randomhouse.co.uk/environment

Editorial director: Albert DePetrillo
Editorial manager: Nicholas Payne
Series consultant: Justin Richards
Project editor: Steve Tribe
Cover design: Two Associates © Woodlands Books Ltd, 2012
Production: Alex Goddard

Printed and bound in Great Britain by Clays Ltd, St Ives plc

To buy books by your favourite authors and register for offers,
visit www.randomhouse.co.uk

INTRODUCTION

It's always an honour to write a *Doctor Who* book; it's an even greater honour to have it revisited for the programme's 50th Anniversary celebrations.

Fear of the Dark was an unexpectedly personal novel. Until this book, I had written exclusively for BBC Books' then current Eighth Doctor range. Those books were taking the series forward at a time when it was no longer on TV. It's almost impossible to believe it was ever actually off TV now.

So *Fear of the Dark*, starring the Fifth Doctor, was my first 'past Doctor' book. I don't really have a favourite Doctor – it usually depends who I'm watching at the time – but most people have a soft spot for the Doctor they saw first, often as a child. I grew up with Jon Pertwee and Tom Baker as the Doctor, but Peter Davison's Doctor was just as special to me: he was the first Doctor I watched as a grown-up (as I liked to think of myself then...), and my critical faculties were in full flow. The stories, the scripts, special effects, companions – all fell under my unforgiving and supercritical gaze.

But I could never find fault with the Fifth Doctor himself.

Youthful, energetic, courageous, trainer-wearing, cricket-loving, quietly clever, unfailingly polite, and – above all – *fallible*.

This Doctor made mistakes. Not everything went his way. Sometimes he was just plain unlucky. But he never gave up, never gave in, and held fast to what he believed in.

He had all the best attributes of the Doctor, but he was also vulnerable. There was a charming humanity to the Fifth Doctor that has never been replicated.

In other words, he was a hero. And I loved writing for him. There was a fantastic sense of joy and privilege, to be returning to this hero and his friends and times and inventing new problems for him to solve and new enemies to overcome.

The Fifth Doctor had already been tested by the best: Cybermen, Daleks, Silurians and Sea Devils, Omega, the Master – even the Black Guardian, for goodness' sake – had taken him on and lost, so I had to come up with a new challenge. Something that would allow the best of this Doctor to shine. Often, in the TV series, he would come up against some of the bleakest and meanest of worlds: mercenaries and machine guns, voracious corporations, cold-war computers – and they were just the product of human beings. Our most 'human' of Doctors was often faced with our species at its most *inhuman*. How painful, how depressing, how cruel that must have seemed – to always be so very, very far away from a game of cricket on a sunny afternoon.

But the Fifth Doctor stands out brightly in a glut of harsh, unforgiving futures, and never more so when battling against the violent and the extreme.

And so I decided to take him back into just such an environment, as far from civilisation and cricket and a nice cup of tea as it's possible to get; an absolute hell for him, in fact, where lives are lost in appalling fashion, where the humans are fighting for their lives and willing to do anything to survive, where the monsters are implacable, savage and unknowably alien. Where the Doctor must finally stand toe to toe with death itself: the great unknown, the lurker in the dark.

To be truthful, our dear old Doctor quite goes through the mill in *Fear of the Dark*. It was deliberate. I wanted to take this most vulnerable of heroes to breaking point – and beyond. To take away those tiny little nuggets of humanity that he craves, to remove his options and his hopes, and to bring him physically, and metaphorically, to his knees.

Of course, he takes his friends with him: the Fifth Doctor's very best companions, Tegan and Nyssa. Tegan was the brash, no-nonsense Australian air hostess, and Nyssa was the quiet, contemplative young scientist from the peace-loving alien world of Traken. Both had known tragedy. Both were travelling with the Doctor by choice. Both would be tested in *Fear of the Dark* along with their friend. There would be no hiding places on the blighted moon of Akoshemon.

Then there is the supporting cast: Jyl Stoker, the no-nonsense leader of the humans, trying to hold her team together as disaster strikes; Bunny Cheung, big, powerful, but soft-hearted; Vega Jaal, the gloomy alien mining expert (take a look at Vega Nexos in *The Monster of Peladon* if you want to know what one of his species looks like), the ancient scientist Ravus Oldeman, Captain Lawrence, Silus Cadwell and the crew of the *Adamantium*… these were all characters who became people to me as I wrote the book, who did what I thought was impossible: to surprise me, to make unexpected decisions, to affect the story as I wrote it. The plot is always paramount, but these characters, these people, felt unnervingly real to me. There's even a love story in there.

Looking back on *Fear of the Dark* now, two things immediately strike me: how proud I am to have written this story for the Fifth Doctor, and, blimey, how small the print was. Maybe I'm just getting old, but in the original paperback version the type size is *tiny*. The word count must have been huge, though I didn't notice it at the time. I must have really enjoyed writing it.

There was a problem with the original cover: the design I'd requested was for a plain black cover, and a simple, monochrome image of the Doctor's face, with one side slightly shadowed but visibly that of a skull. It looked very striking on the proof copy – but on the final version the Doctor's face was too much in shadow and the skull became an almost subliminal presence. Some people have told me they preferred it that way, and I think I can see why: the Doctor's face is almost consumed by shadow, and rightly so. The Dark takes no prisoners.

Ah yes… the Dark.

If you're still reading this then you may notice that I haven't said anything about the monster in this novel – and that is deliberate.

I'm not going to give you any details about that now: you should discover it for yourself, like many of the characters in the story, alone and in the dark, moment by horrific moment…

Trevor Baxendale
August 2012

For Martine, Luke and Konnie –
three very bright lights in the darkness

PROLOGUE

Every dream exists on the precipice of nightmare. Nowhere else but in the subconscious is the divide between comfort and horror so narrow, and so fragile. It is almost as if a dream is just waiting to be toppled, its hopes dashed, its promises broken.

Nyssa sometimes dreamed of Traken, but the dream always tipped over into nightmare.

And the nightmare always ended the same way: she would be hurrying through the gardens and cloisters, calling for her parents, warning them of the disaster she knew was coming. But no one could hear her.

Worst of all, she couldn't even find her parents.

In her dreams, her mother was still there, a half-remembered face made dear by the imagination. But in the nightmare, Nyssa couldn't find her. She ran and ran, and searched every secret garden and grove, all the while knowing that time was running out.

Her father had disappeared too. In his study sat a man with a dark beard and even darker eyes. He would laugh at her when she arrived, breathless and soundless, at the very moment Traken vanished from the heavens.

And she saw *that* as if from a distance, the whole planet fading away into the awful blackness of space as if it had never existed.

Nyssa woke up, breathing raggedly, the bed sheets tight around her sweating body. She was shivering, although it wasn't cold. It was dark, but she had her eyes shut anyway. There was something nagging at her memory, something she had read in one of the books in the TARDIS library. Nyssa usually stuck to the extensive science journals and textbooks, but she had come across this slender, dusty volume of Earth poetry wedged between *Wisden's Almanack* and *A Brief History of Time* only a few days ago. It said 'Keats' on the spine, and it had fallen open on a page where two lines had been circled in green ink:

> *The thought,*
> *The deadly thought of solitude.*

For some reason it had stuck in her mind, and now she realised why. When Traken was erased from the cosmos, it had left her the sole remaining person from that world in existence.

She had felt so very alone.

She felt alone now, sitting on her bed in the dark, listening to the hum of the TARDIS around her. With nothing else to distract her, she was able to concentrate on that noise: the soft reverberation of distant, mysterious engines powering the vessel through the space-time vortex. If she listened carefully, she could imagine that the engines were made quiet only by distance, that the almost subliminal hum was just the final echo of massive, churning machinery. Somewhere deep in the TARDIS, its ancient dynamos thundered with terrific, unending exertion. Nyssa found the image quite disturbing.

Only then did she realise that normally, on her waking, the TARDIS would automatically activate the lights in her room. Softly at first, gradually increasing the lambency as she threw off sleep. But now it was pitch black. She couldn't see a thing. And yet she had the feeling, growing in intensity, that she was not alone.

'Is there anybody there?' she heard herself asking plaintively.

There was no reply. Nyssa pulled her knees up and wrapped the sheets around her more tightly. She peered into the gloom, hoping that perhaps her eyes would soon grow a little more used to the dark and she might be able to see something. Her ears strained to pick up the slightest sound, but all she could hear was her own heartbeat and the deep, alien breath of the TARDIS.

'Wh-where are you?' she asked the darkness. There was no reply.

Nyssa immediately decided that she had imagined a half-formed phantom left over from her dream of Traken. The perspiration was cold on the exposed skin of her back now, and she felt a droplet trickle down her spine like an icy caress.

Why wouldn't the lights come on? Perhaps the TARDIS had malfunctioned; it wouldn't be the first time.

Her eyes were indeed now more accustomed to the blackness. She could just make out the bedclothes in front of her as a dull grey rectangle in the gloom. Staring, Nyssa picked out the edge of the bed itself, although beyond it there was nothing but the dark. It was exactly the same darkness that Traken had left in its place. Nyssa experienced a nauseating sense of peering into an abyss; of her bed floating like a miniature island in an ocean of night.

And then she saw it.

At first it was just a smudge of black against the greyness that marked the end of her bed. Then it inserted itself like a dark finger into the sheet, plucking at the material as it was dragged along the edge of the mattress.

Nyssa stopped breathing. But she could hear a low, rasping susurration in the air around her. There *was* something in her room with her. Something that breathed.

Rigid with fear, she watched the finger of blackness spread out into something the size of a hand. Then it started up the bed towards her, expanding like a dark stain across the bedclothes.

She cringed as the darkness approached, convinced it would feel cold and wet to the touch. And as the blemish crept up towards her, so the shadows gathered around her, above her, behind her.

Soon she would be submerged in the blackness.

She opened her mouth to cry out, to call for the Doctor and Tegan. But at the last moment she halted, frozen by the sudden, sickening fear that her voice would be as silent as it was in her Traken nightmare.

The darkness rose up and engulfed her like a shroud. The loss of vision was so absolute that, for a long moment, Nyssa thought that her eyes had been taken from her.

She sat, blind and paralysed with fear.
Then something in the darkness touched her.

MESSAGE STARTS

'OK, sweetheart, you can start talking now.'

'Is it on?'

'Yes, it's running. You can talk to Daddy now.'

'Will he hear me?'

'Sure he will. When this gets to him. It'll take a little time, it's got to go a long, long way.'

'How far?'

'To the edge of the galaxy.'

'What if it goes too far and falls off the edge of the gaxaly?'

'Galaxy, not *gaxaly*! Now speak up and Daddy will be able to listen to your message later.'

'OK. Now? OK. Hi Daddy. It's Rosie. Mummy says you'll see me on your viewer when you get this. She says I can talk to you later, too. And then you'll be able to talk back. That will be better, because I want to ask you some things. I've been having bad dreams at night again. Last night I dreamed a bear and a lion were chasing me and I was scared. Is it silly to be scared of dreams? Mummy lets me sleep in her bed at night but it's still dark. I don't like it when it's dark. Mummy says there are no bears or lions here but how can you tell if it's so dark? Mummy says you work in caves where it's dark all the time and you're not scared one bit. Is that right? How come you're not scared? What if a bear or a lion comes? Please come home soon, Daddy. I don't like it when you're away. Neither does Kooka. His arm's come loose again. Mummy says it's going to drop right off soon, so you'd better come back home and fix it real quick. I'm out of

5

time now so I've got to say bye. Oh, but Daddy, be careful you don't fall off the edge of the gaxaly. We miss you. Bye.'

MESSAGE ENDS

PART ONE
INTO THE VOID

Thoughts are but dreams till their effects be tried
William Shakespeare

CHAPTER ONE

The dust hadn't settled yet. It hung like a miasma of filth in the cavern, and Stoker thought she was going to choke. She managed a dry cough and picked her way through the men clearing away the debris, until she reached the edge of the rock fall.

A large, broad-shouldered man was helping to shift fallen rocks out of the way, and Stoker tapped him on the shoulder. He turned round slowly, eyes fierce above a big jaw covered with a four-day beard. His hands were big and solid, covered with dust and scratches. Stoker wasn't the least bit bothered. 'What the hell d'you think you're playing at, Cheung?'

She only ever called him Cheung when she was really annoyed, and he had the good grace to look abashed. 'I dunno what went wrong, I'm sorry.'

'You're supposed to be my explosives expert,' Stoker said. 'It'll take days to clear up this mess.'

'It's not as bad as it looks.'

'Oh, I forgot, you're the expert!' Stoker laughed harshly. '"Ex" as in *not any more* and "spurt" as in *a drip under pressure*.'

She saw the wounded look even through her anger, and realised it was time to turn it down. They didn't need any more fireworks at the moment. 'I'll see you later,' she told him, with slightly less rancour.

Cheung nodded. 'How are the casualties?'

'Lucky. The woman's just cuts and contusions. I'm on my way to check on the other two now. They're probably filing a massive compensation claim as we speak.'

Cheung smiled grimly.

Stoker watched him turn to pick up another rock and said, 'Leave that, you big lummox. Go and help with the analysers, they could do with your muscle.'

The big lummox pulled a face and stood up, towering over her. Stoker was tall, an easy six feet, but Cheung was like a giant and he could, quite literally, bend iron bars with his bare hands. The other men loved him because he combined that kind of physical power with a surprisingly gentle manner and good humour.

'Go on,' she told him, whacking the knuckles of her left hand against his shoulder. 'Scoot. I'll handle this.'

Cheung mock-saluted her and moved off. Stoker pushed at a rock with the toe of her boot. It was half buried and wouldn't budge. She let out a sigh of frustration, then gagged on the dust.

A figure appeared in the haze: tall, horned, with a sharp-looking face and huge, staring eyes.

'Oh, it's you,' Stoker muttered after an initial flutter of panic. She distracted herself by fixing her blonde hair back in a short ponytail. She guessed she looked a mess.

'This is not good,' said the horned figure ominously.

'Tell me something I don't know, Jaal.'

'I warned you that this was a Bad Place,' Jaal insisted. 'I can sense the evil around us, living in the rock, waiting for its chance to strike.'

'Give it a rest, Jaal. The situation is bad enough without your endless prophecies of doom. Don't let me catch you telling any of the others that rubbish, d'you hear?'

Vega Jaal looked at her balefully. Stoker couldn't tell if she'd hurt his feelings, but she needed him on her side. 'Come on, Jaal: I know it's not *possible* for you to lighten up, but we all need to muck in here.'

Vega Jaal gave a solemn nod, the best she could hope for.

'Right,' Stoker said. 'Where are the casualties?'

He pointed back into the swirling fog of dust.

'OK,' she said. 'Leave this to me.'

Stoker walked across to where a camp bed and a power lamp had been hastily set up. The dust seemed to have thinned out a bit here, and for a few seconds she just stood and watched the Doctor attending to his patient. He was tall, almost boyish with his fair hair and smooth skin, but he had broad shoulders and an intelligent look in his eyes. The white running shoes he wore indicated an active lifestyle, but the rest of him – pale striped trousers and a long fawn-coloured jacket, presented as much a mystery to Stoker as his name.

She was determined to keep an open mind, however. Stoker's nose had been broken in a bar fight twenty years ago with the result that she now looked a hell of a lot tougher than she really was. She played up to the image when it was useful, but it had taught her to never judge by appearances.

'How's she doing?' Stoker asked, crouching down by the camp bed. There was a girl lying on it, she could only have been twenty, with long chestnut curls and very pale skin. There was a nasty gash on her forehead, which the Doctor was dabbing gently with a white cloth.

He inspected the cloth, noting the red blotches with a sigh. 'She's unconscious,' he told her. 'I won't really know until she wakes up.'

'Which will be when, do you think?'

'I don't know. She's badly concussed.' There was a note of accusation in his voice.

'I thought you were a doctor.'

'Not that kind of doctor, unfortunately. And even if I were, head injuries are notoriously difficult to diagnose properly.'

Stoker thought for a moment. 'We need to move her.'

'Must we?'

'It isn't safe here. There could be another rock fall. I've got men moving equipment out of harm's way, but…'

'All right,' said the Doctor impatiently. 'I'll see what I can do. Where's Tegan?'

'Back there with the others,' Stoker indicated the rear of the cavern. 'She wanted to stay with you, but the cut on her leg needed attention. One of my men, Jim Boyd, is dealing with it. He's got a medkit.'

'Will it have synthetic skin patches?' asked the Doctor.

'Yeah. Jim was looking for one big enough to cover your friend's mouth last time I looked.'

The Doctor smiled despite himself. 'The words "patient" and "Tegan" don't go together easily. If you could arrange for some of your fellows to help me, Miss Stoker, we can try to move Nyssa here to a position of greater safety. Who knows, there may even be something in Mr Boyd's medical kit that might help.'

'Sure.' Stoker stood up. 'I'll get a couple of my "fellows" to come over.'

'I'd appreciate it.'

Stoker backtracked through the rubble, feeling dusty and confused. She needed a drink and some fresh air, but above all she needed these complications *gone*. She checked her wrist chrono again and quickened her pace. As she neared the back of the cavern, where the rock opened out a little and the dust hadn't quite reached yet, she heard the voice: an unfamiliar, twangy accent with the sharp note of rising panic buried somewhere inside it.

'Never mind the booze, just take me to the Doctor. Where is he? I want to see him.'

Stoker clambered down the rocky slope that led into the work area. Jim Boyd was just finishing up, and Cheung had stopped to offer a hand. 'OK, Jim, you can go,' Stoker said. 'We'll handle this.'

'Are you in charge here?' demanded the woman sitting on a supply crate. She had short auburn hair and a determined look. She was young and pretty, underneath all the anxiety.

'Yes,' said Stoker. 'Your Doctor friend is coming over now.'

'What about Nyssa?'

'I'm going to send a couple of men over to help. They can't stay by the rock face, it's too dangerous.'

'You're telling me it is!'

'I'll go,' said Cheung, straightening up. 'We've stacked all the analysers now, they'll keep for the time being.'

'So long as we can get them when we need them,' cautioned Stoker, fighting down the urge to glance at her chrono again.

Cheung spread his hands and grinned his infuriating grin. 'I told you, it's sorted. Now let me go and help with our two new friends over there.'

'OK,' agreed Stoker. 'But don't take too long about it, Bunny.'

He moved off, his long legs scrambling quickly and confidently over the loose rubble.

'Thanks,' said the girl, Tegan. She sounded genuine. 'Your mate's a real trooper.'

'Bunny Cheung, my right-hand man,' said Stoker. 'Strong as an Ogron, soft as a puppy. But he's no fool.'

'Bunny?'

Stoker smiled. 'He'd prefer it if we called him "Tiger" or something.' She paused to take a slim cigar from her jacket pocket and lit it with an old real-flame lighter. 'Don't want all that muscle going to his head, though, so Bunny it is. Fancy a smoke?'

Tegan shook her head. Stoker blew out a cloud of blue smoke and noted the look of irritation that crossed Tegan's face. 'I don't want anything except the Doctor and Nyssa.'

'Persistent, aren't you?'

'It has been said.'

'How's the leg?'

'Awful.' There was a large patch of Synthiskin stuck to Tegan's left thigh, where she had been cut during the rock fall. Stoker stared in puzzlement at the pale material of Tegan's shorts; she was wearing a camisole top and a thin jacket to match. What the hell was she doing around here dressed like that?

In fact, the more she thought about it, the more these people didn't make any sense to Stoker. She never worked to what you'd call an actual *plan*, but this lot, at best, could only be trouble. At worst, they could constitute a real threat to her operation here. She took another drag on her cigar and sat down on the crate next to Tegan.

'So. We've got a few minutes. Why don't you tell me what you're doing here?'

Tegan's shoulders slumped in defeat. She was evidently tired and confused. 'It's a long story.'

'Great.' Stoker gritted her teeth around the cigar. 'Let's hear it.'

CHAPTER TWO

It had been Tegan's first morning back on board the TARDIS.

She remembered touching one of the softly glowing roundels that were arranged in columns around the console room and being rewarded with a warm, comforting hum that she could feel through her fingertips.

She had never believed that would feel so reassuring.

Soon after she had first blundered into that police call box on the Barnet bypass, Tegan had despaired of ever seeing 1980s Earth again. But just when she had resigned herself to a life of wandering through time and space, the Doctor had accidentally left her behind at Heathrow airport in 1982.

And then things had *really* started to go downhill. She'd lost her job, of course. And she had suffered recurrent nightmares, often featuring snakes. Depression had followed.

After a while, Tegan had realised what she was missing: the simple truth was that she had never felt more alive than when helping to defeat the Cybermen, or Terileptils, or the Master or Omega. Tegan was at heart a practical woman and more than anything she wanted to *help*. Travelling with the Doctor had given her adventure, excitement, and above all, the chance to make a *difference*.

Quite simply, she wanted to *do* something with her life.

Her enforced stay on Earth had turned into an epiphany of sorts. Whereas once she had longed to return to her original life, now she was forced to confront the prospect of living a very humdrum human existence. And that, as Aunt Vanessa would have said, would simply never do.

Tegan had cut off all ties, and armed only with a sassy new haircut

14

and the bare essentials she had decided to see the world – on her own. Looking back, it seemed almost like destiny, running straight into the Doctor and Nyssa in Amsterdam.

'Never look a gift horse in the mouth, Tegan my dear,' Aunt Vanessa had always told her. Tegan took the advice without hesitation; leaping at the chance to rejoin her friends in the TARDIS as if she had never been away.

And now this room, this humming white space, seemed more like home to her than any place on Earth.

'Good morning,' said the Doctor as he breezed into the console room, carrying a toolkit. 'You're up early.'

Tegan felt a rush of warmth at the banality of the greeting in such fantastic surroundings. 'Couldn't sleep. I'm just so glad to be back.'

'Er, yes, well… we're glad to have you back.' The Doctor dumped the toolkit on the console and flipped it open. He hadn't mentioned Heathrow at all, and it suddenly struck Tegan that abandoning her there could have happened a fair while ago from his perspective. She'd been stuck on Earth for months – but for the Doctor and Nyssa, it could easily have been *years*. It was an uncomfortable thought: they might well have been travelling around having adventures in time and space without her. The Doctor never seemed to age, and as for Nyssa – well, who could say? She was Tegan's friend, but she *was* from another planet. And maybe she *did* seem a little more mature now, come to think of it.

'You know, I really must get around to finding another sonic screwdriver,' announced the Doctor, holding up a couple of odd-looking instruments from the toolbox and comparing them. 'Repairing the TARDIS is going to be a long job without one.'

'Is there something wrong with the TARDIS?'

'That's what I intend to find out.' The Doctor reached underneath the control desk and opened an access hatch. 'I've got the distinct impression that the Time Lords were poking around in here during my last little visit to Gallifrey. I want to make sure there's been nothing added or taken away.'

Tegan crouched down to peer over his shoulder into the hatch.

All she could see was a load of complicated circuitry and flashing lights. 'Such as?'

'Oh, the odd directional control unit, perhaps. Conterminous materialisation dampener. Possibly even a direct transfer blurgle ogler.' The last bit was unintelligible due to the fact that the Doctor's head was now completely immersed in the interior of the console. There was a series of concerned grunts and then he emerged, a smudge of oil on his nose. 'I certainly wouldn't put *that* past Maxil and his uniformed twits.'

'Doctor,' said Tegan, 'I haven't got a clue what you're talking about. But it's good to be back.'

He gave her his most winning smile. But the smile turned into a quizzical frown and he said, 'Can you smell burning?'

They both started sniffing the air. 'Phew,' said Tegan. 'Something's cooking.'

The Doctor disappeared back into the console, sniffing worriedly. 'If those nincompoops have touched the fluid-link bypass…' he growled. Then there was a bright flash and the Doctor leapt back out of the hatch in a cloud of smoke.

'Do you have a fire extinguisher?' asked Tegan.

'That was the telepathic circuit overloading,' he said, managing to look both puzzled and affronted at the same time. He leapt to his feet and began to flick switches and stab buttons on the console. 'Some kind of powerful psionic feedback…'

At that moment the interior door opened and Nyssa walked in. She was looking pale and ill, and was still wearing her dressing gown. Tegan immediately helped her to the wicker chair on one side of the console room. 'Nyssa! Are you OK? You look awful…'

'What's the matter?' asked the Doctor.

'Oh, Doctor,' Nyssa said, her voice strained and weak. 'I've just had the most terrible nightmare…'

With a sharp crack a section of the rock face fell away. Splinters of rock and jagged stone cascaded down the slope, throwing up more dust. The Doctor darted forward and pulled Bunny Cheung away, just as a large boulder hit the ground where he had been standing. The noise reverberated around the cavern like gunfire.

'Come on,' called Stoker from the mouth of the cave. 'Time to retreat.'

Bunny gently lifted the makeshift stretcher, with the girl still on it, and carried it away from the pile of fallen rock. The Doctor scooped up the lamp and blankets and hurried after him.

The mist of dust was fading slowly, leaving a flat, stony taste in the mouth. Despite herself, Stoker was impressed by the degree of devastation. When she took a moment to survey the damage, the mass of rubble and granite that now covered the cavern floor in a wide fan from the detonation point, it seemed even more amazing that the Doctor's little party had survived at all, let alone with only minor injury. But that was the thing with CG bombs: the whole idea was to minimise structural damage within a pre-set gravity field. Bunny might have cocked up the field setting but it had probably saved the lives of these people.

Stoker took the opportunity to watch the Doctor carefully as he picked his way across the fallen rock. He moved across the debris of the cavern with a sure-footed poise, but his pale clothes looked curiously unsuitable and antiquated.

'Down here should be fine,' the Doctor said to Bunny Cheung, indicating the space where the analysers had been stored in the secondary cavern. It wasn't perfect, but it would have to do for now. The girl on the stretcher was starting to moan.

The Doctor immediately knelt down and rested a hand on her forehead. 'Nyssa! Can you hear me? It's the Doctor. Everything's all right. You're in safe hands.'

It was vague and not entirely correct, but Stoker couldn't fault the man's bedside manner. Nyssa's eyes were fluttering as she started to come around.

It was Tegan who spoke next, pushing past Stoker to be with her friends. 'Nyssa! Doctor, is she OK?'

'Ah, Tegan. Nyssa's as well as can be expected, I think. She's had a nasty knock on the head. How's the leg?'

'Painful!'

The Doctor patted her arm. 'Good, that's the spirit.' He turned to speak to Bunny Cheung. 'Thank you very much, I couldn't have moved her so quickly without your help.'

Bunny clapped the Doctor on the shoulder. 'Forget it. Always happy to help a damsel in distress.'

There was a thunderous echo as more rock collapsed in the main cavern.

'And just in the nick of time too, by the sound of it,' he added with a grin.

The Doctor returned the smile. 'Absolutely.'

Bunny turned to Stoker. 'Can I take that call now, boss? It's been waiting since before the blast.'

Stoker grimaced, suddenly remembering. 'Oh, hell, yes, if you must. But I haven't finished kicking your backside properly yet, Bunny. So get out of here while you still can.'

With a huge grin, which took in not only Stoker but the Doctor and Tegan too, Bunny lumbered off towards the equipment area.

'He's got a personal call on hold,' explained Stoker to the Doctor. 'The big lummox can hardly wait.'

'He's as strong as an ox,' remarked the Doctor, rubbing his shoulder. 'He lifted Nyssa as though she weighed nothing.'

'Yeah, he's a real hero,' Stoker said drily.

'Don't be so hard on him,' Tegan said. 'I'm going for some fresh air. Do you mind?'

Stoker shrugged. 'You won't find any of that down here.'

'I wasn't talking to you.' Tegan looked at the Doctor. 'Is it all right?'

The Doctor cleared his throat. 'Certainly. I'll make sure Nyssa's comfortable here and then catch you up.'

Stoker watched Tegan limp away and raised an eyebrow. 'Is she for real?'

'She's plain-speaking,' the Doctor admitted. He looked at Stoker. 'There's a lot of it about.'

The Doctor knelt down to check Nyssa again. He felt her pulse and then gently raised each eyelid to examine her pupils. She had stopped moaning now and seemed a little more settled, with some colour in her cheeks. There was an ugly swelling beneath the cut on her forehead but the bleeding had stopped. The Doctor pulled the blanket up gently to her chin and then stared at her thoughtfully for a long moment.

'Problem?' wondered Stoker.

The Doctor stood up. 'I don't know,' he said. He gave her a quizzical look. 'What are you doing here? If you don't mind me asking.'

'I might ask you the same question,' replied Stoker. 'Only your plain-speaking friend has already filled me in on some of the details.'

Undaunted, the Doctor stuffed his hands into his trouser pockets. 'Well, then, perhaps you could answer my question with similar candour. You seem to have some kind of operation going here. What are you? Miners? Mineralogists?'

Stoker paused to light a cigar. 'Archaeologists.'

'Really?' The Doctor raised both eyebrows. 'How interesting.'

Tegan found Bunny Cheung in the comms area, a secluded part of the cave where Stoker's people had erected some kind of equipment bank. There was a chair and a communications console. Bunny had his back to her when she came in. He sat hunched over the controls like Desperate Dan tuning a wireless. Tegan was about to call over to him when a screen fizzed into life and a 3D image flashed into view.

It was a hologram of a little girl, about five or six years old, with big, bright blue eyes. She was clutching some kind of soft toy.

'Hi there,' said Bunny Cheung. 'How's my baby?'

The girl beamed. 'Hi Daddy. Guess what: a cat poo'd in our garden yesterday and Mummy had to pick it up with a stick.'

'What, the cat?'

'No, silly! The poo. She put it in the bin. And Hannah Goodison was sick in school today.'

Tegan smiled, hanging back, and she heard Bunny laughing too. The hologram crackled and broke up a bit, as if there was a transmission problem. Tegan wondered from how far away it was being beamed.

'She's always ill. Hey, I got your message.' Bunny's voice softened to a warm growl. 'Don't be scared, princess. You're with Mummy, remember. Nothing can hurt you at home.'

Rosie digested this for a while. 'What about you?'

'Me? I'm fine, sweetheart. I'm not scared of anything.'

'Not even lions or bears?'

Bunny grinned. 'Especially not lions and bears!'

Rosie nodded solemnly. 'Will you send me a message later? Mummy says we can't talk like this too often 'cos it costs too much.'

'Sure. I'll beam a message right back at you, soon as I get the chance. Promise. How's Mummy?'

'Fine. Daddy, will you be coming home soon?'

'Just as soon as I can, sweetheart. Why, are you missing me?'

'No, but Kooka's arm needs fixing again. It's come right off this time.' The girl held up the soft toy, some kind of orange thing with a peculiar face and three eyes. In her other hand was the thing's arm.

'Oh, right. D'you think he can manage until I get home?'

The girl looked dubious. 'Well…'

'I mean, it's kind of all right, isn't it?' pressed Bunny. 'A one-armed Earth Reptile, it's just like a one-armed human. Don't you think?'

'All right,' the girl conceded the point with some reluctance. 'So long as you fix him as soon as you come home.'

'I will, sweetheart. I promise.'

'I've got to go now, Daddy. You said we mustn't stay too long on the hypernet. So bye.'

Bunny Cheung paused to swallow. 'Bye, honey.'

The girl gave a little wave and a grin and vanished. Bunny sat at the console for several seconds in silence, staring at the empty space where the hologram had been. Then he pressed a series of buttons and, making a huge fist with his right hand, inserted the ring on his middle finger into a small socket by the hologram projector. There was a series of bleeps and whirrs and then he pulled the ring out. For a long moment Bunny stared into the stone on the ring, which glittered in the lamplight.

Tegan cleared her throat quietly to get his attention. 'Long way from home?'

He turned his head, surprised. 'Blimey, do you always creep up on people like that? I could've had a heart attack.'

'Sorry. I just wanted to say thanks, for helping out with Nyssa. That's all.'

Bunny sat back in his chair, the plastic creaking ominously beneath his weight. 'OK. Sorry if I sound a bit grumpy. I was miles away. Light-years away, in fact.'

'Your daughter?'

Bunny's smile lit up his whole face. He had rather small eyes, but, as Tegan now noticed, they sparkled with genuine good humour. 'The one and only. My very own little monster.'

Tegan forced a laugh. 'She's very pretty.'

'Not at all like her dad, eh?'

'What's her name?'

'Rosie.'

'That's nice. You must miss her.'

Bunny rubbed a hand down his face and scratched at the thick stubble on his jaw. 'Only enormously and during every waking moment. Why, does it show?'

'I recognise a long-distance call when I see one,' Tegan said as she perched on the edge of the console unit.

'Direct hyper-wave, bounced all around the Karula Koza system net and pulse-beamed right out here to the very edge of the galaxy. It's virtually untraceable, and very expensive – but worth every credit.'

Tegan glanced at the communications suite. To her it looked lashed together, bits of various computers and transceivers piled on top of one another. These people were working on a shoestring.

Bunny caught her look. 'Just don't tell Stoker.'

'I won't! She does seem a bit sharp-tongued if you ask me.' Tegan felt uncomfortable, suddenly realising that this was like the pot calling the kettle black.

Bunny was shaking his head. 'Stoker likes to act tough. Actually, she *is* tough. But there's not a man here who wouldn't follow Jyl Stoker to the edge of space and back. In fact, they already have.'

'Including you?'

'Well, yes and no. Officially I'm retired, you see. Wanted to spend some time with my family.' Here Bunny flashed her a quick, mirthless smile. 'But Stoker called in an old debt.'

'You owe her money?'

'I owe her my life,' Bunny said. 'But that's another story. It doesn't matter now. All I know is that when this operation's over, I'm off back to Earth and my family for good. But that's me. What's your story? How does a half-dressed girl like you wind up on a godforsaken rock like this?'

CHAPTER THREE

'I didn't think anything could get inside the TARDIS,' Tegan had argued.

'Ordinarily, no,' agreed the Doctor. He regarded Nyssa with a look of consternation. 'But in this case, I think it could be something rather extraordinary. Tell me about the dream again.'

'The nightmare you mean,' said Nyssa. Her voice trembled slightly. 'Traken?'

The Doctor leant closer. 'Specifically the thing in the dark, the thing you couldn't quite see.'

Tegan said, 'I thought we'd been through all this already… Can't you see she's upset, Doctor?' In truth, all this talk of nightmares was making Tegan nervous; she had suffered the night-time heebie-jeebies on many occasions during her sojourn on Earth, mostly bad dreams featuring serpents and jungles and caves and the like, which she had simply put down to her experience on Deva Loka.

Apparently oblivious to Tegan's reservations, Nyssa continued, 'It really wasn't like a dream at all. There was definitely something or someone in the room with me, in the shadows. I got out of bed and followed it into the darkness… I didn't want to, but I had to. Some kind of compulsion, I suppose. It seemed so cold, and dark, like the deep space between galaxies. Empty and merciless…'

Tegan hugged herself and shivered at the thought. The cheerful brightness of the console room had become harsh and clinical.

'And then what?' the Doctor prompted softly.

Nyssa drew a deep breath. 'As I said, the lights came on in my room then. *And it was empty.* There was no one else there… but there *had* been, Doctor, I'm convinced of it. You must believe me.'

The Doctor was frowning. 'You're saying something actually manifested itself in the TARDIS?'

Nyssa shrugged helplessly. 'But Tegan's right, surely. It's not possible for something to penetrate the real-world interface, is it?'

'No,' replied the Doctor confidently. 'Unless, of course, it found another way in.'

'Such as?'

'Your mind.'

Tegan looked confused. 'The dream?'

'Not quite.' The Doctor turned and fixed her with a sudden, piercing stare. 'Do you recall the fault in the telepathic circuits?'

Tegan nodded. 'I thought it just blew a fuse or something.'

'Psionic feedback, I said. Something was trying to force its way past the TARDIS defences.'

'Using my mind?' Nyssa sounded appalled, but the notion seemed to galvanise her. Tegan could tell Nyssa's brain was already working through the consequences with her customary logic, sloughing off the earlier panic.

The Doctor was nodding vigorously as he paced around the console room. 'Your subconscious mind, to be precise, probably while you were asleep.'

'But all this occurred when I woke up from the nightmare.'

'Which is right when the telepathic circuits went *phtt!*' realised Tegan.

'Yes,' said the Doctor thoughtfully, leaning on the console. 'Whatever it was must have hitched a ride from your dream state, Nyssa. Interesting!'

'But what could do that?' Tegan sounded alarmed. 'Is it still here?'

'Very unlikely. The short circuit would have prevented any real temporal incursion. But it might be possible to trace the original telepathic signal…' The Doctor began to operate the controls on the panel in front of him, his face a sudden mask of concentration.

Tegan felt the old, familiar tingle of excitement in her stomach: part fear, part anticipation. But this time, she decided, she was going to be ready for it. She was going to help.

'Of course,' the Doctor was saying as his fingers travelled across the console, 'it might be a bit tricky with a system malfunction, but – Nyssa, try initiating a repair program, would you?'

Instantly, Nyssa stepped up to the opposite side of the console and began operating the switches. Tegan felt a minute prickle of envy, watching them work together like a team. It was almost as if Nyssa had become the Doctor's assistant. But then Nyssa had a strong science background, which Tegan supposed must be an advantage.

'The fault locator won't identify the relevant subroutines for a repair program,' complained Nyssa.

The Doctor hesitated, then said, 'Never mind, we'll try a short cut.' He hurried around to join her. 'If I can tap into the residual energy in the telepathic circuits, the TARDIS may be able to calculate an exact point of origin.'

'Won't that be dangerous?'

'No more than leaving whatever it was that tried to invade the TARDIS via your dream free to try again.'

'But you'll have to link directly with the TARDIS telepathic circuits.'

'I thought they were damaged!' protested Tegan.

Nyssa said, 'It's a terrible risk!'

'Nonsense,' the Doctor declared. 'All I have to do is tune my thought waves into the TARDIS artron signature, and…' He placed the flats of his hands onto two metallic plates located on one of the console panels, and then closed his eyes.

'I don't like the sound of this,' said Tegan flatly. 'What's he trying to do?'

Nyssa examined the various readouts and displays before her. 'He's trying to align the TARDIS telepathic processor unit to the coordinate panel. If he can –'

There was a violent crackle like a firework going off and the Doctor jerked back from the console, hitting the wall behind him heavily. There, he slid down until he lay sprawled across the floor.

Tegan ran across and knelt down by him. He looked pale and stunned but otherwise unhurt.

'Is he all right?' asked Nyssa.

'He's out cold. What happened?'

They looked back at the control console, where wisps of smoke were drifting from the telepathic circuits. As they watched, the glass column at the centre of the console began to slow in its rhythmic movement.

'The TARDIS is materialising,' said Nyssa.

The central column came to a rest with a soft chime. For a moment all they could hear was the gentle hum of the TARDIS around them.

'We've landed.'

'The question is,' said Tegan, 'where?'

The Doctor reached out to touch the cave wall. 'Curious rock structure. Is it crystalline?'

'Not quite, although you'd be forgiven for thinking so,' Stoker said.

The rock was smooth and glass-like, black but with a hint of a deeper, darker green. It had an almost organic quality that Stoker still found unsettling.

'I think we're the first human beings to set foot on Akoshemon's moon,' she went on. 'It's still a bit of a closed book.'

'What are you looking for?'

Stoker hadn't been expecting such an abrupt change of subject, so she paused just long enough to take another drag on her cigar before answering. 'Fortune and glory, isn't that what they say? Fortune and glory.'

'Straight to the point,' admitted the Doctor, 'but hardly informative.'

They were walking back through the cave system, away from the area where the explosion had occurred. The air was a little better here, but it had the dank and closed smell of compacted soil and granite the galaxy over. There were electric lights fixed to the glossy walls of the passages connecting the main caves, bright and yellow but horribly unflattering. Everyone instantly gained a pasty, sick-looking complexion.

'Somewhere inside this rock is the remains of a forgotten civilisation,' Stoker told the Doctor. 'I'm hoping to dig up something very, very old and valuable, or something very, very pretty and valuable. But preferably both.'

'And therefore doubly valuable.'

'You got it.'

Stoker's men were busy in the ancillary cavern moving heavy equipment and storage crates. There were only five of them, and all but one was human. The Doctor glanced at Vega Jaal and then turned back to Stoker.

'Forgotten civilisation?'

'There won't be much left except dust and bones. Maybe a few trinkets. Something that can give us an inkling of the kind of people who used to live in these parts.'

'When you put it like that, it doesn't sound very lucrative,' the Doctor commented.

'Depends what you're interested in,' said Stoker. She stubbed out the cigar against the rock wall. 'My sponsors just *love* bones and dust and old trinkets.'

'They'd have to. This looks like a very difficult operation. You're a long way from any major star system, there are no obvious signs of any ancient civilisation that I've noticed, and...'

She stopped him with a look that was as cool and impenetrable as the stone that surrounded them. 'And?'

The Doctor met her stare levelly. 'And I've never met an archaeologist yet who preferred high explosives to patient work with a trowel and brush.'

Stoker gave an irritated snort. 'You ask a lot of questions.'

'I'm just curious.'

'Lucky you're not a cat, then.' Stoker turned and called out to one of her men. 'Hey, Bunny!'

Bunny Cheung turned and Stoker beckoned to him. The non-human with the owl-like eyes and sharp features followed Bunny over.

'Our new friend here doesn't believe this is an archaeological dig,' Stoker told him.

Bunny grinned. 'What *does* he think we're doing here?'

'I'm not sure. A holiday, perhaps?'

'You were using high explosives,' the Doctor pointed out. 'Or had you forgotten how we came to meet in the first place?'

'Maybe you think we're gun-runners or something,' smirked Stoker. 'Smugglers. Pirates. Terrorists, even.'

'We have the necessary credentials,' said Bunny Cheung. He reached into a wide pouch hung on his left hip and produced a coloured plastic document. 'This gives us authority, from the Department of Alien Antiquities at the University of Tyr itself. We're here to uncover the secrets of the Akoshemon system.'

The Doctor flipped through the permit and handed it back. 'I beg your pardon. Please forgive me, but I'm still a little confused. Probably a touch of shell shock, I expect.'

Stoker eyed him carefully. He was hiding something behind all that courtesy; she was about to say something when the Doctor turned to Vega Jaal and started talking to him in a strange, fluting dialect punctuated by clicks and glottal stops.

Jaal replied in kind, inclining his head politely, almost deferentially, to the Doctor.

'What was all that about?' asked Stoker. Her irritation with the Doctor had given way to bemusement.

'I was introducing myself properly to Vega Jaal, here. That is to give him the correct form of address, of course. The people of Vega have a venerable tradition of honour and respect for proper names.'

Stoker glanced at Jaal. 'Do they really?'

'Oh, yes,' the Doctor said.

'You've been to Vega, then?'

'Actually, no.'

'You spoke to him like a native.'

'I have a flair for languages.'

'That might come in useful, if we hit on any ancient hieroglyphics or runes.'

'Is that likely?'

Stoker shrugged. 'Who knows? We're still digging.'

They moved off, the Doctor following Stoker again, leaving Vega Jaal and Bunny to carry on with their work. There was some muted conversation among the men behind them and then a burst of laughter.

'It must be very useful having a Vegan on your team,' said the Doctor. 'Vega has produced more mining engineers and pot-holers than practically any other planet in the galaxy. Just the thing for an archaeological dig.'

'You said it.'

The Doctor stopped her with a touch on her arm. 'By the way,' he said, 'apology accepted.'

'What?'

'For very nearly blowing us all sky high. You did say sorry when you first found us, but I was a little busy at the time.' He flashed a smile. 'Not to mention slightly deaf.'

Stoker let the tension go, her shoulders visibly sagging. 'It's OK. Let's forget all about it. Sorry for snapping like that back there, but…' she let the sentence hang, finishing it in her head: *I'm a little jumpy right now.*

He was looking at her again in that way, slightly guileless, but somehow sharp as a laser. 'But?' he prompted, unwilling to let it drop.

Stoker took a breath. 'It's just this place, I suppose,' she replied, waving a hand at the glossy green rock surrounding them. 'It's pretty grim down here.'

The Doctor nodded, frowning slightly as he stuck his hands into his pockets. 'Yes. It's pretty grim on the surface too, I seem to recall…'

The TARDIS had materialised in the shade of an enormous outcrop of rock, some forty feet high and half as wide. The jagged stone surface was the colour of putrescent meat, coated with some kind of mould or lichen. Nyssa was examining the growth minutely, and

Tegan thought she must have been trying to conceal her anxiety with calm, scientific interest in her new surroundings.

'The whole moon appears to be covered in this lichen,' Nyssa observed. 'I suppose something must account for its atmosphere.'

The air was thin but breathable, and uncomfortably cool. Watching her breath steam in the air, Tegan said, 'No other sign of life, at any rate.'

'And yet…' Nyssa sounded troubled.

'What?'

'I have the distinct feeling we're being watched.'

Automatically, they looked skyward. Looking down on them like a giant, bloodshot eye was the planet, a bloated mass of churning scarlet and black. It was both strangely compelling and utterly repellent. The scabrous colours swirled across the surface in volcanic torment, and it looked to Tegan as though nothing natural or good could exist there. Repulsed, she looked away.

The Doctor stood some distance from the TARDIS, hands in trouser pockets, Panama hat perched on his head, for all the world looking like someone expecting to attend a garden regatta. His white trainers had left a track of footprints in the crusty sand.

'Feeling better?' Tegan asked him, folding her arms. It was definitely a bit chilly.

'I suffered a tremendous psychic blast, Tegan,' he said without looking at her. The eyes beneath the brim of his hat were fixed on the horizon. It wasn't all that far away; the moon seemed quite small.

The Doctor had come round in the console room pretty quickly, jumping to his feet with unlikely vigour. He'd shrugged off Nyssa's concerns and Tegan's offer of a stiff drink. Instead, after glancing at the stationary time rotor, he had simply unfurled his Panama and flicked the door lever down. Now Tegan was struggling to think of something useful to say. 'Breathe deeply and –'

'And relax, yes, I know.'

'Sorry. Just wanted to help, that's all.'

'In that case, tell me what you see. I want to make sure my perceptions haven't been interfered with.'

Tegan pulled a face and then examined the scene around her once more. The mould-coloured plain was dotted with huge, thrusting rocks, jagged as knives. The crag the TARDIS had landed next to was one of the smaller ones. It looked as though the whole moon was covered with them. And it was a smallish moon, right enough: she even fancied she could see the curve of the horizon. And up, beyond that, outer space.

For a long moment, Tegan simply stared at it, and she noticed the Doctor was doing the same. Even he seemed impressed.

Beyond the blood-red planet, the sky was split in two. One half was a great wash of colour, blue and purple and burgundy speckled with a million stars. Tegan knew that every star was a distant sun, and for a second she felt a dizzying sense of vertigo as the scale of what she saw hit home. I'm so *insignificant*, she thought.

She switched her attention to the other half of the sky, which was the complete absence of colour: total blackness. There were no stars, however distant, just a void of unremitting darkness. She shivered.

'What's out there?' she asked the Doctor. Her breath wisped away on the cold breeze.

'Nothing,' said the Doctor bleakly. 'Well, nothing until you reach the next galaxy. That, Tegan, is intergalactic space, the empty void separating the galaxies.'

'It's awesome. It's so empty it's creepy.'

'Whereas that,' the Doctor gestured to the sparkling luminescence on the other side of the sky, 'is full of life and light and energy. The galaxy that this world belongs to, seen in all its glory.'

'And the planet?'

'I doubt there's anything much alive there, but you never know.'

'We must be on the very edge of the star system,' observed Nyssa as she joined them.

'Yes,' agreed the Doctor. 'The last planet before the void.'

'Why did the TARDIS bring us here?' wondered Tegan.

Nyssa was staring out into the pitch black of empty space. 'It's like my dream… So cold, and merciless. Abysmal.'

'Oh, I don't know,' said Tegan. 'It's kind of scary and exciting, like reaching the top of a rollercoaster.'

'No,' said the Doctor. 'Nyssa meant what she said: *abysmal*. Bottomless, immeasurable depth. The edge of nothing but primal chaos.'

'Can you feel it too?' asked Nyssa, her voice wavering. She pulled the collar of her jacket tighter.

The Doctor nodded. 'It's here. Somewhere close, waiting. Impatient.'

'What is?' demanded Tegan.

Nyssa said, 'The thing that came to me in the TARDIS.'

'You can both sense it? Now you're giving me the willies. Why don't we just go?'

'There's no point,' said the Doctor. 'It would find us wherever we went.'

'What? How?'

'It came to me while we were in the space-time vortex, remember?' explained Nyssa. 'It wouldn't matter where we tried to go, if it can find us in the vortex.'

'Right, that's it,' Tegan declared. 'Let's find this thing, whatever it is, and get rid of it.'

But neither the Doctor nor Nyssa seemed to be listening; they were both staring up into the darkness.

And it was then that the ground had exploded beneath their feet.

CHAPTER FOUR

Nyssa woke up suddenly.

Her throat was dry but she was unhurt, apart from a pulsating headache. And a very tender swelling on her forehead. There was some sort of dressing on the wound, but she reasoned that it could not have been that bad an injury if she had actually woken up.

'Take it easy,' said a familiar voice. Gentle hands helped her into a sitting position.

'Tegan,' Nyssa gasped. She felt nauseous. 'What happened?'

'Never mind about that now,' said Tegan. 'Would you like a sip of water?'

'I think I'm going to be sick.'

'Relax, you're all right. It's just a mild concussion.'

'Where's the Doctor?' Nyssa's memory felt cloudy, the events leading up to the explosion a patchy blur. *Explosion.* She remembered that well enough. The earth had leapt beneath them, a sudden wrench that hurled them all into the air, tossing them like leaves in an autumn squall. She recalled the noise, a thunderclap, her ears buffeted and instantly silenced. Even now they were ringing.

Then the fall, the long, painful descent through stone and dust and debris, losing contact with the Doctor and Tegan in the choking slide of shattered rock. And just before losing consciousness, Nyssa had seen the sky above them for the briefest moment before it was replaced by the sudden darkness of oblivion.

Tegan said, 'The Doctor's talking to someone called Stoker. She's some kind of archaeologist, got a whole team down here. I think they were using explosives to help dig a tunnel or something.'

'We're underground?'

'Yeah. The explosion blew a hole straight through to the planet's surface, right where we were standing!'

'And we fell through the hole?'

'That's about the size of it, yes.'

'Then we're lucky to be alive.' Nyssa eased her legs gently off the bed. The material of her trousers was covered in rock dust, and she patted it without much effect. 'Where are we, exactly?'

'We're on a moon that orbits the planet Akoshemon. Stoker's lot are hoping to dig up the remains of some ancient alien civilisation, apparently. They sort of dug us out of the rubble first, though.'

In the main cavern, Stoker was attending to a minor dispute between two of her men concerning faulty equipment. For the moment she seemed to have forgotten about the Doctor, and so he took the opportunity to strike up a conversation with Bunny Cheung and Vega Jaal.

'Did you say your sponsor was the University of Tyr?'

Bunny nodded. 'That's right. Stoker received a grant from the Department of Alien Antiquities. They've quite an interest in this region of space. If Stoker finds what they're looking for, she'll be well rewarded.'

'And you?'

'Percentage of the profits.'

'Excuse me a moment,' said the Doctor, squatting down. He picked up a fragment of rock from the cave floor and examined it in the light of the nearest lamp. He showed it to Vega Jaal. 'What do you make of that?'

'Porizium,' said the Vegan instantly.

'Are you sure?'

'I'd recognise it anywhere.'

'Bit of a geologist, are you?'

'We are all geologists on Vega, Doctor. It is one of the fundamental skills of my people. On my planet, the basics of geology are taught in the nursery.'

The Doctor smiled. 'Of course. Porizium's quite valuable, isn't it?'

'I believe so, if there is a rich enough seam.'

The Doctor seemed to ponder this for a moment, before carelessly discarding the stone and dusting his hands. 'What ancient civilisation are you hoping to find the remains of here?'

'Ah.' Vega Jaal suddenly appeared troubled. 'You will have to ask Stoker about that…'

'Don't you know?' the Doctor asked, puzzled.

Bunny was grinning wolfishly. 'Jaal's under orders not to say anything about it, Doctor. He's obsessed with the ghosts and ghouls of Akoshemon, and it drives Stoker up the wall!'

'Really!' The Doctor sounded very interested. 'Ghosts and ghouls?'

Vega Jaal said, 'The planet Akoshemon is infamous in this sector of space. Its name is synonymous with cruelty and death. It is said that its diabolical inhabitants will never rest in their graves until…'

'How come you two have got time to stand around chatting?' demanded Stoker, stepping abruptly between Bunny and Vega Jaal. She looked to be in a furious temper. 'We've got a deadline to meet, remember!'

'I've never seen an archaeological dig in a hurry before,' commented the Doctor.

Stoker cast him a black look and rounded on her men. 'Bunny, I want that word – *now*. Jaal, stop telling your ghost stories and get cracking on the cave survey, double quick!'

'We may get the opportunity to talk again later, Doctor,' said Jaal.

'I hope so!' said the Doctor. 'I always enjoy a good ghost story.'

Stoker glowered at them both, and Vega Jaal, after a slight bow to the Doctor, left to attend to his duties.

'I'm way behind schedule and my best survey equipment's on the blink,' grumbled Stoker. 'I don't need any more gloom and doom from him, thank you.'

'Is there anything I can do to help?' asked the Doctor.

Stoker lit a cigar and blew out a stream of smoke. 'Nope. Thanks for the offer, but my next job is kicking Bunny's hairy backside until it glows, and frankly, you ain't got the footwear for it.'

The Doctor looked at his white sports shoes and then at Stoker's steel-capped boots. 'Er, quite.'

'Now, if you'll excuse me,' Stoker muttered, and, chomping down on the cigar, set off after Bunny Cheung.

The Doctor suddenly found himself alone.

Stoker hauled Bunny Cheung into her makeshift office, a small space behind the communications bank where he had spoken to Rosie. She was straight to the point. 'Your mistake, Bunny, could have cost us more than just time, but time is a real issue for us here. You know we're working against the clock: if we don't find what we've come here for within the next couple of hours, I can't guarantee we won't be rumbled.'

'I wasn't to know there was anyone up there,' replied Bunny. He was trying to stay calm and reasonable, but Stoker was clearly under mounting pressure.

'That's not the point, and you know it!'

'So what *is* the point, Jyl?'

'The point is, I trust you to get it right. Every time. You're supposed to be an explosives expert. Act like one.'

'That's not fair.'

Stoker cut him down. 'Fair isn't the issue here. I don't know what the Doctor and his girlfriends are doing here, hut you could've had them killed. Have you thought of that?'

'Of course I have. But you said it yourself: we're working against the clock. You want those rock samples tested like yesterday. Fine. I set the CG bombs as normal, and I checked everyone was clear. I didn't realise there would be other people snooping around. We're supposed to be on our own here, remember?'

'I am aware of that fact, yes!' There was a moment's angry pause. Then Stoker said, 'Sorry, Bunny, but I can't help thinking your mind's not on the job.'

'Meaning?'

'Rosie.'

'Rosie! What's this got to do with her?'

'Come on, Bunny. Everyone knows you didn't want to come on this trip. We all know you can't wait to get back home. Rosie's a great kid, Bunny, the best. I envy you her, I really do. And you're a good father.'

'But?'

Stoker took a deep breath. 'But you're spending too much time on the hypernet, and maybe not enough time on your job. Besides, it's way too risky: what if someone picked up the simcord transmission stream?'

'Jyl. If I wasn't stuck here on this lousy lump of crap in the middle of nowhere, I'd walk out on you right *now*.'

Perhaps Stoker hadn't anticipated the full extent of Bunny's feelings, because she seemed to be lost for words. The silence steamed between them.

'But as there is no way off this rock,' Bunny continued eventually, 'I'll stick with you and do my best. But *nothing* is going to stop me speaking to my daughter. Nothing.'

Stoker had to concede defeat. She slapped a hand against the man's arm. 'OK, maybe I'm just getting jumpy. It's this damn moon. I hate to admit it but Vega Jaal's right, there's something strange here… I just don't know what, exactly.'

She was clearly concerned, and Bunny's attitude softened accordingly. 'Do you think this Doctor is going to be a problem?'

'I don't know.' Stoker reached a conclusion. 'Maybe I'd better find out.'

Left to his own devices, the Doctor had been taking a look around. He had come across a stack of packing crates against one wall, and, as there was no one in the immediate vicinity, he decided to take a quick peek.

He'd seen this variety of crate before: ex-military issue. Nothing untoward about that, of course. Cheap military surplus equipment was widely used all over the universe. But he did wonder what was inside them. The Doctor felt sure that he and his companions had been caught in some kind of controlled-gravity blast, but neither

Stoker nor Bunny Cheung had reacted when he had specifically referred to high explosives earlier. And military-issue CG bombs were most definitely not your average high explosives.

Of course, the packing crates were all sealed. After only a moment's hesitation, and another quick check to make sure the coast was clear, the Doctor fished out a screwdriver from his coat pocket and began to prise open one of the crates.

'Looking for something?' Stoker asked from behind him.

The Doctor leapt away from the crates, scratching his head in an obvious attempt to distract her from what he had been doing. He dipped his other hand towards his coat pocket, missed it because of the flap, and was left with no choice but to slowly hold up the screwdriver for her to see.

'That's no use,' Stoker told him. 'Those crates have sonic locks.'

The Doctor glared ruefully at the screwdriver. 'Do they, indeed.'

She took the tool off him. 'Bit antiquated, isn't it?'

'I generally find old-fashioned methods are the best.'

She eyed him thoughtfully. 'I'll just bet you do.'

The Doctor thrust his hands into his trouser pockets. 'Tell me about Akoshemon.'

'Jaal spooked you already, has he?' Stoker sighed. 'There's not all that much to tell, to be honest. It did have a pretty heavy reputation in these parts. A lot of bad stuff went on, war, famine, pestilence, that kind of thing. But it all happened a long time ago. It's completely lifeless now: highly toxic atmosphere and a surface that's little more than an ocean of boiling mud and molten lava.'

'Sounds delightful,' said the Doctor.

'Jaal likes to tell his stories, though. You know the kind of thing: evil spirits haunting a dead planet, ancient evil waiting for the chance to live again. Good campfire stuff, but I don't like him upsetting the others.'

'Is he that convincing?'

Stoker pulled a face. 'He has a way with him, you know? He likes to do the mystic bit: like he has a sixth sense where he comes from.'

'Vegans are generally very attuned to the physical world around them,' the Doctor said. 'Some believe that connection exists on the spiritual level too.'

'Whatever,' said Stoker with a dismissive wave of her cigar. 'I just haven't got the time for it.'

Any further comment was interrupted by the arrival of one of Stoker's men. He looked flustered. 'Boss, there's some kind of fault on the analysers.'

Stoker looked heavenward. 'This is all I need. All right, Jim. I'm coming.' She turned to the Doctor. 'Sorry, duty calls. I'll see you later.'

Tegan led Nyssa through one of the short tunnels that interconnected the caverns. Tegan was starting to get her bearings now, using bits of equipment or particular lamps as rudimentary landmarks.

When they found the Doctor, he was alone in a tunnel, staring thoughtfully at the rock wall. 'Fascinating geological structure, don't you think?' he asked as they approached.

'Doctor!' said Tegan. 'Nyssa's here.'

He whirled around with a delighted grin. 'Splendid! How are you feeling? Better? Good! Now, what do you think of this, hmm?' He turned back to inspect the rock. 'Not quite crystalline, is it?'

Reaching out to touch the surface of the wall, Nyssa said, 'It's like glass that cannot be seen through.'

Tegan said, 'Or a whole pile of broken wine bottles jammed together.'

'It is opaque to your eyes, but translucent to mine,' said a voice from behind them. They turned to see Vega Jaal standing in the tunnel, arms folded across his chest. His eyes glowed faintly in the semidarkness.

'Allow me to introduce Vega Jaal,' said the Doctor. 'He enjoys a very good working relationship with every kind of rock. You could say it's in his nature.'

'Not this rock, Doctor,' said Vega Jaal. 'This rock keeps a secret.'

'Really! And what might that be?'

'I don't know. It's a secret.'

The Doctor's face fell. 'Ask a silly question…'

'Have you tried to find out what it is?' asked Tegan.

Vega Jaal shook his head. 'Its secret is as dark and impenetrable as the rock itself.'

The Doctor was clearly intrigued. 'You know more than you're letting on, Vega Jaal.'

'Stoker thinks I am a doomsayer,' replied the alien, 'but I simply speak my… mind.'

'I don't understand,' Nyssa said.

'I sense things: hollows in the rock. Voids.'

Nyssa stiffened. 'Voids?'

'There is a great void here, in this moon… an empty place, and yet not empty. It is filled with something I cannot describe, but I know it is this moon's darkest secret.' Jaal's eyes seem to glow brighter. 'And there is a door…'

'I hate riddles,' complained Tegan.

'A door to what?' asked the Doctor.

'The void. The non-void.' Vega Jaal hesitated. 'The… hunger. The craving.'

'We're going around in circles now,' Tegan muttered.

'Hush,' said the Doctor. 'This could be important.'

'But I have said more than I know already,' said Vega Jaal. 'And it can sometimes be difficult to separate feeling from conjecture. I could simply be mistaken.'

'But?'

Vega Jaal fixed the Doctor with a baleful glare. 'I am certain that the door will be found, Doctor. And that it shall be passed through.'

'Into the void?' asked Nyssa.

Jaal shrugged. 'Or the void may come through to find us.'

'Hey, Jaal!' echoed a voice from further down the tunnel. 'Come and lend a hand with this: the scanner's still messing us about.'

'I must go,' said Vega Jaal. He bowed stiffly and followed the passageway towards the voice.

'What was all that about?' Tegan wanted to know. 'Doors and voids and things: it doesn't make any sense.'

'Well, Vegan geology relies as much on mysticism as scientific fact. Plus a healthy dose of good old-fashioned extra-sensory perception.'

'Terrific.'

The Doctor seemed to reach a decision, and said, 'If we're going to get anywhere here, we'll need Stoker's help. Come on.'

'Where are we going?' Tegan asked, as she and Nyssa fell into step behind him.

'To make ourselves useful!'

They found Stoker crouching over a bulky machine, surrounded by nearly everyone in her team. Like most of Stoker's equipment, the machine looked worn and frequently repaired: one of the access plates was held on with gaffer tape.

Jim Boyd was sitting at a seat in front of a keyboard and screen, tapping at the controls without effect. 'See! Not a spark. We can't do anything unless this heap of junk actually *works*.'

'Hey,' said Stoker. 'This heap of junk cost over forty grand. You've got to treat it with care.' She banged it hard with the flat of her hand, raising a laugh from the men.

'Is that a spectron analyser?' asked the Doctor, inserting himself between a couple of the men.

Stoker looked back at him. 'What if it is?'

'I might be able to fix it. I'm quite a whizz with computers.' A pause. 'And the gentleman is quite right: you'll never find what you're looking for without it.'

Stoker sat back and crossed her arms. 'You've got it all worked out, haven't you?'

'This is no archaeological dig,' said the Doctor bluntly.

By now, the entire team was listening intently to the exchange. Stoker was watching the Doctor with a shrewd, slightly amused expression. 'Go on.'

The Doctor took this as an invitation to start work. He leaned over and began to tap the keyboard in a rapid, confident manner. He talked as he worked. 'As I said, in my experience archaeologists rarely use high explosives – or even army surplus controlled-gravity bombs. That in itself was enough to get me thinking.' The Doctor glanced apologetically at Bunny Cheung before adding, 'And then there were your credentials. All forgeries, I'm afraid.'

'Forgeries?'

'There is no Department of Alien Antiquities at the University of Tyr. It specialises in temporal compression research.'

Stoker looked at Bunny. 'You knucklehead.'

'And then there's Vega Jaal,' said the Doctor, his fingers rattling over the keyboard. 'He correctly identified a lump of natural porizium ore on sight, the sort of thing an experienced miner might be capable of, but not an archaeologist. And while that might not be unusual for a Vegan, it confirmed that I was on the right track. This moon could be rich in many kinds of minerals. All your equipment, including this machine, is calibrated for mineral analysis. And the fact that you're all in such a terrible hurry is the final clue: at a guess, I'd say you want to secure exclusive mining rights for this moon before anyone else has a chance to jump your claim.'

'Such as you?'

The Doctor made a series of final keystrokes and sat back. 'I'm not a claim jumper.'

'I'm glad to hear it. OK, so you've seen through our little deception. We can't be too careful in our line of business, I'm sure you realise. But there is one question I'd like an answer to, right now.'

'What?'

'Can you fix our analyser?'

'I already have.'

Jim immediately moved in, checking the readouts thrown up on the analyser's screen. 'He's right. This thing's running like a rabbit. It's scanning right now.'

'What's it do?' Tegan asked Nyssa.

'I think it's designed to scan the surrounding rock for particular minerals. It probably utilises some kind of isotopic recognition wave.'

'Well done, Nyssa,' said the Doctor.

'Will you look at this!' exclaimed Jim suddenly, his whole body stiffening. 'Hot *damn!*'

Everyone crowded in to see the screen. Numbers and graphics scrolled up in a rainbow of information.

A strange quiet came over the group as the readings settled down.

'Is that what I think it is?' asked someone.

'It's lex,' said Stoker simply. Then, shouting, 'It's *lex*, for crying out loud!'

'But it's practically off the damn scale!' said Jim. His voice rang with disbelief.

Suddenly, Bunny Cheung let out a massive *whoop!* of joy and Tegan yelped in surprise.

'By all that's good and holy,' Jyl Stoker was shaking her head in disbelief.

'You've done it, Jyl,' said Bunny Cheung. 'You've *done it*!'

'Done what?' asked Nyssa, raising her voice to be heard over the sudden clamour of excited shouting and laughter. 'What's going on?'

'The analyser's detected a huge seam of a very rare mineral called lexium,' explained the Doctor.

'What does that mean?'

'Fortune and glory!' shouted Stoker with relish. 'Fortune and glory! *We're gonna be rich!*'

CHAPTER FIVE

Tegan hadn't been to a party in ages.

In fact, when she thought about it, the last time she could remember having a good old knees-up, as Aunt Vanessa would have called it, was at Cranleigh Hall in 1925.

But this was different. Here there was no fancy dress or indeed anyone even attempting the Charleston: there weren't even that many people. But between them, Stoker's half dozen had managed to fill the cavern with the shouts and whoops of people finally allowed to have some fun. There was drink of course; a pretty potent beer and even a bottle of wine. It seemed Stoker's team had come prepared for success and ready to party.

Jim Boyd was asking her something.

'Sorry,' laughed Tegan. 'I can't hear you!'

'Do you want to dance?' Boyd yelled.

'Sure!'

And why not? Tegan needed to have some fun too, if only to help blot out the chilly atmosphere of the caves. And, if she was totally honest, blot out the last few months of her life.

The Doctor watched Tegan get up to dance and smiled.

'It's good to see Tegan enjoying herself,' remarked Nyssa, noticing the Doctor's look of amusement.

The Doctor dipped his head closer so that he could hear her over the din. They were sitting together with Stoker and Vega Jaal, around a portable heat generator. It provided a happy red glow in the centre of the cave, throwing up huge wavering shadows of the dancers around the walls.

'It's good that she can relax here,' Nyssa added wistfully.

'You don't share her happiness?'

'Do you?'

The Doctor appeared to think carefully about this. 'I'm still concerned about the reason we came here in the first place, Nyssa. There is danger here, somewhere. I wish it wasn't the case, but it'll find us soon enough.'

'Or we will find *it*.'

'Yes. We can't afford to relax too much. But on the other hand, Stoker and her men have a lot to celebrate, and I don't begrudge them that.'

The party had evolved naturally from the raucous carousing that had followed the discovery of the lexium. The Doctor had received some hearty slaps on the back for fixing the analyser, along with a bone-crushing hug from Bunny Cheung. Someone started passing cans of beer around. Someone else produced the sound system and started to play dance music. Jyl Stoker went around each of her men and shook them by the hand, touching their faces and heads and shoulders in natural camaraderie. The affection she demonstrated for these men was almost maternal. They all, to a man, thanked her profusely.

She cut an oddly masculine figure, dressed in a jump-suit of some tough, black material covered in zips and pockets. Over this she sported a sleeveless padded jacket, and in the inside pocket of this she kept her cigars. When she had finished talking to her men, Stoker had sat down on a crate and taken out a fresh cigar with cool deliberation. Then, with equal consideration, she had lit it with an antique stainless-steel lighter. For a while she sat there, quietly watching the smoke curl away from the tip of the cigar and disappear into the darkness overhead. While the others cheered and joked and told each other how they were going to spend their share of the fortune, Stoker simply reflected on her own personal journey here.

She'd taken the hard road, of course.

Stoker could have settled for a comfortable career with the Consortium, but from an early age she had believed in making her own successes. She had firmly rejected the offer of corporate sponsorship during her training, and all the ties that went with it, and cut loose from Earth Central at the earliest opportunity. It had cost her an easy life, for sure, but all she had earned – her ship, her crew, and her reputation as one of the most formidable independent miners in the sector – she had achieved by her own rock-hard work and determination.

So she looked older than she was, she'd got a busted nose and a temper to match, but results were what mattered most to Jyl Stoker and she never compromised.

This moon was her reward, the end of her hard road.

'I assume congratulations are in order.'

Stoker opened her eyes and found the Doctor sitting down next to her. She stretched like a cat, freeing her shoulder and neck of the binding tension that had been building up over the last few days. 'You're not the least bit bothered about the lex, are you?'

The Doctor shrugged. 'I've never really seen the point of personal wealth. "There is nothing that makes men rich and strong but that which they carry inside of them".'

'"Wealth is of the heart, not of the hand",' responded Stoker, meeting his gaze. 'See, I know John Milton too.'

'Ah, but I knew him *personally*.'

Stoker found herself laughing. 'You're really *not* interested in the lex, are you?'

'Perhaps I'm not sure what all the fuss is about. Tell me.'

Stoker raised her eyebrows, wondering how to begin. 'Lexium is *the* find; the rarest, most fashionable commodity an independent mining outfit like this could hope to come across: the profits from this trip alone could make us all millionaires. Or if not actual millionaires, then pretty damn comfortable. For the rest of our lives.'

'There's good money to be made out of space mining, then,' remarked Nyssa.

'If you can get to the right place before anyone else, yeah.'

'What made you come looking here? Akoshemon is on the very edge of this galaxy, a long way from anywhere.'

Stoker blew out a ring of smoke, wondering how much she should reveal. The trouble was, she couldn't help wanting to trust the Doctor. 'The usual way,' she said eventually, gauging his reaction. 'A tip-off, that the Akoshemon moon could have some lexium, among other things.'

The Doctor nodded thoughtfully. 'Black-market information, to which the large mining corporations may not have access.'

Stoker was careful not to confirm or deny the source, but the conclusion was sound. 'It's a race. There's a lot of folks out there looking for a way to get rich quick, and that includes the major operators like IMC and the Consortium. We're just the small guys, the independents. We have to use whatever methods we can to keep ahead. And they use whatever methods *they* can to do the same. The Consortium has got all the advantages, the best resources and equipment. Sometimes they even tag on to an independent team and then snatch the claim right out from under it.'

'Hence the urgency.'

'It's our only advantage: because we're small we can move fast. I arranged for my team and survey equipment to be dropped off here by a passing hyperspeed freight cruiser, under the cover of an archaeological dig.'

'How will you get back?' asked Nyssa.

'My own ship is due here in two days. Just long enough to complete the survey and lay a claim. The Consortium won't even know we're here.'

A shout of laughter broke out from across the glowing heat generator. They turned to see Bunny Cheung entertaining some of the men by juggling tools and pieces of equipment. With great speed, he was keeping a torch, a bunch of sonic keys and a wrench moving through the air. Some of the men were starting to clap and stamp their feet, marking time.

'Come on,' said Bunny. 'Throw me something else.'

Someone tossed a can of beer towards him, and with a deft

47

movement he incorporated it into the juggling. 'Easy! Only four items. Come on!'

Jim Boyd, standing with his arm around Tegan's waist, produced a flick-knife. He sprung the blade, and then threw it over.

Bunny caught it easily by the hilt and it joined the other items in a rapid spin. The men whooped and cheered.

'He's really very good,' said the Doctor, with genuine admiration.

'He's a damn show-off,' said Stoker. 'He's always like this when he gets a drink inside him.'

'He's doing all that while inebriated?' asked Nyssa wonderingly.

'D'you think he'd try it sober?'

They watched the various objects whirling through the air, Bunny's hands a blur. The knife blade glinted red every so often in the light of the generator. The clapping had reached a driving crescendo.

'Come on!' challenged Bunny, his eyes never leaving the flashing arc. 'One more!'

'Try this,' called the Doctor. He lobbed a cricket ball over, and Bunny barely faltered.

'Amazing!' said the Doctor. 'Such dexterity!'

'More!' shouted someone. Then it became a chant. 'More! More! More!'

Bunny was grinning, the sweat glistening on his face. His shoulders dipped and swayed as he struggled to keep the objects moving. He was having to throw them a lot higher now to maintain the rhythm, still catching the flick-knife by the handle every time. 'More?'

'More!' everyone yelled.

'Here!' someone threw another can over, but it was empty and Bunny misjudged the weight. The whole act disintegrated with a clatter and a roar of sympathy from the audience. But Bunny simply laughed and bowed theatrically at the waist. Everyone was clapping and cheering.

Everyone except Vega Jaal.

The Doctor noticed him staring into the ruby glow of the heat generator, completely uninterested in the juggling. He didn't even seem to have noticed it was over. Then the Vegan simply stood up and walked away, towards the back of the cavern.

'Interesting,' said the Doctor.

Nyssa had noticed the alien's strange behaviour too. 'I haven't seen him drinking or laughing or even talking to anyone during the party,' she told the Doctor.

'I wonder what's on his mind?' Frowning, the Doctor got to his feet and followed Jaal out of the cave as the music started up again.

Nyssa watched him go. She wondered if she ought to follow, but something stopped her. Perhaps it was because Jaal had headed towards the darkest part of the cavern, away from the lights and the generator and the people.

And Nyssa really didn't want to go there.

She turned her attention back to the party. Tegan was still dancing with Jim; he was holding her very close, and Nyssa wondered what that must feel like. Sometimes she felt as though there was more to learn about life than could possibly be squeezed into just one lifetime. She envied the Doctor his seemingly limitless knowledge and experience, and had tried to learn as much from him as she could.

Nyssa's gaze was drawn up to the febrile shadows of the dancers on the rock walls around her. The shadows existed on the periphery of vision, almost lost in the gloom. They moved like ghosts, and, detached from the simple joy of the dancers, appeared to writhe in torment.

'Your friend's been watching us,' said Jim.

'The Doctor?' Tegan frowned and glanced across to where she had last seen him sitting, talking to Stoker.

'No, the girl.'

'Nyssa,' Tegan said. The Doctor had disappeared, and Nyssa was staring at the ceiling. 'She looks bored out of her mind. The Doctor's probably been trying to explain cricket to her again.'

'Cricket?'

'It's a sport, on Earth. Or so they say.' A thought struck Tegan.

'Hey, have you ever been to Earth?'

'I'm from Earth!'

'Oh, me too!' And then Tegan was laughing at the absurdity of it all. 'Thanks for a great time. I've enjoyed myself.'

'It doesn't have to end now.'

Tegan looked at him again, properly this time. He was tall and rather thin, with a studious expression. Tegan thought that maybe Nyssa would be more his type. Academic. But he did seem interested in her, and he was good-looking, in a bookish kind of way.

'What year is this?' she asked.

He laughed nervously. 'What is this, a trick question? Test my sanity?'

'You must be mad to come to a place like this,' said Tegan.

Jim looked into her eyes. 'I used to think that. Not any more.'

Tegan felt her pulse quickening. She glanced back to where Nyssa was sitting, but she was still watching the ceiling. She was looking pale and frightened again.

'Twenty-three eighty-two,' said Jim.

'What?'

'The year is 2382. You did ask.'

'Oh, yeah. I'm sorry, you'll have to excuse me. I need to see my friend a minute.' Awkwardly Tegan broke away from him, although he wasn't even touching her now. She gave him a confused smile, and then left him standing there, sad and bewildered.

The Doctor caught up with Vega Jaal in one of the tunnels. Several of the wall-fixed lamps had been deactivated to conserve power, and the shadows were thick. Jaal appeared as a ghostly apparition, arms tightly folded, chest heaving.

'Are you all right?' asked the Doctor.

Jaal didn't seem surprised that he had company. 'Do I look all right?'

'Well, er, no. That's why I followed you.'

'I knew you would.'

'You did?'

Jaal nodded. 'I can sense these things. I sense that you are a good man, although you are not a human.'

The Doctor slipped his hands into his pockets. 'What else can you sense?'

'My people enjoy a very close bond with the earth, Doctor. And by *earth* I mean the ground, the rock and soil we stand on, and not the planet from which humans originate.'

'The *Vega Vinculum*,' said the Doctor.

Jaal smiled. 'You are familiar with both my people *and* my religion. You are indeed a most extraordinary man.'

'I find that people are often defined by their beliefs.'

'Vegans believe in the soil, the ground, the womb of life. Our connection to the forces that govern the land around us is inextricable. We can sense things that other species cannot. You asked what I could sense here, on this moon.' Vega Jaal turned and his face passed into shadow. 'I can sense the darkness, and I can sense death. *And that is all.*'

The Doctor found the words quite chilling. He took a step closer. 'Is that why you are afraid?'

Vega Jaal let out a snort of derision. 'A mole-man, scared of the dark?'

'I've never cared for that term.'

'It's what humans have always called us.'

'As you have already pointed out, I'm not human.'

Jaal's voice dropped to a whisper. 'Is that why you can sense it too? You can *feel* that there is something wrong here, can't you? Something sick in the heart of this moon.'

'Possibly. I'd like to know what it is.'

Jaal shook his head. 'You mustn't. You *mustn't*. It will destroy you. Go now, while you still can.'

'I can't,' said the Doctor, also in a whisper. 'I can't.'

'Nyssa?'

She jumped. 'Tegan! Can you feel it?' Her voice was brittle, her hands deathly cold as they gripped Tegan's arm.

'Feel what?'

'It's here,' breathed Nyssa. 'And it knows we're here, too!'

She was pale and shaking. Tegan sat down and put an arm around her shoulders. 'Take deep breaths and try to relax. I'll get you a drink.'

Nyssa clutched at her suddenly. 'No, don't leave me! Stay here, please.'

'All right, calm down. I'm not going anywhere.'

Nyssa seemed to make a conscious effort to control her breathing. Gradually she settled down, sagging against Tegan as the anxiety drained away. 'I'm sorry.'

Tegan hugged her. 'It's all right. No worries.'

'I wish the Doctor were here,' whispered Nyssa.

'You have to help me,' the Doctor urged. 'I must know what it is that you can sense!'

Vega Jaal would not face him. 'To know it would be to die. That is all I can tell you, Doctor.'

The Doctor clenched his fists in frustration, walking around the Vegan so that he could look into his eyes. In the darkness of the passageway, it was difficult to see Jaal at all. 'There must be more.'

'But that's just it,' replied Jaal, his voice wavering with despair. 'Darkness! Death! *Nothing* else!'

The Doctor sighed. 'So what do you propose to do about it?'

'Leave. We should all leave. Now.'

'Somehow, I can't see Stoker and her men agreeing to that.'

'Then they are doomed.'

'Stoker says her ship isn't due to arrive for another two days. You can't leave.'

Vega Jaal didn't reply. In the gloom, the Doctor could see that he had crossed his long, thick forearms across his chest so that his splayed fingers hovered over his own shoulders. Each finger was hooked and rigid. 'That is a Vegan sign to ward off evil forces,' noted the Doctor quietly. 'Something's coming, isn't it? You can sense it!'

The Doctor whirled around, alerted by a sound he couldn't hear. The darkness further into the tunnel had become thicker, almost as if the shadows were gathering around them with the patience of hunters.

Vega Jaal was mumbling a prayer in his own tongue; he could hardly be seen now in the darkness. The Doctor turned his attention fully toward the hunting shadows, searching the blackness for sound, movement, anything. He let go of Jaal and slowly moved towards the back of the tunnel.

There was something there. If only he could see it properly, up close.

The knot of darkness drew itself tighter.

The Doctor stepped closer. He reached out a hand, but he could no longer see it.

'What d'you think you're doing?' demanded a voice from behind him.

The Doctor felt the tension snap in his mind with painful force, and he whirled around just as a powerful lamp was switched on. The shadows retreated after only a moment's hesitation. The Doctor was left squinting into the brilliance, raising a hand to block the worst of it. 'Who's that?'

'It's me, Bunny,' the voice boomed down the tunnel, sounding ludicrously confident. 'Is that you, Doctor? With Vega Jaal?'

The Doctor felt physically exhausted. 'I'm glad you're here, Bunny.'

'It's always nice to feel wanted. What's the matter? You look like you've seen a ghost.'

'Shine your torch down here, would you?' asked the Doctor, pointing towards the back of the tunnel wall. Moments ago it had been lost in the blackness, now it was plainly rock. But there was something there.

Bunny gave a low whistle. 'Well. How the heck did you find that?'

'I don't really know,' said the Doctor. 'Perhaps I'm just lucky.'

It was a door. Cut into the rock, tall as a man and perhaps half as wide. The Doctor reached out and brushed away the cobwebs that covered it, revealing an ancient, pitted metal surface.

'I think you'd better fetch Stoker,' he told Bunny. 'Tell her that your mining expedition has just become an archaeological dig after all.'

CHAPTER SIX

Nothing kills a party like bad news.

The discovery of the door caused mixed feelings: confusion, consternation, irritation, even trepidation, and in roughly that order. All translated into *bad news*. Stoker's men were poised to make themselves rich; they didn't want any interruptions.

'I haven't got time for this,' was Stoker's predictable response.

Bunny said, 'We've got to check it out. You know the regulations.'

'Regulations be *damned*, Bunny! We've bent all the rules there are to get here and it's paid off. Don't tell me you're going to throw it all away on this nonsense.'

They were in the comms area, the makeshift office. Stoker was pacing the floor, Bunny Cheung was leaning against the bank of communications gear.

'The door is there, I've seen it. We can't ignore it.'

Stoker fumed for half a minute, hands on hips. 'This could ruin everything, Bunny.'

'I know. I'm sorry.' Bunny put his hand on her shoulder. 'We have to take a look, at the very least. It may be nothing.'

'I doubt that,' said the Doctor.

'Who asked you?' snapped Stoker. 'If it weren't for you, we wouldn't be in this mess. No one would've have found it.'

'That doesn't make it right. You can't rip the mineral wealth out of this moon knowing that someone, or something, is buried here.'

'It could be thousands of years old,' Bunny pointed out.

The Doctor shook his head. 'Judging by the corrosion of the metal, I'd say it was no more than a century old, possibly two.'

'Ironic, isn't it?' said Stoker, utterly deflated. 'All that guff about being archaeologists. What a joke. All right: what do *you* think is down there?'

'I'm afraid I'll have to take a look before we can find that out.'

She swore, once and with passion. 'Let's get it over with.'

Tegan and Nyssa finally caught up with the Doctor when he emerged from his meeting with Stoker and Bunny Cheung.

'Hey, what's going on?' Tegan demanded to know, falling into step. 'Is there a problem?'

The Doctor was clearly energised and ready for action. Sometimes it could be exhilarating to ride on his coat tails; other times it could be simply infuriating. 'Nyssa, how are you feeling?' he asked cheerily. 'Bearing up?'

'Just about.'

'Jolly good!' The Doctor strode on. 'Come on, keep up!'

'Hold on a minute!' Tegan grabbed hold of the Doctor's arm. 'Explanation. Now.'

The Doctor caught the look in both Tegan and Nyssa's eyes. 'All right…' He stuffed his hands into his trouser pockets. 'There's a distinct possibility that there is more to this moon than an abundance of lexium, There's a sign that it could have been previously inhabited, or used for some purpose by intelligent life.'

Tegan said, 'Stoker doesn't look very happy about that.'

'Galactic law states that consecrated planets, moons and asteroids cannot be subject to mining operations. It's highly illegal. If this turns out to be a buried crypt or something, Stoker will lose everything.'

'Looks like her archaeology cover's backfired, then.'

'It would seem so, yes.' The Doctor was clearly impatient to catch up with Stoker. 'Why don't we all go and take a look?'

'Do you think that's wise?' wondered Nyssa.

'What choice do we have?' The Doctor stared at her for a moment and then turned on his heel.

They had moved some lamps so that they could all see the door properly. The door was recessed about a band-length into the rock wall, but the light was reflected wherever the dust had been brushed away to reveal the old, scarred metal beneath.

Bunny Cheung said, 'The CG blast must have cleared away some loose rock.'

'I still don't see how anyone could have missed it,' said Stoker peevishly. 'I mean, we've all been down this tunnel a dozen times at least.'

Bunny Cheung said, 'It was covered in cobwebs; unless you'd known what you were looking for, it would have been practically invisible.'

'Hmm,' said the Doctor. He was crouched down by the base of the door, examining the metal.

'OK,' said Stoker, clapping her hands once. 'Let's open it. Any suggestions?'

The Doctor straightened up. 'Push?'

Stoker gave it a shove with the flat of her foot, but the door didn't move.

'Maybe it opens outwards,' said Tegan.

The Doctor shook his head. 'No, it would hit the edges of the surrounding rock. It must open inwards.'

'Let me try,' offered Bunny Cheung. He moved forward and set his right hand squarely in the centre of the metal. 'It probably just needs a… good… *heave*.'

With a grinding protest, the door began to move. It tipped forward slightly, and Bunny repositioned himself for greater leverage. Slowly he pushed the metal slab up and back until it lay flat, parallel to the floor. Beyond there was nothing but blackness. Stoker shone a torch into the shadows, but the light simply disappeared.

'Get something to prop this open,' Bunny ordered. 'We don't want it swinging shut behind us.'

It was Stoker who asked the obvious question. 'You're going in there?'

'Why not?'

'Come on,' said the Doctor, taking Stoker's torch. 'I'll go first.'

Bunny quickly grabbed another light and followed him in. 'I'm right behind you.'

Tegan and Nyssa looked at each other and shrugged before stepping into the darkness after him.

'I'm going to regret this,' grumbled Stoker, following them.

There was a short passageway, markedly different from any of the cave tunnels in that the walls were perfectly straight. The torch beams reflected off rock in sharp angles, throwing unnatural shadows back along the passage. Their footsteps scraped along the ground until the Doctor's voice came echoing back. 'Careful, there are some steps here. Leading down.'

'Typical,' muttered Tegan.

'I don't like this,' said Stoker.

'You can hold my hand if you like,' Bunny suggested mischieviously.

'Good idea,' the Doctor's voice called back. 'Everyone stick together.'

Holding on to each other, they descended around twenty stone steps until they reached a small square space just big enough to contain half a dozen people. They filled the little chamber, feeling both nervous and silly, trying not to bump into one another.

'There's another door,' realised the Doctor, shining the beam of his torch on another slab of metal. This was in better condition than the first, the burnished surface glinting in the light.

'What's that?' wondered Bunny, aiming his own torch at a rectangular panel set in the metal at head height. 'A window?'

The Doctor rubbed at the panel with his handkerchief. 'It's thick with dust, but yes, it *is* a window.' He tapped it with a finger. 'Plastic, too.'

'Can't be a burial chamber, then,' said Bunny. 'Who'd need a window in a crypt door?'

Stoker said, 'Can we go now? This place is giving me the flaming creeps.'

The Doctor was trying to shine his torch through the grimy square of plastic. 'I can't see anything.'

'I'll try opening it,' suggested Bunny, putting his shoulder to it. '*Umph.* Won't budge. This one must be jammed tight, or seized up maybe.'

'I doubt that,' said the Doctor. 'I think this door is locked.'

'Locked?'

'Yes. From the inside.'

There was a moment's pause.

'That's it,' said Stoker. 'Let's get out of here.'

'Wait a second, Jyl,' hissed Bunny. He turned back to the Doctor. 'Locked from the *inside*?'

The Doctor smiled. 'Interesting, isn't it?'

'Interesting?' repeated Stoker. 'Come on, Bunny. Let's go. You know the kind of reputation Akoshemon had. This can't be good.'

'We've come this far,' said the Doctor. 'We can't stop now.'

'You're very keen to get in there,' snarled Stoker.

'I can't resist a locked door.'

'All right, break it up,' said Bunny. 'I'll go back up and tell Jim and Nik to bring down some cutting gear. We need this door opened and pronto.'

The laser cutter made reasonably short work of the metal door, but it wasn't long before the air turned hot and thick with the smell of scorched metal and human sweat. Nobody spoke. For several minutes all that could be heard was the whine of the laser cutter. Tegan thought it sounded like a dentist's drill.

'We're through,' grunted Nik at last, sitting back and wiping his brow with the back of his glove. He switched off the cutter, much to everyone's relief.

A glowing red line had been traced around the edge of the door. 'Better knock it out before it cools down too much,' suggested Jim.

Bunny Cheung stepped forwards and knocked the rectangle of metal out of its molten frame with one punch. The door fell away with a clatter. Musty air blew out of the dark, square mouth like a dying man's cough.

'OK,' said Stoker. '*I'll* go first this time.'

She stepped through the opening, careful to avoid the red-hot edges. Bunny Cheung followed her, his face pale in the torchlight.

'Well?' said Tegan to the Doctor.

'You'd both better stay here for now,' the Doctor told them. 'We don't know what's in there.'

'We want to stay with you,' insisted Tegan.

The Doctor hesitated. 'It could be dangerous.'

'It usually is.'

'Tegan, just for once, don't argue…'

'Arguing's what I do best,' she retorted. 'Now let us through.'

Taking a deep breath and looking to heaven for strength, the Doctor stepped back and did as he was told. Tegan stepped bravely into the blackness, and Nyssa followed, albeit with less enthusiasm.

Jim and Nik were left looking on in bemusement. The Doctor gave them a tight, forced smile and then followed his companions.

'That Tegan's really something,' said Jim wistfully.

'She's sure got balls,' agreed Nik.

'I think I'm in love.'

'I quite fancy her friend.' Nik started to pack up the laser cutter, then paused to look into the darkness beyond the doorway. 'Think we should go in after them?'

Jim glanced at his friend. 'Are you crazy?'

Stoker's torch beam illuminated nothing more than a haze of dust thrown up by the falling door.

To her left she could see the Doctor's light, roving through the darkness. She aimed her torch at him, picking out his face in the black. He was looking tense.

'I can't see a thing,' she whispered irritably. She didn't even know why she was whispering. Perhaps it was the sepulchral atmosphere, the powerful sense of being intruders in some kind of tomb. Any second now, she thought, they would stumble across a sarcophagus or something.

She gasped as something brushed her face, panicking, and suddenly the Doctor was by her side.

'It's all right. It's only a cobweb.'

In the light of his torch, the Doctor's fingers were coated with fibrous grey strands. 'Very old and brittle,' he noted. 'Its owner is probably long dead. Come on.'

'Quick, shine your lights over here, we've found something,' called Tegan.

They moved in the direction of the voice, the torch beams eventually finding both Tegan and Nyssa in the gloom. Their faces, washed of all colour, looked ghoulishly stark.

Stoker's light slid over a long flat slab of metal standing waist high.

'We walked right into it,' said Nyssa.

Further investigation found it to be about three metres long and a metre wide, its surface silvery and smooth.

'Don't tell me,' groaned Stoker. 'It's a tomb. We're trespassing on the ancient burial sites of Akoshemon. Any second now we'll be cursed for eternity.'

'It's not a tomb,' said the Doctor. 'It's a table.'

The anticlimax was almost physical; Stoker felt herself shudder with relief.

'It's thick with dust, too,' added the Doctor, drawing a line across the table top with one finger. 'Someone's been neglecting the housework.'

'And look over here,' said Bunny. 'A chair.'

'This is hopeless,' complained Tegan. 'We need some proper lighting down here.'

'First sensible suggestion I've heard all evening,' Stoker grumbled.

'You're right,' said Bunny. 'I'll go and organise some lamps.'

'I'll come with you,' said Nyssa. Her voice sounded strained.

'Nyssa? Are you all right?' asked Tegan.

'I don't know. I don't feel very well…'

'Doctor?' Tegan sounded unsure.

'Go with her, Tegan,' ordered the Doctor. 'She's still recovering from the explosion. Stoker and I will carry on down here.'

'Righto, Doctor.'

As Tegan and Nyssa headed for the dim rectangle of the entrance, Stoker shivered. The temperature seemed to have dropped suddenly, and she wasn't sure she entirely liked the way this was going. Somehow the Doctor had taken charge, and it rankled. The truth was she found all this creeping around in the dark very disturbing. She could feel the primal anxiety of not being able to see properly building up to panic. But panic was something she *refused* to do.

'Over here,' said the Doctor. 'I think I've found another chair. Only this one's on its side.'

Stoker gritted her teeth. 'Do we have to skulk around in the dark like this? Can't we just wait for Bunny to come back with some decent lights?' Too late, she realised that she had asked the Doctor for guidance and, in doing so, placed him fully in control.

She heard a metallic scrape as the Doctor righted his chair. 'You can go back if you want,' he said. 'I'm staying here.'

Alone, she thought. 'Aren't you frightened?'

'Not until I find something to be frightened of, no.' Stoker found his dry, confident voice strangely reassuring. 'At the moment,' he continued, 'all we've got is a room, a large table and a couple of chairs. Not quite the Hammer House of Horror, is it?'

Tegan had led Nyssa out into the antechamber at the foot of the stairs. Jim and Nik were waiting in the semi-darkness, talking to Bunny Cheung.

'What did you find?' asked Jim.

'So far, a table and some chairs,' said Bunny.

'This could be the find of the century.'

'I'll get on to the major news networks straight away,' said Nik.

'Oh belt up, the pair of you. Come and help me find some spare lamps.'

'Can someone help me, please?' said Tegan. 'My friend's sick.'

They took Nyssa back up into the main cavern and sat her down on a packing crate. The heat generator was still throwing out its merry red light, and Nyssa huddled closer to it, shivering. Jim found her a blanket and draped it over her shoulders before going off for the lamps.

'How are you feeling now?' asked Tegan.

'Better,' said Nyssa. She assumed that she was suffering from shock, a delayed reaction of some kind to the explosion. 'I just needed a little air, I think.'

'It was pretty stuffy down there.'

'You'd best get back to the Doctor,' Nyssa said. 'You know the sort of trouble he'll get into if someone doesn't keep an eye on him.'

'You're sure?'

'Of course.'

'I don't know, Nyssa. You still look a bit wobbly, if you ask me.'

'Please, I don't want to be a nuisance. I just need to sit for a while.'

'Do not concern yourself,' said a soft voice. They looked up to see Vega Jaal standing there. 'I shall sit with your friend, if she will permit me.'

Nyssa smiled weakly. 'That's kind of you.'

'OK,' said Tegan, getting up. 'Thanks. I'll go and help Bunny and the others.'

Vega Jaal watched her go, and then sat down next to Nyssa. 'We are kin, you and I.'

Nyssa frowned. 'We are?'

'We are both more sensitive than these humans.'

Nyssa pulled the blanket tighter. 'I've never really thought about it.'

'You don't need to think about it,' Jaal said. 'You can feel it.'

But Nyssa did think about it. It was what she was trained to do, after all, as a scientist. 'Down there, I felt cold… but cold *inside*. Somewhere inside my head. As if I could sense a great void on the edge of the darkness, something I couldn't quite see but I *knew* was there. Like the emptiness of space, all around us. Oh, I'm not making any sense.'

'It doesn't matter,' said Jaal. 'Sense and reason are secondary to the things we feel.'

Nyssa was confused. She was doing her best to analyse all this, to apply a logical thought process to her feelings. But all she could sense were the phantoms of oppression and doom, like the memory of a nightmare. 'What's going to happen to us here?'

Vega Jaal shrugged. 'Soon, I will have to go down there too, and feel the coldness you have felt.'

At that moment, Nyssa couldn't imagine anything more awful. 'Why?'

'Because,' and here Vega Jaal smiled gently, 'your friend the Doctor will ask me to.'

Tegan found Bunny Cheung in the comms area. He was replaying the holographic message from his daughter.

'… *Kooka's arm needs fixing again. It's come right off this time.*'

Bunny smiled sadly and flexed his hand. The image of Rosie froze mid-sentence, '*So long as you fix him as soon as you come–*'

'Are you OK?' Tegan asked quietly.

This time he didn't jump. He just wiped one massive hand down his face and beard, as if to clear his mind. 'Still a long way from home,' he said.

'This business is going to delay things even more, isn't it?'

'I should say so.'

'We'd best get a move on, then.'

Bunny stared for a moment longer at the glowing statue of his daughter. Then he made a fist with his hand and the hologram vanished. 'I downloaded her from the hypernet earlier,' he explained, waggling the large ring on his middle finger. 'Easier to carry with me. I'm supposed to be sending her a message, but…'

Tegan just nodded, not really knowing what to say. Jim and Nik had arrived anyway, with a hover trolley loaded up with portable lamps.

'Won't we need some cable?' asked Tegan.

'Nah,' said Nik. 'These have remote power units. They get their juice transmitted directly from the generator. Nice bit of kit.'

'Right then,' said Tegan. 'The Doctor will be waiting for these. Let's get cracking.'

*

The Doctor and Stoker had made some progress. By now their eyes had become accustomed to the very limited light available, and they were able to pick out some more objects in the silvery gloom. In addition to the table and four chairs, they had discovered two large wall-mounted cabinets and a series of knee-level storage units ranged against one wall. The doors to these all appeared to be locked.

Stoker was holding a torch for the Doctor, who was squatting down to examine the locking mechanism on one of the units. 'You've done this kind of thing before, haven't you?'

The Doctor didn't reply straight away. Something had caught his attention. 'These locks are electronic!'

'Aren't all locks electronic?'

'Well, probably, in this period,' the Doctor conceded.

'So?'

'So these locks are still operating. There must be a live current going through them.'

Stoker frowned. 'Are you sure? But that would mean…'

'There's some kind of power source here, and it's still operational.'

'That's the lot,' said Bunny, placing the last of the disc-shaped lamps onto the stack.

'That didn't take too long,' Tegan said, feeling a little flushed with all the exertion. 'I wonder how the Doctor's getting on?'

She turned to call through the black hole that was the doorway, but to her surprise found the room beyond suddenly flooded with light.

The Doctor was standing on the far side of the room, one hand resting on some kind of wall panel. Stoker was standing next to him, her eyes screwed up against the harsh electric glare.

'We, er, seem to have found the light switch,' said the Doctor, managing to sound both apologetic and self-satisfied at once.

'You mean we've just lugged all those wretched lamps down here for nothing?' Tegan tried to glare at him but she couldn't compete with the brilliance of the overhead strip-lights.

'Not to worry,' said the Doctor. 'The exercise will have done you good, if nothing else. Now come and see what else we've found.'

Tegan stepped through the doorway into what might once have been some kind of workshop or laboratory. Apart from the large central table and chairs and a few lockers on the walls, it was sparsely furnished. The surfaces were functional metal, with what she guessed were a couple of computer workstations. Small lights flickered on various control panels, and a quiet rushing noise alerted her to the presence of an air-conditioning unit in the ceiling.

'It's amazing,' said Bunny Cheung. 'No one can have been here for years, but it's all still functioning.'

'There must be another room through here,' said the Doctor, indicating a wide door at the rear.' At least we won't have to cut our way through. With the power back on... aha!' He pressed a switch and the door slid smoothly open.

The next room was larger and quite obviously a lab of some sort: there were humming computer banks and monitor screens ranged along the walls and a number of workbenches full of scientific apparatus. The Doctor immediately began to inspect the equipment.

'But what is this place?' wondered Tegan. 'Some kind of secret base?'

'More likely some sort of scientific research establishment,' the Doctor said. 'Entirely self-contained, but very probably secret, judging by its location.'

'Research into what?' asked Stoker.

'Well, there's a lot of calibration equipment for stasis field generators and such like here. I'd say that they were researching suspended-animation techniques.'

'"They"?' queried Bunny.

'Whoever worked here.'

'And where are they now?'

'Good question.'

'Maybe they finished up and left,' suggested Stoker hopefully. 'The place looks abandoned.'

'You're forgetting two very important things,' the Doctor pointed out. 'Firstly, the power had been left on. Somewhere there's a generator still running. Not usually the action of someone abandoning a place for good, unless they had to leave in a terrible hurry.'

'And secondly?'

'The most interesting thing: the outer door was locked from the *inside*, remember.'

'You mean, whoever lived or worked here… should still *be* here?' Tegan hugged herself as she looked around the empty room. 'That feels kind of weird, Doctor.'

'Hmm,' the Doctor seemed suddenly distracted, squatting down again to pick up a fallen beaker. He examined it closely for a moment, then looked across the lab to where a plastic tray lay propped up against the wall.

'You're about to add a third "interesting thing" to the list of things we've overlooked, aren't you?' Stoker realised.

The Doctor nodded thoughtfully. 'The items on the floor in here, and the overturned chair in the first room. Signs of a struggle of some sort, would you say?'

Bunny Cheung said, 'I really don't like the sound of this.'

'I'd like to ask Vega Jaal to come down here,' the Doctor said as he stood up.

Stoker looked puzzled. 'Jaal? Why?'

'I think he might be able to help. We're underground, in his element.'

Stoker considered the request for a second and then sent Bunny to fetch the Vegan. Then she took out a cigar from her jacket pocket and lit it. 'Y'know, I really don't like the idea that someone has been here *before* me.'

'You're just worried about losing your precious lexium,' said Tegan.

Stoker blew a perfect smoke ring. 'I'm not allowed to stake a claim on consecrated ground or anywhere with specific religious significance. I haven't seen evidence of either yet.'

The Doctor looked at her curiously. 'Loopholes, Ms Stoker?'

'You bet. Quite apart from my own personal ambitions, Doctor,

I have my men to think about. They rely on me for a living. If there's any way I can complete my claim for mining rights to this moon, I will.'

'That sounds very mercenary,' said Tegan.

'We all have to make a living. And I owe it to my team to see them right. I'm not giving up this moon without a fight.'

Nyssa sat quietly with Vega Jaal. She had found him to be intelligent and considerate, but he was rather gloomy company. She felt unaccountably relieved when Bunny Cheung arrived and said, 'Stoker wants you, Jaal.'

'You mean the Doctor wants me.' Vega Jaal gave Nyssa a sad smile and got up to leave.

'I'll come with you,' Nyssa said, standing up. She already felt a little guilty.

'You are not well enough,' Jaal said.

'No, I insist. I feel a lot better thanks to you.'

'I'm sure I've done nothing.'

Nyssa smiled. 'On the contrary, you have made me realise that my feelings, my instincts, are every bit as valuable as my intelligence. It is only a question of interpretation.'

'We'd better go,' said Bunny Cheung. 'Wouldn't do to keep Stoker waiting.'

Nyssa was surprised and heartened by the sight of a well-lit, functional laboratory complex. Its mundane appearance lent her strength.

'Hi there,' said Tegan. 'Feeling better?'

Nyssa said, 'You've been busy.'

'Not really. The Doctor found the light switch, that's all.'

'Ah, Vega Jaal,' said the Doctor. 'Good of you to come.'

The Vegan nodded formally and then cocked his head slightly, as if listening for something. 'Can you hear it?' he asked.

'Hear what?'

'The cry of a dying planet: born on the wind of time and trapped in

67

the rock that surrounds us; the eternal scream of a world desecrated and turned into evil.'

A stunned silence was met with Stoker's slow hand-clap. 'Oh, bravo.'

Even the Doctor looked a little flustered. 'Well, er, Vega Jaal… now we know what you can, er, hear. Could you please tell us what you *feel* down here? I was hoping to make use of your natural geological senses.'

'I feel death,' said Jaal simply. 'All around us, and near every one of us.'

'Oh, for pity's sake!' exploded Stoker as her patience finally wore through. 'I don't employ you to frighten everyone with this pseudomystical claptrap, Jaal!'

'No, wait, please,' the Doctor urged.

Vega Jaal raised a hand to cover his eyes, clearly distressed. He said, 'It is very bright in here. But death is waiting in the darkness. It watches us from the shadows.'

Tegan said, 'I'm sorry Doctor, but this is giving me the creeps.'

'See?' Stoker demanded.

The Doctor ignored them both, stepping closer to Jaal and saying, 'There's more, isn't there? Something you're not telling us.'

Jaal shuddered. 'Death is coming for all of us. Me. Stoker. Bunny. Your friends. Even you, Doctor.'

'Nobody lives for ever,' said the Doctor.

Jaal's eyes burned. 'But you will die many times over, Doctor.'

'I already have.'

'Not like this!' Jaal's voice was a rasping whisper now. *'Death after death…!'* For a long moment he and the Doctor stared at each other, and then the Vegan abruptly collapsed. The Doctor only just managed to catch him as he fell. Stoker helped him to lower Jaal into a chair.

'Get some water, quick,' Stoker ordered, and Tegan left immediately.

Satisfied that Vega Jaal had only fainted, the Doctor turned to Nyssa. 'How are you feeling, Nyssa?'

'Scared.'

'Jolly good! That's only natural. I'd have been more worried if you weren't.'

'Why did you make him do that?' Nyssa asked. Her anxiety was giving way to anger. Sometimes the Doctor's casual disregard for other people's fears irked her. She grasped Vega Jaal's hand and his large eyes flickered open.

'I apologise,' the Vegan murmured weakly.

'It's all right. The Doctor had no right to let you –'

'The Doctor had every right' Jaal contradicted her firmly.

The Doctor said, 'Something is affecting us all: Vega Jaal is acutely sensitive to it, whatever it may be. At the moment, Jaal is our best chance of determining what it is, or where exactly it might be.'

'You're using him,' stated Nyssa.

'I know.'

'Let's not argue the rights and wrongs of it,' said Bunny Cheung. 'Let's just get it over with. Jaal, have you any idea what's going on?'

The Vegan shook his head sadly. 'No. I still sense only death, and total, irredeemable darkness.'

'Well that's just great,' said Stoker.

'It could be anything from an ultra-dense psionic field to a particularly high level of positive ions in the atmosphere,' said the Doctor.

Nyssa felt on more familiar ground now. 'Which do you think it is?'

'Neither, to be perfectly honest. But something is manipulating our perceptions down here, both ordinary and extra-sensory. But it's very subtle. I want Vega Jaal to tell us if he can detect any kind of focus.'

'Through there,' said Jaal, pointing.

They all looked at the wall, where the Vegan had indicated.

Stoker sighed. 'It's just a blank wall, for goodness' sake.'

'But what's on the other side of it, I wonder?'

'A load of rock,' Bunny said.

'No, I don't think so,' the Doctor said. 'Remember, Vega Jaal can sense cavities and voids through solid rock.' He moved to the wall and examined it, tracing the edges of the metal panelling with his fingers. 'I think this is another doorway. A secret door.'

'You're right,' Nyssa agreed. 'That is the only area of the wall clear of obstruction.'

Bunny joined the Doctor. 'There must be a way of opening it.'

'Do we really want to, though?' Stoker said. 'I mean, if what Jaal says is true, it might be better to leave it shut.'

But the Doctor had found the switch, and the wall panel slid up into the ceiling with a buzz. A cold draught flicked at his hair.

'Too late,' said Vega Jaal.

'Dark again,' noted Bunny, peering into the black hole. 'Give me a torch, someone.'

Nyssa felt a stab of fear the moment she saw the darkness. She felt as though she was standing on the brink of terror, but even as she swallowed down the cold lump of dread in her chest and opened her mouth to warn them, the Doctor had already followed Bunny through the opening.

'Too late,' said Vega Jaal again.

'This is getting to be a habit,' Bunny joked.

'Careful,' the Doctor warned him. 'More stairs.' Their shadows, cast in front of them by the light of the laboratory, ran down the short flight of steps like liquid.

They reached a large circular chamber where the air seemed frozen solid, as though something was waiting for them down here, holding its breath. There was a strange smell, dry and leathery, but the cold made it elusive.

'Another lab?' Bunny guessed, his deep voice echoing loudly.

'Or a morgue,' said the Doctor quietly. 'Look at this.'

His torch had found a bundle of rags on the floor; or at least it looked to Bunny like a bundle of rags. Then he realised with a jolt that they had found a body.

It was humanoid, emaciated and skeletal, its hands curled into claws across its chest. The skin was thin and withered, so much so that the eyes were simply empty holes in the skull and the teeth had been exposed in a hideous, hysterical grin.

The Doctor's torch beam roved across the floor, picking out yet more bodies; corpse after corpse strewn across the chamber.

CHAPTER SEVEN

The first body to be examined in any detail was a human adult male, and little more than a dried-out husk. A thick layer of dust had settled on the brittle skin, indicating that the corpse had lain here on the floor of the lower chamber for some time, possibly many years. The slightest touch caused the desiccated tissue to crumble into a brown, flaky powder.

Lamps were brought down into the chamber so that all the bodies could be examined properly. There were five in total, lying in the centre of the room, which appeared to have been carved out of the solid rock. The Doctor was conducting brief *in situ* post-mortems, kneeling on the stone floor and peering at each cadaver in turn through a pair of antiquated half-moon spectacles. Closer examination involved the use of a magnifying glass and occasional murmurs of 'interesting' and 'hmm…' and 'oh dear'.

'Well?' Stoker prompted eventually, tired of being a spectator. 'What's the verdict?' She slipped a cigar between her teeth and flicked open her lighter.

'Death by chronic blood loss,' said the Doctor, standing up. 'Each of these poor fellows has been completely dried out. There is advanced calcification of all muscle, tissue and skin. I can't say for sure without conducting full autopsies, but I'd be willing to bet that all the internal organs are in a similar state of dehydration.'

Stoker nudged one of the corpses with the toe of her boot. The whole body moved with a dry, rustling noise. He was as light as a feather. 'Do you want to do a full autopsy?'

The Doctor carefully folded his glasses and put them away. 'Not unless I have to, no.'

'Do you think they locked themselves down here all those years ago and just… dried?'

She was rewarded with the briefest of smiles. 'It's impossible to say. I doubt it. If we can access the computer records upstairs, we might be able to find out more.'

'Maybe they had some kind of disease,' Bunny Cheung realised nervously. 'You said this place looked like a research lab. Maybe they were researching into an infectious disease or something. Bacteriological weapons, even. They made a mistake, something toxic leaked. Wiped them all out.'

'If there was any biohazard down here, then we will already have been exposed and contaminated.'

'You're a real comfort, you know that?'

'For what it's worth, Bunny, I don't believe that these people died as a result of any disease. It's difficult to say, but it looks to me as though they were simply… sucked dry.'

'Sucked dry?' repeated Stoker.

'Whatever happened to them happened very quickly. The result was practically instant mummification. The level of decay in the remains is almost negligible.'

Stoker let her breath out slowly through her teeth. She felt very tired. 'So what do we do now?'

'This has to be reported to the relevant authorities,' Bunny said.

Stoker snorted. 'Yeah, right. Blow our whole lexium claim out of space, why don't you?'

'Jyl, we have dead bodies here. It needs to be investigated.'

'Can't we let sleeping dogs lie? No one's missed them for a hundred odd years. Why stir it all up now?'

Nyssa was sitting with Vega Jaal in the main laboratory. The Vegan was rocking slowly back and forth, staring straight into nothing. 'This is only the beginning,' he said.

'I don't understand,' Nyssa said.

'The beginning of what?' Tegan asked bluntly.

'Think about it,' Vega Jaal said. 'Every door leads down into darkness. The door in the cave led into the antechamber. The second door led into here, where it was also dark. That door over there…' he nodded at the rectangular hole in the wall where the Doctor, Stoker and Bunny had gone earlier, 'the same again. Only this time we find dead bodies. Each time we find a door, we go further down. Nearer the darkness.'

Tegan folded her arms. 'So?'

'There is another door to come,' Jaal said quietly. 'But we will not find the darkness beyond it. The darkness will find *us*.'

Nyssa felt herself beginning to perspire again. 'How would we know if this… darkness had already found us?'

Jaal stared at her. 'We'd be dead.'

'Are you OK, Nyssa?' Tegan asked. 'You don't look well. You shouldn't let this guy get to you.'

Vega Jaal smiled humourlessly at this. 'It is not me you should fear.'

'I'm talking to my friend,' Tegan told him. 'Nyssa, do you want me to fetch the Doctor?'

'No, I'm fine, honestly,' she lied. 'I just feel… I just feel as though we're being watched. It's probably my imagination.'

Tegan nodded. 'This place is getting pretty spooky.'

At that moment the Doctor stepped through the hole in the wall. Stoker and Bunny Cheung followed him out looking pale and drawn. Stoker sat down heavily in one of the lab chairs and closed her eyes.

'What have you found?' asked Vega Jaal.

The Doctor sighed and stuck his hands in his trouser pockets. 'At the moment I haven't the slightest idea.'

Vega Jaal turned and stared intently at the doorway to the lower chamber.

'If only we knew who those poor people were,' said Nyssa.

'The overalls they wore all have name tags. I've jotted them down.' The Doctor took out his notepad and tore off a sheet of paper, handing it to Tegan. 'We know *who* they were… we really need to know what they were doing.'

'Do you think the answer might lie in these old computer banks?'

Nyssa asked, indicating the various workstations around the room.

'Capital idea!' The Doctor inspected the nearest VDU. 'Shouldn't be too much trouble to get them working... there's power running through them, after all.' He tapped a small LED glowing on the side of the computer. 'It's simply a question of finding the correct start-up procedure.' He began to stab experimentally at the keyboard.

Stoker watched the Doctor, Tegan and Nyssa crowd around the computer. Those girls hung on his every word, she thought. Oddly, she didn't find it all that surprising. He was a strangely inspirational figure. If anyone could get to the bottom of all this, then Stoker was sure he could. The only question was whether she really wanted to get to the bottom of all this. A huge cloud of doubt was now gathering over her claim to mining rights on this moon.

There was a loud bang from across the room as the Doctor whacked the computer with the flat of his hand. The VDU flickered reluctantly into life.

Tegan laughed. 'When in doubt give it a thump, as my Aunt Vanessa used to say.'

'I'm not sure that's the best way of dealing with advanced technology,' said Nyssa prissily.

'Tried-and-tested methods are usually best, Nyssa,' the Doctor smiled.

Time for a smoke, Stoker decided, and took out her cigar. She looked up just as Bunny Cheung stepped into her light.

'We need to talk,' Bunny said. He stood like a pillar of rock, his hands forming giant fists. 'There are dead people here. Jyl, we have to do something.'

Stoker paused before lighting her cigar. 'What do you suggest, Bunny?'

'Pack up and leave, for one thing.'

'What?'

Bunny sat down next to her. 'This isn't anything to do with us, Jyl. We can't go on with the claim knowing that all this has... happened. We should leave it to the experts. Leave it to the Doctor and Tegan

DOCTOR WHO

and Nyssa if you like. But don't involve us.'

'We already are involved.'

'Our interest is with the mineral exploitation of this moon. Nothing else.'

'Are you forgetting the lexium?'

'Of course not.' Bunny looked uncomfortable. 'But what can we do? We can't make a claim now.'

Stoker sat forward, teeth clenched. 'We are sitting on a fortune here, Bunny. How are you going to explain it to the others if we have to back off?'

Bunny took a deep breath. 'It could be dangerous here, Jyl. We don't know what killed those people down there. I think the men will value their own skins more than the chance of a share of the lex.'

Stoker smiled faintly. 'That's rubbish and you know it. This is a chance in a lifetime for all of us. You and I could afford to retire after this claim.'

'It's pointless, Jyl. We can't go on.'

'I am not sitting back on a sodding technicality only to let some Consortium stooge sail right in and get the lex! No way.'

'There's more than securing mining rights at stake here,' Bunny argued. 'You have to consider the personal safety of your team.'

'You mean *your* personal safety.' Stoker poked a finger into Bunny's broad chest. 'You're only concerned about getting back to your precious family, Bunny.'

'I'm not ashamed of that.'

'Well some of us don't have families to get back to.' Stoker's jaw tightened with suppressed fury as she finished speaking. 'Besides which, until our ship arrives we're stuck here, Bunny. So we may as well make the best fist of it we can.'

Bunny Cheung sat back with a growl.

Stoker finally lit her cigar and took a long drag. 'I thought that if we could help the Doctor with his investigation, we might still find a way to secure the claim.'

'You agree the claim's in jeopardy, then?' Bunny grumbled.

'Of course it's in jeopardy. So let's see if we can turn this mess around and get that lex for ourselves.'

Bunny folded his arms. 'I'm still not happy about it.'

'I'm not asking you to be happy about it, you big lummox. I'm asking you to help. OK?'

Bunny glowered at the holograph ring on his right middle finger. 'OK.'

'It seems fairly straightforward,' said the Doctor. 'Just a matter of finding the right access code now.'

'Is that all?' Tegan asked heavily. They were sitting in front of the computer console. The monitor had filled up with glowing green letters and numbers and then blanked out on them. Tegan hadn't had much experience of computers on Earth, and tended to treat them with suspicion. Her cousin Colin had been a bit of a computer geek; she remembered a dreary afternoon spent playing Ping-Pong with him on his brand-new home computer. Colin had found it enthralling, and told her how computers were soon going to revolutionise the way the world worked and played. Some chance, Tegan had thought.

'Perhaps we should try hitting it again.' Nyssa suggested.

'Sarcasm isn't your strong point, Nyssa,' said the Doctor. 'Let's switch back to more conventional methods: try tapping a few keys and see what happens.'

Nyssa sighed and started to work.

A terrible sound filled the air: a long, agonised shriek of mortal suffering. It was so unexpected, and so shockingly unnatural, that it took several seconds before anyone could properly identify the noise. At first, they did nothing but look at one another.

The scream suddenly died away, becoming little more than an expiring cough of air.

'Down there,' Nyssa pointed at the open portal to the lower chamber. The corpses' chamber. Tegan felt the hairs stiffen all over her body.

The Doctor looked quickly around the lab. 'Where's Vega Jaal? He was here a minute ago – oh, no...'

He whirled around and plunged through the doorway without any further hesitation.

The body was lying in the centre of the room, a little way from the others. The Doctor rushed over to Vega Jaal's withered remains and knelt down. His fingers gently touched the Vegan's face. The flesh was nothing more than dry, fibrous meat.

Bunny had followed the Doctor into the chamber and glanced quickly around. The corpses of the other victims still lay in the centre of the room, but the rest of the chamber was empty.

'He's dead, I'm afraid,' the Doctor was saying, unnecessarily. Vega Jaal's once huge, liquid eyes were now blind, screwed up lumps of blackened tissue.

'Oh, dear Lord,' whispered Bunny. 'It must still be here. Whatever it was that killed all those others… *it's still here!*'

They exited the lower chamber and shut the door behind them. For a few minutes they all stood in the main lab, agitation soon giving way for the need to blame.

'Who the hell let him go down there on his own?' Bunny had demanded fiercely. The skin of his face was bleached with shock.

'I didn't even know he'd gone down there,' Tegan said.

'Someone must've seen him!'

'No one did, Bunny,' said Stoker. 'He must've slipped down there when we were busy.'

'But why?'

Stoker boiled over at this point. 'How the hell should I know?'

'He was curious,' said the Doctor.

'Well he's *dead*, now,' snapped Bunny. Then he sank into a chair and buried his face in his hands. 'Sorry,' he said. 'I'm sorry.'

Tegan put a hand on his arm. She felt immensely sorry for him. All he wanted to do was go home, a feeling Tegan remembered only too well.

'Why *did* Jaal go down there?' the Doctor was asking. 'What could he sense?'

It was Nyssa who spoke up in reply. 'Vega Jaal said there was another door. He said that every time we found a door, it led down into the darkness.'

'That's true enough,' Tegan muttered.

'He said the next door would be the last door,' Nyssa went on. 'And that beyond that there was *nothing* but darkness.'

'I don't understand all these riddles,' protested Stoker. 'What does it matter, anyway? He's dead.'

The Doctor was pacing the room, without taking his eyes off the door. 'Vega Jaal knew there was something down there. Something dangerous.'

Tegan frowned. 'And yet he still went down there? Without telling anyone?'

'Yes, without telling anyone,' the Doctor repeated thoughtfully. 'Because he knew someone would try to stop him, or else go down there with him.'

'Damn right,' Bunny confirmed.

'That could only mean he didn't want anyone else to share the danger,' Stoker said.

'He wanted to face it alone,' the Doctor agreed.

'Are you trying to say Vega Jaal went down there alone because he *knew* something would try to kill him?' asked Bunny.

'Yes, I think that's exactly what he did.'

Tegan was aghast. 'But that's awful! Why would he commit suicide like that? It doesn't make sense!'

'It would to a Vegan,' the Doctor said. 'Jaal warned us that we were all going to die. He had already accepted his fate. Taking the initiative, confronting the probable cause of his death, would guarantee him a place in the Vegan afterlife. And it would also serve as a warning. To us.'

'He sacrificed himself?' Nyssa said. 'That's horrible.'

The Doctor shrugged. 'It's also academic, I'm afraid, Vega Jaal has proved his point: there *is* something deadly here, something with the power to drain a body of blood in a matter of seconds. He's alerted us to a very real danger.'

'We shouldn't be staying here,' said Bunny. 'We should all move back up into the caverns. It's got to be safer.'

'There's no point in us an staying down here, I suppose,' the Doctor agreed.

'Don't tell me you *want* to stay?' said Stoker. She pointed at the wall. 'You're telling me there's some kind of killer on the other side of that. To me the next step is obvious: we should lock this place back up and seal it in.'

The Doctor shook his head. 'We have to find out what it is. We can't leave until we do.'

Stoker looked to Bunny. 'What do you think?'

'I don't know any more, Jyl. I just don't know.'

'But we can still save the claim,' Stoker insisted. 'Seal this place up, blow it up, flatten it: I don't give a damn. The sooner we get back to our proper job, the better. For all of us.'

Bunny banged his fist down on the bench top, denting it. 'Oh come on, Jyl – Vega Jaal's dead! We haven't even told the others yet. If we do anything now, it should be to pack up and leave. Forget the lex.'

'We can't leave until the ship gets here, you know that.'

'Then we send a mayday call. Interstellar. Someone's bound to pick it up.'

'Yeah – like the Consortium for starters.' Stoker let out a hiss of despair. 'Can you just stop and think about this first, Bunny? I've got a claim to protect here. I don't want you going all jittery on me just because you're due some home leave!'

Bunny growled and stood up. 'Do what you want, you always do.'

As Bunny stalked out of the lab, Stoker suddenly jumped up and ran after him. She stopped at the doorway and bellowed after him, 'Don't you dare send that mayday, you bastard!' Her voice echoed back at her, full of desperate anger and rear. She closed her eyes. 'Oh, hell and damnation.'

'I'll go after him,' said Tegan, brushing past. 'He's just upset, that's all.'

Stoker opened her eyes and looked wearily at the Doctor, who had sat down and put his feet up on one of the benches. 'Are you quite finished?' he asked pointedly.

'Don't get snappy with me, Doctor, I'm not in the mood.'

The Doctor swung his legs down. 'In case you're forgetting, Vega Jaal's body is still on the other side of that door. We have to get it back. We have to find out what killed him. We have to find out what is going on here.'

'What's all this "we" business?' Stoker said. She ran a hand over her head and leaned against the exit door. She felt extraordinarily tired and confused. 'I hadn't bargained on all this,' she added quietly.

Nyssa said, 'You cannot leave Vega Jaal's body down there.'

Stoker looked up at the wall where the secret door was. It looked blank, innocent. She really didn't want to know what lay on the other side any more. But Stoker knew that Nyssa was right: she had a duty to Vega Jaal. 'OK,' she said. 'Let's do it.'

Vega Jaal was still screaming, even though he was dead.

It was soundless and without breath, but you could see it was a scream: his mouth was open, wide enough to see the shrivelled tongue inside. Sharp yellow teeth protruded from shrunken gums, the lips pulled right back by the harsh angle of the jaw.

Stoker swallowed back the bile in her throat and stepped closer to the corpse. Jaal's remains had been carried out of the lower chamber and placed on one of the workbenches in the main lab. Under the strip-lights he looked as yellow as parchment.

The Doctor was examining the body in minute detail. Stoker felt she owed it to Vega Jaal to be present, but it was all she could do to stop herself throwing up. She wanted to look away, but she wouldn't allow herself that luxury. Jaal was dead. She was alive. What comfort did she deserve?

'Look at this,' said the Doctor. He was inspecting the side of Jaal's skull through his magnifying glass.

Stoker forced herself to take another step closer. The Doctor was pointing to a series of irregular pockmarks in the paper-like skin on the Vegan's head.

'What are they?' Stoker asked thickly.

'Holes,' the Doctor said. 'Various sizes, some no more than pinpricks and others the size of a small coin. These particular holes lead directly into the skull.' The Doctor looked up at her, and then added, 'Something penetrated flesh and bone to get to the blood within.'

Stoker pulled a face. 'It drank his blood?'

'Yes. All of it.'

'Can't we cover him up?' The yawning mouth was really starting to get to Stoker now.

'Of course,' said the Doctor. 'We'll get a blanket or something from upstairs.'

'I really didn't want any of this,' Stoker told him.

'I know.'

Stoker frowned. 'What's up?'

The Doctor was looking at Nyssa. She was sitting quietly, staring straight ahead – utterly motionless. It didn't look natural. 'Nyssa? Is there anything wrong?'

'It's hungry…' Nyssa said softly. 'It's hungry and it wants… it wants…'

'What's up with her?' asked Stoker, alarmed.

'It's trying to make contact again,' said the Doctor quickly, excited now. 'Nyssa's sensitive to it.'

'To what?'

'To whatever it was that Vega Jaal could sense! Now that he's dead, it's using Nyssa instead…' The Doctor moved closer. 'What does it want, Nyssa?'

Nyssa's brown eyes had rolled up beneath the lids. All colour had drained from her face. Her head was tilted back slightly, her lips parted. 'It wants… us… it wants us all…'

The Doctor knelt down by her, leaning in close so that he could whisper into her ear, 'What is it, Nyssa?'

Nyssa's lips moved, but for a moment no sound emerged. 'It… it is dark…'

'What does she mean?' asked Stoker. 'It's too dark to see it?'

'Darkness,' Nyssa whispered. 'Darkness… it wants us! It's coming for us!' Then she slumped forward like a puppet with its strings cut, lifeless, boneless. The Doctor caught her awkwardly and lowered her to the floor.

'She's stopped breathing,' he said, feeling for the pulse in her throat. 'Cardiac arrest! Help me!'

Galvanised by the panic in the Doctor's voice, Stoker leapt forward. 'What should I do?'

'We've got to resuscitate her. I'll breathe for her, you try and get the heart started.'

'What? How?'

The Doctor was already leaning down over Nyssa, tipping her head right back and opening her mouth. The fingers of one hand squeezed her nostrils shut and then, taking a deep breath, he clamped his mouth down over hers. He blew into her lungs with sufficient force to inflate her ribcage slightly. He came up for another breath. 'Strike her hard on the sternum when I say,' he instructed Stoker. He bent down and breathed into her again. 'Now!'

Stoker slapped her hand flat onto Nyssa's chest.

'No, like this,' said the Doctor, and, using both hands and the full weight of his shoulders, pressed down with sudden force on her breastbone, directly over the heart. He repeated this twice and then returned to breathing for her.

Stoker copied the Doctor's actions when he signalled, frightened that she was going to break a rib or something, but too scared not to give it everything she had.

'Come on, Nyssa!' gasped the Doctor in between breaths. Nyssa's face was a terrible white colour, the skin around her lips already turning grey as the blood lost precious oxygen. The Doctor pinched the nose shut again and breathed into her mouth.

Stoker thumped on the chest. 'Come on, you silly bitch! Breathe!'

The Doctor came up for air. There was stone-cold terror in his eyes as he watched Nyssa's lips turning from purple to blue. 'Cyanosis,' he said. 'We're losing her!'

Stoker heaved on the girl's chest again. This time she *tried* to break a rib, anything to kick-start the lump of meat inside into beating again. 'Come *on*, girl! You can do it! You can do it!'

'Keep going,' the Doctor ordered, feeling for a pulse again. His fingers trembled against the cold flesh of her neck. 'Come on, Nyssa. I'm not going to let you die. I *refuse* to let you die!'

Stoker pounded once more and suddenly Nyssa convulsed. At first Stoker thought it was just a nervous reflex; maybe she had fractured something. But then Nyssa started to choke and gag until the Doctor rolled her onto her side and she vomited. She drew in a series of shuddering breaths and coughed up a bit more. Then the Doctor gathered her up in his arms and pulled her to him. She was looking pale, but her lips had turned pink again and her eyes were fluttering.

'Is she OK?' asked Stoker, exhausted.

The Doctor nodded and held Nyssa close. 'She's fine, she's fine,' he murmured. His blond hair was stuck to his forehead with sweat and his eyes had a hollow, scared look in them that Stoker didn't like. 'She's fine,' he said again. He didn't sound like he meant it.

Chapter Eight

The next couple of hours were a blur for everyone. The Doctor took Nyssa back up into the main cavern and laid her down to rest on a stretcher. Tegan didn't seem to notice the empty, haunted look in the Doctor's eyes as he laid Nyssa down.

The men were sitting around playing cards and computer games; Stoker tore them off a strip and got them shifting some of the heavy-duty analyser machines into position. She was working on the principle that they might as well do the job properly while they were here. There was no doubt about the lexium, but with the big machines they could get an accurate assessment of exactly how much there was, where it was, and what kind of grade it might be. The men seemed happy to get back to work, or at least happy to be checking on the lex. Stoker just wanted them kept busy.

She found Bunny Cheung in the comms area. For one awful moment Stoker thought he had sent the mayday, but he just looked up at her and shrugged.

'Finished your sulk?' Stoker asked, lighting a cigar.

'I don't sulk. I brood manfully.'

'Finished brooding?'

'More or less. Tegan came up and talked at me for a while.'

'So what gives?'

'I didn't send any mayday signal if that's what you mean,' Bunny told her. He looked her in the eye. 'But I still think we should.'

'OK. So what's stopping you? Besides a flea in the ear from Tegan?'

'Another kick up the backside from you,' Bunny suggested.

Stoker nodded thoughtfully. 'I won't give up on this place, Bunny. It's important.'

'I know. But so was Vega Jaal.'

'Point taken. So where do we go from here?'

Bunny leant forward in his chair. 'Let's wait and see what the Doctor comes up with. In the meantime we carry on as best we can. But if anything else happens, if we lose anyone else, then I'm quitting. Understand?'

'We won't lose anyone else,' Stoker promised. 'I'm having that place sealed up. Whatever's down there, whatever got Jaal, is staying down there. For good.'

'All right.' A little of the tension left Bunny's shoulders and he sat back. 'What's happening with Vega Jaal's body?'

'The Doctor says he should be buried; apparently that's the custom on Vega. Returned to the earth and all that. Personally it gives me the creeps.'

Bunny smiled faintly. 'I think Jaal would've appreciated that.'

She smiled back. 'Yeah. More than likely.'

'So what do you think?'

'I think if we leave him down there any longer, he's going to start smelling. Now that the power's back on, it's not so cold. The air con is warming the place up nicely. I say we get him up here, bury him, and then blow the door to that place to hell and back.'

'Right,' Bunny said. 'I'll take care of it, if you like. Get a couple of men to help.'

'Thanks, Bunny, but I should do it. The others would expect it. At least,' she took a deep breath, 'they will when I tell them about it.'

Nyssa dreamed again. She dreamed that she was back in the TARDIS, where it was safe and warm and brightly lit. The Doctor was showing Tegan how to operate the scanner controls properly; neither of them was taking much notice of Nyssa. It was odd, but ever since Tegan had returned, the Doctor had shown less and less interest in Nyssa. There had been a time when he had taken pleasure in showing her how to operate the convoluted control systems. In fact, Nyssa had proved an attentive and eager pupil, and she had mastered several complex operations. She could read the star charts, or some of them, anyway, and plot a course. She knew how to enter particular spatial coordinates on the appropriate control panel.

But for the life of her, she couldn't remember how to work the scanner.

This was absurd, because it was one of the first and simplest things she had learnt. But now, even as the Doctor showed Tegan the relevant switches and dials, Nyssa could not recall the correct procedure. As Tegan learnt it, Nyssa forgot it.

It was intensely irritating. For the first time in a very long time, Nyssa felt like an outsider. An orphan, homeless and unloved. Forgotten about.

Now the Doctor even had his arm around Tegan. Nyssa shivered and turned away.

And saw the interior door open before her. Beyond it, rather than the usual bright corridor, was nothing but blackness. Standing in the doorway was a short, muscular figure with wiry, reddish hair and a sharp, pinched face. His eyes were like huge orbs of translucent amber, staring at her from the darkness. Nyssa found him strangely familiar, although she couldn't recognise him. He beckoned her to follow him, and then turned and disappeared.

Without a backward glance at the Doctor and Tegan, Nyssa followed.

The console room door closed softly behind her, sealing her in the absolute blackness beyond.

She knew with certainty that she was no longer in the TARDIS. She was floating in a void, weightless and sightless. There was nothing to touch; no wind on her face or sounds to hear. There was no way to judge distance, or time. It was total sensory deprivation.

Only then did she feel the first ripple of panic, as the exact nature of her circumstances dropped like a cold pebble of fear into the centre of her mind.

She expected to wake up, then.

But she didn't.

*

'I'm not happy about this, Doctor.'

The Doctor sighed. 'Why doesn't that surprise me, Tegan?'

'If Nyssa's ill, I should be with her. Not wasting my time down here!'

The Doctor's first response was to cast a quick glance heavenward and plunge his hands into his trouser pockets. Then he met her stare evenly and said, 'There is nothing you can do for her, I promise. She just needs some rest, that's all.'

'What if she has a nightmare or something? You know, another funny turn?'

'I very much doubt that,' the Doctor said. Tegan switched to her dubious, distrusting look and the Doctor finally capitulated. 'All right, all right: I don't know. There's every possibility she may have another psionic episode. But short of waking her up, and keeping her awake, I can't see any way of preventing that.'

'Can't she be shielded in some way?' Tegan wanted to know. It didn't seem fair to leave Nyssa open to such abuse. Whatever the Doctor meant by *psionic episode*, it couldn't be good.

The Doctor shook his head emphatically. 'Now that Vega Jaal is gone, Nyssa is our best hope of maintaining contact with… with whatever it is that's causing all the trouble.'

Tegan's jaw actually dropped. 'Maintaining contact? Doctor, you can't just use her like that!'

'I really don't have any choice, Tegan,' the Doctor said. He sounded pained. 'Believe me. Whatever force tried to gain entry to the TARDIS via Nyssa's mind was simply using her. That link, or conduit, to the enemy is our only connection with it; if we can use it effectively, it might provide us with some small advantage.'

Tegan folded her arms. 'I still don't like it.'

But the Doctor was losing patience now. 'Tegan, if you really want to help, then you will just have to trust me. In the meantime, can we please continue with this?' He indicated the computer screen in front of them. They were alone in the laboratory, trying to access whatever records or files they could before, as the Doctor put it, Stoker started thinking with her explosives.

'She's busy explaining to her men what's happened to Vega Jaal at the moment,' the Doctor had told Tegan as he led her back down into the lab complex. 'They'll probably bury him. But it won't be long before Stoker tries to close this place down, probably by blowing it to pieces.'

Tegan didn't think that sounded so bad an idea, but held her tongue. The Doctor was working against the clock, which was something she did understand, and she really did want to help. 'What do you want me to do?'

'We need to check through the laboratory staff complement: you've got the relevant screens up now. We need to know who was here, and what they were working on.'

'OK, Doctor, I'll give it my best shot.' *Yeah*, Tegan thought sourly, *a shot in the dark.*

They buried Vega Jaal and Stoker said something awkward. No one really remembered what. It was a miserable service, if you could even call it that: a shrivelled-up something that was once their friend, lowered into a shallow grave scraped out of the rock and covered with rubble.

Bunny Cheung got the men back to work afterwards, trying to maintain the rhythm of duty, not letting anyone have too much time to brood. But it was hard not to think about Vega Jaal.

'Well, there's one bright side to all this,' Nik said a little later, when he was standing in a side tunnel with Jim Boyd.

'What?'

'It means a bigger share of the lex for the rest of us.'

Jim glared at him. 'You're one sick puppy, you know that?'

'Every cloud has a silver lining. Haven't you ever heard that expression?'

'Yeah. Here's another expression: you're full of crap.'

Nik smiled. 'You're just sore because that Tegan girl gave you the heave-ho.'

'She did not,' Jim said quickly. 'She had other things on her mind. Her friend was sick.'

'Her friend was sick,' Nik mimicked.

'You're just jealous because I pulled.'

'You call that pulling? One dance and *au revoir*?' Nik smirked. 'You need to get out more.'

'I need some fresh air, that's for sure,' Jim agreed stiffly. 'Something stinks around here.'

'Probably Vega Jaal. I said that hole wasn't deep enough.'

Jim shook his head in despair. 'Go to hell,' he said, and walked away, back towards the main cavern.

Nik watched him go and shrugged to himself. He finished his cigarette and then ground it out under his boot. It was colder and darker in this tunnel than he had thought. He was just about to hurry after Jim when he heard something move behind him.

Tegan tapped at some of the keys and watched the information scroll up and down the screen. After only a few seconds she hit pay dirt. 'Hey, look at this: we've got a list of names.'

The Doctor peered at the display, which said:

PRIMARY CONTROL: PROJECT AKOSHEMON/
PERSONNEL/2319.01.12
PROFESSOR NIJAL AMGA
PROFESSOR JEN GARONDEL
SCIENTIST KAHL STRODER
SCIENTIST HARK ROTAH
TECHNICIAN RETEP MATS
TECHNICIAN RAVUS OLDEMAN

'Six names,' the Doctor said. 'But only five bodies. Which one is missing?'

Tegan checked the hand-written list in the Doctor's notebook. 'The last one – Technician Ravus Oldeman.'

'I wonder what happened to him?'

'I just had a nasty thought,' Tegan said. 'What if it was this Ravus Oldeman character who killed the others? That would explain why his body wasn't with theirs.'

'It's a possibility,' the Doctor conceded. 'The real question is: where is he now?' He stared at the VDU intently, as if the answer might suddenly type itself across the screen. The graphics reflected in his eyes like little green flames.

Tegan swallowed hard. 'He must have killed Vega Jaal too.'

'This is only conjecture, remember,' the Doctor cautioned. 'We still know very little, apart from the names of the people who worked here. Ideally, we need to know what they were working *on*.'

'This Oldeman person's probably died of old age by now. If that's the date this list was compiled,' Tegan pointed at the heading on the screen, 'then it's over one hundred and fifty years ago.'

'Hmm,' the Doctor said, rather unhelpfully.

Tegan stretched. 'Ugh. My neck's getting stiff from sitting at this wretched machine.'

The Doctor patted her on the shoulder. 'We're missing something obvious here, you know.'

'What?'

'Well if I knew that we wouldn't be missing it, would we?' The Doctor straightened up and chewed his lip thoughtfully.

'It's old age, Doctor. Even Time Lords must get absent-minded.'

'I'm not absent-minded,' responded the Doctor tartly. 'Besides, it's more serious than that: something is tampering with our perceptions. Subtle changes in our brain chemistry. Clouding our minds. I've been subconsciously aware of it ever since we materialised.'

'Speak for yourself.'

'Oh, I am, chiefly. And Nyssa. Vega Jaal felt it too, of course. It seems to affect non-human minds more easily; the psi potential is slightly greater, I suspect.'

Tegan shifted uncomfortably. 'Do you mean thought control?'

'Nothing so direct. This feels almost as if something intuitively telepathic is reaching out blindly, probing in the dark for a weakness.'

'There's that word again,' Tegan noted. 'Everyone keeps mentioning the dark.'

The Doctor frowned. 'Yes, they do, don't they?'

'But humans aren't affected, right? By this telepathic probing, I mean.'

'Marginally. We've all been preoccupied with one thing or another, but everyone has experienced something: mood swings, depression, anxiety. Yes, definitely some kind of psionic field effect causing perceptual inhibition. Do you realise that no one even noticed that door in the cave until Vega Jaal and I found it?'

'And don't we wish you hadn't,' Tegan muttered. 'I can't help worrying about Nyssa, Doctor. She seems pretty badly affected by this telepathic thing.'

The Doctor grunted. 'How about you, Tegan? How have you been feeling?'

'Now you mention it, I've been feeling pretty irritable and cranky ever since we arrived.'

'As I said, it doesn't seem to be affecting you very much at all.'

'All right,' said Stoker, 'let's have it.'

The man sitting at the analyser controls licked his lips and said, 'The lexium is spread pretty evenly through the geological structure of the entire moon, but there are heavier deposits of the basic trace ore very near the surface. I'd say seventy to eighty per cent. Possibly more.'

Stoker squeezed his shoulder. 'Couldn't be better, Jim,' she said quietly. 'If you weren't so damn ugly, I'd kiss you.'

'Feel free to insult me,' Jim said. 'I'm going to be very, very rich.'

'We all are,' Stoker said. But suddenly the words sounded hollow, and with a start she realised that she wasn't sure about it any more. This place had damn well got under her skin. Finding the lab complex had rattled her. Losing Vega Jaal had rattled her. The Doctor had rattled her. She was sick of being rattled. She slapped Jim on the back and said with greater confidence, 'We *all* are.'

She looked up at Bunny Cheung. His massive arms were folded across his chest and he was glowering at the analyser display. Stoker thought that she could really do with a little more support from him right now. 'What's up with you?' she demanded.

Bunny cast her a dark look. 'Just thinking, that's all.'

Stoker knew what Bunny was thinking. She had known him for too long, she knew exactly how he thought. Right now he was thinking that it would be an unbearable shame if they should find all this easy lex and then have it snatched away from them. Worst of all, that was exactly what *she* was starting to think too. But the fact that it could happen, that they *could* lose it, made Stoker all the more determined to keep hold of it.

'We could get a more detailed trace if Nik looked at this,' Jim said, tapping the analyser. 'He's the expert.'

'Where is Nik?' Stoker asked.

'Dunno,' said Jim. 'I left him having a smoke in the side tunnel.'

'I don't like the thought of anyone wandering off on their own,' Bunny growled. 'Find him.'

As Jim got up and left, Stoker frowned at Bunny. 'What are you trying to do, scare everyone stupid?'

'*I'm* scared stupid. I don't see why everyone else shouldn't be.'

'Well just stop it. I had enough of that stuff from Jaal. Keep your mind on the job, Bunny. There's nothing to worry about up here.' Despite herself, Stoker felt apprehensive.

Jim Boyd came back with a look of horror on his face. 'You'd better come and see this, boss.'

They recognised Nik's body only by his overalls and jacket. The jacket looked huge on the shrivelled corpse, with dry, wizened little hands poking out of the cuffs. His head was tipped right back, the face sunken into the bone, the eyes wide but opaque. His mouth was still open, the flesh inside grey and withered.

And locked into a perpetual, silent scream that Stoker recognised all too easily.

'Poor bastard,' said Stoker gruffly.

'You know what this means, don't you?' said Bunny Cheung. 'Whatever killed Vega Jaal *isn't* sealed up in that lab.'

Stoker turned on her heel and marched away.

'Where are you going?'

'To see the Doctor.'

'Wait a sec,' said Tegan. 'Didn't you say something about suspended animation before? When we first found the lab – the equipment, you said it was all to do with suspended animation.'

'Yes, that's right,' the Doctor said, frowning. He waited patiently for Tegan to make her point.

Tegan felt a guilty surge of hope: could this perceptual tampering inhibit his thought processes on such a basic level? If the Doctor's brain was becoming muddled, then she could really be of help. 'Suspended animation,' Tegan prompted him again. 'That's all about freezing people, isn't it? Well that's where this Ravus Oldeman could be. Frozen somewhere!'

The penny dropped and the Doctor erupted with excitement. 'Of course! Why didn't I think of that?' He grasped her by the shoulders. 'Tegan, you're a wonder!'

Tegan glowed.

'Although,' said the Doctor, raising a cautionary finger, 'it could just be that my mind is being dulled by the psionic field effect I mentioned. Yes, that must be it. Sorry.'

Tegan slumped. 'I thought I was helping!'

'You are,' the Doctor assured her. 'But it's not always about cryogenics, or, er, freezing people as you put it. Suspended animation covers a multitude of techniques: simple cryogenics, stasis fields, slow-time envelopes, reverse chronon manipulation. The list goes on. But it's still a distinct possibility…' The Doctor whirled to face the blank wall where the secret door led to the lower chamber. 'Maybe if we…'

'Hold it,' said Stoker.

The Doctor turned back guiltily, one hand raised to open the door.

Stoker looked white with anger, Tegan noticed. There was real fire in those amber eyes. 'Nik's dead,' Stoker told them. 'Killed by whatever it was that killed Vega Jaal.'

A thick silence filled the laboratory.

'I'm very sorry to hear that,' the Doctor said.

'Sorry?' Stoker took a step forward, balling her fists. For a moment Tegan really thought she was going to take a swing at the Doctor. Then Bunny Cheung appeared behind Stoker and laid a big hand on her shoulder.

Stoker shrugged it off. 'It's OK, Bunny, I'm not about to do anything stupid. I've already done something stupid: let this joker carry on down here instead of destroying this dump in the first place.'

'It's too late for that now,' Bunny said.

'Whatever it is that killed your men is already on the loose,' the Doctor pointed out. 'You can't seal it in down here.'

'And whose fault is that?' Stoker asked.

'Certainly not mine.'

'Everything was fine until you arrived!'

'Steady, Jyl,' said Bunny. 'Let's hear what he has to say.'

'I'm sick of hearing what he has to say.'

'I can help you,' the Doctor said. 'We are all in extreme danger. Unless we stick together, we could all be killed.'

'What do you suggest, Doctor?' asked Bunny.

'I assume Nik was alone when he was attacked?'

'We think so. He must have been.'

'Just like Vega Jaal,' the Doctor nodded. 'I suggest you gather the rest of your men together and bring them all down here. From now on no one must be left alone.'

'Roger that,' Bunny said.

'It might be possible to afford you all some extra protection if you were to stay in my ship…'

'I'm not interested in your ship,' said Stoker.

'No,' the Doctor said. 'I didn't think you would be.'

'I'm sticking right here until my own ship arrives,' Stoker insisted. 'I'm not letting this rock go, Doctor.'

'I'd still like you to consider –'

She shook her head. 'It's not even up for discussion.'

The Doctor shot a sideways glance at Tegan, who shrugged. 'Very well,' he said carefully. 'In that case we all stay here and try to find out what it is that's responsible for the killing. And then try to stop it.'

'Damn right,' Stoker said. With great effort she seemed to control her anger. 'Have you found out anything useful?'

'We might have,' Tegan said.

'But we're still working on it,' the Doctor interrupted quickly. He patted the computer console. 'Checking the databases.'

'Right,' said Stoker. 'Get on with it. Let me know the minute you come up with anything. Come on, Bunny.'

Bunny Cheung shot an apologetic look at Tegan and followed Stoker out.

'What was all that about?' asked Tegan when they had gone. 'Why didn't you tell her about Ravus Oldeman?'

'It's only a theory at the moment, Tegan. I want proof before we go saying anything to Stoker, she's in a very excitable state of mind.'

'The psionic field?'

'No,' the Doctor said patiently. 'She's just lost two of her men, Tegan. She's upset, and rather understandably, don't you think?'

'All right. Sorry. So what do we do now, then?'

The Doctor pointed at the door leading to the lower chamber. 'Well, there's obviously no point in keeping that shut any more. I think we should open it up again and have a good look round, don't you?'

Casting a dubious look at the door, Tegan slid off her stool. 'If we must.'

'Brave heart, Tegan!' The Doctor called back as he activated the door. It hummed away and he trotted confidently down the steps into the lower chamber. Tegan followed him, muttering all kinds of retribution for the next time he said *brave heart* to her.

This was the first time Tegan had seen inside the lower chamber. It was cold and gloomy, of course, with some strangely shaped pieces of equipment ranged around the circular wall. On the floor lay the withered remains of the original scientists, or five of them at least. Tegan stepped hurriedly over the flaky remains to join the Doctor, who was already examining one of the wide cylindrical machines on the far side of the room. It resembled some kind of large casket or chest.

'I overlooked this in all the excitement earlier,' he confessed. 'After finding the bodies, I never thought of looking in these tanks.'

'Tanks?'

'Rudimentary stasis tanks. They're all of a slightly different design, suggesting that they may be experimental prototypes. That would fit in with the suspended-animation research, I think you'll agree.' The Doctor began to brush away some of the grime and dust that covered the surface of the chest, Metal glinted dully in the lamplight.

Tegan shivered. 'It looks like a freezer. Or a giant coffin.'

'Don't be morbid.'

'That's easy for you to say,' Tegan said. 'Don't forget we're sharing this room with a pile of old corpses.'

'Look at this,' the Doctor said. He was pointing to a small row of flashing LEDs he had uncovered. 'Self-contained power generator.'

Tegan was intrigued despite herself. 'It's still switched on?'

'Apparently. I wonder what's inside? There should be an inspection hatch here somewhere…' The Doctor took out his handkerchief and scrubbed vigorously at a panel on the metal casing. A few seconds' work revealed a square window of plastic. Tegan stood on tiptoe but it was impossible to see inside; it was simply too dark.

The Doctor fished out his pencil torch and shone it through the window. The beam fell into a dark green haze.

'It looks like it's full of water or something,' said Tegan. 'Bit murky, though.'

'Wait a minute,' the Doctor said, shifting the angle of the torch. 'There is something. Can you see it?'

Tegan peered into the hole. The light of the pencil torch didn't reveal much: just a faint shape floating in some kind of fluid. But as she looked, the shape seemed to rise toward the window, becoming clearer as it neared the light. Tegan felt her heart hammering in her chest. She wanted to look away, but she couldn't. She had to see what it was.

The shape floated into view. Tegan's gut twisted as she recognised it as a human head. It rolled around to face her through the porthole. A pair of large round eyes stared madly out at her.

CHAPTER NINE

'Can you wake him up?' asked Stoker. She was staring into the stasis tank window with a look of mild distaste. She wasn't keen on the way those eyes were staring out. They looked like the pale and useless eyes of a blind man.

The Doctor was fussing around the tank's control panel. Lights flashed across its little display as he pressed switches and turned dials with great concentration.

'I said can you wake him up?' Stoker asked again when it became obvious the Doctor either hadn't heard her the first time or wasn't going to reply.

He stood up. 'Technically, he's not asleep.'

'He's in suspended animation, yeah yeah.' Stoker wrinkled her nose irritably. 'That kind of thing went out with Mechonoids, Doctor. As far as I'm concerned if he isn't asleep he's dead. Can you either wake him up or resurrect him? Either will do, so long as he can answer my questions when he comes round.'

The Doctor sighed and ran a hand along the steel surface of the casket. 'I think we can bring him back to full consciousness, yes. The stasis tank is fully functional, albeit a little primitive. The gel inside preserves the bodily material without the need for cryogenic freezing. The heart rate, motor functions and brain are all reduced to a catatonic state via –'

'Spare me the lecture. Just ring his alarm clock.'

'This may take a little time,' the Doctor warned her sourly, and returned to fiddling with the controls.

Nyssa was sleeping peacefully on one of the tables, covered with a foil blanket. She looked wan beneath the electric lights, with dark circles under her eyes, but otherwise all right. The Doctor had advised complete rest anyway.

Next to the table sat Jim Boyd. He was very pale and sat staring at the floor between his feet. Tegan sat down next to him and he looked at her with red-rimmed eyes.

'Sorry about your friend,' Tegan said.

After a lengthy pause Jim said, 'I can't believe he's gone.'

'Had you known him for a long time?'

'Long enough to argue with him,' he said bitterly.

'You had a fight?'

Jim took off his spectacles and wiped brusquely at his eyes with the back of his hand. 'It was nothing. He was only mucking about. Nik did that kind of thing: he knew how to rile me. I just didn't expect him to… I didn't want him to…' Jim's voice trailed off as the words became inadequate, or perhaps simply too cruel. No one deserved such a violent and unnatural death. But violent and unnatural death was, sadly, something that Tegan had seen before. She tried to imagine how she would feel if it was the Doctor or Nyssa who had been killed. Almost instantly she remembered Adric's death, and with it came a pang of guilt. How could she have forgotten *that*?

'I think I can imagine how you feel,' she told Jim. 'I had a friend once… not a friend like Jim, but someone I knew pretty well… and he was killed. He was just a kid. It's too awful.'

Jim didn't say anything. It took a full minute of him not saying anything for Tegan to realise that he simply *couldn't* say anything. To open his mouth to speak would let all the emotion out. Tegan could see that his eyes were glossy with tears. She simply didn't know how she could help now, and felt wretched. She touched him and he gripped her hand tightly, desperate for human contact. 'I'm so sorry,' Tegan whispered.

He glanced up at her and managed a weak smile, still holding on to her hand. For a fraction of a second, Tegan recalled the warmth of his body against hers, only a few short hours ago. When everything had been lively and joyful, when they had danced and Bunny had juggled and Jim had made a pass at her. Now Tegan looked away, feeling awkward and ashamed of such careless jubilation.

Thankfully, something distracted them both: Nyssa was stirring.

'I think Nyssa's coming round,' Tegan said.

Nyssa had given herself over to the darkness. She had no choice; the darkness was all there was, an unending, depthless void.

She spun slowly through the unmoving blackness, or perhaps she was unmoving, and the blackness spun slowly around her. It was impossible to determine which. She had given up trying to analyse the experience scientifically: there was nothing to measure anything against. The only danger with abandoning her scientific rationale was the increased chance of it giving way to panic; already she could feel the first spark of what she knew would become a burning terror if she allowed it to kindle.

But she could feel her heart beating faster and faster. Its heavy thudding was all that she could hear. The blood roared thickly in her ears. She imagined she could hear other sounds behind the pounding beat: the TARDIS engines, humming distantly, just beyond comprehension. The whispering voice of a lover never known.

I am here Nyssa

Startled, Nyssa wondered if she had heard herself say something aloud. She was, after all, completely alone. Pointlessly, she opened her eyes. She saw only blackness; or rather she saw *nothing*. Emptiness. No light at all.

'Where am I?' she asked the void.

Traken

'I don't understand. Traken is gone. Destroyed.'

You are in the space left by Traken. A cavity in reality. A wound in the universe

'Who are you?'

I am all that is left. I am the dark

'What do you want?'

Life

'You want to live?'

All life

Nyssa swallowed. What was she doing talking to herself like this? She was utterly alone she reminded herself firmly. Alone. There was no one else with her here in the void, she was certain of it. She had never been more alone.

You are not alone, last daughter of Traken

'I don't like what you are doing to me,' Nyssa said carefully.

I know

'Please stop it.'

You cannot stop darkness. It is everywhere. I am everywhere. I surround you. I am inside you now. In your mind and your heart and your blood

'No!'

Your blood runs black with me

'No!' Nyssa could feel the blood thickening in her veins as it congealed with the blackness, feel her heart straining to move it, thudding desperately, harder and harder.

She woke up and saw Tegan and hugged her.

'Easy now,' Tegan was saying. 'It's just a nightmare.'

There's no such thing as *just* a nightmare, thought Nyssa. Not any more. But she nodded and held her friend tightly for a long time.

'What's going on?' Nyssa asked. 'Why is everyone down here?'

'Something pretty awful has happened.'

Nyssa tried to listen as Tegan described the events leading up to Nik's death and the discovery of Ravus Oldeman's stasis tank. Tegan clearly didn't want to alarm her, but equally felt it only fair that Nyssa should be in full possession of the facts. Nyssa allowed herself a momentary, slightly sardonic smile: *the facts*. What *were* the facts here? No one really knew. No one knew the secret of the darkness here, the black, impenetrable void locked away in the heart of this ghastly moon. Not even her.

'So now the Doctor's trying to bring this Ravus Oldeman person back to life, or whatever it is,' Tegan was saying. A pause. 'Nyssa?'

But Nyssa wasn't really listening. All she could hear was the thick, black blood drumming in her ears.

*

'You're very quiet,' Stoker told Bunny Cheung. She sat down next to him, turning the plastic chair backwards so that she had to straddle it.

Bunny gazed up at her. He looked tired. 'Just thinking.'

'Whoa,' Stoker said. 'You're doing too much of that lately: you're going to do yourself a real injury soon. Stop it.' She unwrapped a fresh cigar and lit it.

Bunny looked back over to where the Doctor was still making adjustments to the stasis cabinet containing Ravus Oldeman. There was a brooding, contemplative shadow in the big man's eyes as he watched the process: the preservative gel was being drained into a receptacle beneath the stasis tank. The dull whine of the pump machinery could be heard quite clearly. All that remained was for the casket computer's automatic resuscitation program to take effect.

Stoker watched Bunny and blew smoke. Then she said, 'So, out with it: what's up?'

Bunny sat back and folded his arms. 'I'm not happy leaving the comms unit up there,' he jerked his head to indicate the caverns above the lab complex. 'We've got no way to contact anyone down here. We're completely cut off otherwise.'

Stoker looked at him stonily. 'No mayday signals, Bunny.'

'We may have to, Jyl.'

'Only on my direct order,' Stoker said flatly. 'Or over my dead body. Whichever comes first.'

'So we can't call for help until you're killed, is that it?' Bunny snorted. 'Bit late then.'

'I'm serious. We can sit this out. Let the Doctor wake this Oldeman guy up and we can get some answers; he must know what killed the other scientists here. Then we can decide what to do for the best.'

Bunny said nothing; he just sat and played with the hologram ring on his finger.

'Hold it,' said Stoker suddenly sitting up. 'Something's happening.'

The Doctor was opening the stasis tank. The lid split with a hiss and slid aside, revealing the man within. He was completely naked, that was the first thing Stoker noticed. The second thing she noticed was how *old* he looked.

And, finally, that he was actually alive.

The Doctor helped the old man up into a sitting position and asked for a blanket. Tegan wrapped a foil sheet around Oldeman's bony shoulders as he sat shivering and coughing.

'It's all right,' the Doctor was saying, 'you're bound to feel disorientated at first. Relax and you'll soon feel better. You've been asleep for a long time.'

Oldeman gagged and spluttered like a geriatric choking on a fishbone. White hair was plastered to his skull and his skin was slick with the remnants of the gel. He seemed to be trying to speak. 'I...'

Stoker went over. 'You're Ravus Oldeman?'

The man stared at her blankly, his mouth hanging open.

'Is your name Ravus Oldeman?' Stoker persisted.

The Doctor said, 'I think we ought to give him a little time to come round before subjecting him to an interrogation.'

'We haven't got time,' Stoker said.

'Need...' said the old man. 'I need...'

'What? What do you need?'

'Need new... new... neuro... Need neuro...' he spluttered.

'What's he talking about?'

'Neurolectrin!' exclaimed the Doctor. 'Of course, there must be some around here somewhere. Help me find it.' He began to rummage through the lockers on the wall.

'What is it?' asked Tegan.

'Neurolectrin is a drug commonly used in resuscitation from suspended animation,' explained the Doctor. 'It helps reverse synaptic decay. Without it the subject can fall prey to irreversible mental illness very quickly.'

'You mean he'll go senile?' asked Tegan.

'That's all we need,' groaned Stoker. 'We're supposed to be getting some answers from him, not nonsensical rambling.'

'Could this be it, Doctor?' Tegan held up a small plastic tube she had found in a medical box.

The Doctor grabbed it and checked the label. 'The very thing, Tegan, well done!' He turned immediately, snapped the end off the injector and jabbed it into Oldeman's neck. The man was slumped over, leaning heavily against the lid of the stasis tank, but he seemed to have stopped trembling and was breathing normally.

'Did it,' he mumbled. 'I did it…' He opened his eyes. They were watery but alert as he looked around him, taking in the lab and the host of strangers surrounding him. 'Who…?'

The Doctor introduced himself quickly. 'I take it that you *are* Ravus Oldeman?'

Oldeman nodded. 'Did you… activate the stasis tank?'

The Doctor said that he had. 'This may come as a bit of a shock to you,' he went on, 'but you've been asleep for over one hundred and sixty years.'

Oldeman glared at them all, his eyes bugging out with fear. He reached up with one bony hand and grasped the Doctor's lapel. 'You've got to get me away from here. You've got to get me away from here!'

The Doctor held on to the man's hand. 'Why? What's the matter?'

'It won't be dead yet!' Oldeman gasped. 'It will still be here! Still alive. *It'll kill us all!*'

'It was supposed to be perfect stasis,' Oldeman grumbled as he sat down a little later. They had found a set of grey overalls for him and a towel, and given him half an hour to wash and get dressed. He looked a lot healthier now as he gratefully accepted a mug of hot coffee from Tegan, although it was impossible not to notice how gnarled the fingers that grasped the cup were. His hair stood out from his scalp in white tufts and his eyes looked pink and rheumy.

'Nothing's perfect,' the Doctor said, not unkindly.

'I must have forgotten to check the amniotic gel for electron decay,' Oldeman added.

'I expect so.'

'I was in such a rush.' Oldeman's voice was cracked and tired, his eyes squinting as he peered into his blurred memory. 'I think.'

'When will you be due for another dose of neurolectrin?' the Doctor asked.

'What?'

'Neurolectrin. You'll need another dose.'

Oldeman nodded slowly. 'Yes, probably quite soon. I didn't make a note of the time when… when… what time is it, by the way?'

'Time you started giving us some real answers,' said Stoker. 'We need some info that only you can provide, Oldeman.'

'I'm afraid, my girl, that you will have to bear with me a little longer,' he said, peering myopically at Stoker. He tapped the side of his head and added, 'Still waiting for everything to settle down in here. I've had quite a shock, you know! It isn't easy coming round from stasis, but doubtless you know or care little about that. How would you like to go to sleep feeling young and fit, only to wake up old and weak?'

Ravus Oldeman may have been pushing two hundred and thirty, thought Tegan, but he was pretty spry for an old timer.

The Doctor must have been thinking the same thing. He said, 'Come now, Mr Oldeman, you're very well preserved for your age.'

Oldeman smiled thinly. 'Ah, better is a poor and wise youth than an old and foolish king.'

'Ecclesiastes,' said the Doctor.

Oldeman beamed at him. 'At least I find myself in the company of a true intellectual,' he said. 'Last time I was here, I was surrounded by buffoons and ingrates.'

'Your fellow scientists?'

'You might call them that,' Oldeman spat derisively. 'I wouldn't. They never could recognise genius when they saw it.'

'And that would be you, would it?' asked Stoker. She fixed him with a measured stare. 'Didn't get on with them much, I take it?'

'Not really. Although I would never have wanted… *that*… to happen to them.' He frowned, suddenly appearing frail. 'Not to anyone, in fact.'

'But you must have argued?' Stoker pressed.

'Of course, we were all scientists, good or bad,' Oldeman replied testily. 'We fell out regularly over technical problems and research methods. None of them would listen to me. I warned them of the danger, but they didn't want to listen to an old fool.'

'Or maybe it was because you were just a technician,' Stoker suggested. 'Maybe they felt happier listening to the *professors*.'

Oldeman responded with a watery glare at Stoker.

'Pardon me,' the Doctor said, 'but you do seem rather mature for a humble technician.'

Oldeman switched his sharp look to the Doctor. 'It's a question of *fields*, young man. I was an expert in the field of gene manipulation. The bulk of the research going on here is – was – biotechnology.'

'And its application to suspended-animation techniques, I presume,' the Doctor nodded thoughtfully.

'The stasis tank was a working prototype,' Oldeman said. 'It was never meant to be used in anger… but in the end, I had no choice. It was the only way I could think of to… survive.'

'Tell us about it,' the Doctor urged.

'Very well.' Oldeman sat back and took a sip of his coffee. The cup trembled in his hand. 'I'll start at the beginning, shall I? I actually qualified as a theoretical geneticist at the Human Sciences Academy on Mars. I wrote a paper on biomechanical gene manipulation in long-term stasis when I was a student. It was quite good, even if I say so myself, for someone of such a relatively tender age. But some time later I was working as a senior technician on Titan when I met Professor Garondel. We seemed to hit it off all right then, and he must have been impressed with my paper – or at least simply liked me – because, years later, he invited me to take part in a research project he was heading up. An investigation into the possibility of using genetic manipulation techniques to improve the efficacy of long-term induced animal-hibernation systems.'

Tegan stifled a yawn, earning a reproving glance from the Doctor. Jim Boyd smiled and whispered, 'This making sense to you?' Tegan shrugged. She turned to Nyssa and asked her the same question.

'Perfectly,' Nyssa replied quietly.

Something about the way Nyssa spoke made Tegan frown. Was that a tiny, supercilious smile playing at the corner of Nyssa's mouth? She tapped her again. 'You all right?' she mouthed.

'I'm fine,' Nyssa said. 'Honestly.'

At least she was looking better, Tegan thought. This science stuff must be a real tonic for her.

'It seemed like an interesting thing to do at the time,' Oldeman continued without a trace of irony, 'and I welcomed the opportunity to prove myself. Garondel had recruited a small band of specialists to form a research team and set up this facility. I can see you're all wondering why we ended up here, of all the places in the galaxy... and it's a good question. I asked the same question back then, right at the beginning. Garondel wanted the research to be conducted in secret, you see. There was a lot of competition in the scientific community and Garondel was determined to be the first to pull off *this little trick*, as he called it. This little trick, I must add, being the eventual and complete bastardisation of the original aims and intentions of the project I had signed up for. I'll never forgive Garondel for that.

'Little did I know then, to use a popular and well-worn phrase, that I was to be engaged in work that would result in the creation of a *monster*...'

At that moment Tegan was distracted by Jim, who was surreptitiously pointing across the lab to the exit. Bunny Cheung was just slipping out through the door without anyone else noticing, which was quite a feat for someone of his stature. But everyone else was concentrating on Ravus Oldeman.

'Where's he off to on the quiet?' Tegan wondered.

'He shouldn't go up there on his own,' Jim said.

Tegan whispered, 'I'm going after him.'

'Wait for me!' Jim mouthed, and quickly followed her.

Ravus Oldeman, meanwhile, was warming to his theme and the little crowd of interested faces surrounding him. 'The first thing that struck me as odd about Professor Garondel was his insistence that we adhere to the genetic matrix of Akoshemon.'

'The planet itself?' queried the Doctor.

'Samples taken from the surface, yes. Rocks and minerals mostly.'

'Whoa,' said Stoker, raising a hand. 'Akoshemon has got one hell of a reputation in these parts. It's never been a good place to be: in fact its name is a byword for depravity and wickedness of every kind. Whatever it was they did on that planet when there were people there – and I use the word *people* loosely – it wasn't in the best interests of humankind.' Stoker paused, aware that she had the full attention of the Doctor, Nyssa and Oldeman. 'I mean, I'm not really into all that superstition crap but *everyone* knows about Akoshemon. The problem being that whatever it was that went on down there killed the whole damn planet stone dead. There's nothing there but poisonous mud and an atmosphere that can, at best, be described as highly toxic.'

Oldeman nodded and looked regretful. 'The specimens were collected by robot landers and transferred directly to this laboratory on the moon. I was not unaware of the planet's unsavoury moral reputation. But Garondel insisted: whatever had happened on Akoshemon in the distant past, good or bad, its people were also renowned for their physical longevity.'

'That could have been the result of regular cellular regeneration,' commented the Doctor.

'It was the result of controlled cellular stasis,' Oldeman corrected him gently. 'Garondel wanted to use genetic material from the planet Akoshemon as a baseline constituent of an artificially generated organism, one that could carry within its genetic code the secret of cellular stasis: the ability of living tissue to enter a completely dormant state and then revive itself naturally without any harmful decay.'

'Yes, that might be useful,' said the Doctor. 'But extremely hazardous without a full breakdown of the Akoshemon genome.'

'I know, Doctor,' Oldeman nodded sadly. 'I know. I did try to warn Garondel, but he was an arrogant fool. He insisted on going ahead with only a basic understanding of Akoshemon microbiology.'

'That doesn't sound very intelligent,' said Nyssa.

Oldeman smiled at her. 'Intelligence was never his strong suit, my dear. Knowledge and practical expertise, yes, but not intelligence.'

'So what happened?' asked Stoker.

'Garondel tried to combine the Akoshemon material with human DNA. He then force-generated the resultant life form in the hope of using it as a viable test subject for experimentation.' Oldeman looked down in contrition at this point. He had to take a deep breath before he could continue. 'To my lasting shame, the experiment was an unqualified success... and completely uncontrollable.'

Bunny Cheung was doing something very stupid, and he knew it. Or rather, he was doing two very stupid things.

Firstly, he had left the relative safety of the lab complex and headed back up to the caverns on his own: clearly a stupid thing to do. Somewhere in these caves was a killer, probably lurking in the shadows or waiting just around the next corner to strike. Bunny didn't fancy being drained of all his blood by an unseen monster, but he really had no choice. He *had* to come up here: he had to get to the comms unit.

Which was the second stupid thing. Even if he managed to bypass the killer, even if he managed to reach the comms unit safely and use it, and then get back to the lab complex still without being killed... *then* he would have to face the wrath of Jyl Stoker.

But he had done that before, and lived. And living, for Bunny, was the most important thing right now. Living, staying alive, getting back home to his family. Nothing else mattered to him any more. Not Stoker, the Doctor, the lexium, the lab, the killer, anything. All he had to do was get out of here alive and get home.

He kept picturing Rosie, smiling, calling him home. Holding out her cuddly Earth Reptile for him to fix again. A new arm for Kooky. Bunny almost laughed, clenching his right fist and looking at the holograph ring. 'Not long now, Rosie, I promise,' he whispered.

He was breathing heavily by the time he reached the main cavern. The sound of his boots on the ground was echoing loudly through the tunnels, and Bunny suddenly realised that he wouldn't be able to hear anything that might be trying to sneak up on him.

He forced himself to stop and listen, holding his breath. He strained to hear anything that might indicate he was being followed, or tracked, or watched. But he could hear nothing over the sound of his own heartbeat.

He was about to press on when he thought he saw something up ahead: something moving in the shadows. He took a step forward. 'Who's there?' he croaked.

The shadow moved again. Bunny's heart missed a beat until he realised that it was his own shadow, cast ahead of him by the lamps on the cave wall behind. 'You idiot,' he sighed, and moved on.

'Garondel had created a terrible creature,' Ravus Oldeman said with a slight tremor in his voice. 'An inhuman monster.'

'With an unbelievable appetite for human blood,' the Doctor noted.

Oldeman nodded. 'We didn't know that at the time of course. But eventually the… animal… broke free and attacked anyone it came into contact with.'

'Hold it,' snapped Stoker. 'Broke free? How?'

'We grew it in a containment vessel following the normal procedure for such an experiment. We did not reckon on its immense physical strength.' Oldeman shuddered at the memory. 'One night, it simply smashed its way out.'

'And the blood hunt began,' said Nyssa.

The Doctor looked at her quizzically. 'Blood hunt?'

'I mean killing. The killing began.'

'Yes, my dear,' Oldeman said. 'The killing began. I can't even remember who was the first to die. It was all so fast, so unbelievable. In the end there were only two of us left: Garondel and myself. We had a bitter argument, the kind of argument men have when they are scared out of their wits. We were trapped. We knew it would track us down and kill us both before a relief ship could be sent to rescue us. Neither of us could agree the best way to deal with the creature.' Oldeman's eyes glazed over at the memory. With difficulty, he continued, 'I fear that I chose the coward's way out: I used the prototype stasis tank in a desperate attempt to escape. I thought that if I could hide from the creature, enter a state of suspended animation, then I might just survive.'

'And you were right,' said Nyssa.

'But you took a terrible risk,' Stoker said. 'You couldn't have been sure that anyone would come by and wake you up. It's only by chance that we found you one hundred and sixty years on.'

'In the circumstances,' Oldeman told her simply, 'it was no risk at all. Not to enter the stasis tank would have meant certain death.'

'We're overlooking something here,' the Doctor said. 'The creature sucked its victims completely dry of blood...'

'An incredible biological machine in many ways,' Nyssa said.

Oldeman glared at her. 'My dear, it is much more than that. It is frighteningly powerful, totally unique, utterly alien.'

'And pointless,' remarked the Doctor, frowning deeply.

'And still here,' Stoker said. She turned on Oldeman. 'You damn fool, what have you done? Your stupid experiment has cost the lives of two of my men!'

'But the experiment was a success,' Nyssa said. 'In one way,' she added, when everyone looked at her sharply.

'Define success,' Stoker ordered. 'Without forgetting Vega Jaal and Nik.'

'I mean, this specimen was created in this laboratory one hundred and sixty years ago,' Nyssa went on. 'It killed the scientists responsible but it has had nothing to feed on since then. And yet it has survived.'

Stoker said, 'I can't say I'm thrilled.'

'It's a good point, though,' said the Doctor. 'As a life form capable of autonomous self-stasis, it certainly seems to work. But I can't help feeling that we're missing something...'

Stoker made an angrily dismissive noise. 'Sod that. It's still out there somewhere. What are we going to do about it?'

Bunny had almost reached the area where the comms unit had been left. He had slowed his pace because he was now certain something was following him through the cavern. At one point Bunny thought he had seen a pale shape in the gloom at the end of the tunnel, moving quickly, glimpsed only out of the corner of his eye. He stopped to stare, but saw only shadows. Swallowing hard, he had moved swiftly on.

He hadn't actually seen anything else or heard anything else since, but Bunny was certain it hadn't been his imagination. *Something* was here in the caves with him, he knew that for a fact. After all, *something* had killed Vega Jaal and then Nik. The thought of that same something killing *him* made Bunny's heart pound with dread. He couldn't bear the thought of never seeing his daughter again. He couldn't bear the thought of Rosie never seeing *him* again. But the images of Vega Jaal's and Nik's shrivelled-up bodies kept coming horribly to mind.

At last he reached the comms area. He felt a ridiculous sense of relief when he saw the comms unit with its control lights still blinking.

'What are you up to?' asked a voice behind him.

Bunny whipped around, his legs almost buckling. 'Tegan! You frightened the life out of me, girl!'

Tegan stepped forward. She looked serious. 'What d'you think you're doing, creeping up here on your own, Bunny? Don't you realise how dangerous it is?'

Bunny almost laughed. 'That's precisely why I have come up here. Because there's something I have to do – and I can only do it alone. Speaking of which, did you come up here on your own too?'

'No,' said Tegan. 'Jim's with me.'

'Where?'

Tegan looked behind her, but Jim wasn't there. 'I don't understand. He was right behind me a minute ago.'

She looked back at Bunny then, her eyes wide and fearful. The scream that tore through the air was long and terrible.

'Jim!' Bunny snarled, leaping forward.

He ran with Tegan towards the cry, but the awful screeching had already stopped. A hideous, final gurgle took its place as they rounded the corner and saw –

Jim thrashing on the ground with something bent over him, something squat, dwarf-like and the colour of an earthworm. A tangle of glistening tubes connected its bulbous head to Jim's body; Jim was shuddering now as the thing sucked the blood out of him with terrifying speed. Even as they watched, Bunny and Tegan could see Jim physically shrinking beneath the creature.

The thing, alerted somehow, twisted around as they approached. A cluster of blood-red eyes stared out from the centre of its head, just above the nest of writhing tubers. The tubes squirmed and retracted, squirting fluid into the air, and then the thing was gone, moving away swiftly, ape-like, into the shadows.

'He's still alive!' Tegan gasped suddenly.

Galvanised from his state of shock, Bunny lunged forward and helped Jim sit up. Thick, dark blood ran freely from puncture wounds all over his shrivelled body. Bunny felt something warm and wet on his hand as he held Jim's head, and he knew there and then that the man was as good as dead: everything inside that mattered was gone, or was leaking out right now between his fingers. Jim's eyes were closed and wrinkled and shrunk right back into their sockets. His mouth hung open and dry, his last breath already slipping free.

'Too late,' Bunny said hoarsely. He lay Jim's body down gently on the ground and stood up. He was shaking with rage. 'This has gone far enough.'

PART TWO
CRASH AND BURN

The evil that men do lives after them;
The good is oft interr'd with their bones.
William Shakespeare

CHAPTER TEN

Captain Lawrence surveyed the bridge of his ship with an exacting eye for detail. He was an imposing figure, and he knew it. The crew respected him, and he had earned that respect, but there was no harm in maintaining the image.

He was tall, with black hair cut short in the regulation manner. Sharp eyes glittered above a straight nose and a straight mouth. He stood straight too, boots slightly apart, slate-grey uniform neat and well pressed, hands clasped behind his back. Stomach in, chest out, he reminded himself. Maintain the image.

One of the younger crewmen glanced up at him from the helm controls. Lawrence caught the flicker of movement and looked down at him, instantly recalling the recruit's name: Jenks.

Jenks paled as he realised the captain was looking straight at him and returned his attention to the flight controls.

'Problem, Jenks?' Lawrence asked tersely.

'No, sir!'

It was all Jenks could do not to quiver under his captain's steely gaze. Lawrence sighed. He could have flown this ship by himself if required: the comtech was sophisticated enough to allow just one qualified man to act as pilot.

The *Adamantium* was a Consortium Survey Vessel outbound from the Antares system, on a routine deployment to the galactic fringe. There were few navigational hazards in this region of space, apart from one minor asteroid cluster and a high-density binary star of which the *Adamantium* would steer well clear. Another three months of regulation survey scans would find them right back at Earth Central. Captain Lawrence was happy with this projected flight plan, and he didn't see any reason to alter it.

But something was nagging at Jenks, and that irritated Lawrence.

'Come on, Jenks! Spit it out!'

Jenks swallowed hard. 'Nothing, sir, really. I just wondered if we were ever going to pick up a decent scan result.'

Lawrence nodded, satisfied. 'This is your first posting to this sector, isn't it, Jenks?'

'Sir.'

'And you're bored.'

'No, sir,' Jenks said, a little too quickly.

'There are very few explored worlds in this sector, Jenks,' Lawrence said with a knowing smile. 'We could find anything, at any moment. Or nothing at all. If all you want is an active life in the Consortium, you should have signed up for a load lifter on the Betelgeuse run. But if you want the chance to see uncharted stars, and the opportunity to discover new and valuable sources of mineral wealth, you could do worse than to employ a little patience. Patience is our watchword, Jenks. Patience and method.'

'Sir,' Jenks said, although it was difficult to tell if he had been inspired or simply had his worst fears confirmed. Lawrence made a mental note to keep an eye on his performance.

The door to the bridge hissed open and Silas Cadwell entered. Lawrence regarded him with some suspicion; Cadwell was new to the crew of the *Adamantium*, although he was an experienced 2IC. He certainly didn't seem to be in awe of Lawrence, but it wasn't that which bothered the captain. Rather it was the way in which Cadwell cut an even more imposing figure than he did: whip thin, taller than Lawrence by several inches, his hair shaven down to the skin. His eyes were the coldest grey Lawrence had ever seen, like little chips of ice. The creases in his uniform looked to be razor sharp.

'Captain,' acknowledged Cadwell, as he stepped up to the command podium. He all but saluted. 'We have a priority class 1-A distress call on the signals scan, sir.'

Lawrence frowned. 'A mayday?'

'Interstellar beamcast,' Cadwell said. 'Originating in the Akoshemon system.'

'Akoshemon?' Lawrence raised an eyebrow.

Cadwell handed him a data card. 'I thought you might like to see it first, sir.'

Lawrence read the card. One name leapt out at him from all the information, causing his jaw to tighten. He distinctly felt a facial muscle jump. 'Jyl Stoker,' he said tonelessly.

'Sir.'

Lawrence looked up into Cadwell's clear grey eyes but the 2IC's expression was unreadable. Perhaps Lawrence had misjudged the man; perhaps he wasn't as heartless as he had first believed. 'Thank you, Cadwell. You may proceed.'

'Sir.' Cadwell swivelled on his heel and addressed the helm. 'Jenks, set a course for the Akoshemon system, maximum speed.'

'You've done *what*?' Jyl Stoker asked, teeth clenched and face blanched with fury.

Bunny stood solemnly before her, his giant hands clasped in front of him, almost in prayer. He could barely meet Stoker's gaze, so Tegan decided to answer for him.

'He's done what he should have done a lot sooner. He's sent a mayday call out.'

Her voice rang out in the brittle silence of the lab. Stoker's eyes didn't flicker from Bunny.

'We need help,' Tegan added desperately. 'Can't you see that?'

'This has nothing to do with you,' hissed Stoker.

'But –'

'*Nothing.*'

Bunny said, 'Jim's dead. How many more have to die before we admit we've lost, Jyl?'

Stoker simply stared at him, rendered speechless by anger. There were tears of frustration glinting in her eyes.

'It's got out of hand,' Tegan insisted, looking to the Doctor for some moral support.

The Doctor was leaning against one of the benches, looking contemplative as he observed the exchange. Nyssa sat on the bench beside him, her face pale and serious, but her mind clearly elsewhere. On the Doctor's other side, in a chair, sat Ravus Oldeman, also watching the argument carefully.

'We're finished here, Jyl,' Bunny said sadly.

'You're so right,' Stoker replied. Her tone was as cold as the rock that surrounded the lab complex.

'Personally,' said Ravus Oldeman, 'I think you've done the right thing, Mr Cheung. I've been waiting to escape from this moon for one hundred and sixty years.'

No one smiled at the joke, but Stoker leapt to her feet and bunched her fists.

'I think we all need to calm down,' the Doctor said. He addressed Stoker specifically. 'What's done is done. Perhaps it will be for the best.'

Stoker glared at him for a second and then slumped back down into a seat. She closed her eyes and began to massage the side of her skull with one hand. The knuckles showed white.

'I'm sorry, Jyl,' Bunny said.

She regarded him venomously from beneath hooded lids. 'Forget it. You and I are finished.'

'The Akoshemon system,' Silas Cadwell announced. 'One M46 type star, three planets: an airless rock, a gas giant and then Akoshemon itself.'

'Ugly-looking place,' Lawrence commented. The planet was up on the forward viewscreen, a big disc of steaming black and red mud. Lawrence felt as though he was peering into a cauldron of bubbling poison.

'The mayday signal originates from the moon of Akoshemon,' Cadwell said. 'A routine survey scan conducted seven years ago indicated the moon to be a low-grade planetoid coded NWP.'

NWP: *not worth pursuit*. Lawrence stared at the pulsating orb on the screen, mesmerised by the swirling, bloody colours. Silhouetted against the scarlet mass was a tiny circle of black: the moon.

'And yet Jyl Stoker is there,' Lawrence said quietly. 'How very intriguing.'

Cadwell looked up at the captain. 'You think the original scan result may require an update?'

'It doesn't matter,' Lawrence said after a momentary pause. 'We can't ignore a cry for help.'

Stoker sat in the corner of the lab, smoking a cigar with some aggression, and glaring sourly at everyone else in the room. She felt distinctly outnumbered. Everyone seemed to be on Bunny's side.

The Doctor was still fussing around Oldeman, having administered a second dose of neurolectrin. In hushed tones they were now discussing the experiments Oldeman had conducted one hundred and sixty years ago – the same experiments that had led directly to the present situation. Stoker could barely look at the old fool without wanting to kill him.

The Doctor's assistants were both behaving oddly, if it could be said that anyone left alive here could behave normally. Nyssa was sitting primly on a bench, listening to the Doctor's conversation with Oldeman. She appeared to be paying great attention, but there was something in her eyes, something flat and unfathomable, that made Stoker think that she was in fact concentrating on something else entirely. It crossed Stoker's mind that the girl might have sustained some kind of brain damage as a result of oxygen starvation when she had arrested earlier. Stoker felt a wave of pity. You poor little cow, she thought, you were as good as dead.

Stoker stiffened slightly as she saw Tegan Jovanka coming over. The woman was giving her a strange look.

'You've got to deal with your anger,' Tegan told her bluntly. 'Otherwise it'll just eat you up. Take it from one who knows.'

'Don't patronise me,' Stoker said.

'I'm only trying to help.'

'Go and help Bunny. He might need a hand rolling out the red carpet for the next Consortium ship that responds to his mayday.'

'You don't know it will be a Consortium ship.'

Stoker took a long drag on her cigar. 'There are only two types of starship patrolling this sector of space: cut-throat mineral pirates and mining survey vessels belonging to the Consortium. The pirates won't answer a mayday.'

'How do you know?'

"Cos I'm one of them.' Stoker flashed a mirthless smile.

'I think we'd be better off with a Consortium ship, then,' Tegan said.

'You might be. I won't. Any Consortium ship that lands here will whip this claim right out from under me, before I can say "shafted by my best friend".'

'That's not why Bunny did it,' Tegan said. 'We need help here. Unless we get help, we could all be killed.'

Stoker looked bored. 'Oh yeah, that.'

'Aren't you scared?'

'I'm too angry to be scared.'

Tegan seemed to consider this. 'Funny, but I think that's what happened to me. When I first joined up with the Doctor. I was too angry to be really scared.'

Stoker was intrigued despite herself. 'But that's changed?'

'I think so.'

'Now you're just scared?'

'No. I mean yes, I'm scared, but I sort of take that for granted. Being with the Doctor means you're going to be scared. He fights scary things.'

Stoker gave her a sardonic look. 'He's in his element here then.'

Tegan looked across the lab at the pale, blond figure in the cricket clothes. He was talking earnestly to both Oldeman and Nyssa. 'Oh yes, he's in his element, all right.'

Lawrence shut the door of his private cabin aboard the *Adamantium* and sat down at his desk. He laid down the mayday report and stared at it for a minute before activating his computer terminal. The puter was command-access only, and not linked to the ship's main system.

'Standing by,' said the puter.

Lawrence said, 'Access Consortium data record for Stoker, Jyl.'

The puter buzzed. 'Stoker, Jyl. Female. Height: six foot. Hair: blonde. Eyes: amber. Born 2341 Earth Colony E5150. Transferred to Earth Central Academy of Science 2359. Studied Exogeology. Failed to graduate. Departed Earth Central 2363. Last known whereabouts: Kaltros Prime. Occupation: rogue trader.'

Lawrence snorted. There was little here he didn't know already, of course, but it was in his nature to check. In fact it was surprising how little information there was; he felt sure Stoker would appreciate that. Rogue traders – the puter's euphemism for pirates – didn't like too much information about them in databanks of any kind, let alone those of the Consortium.

The cabin door chimed and Lawrence switched the puter off. 'Come.'

The door slid open and Silas Cadwell stepped into the cabin. 'You asked to see me, Captain.'

'Are you bored, Cadwell?' Lawrence asked without preamble.

'No, sir.'

'Liar. You're bored rigid, man. Everyone on this ship is bored. It's all very well being patient, but this is ridiculous. Small wonder Jenks is feeling disgruntled. We've found absolutely nothing out here on the rim, and no indication that we will find anything in the near future.' Lawrence paused for effect. 'Until now.'

'Sir?'

'This mayday signal,' Lawrence said abruptly. 'What do you make of it, Cadwell?'

Cadwell did his best to shrug, but he was not a shrugging person. To Lawrence it looked strangely affected, almost rehearsed. Trust him to have anticipated the query. 'Standard signal generator, sir. According to the regulations we have to investigate.'

Lawrence nodded. 'We have to *help*, Cadwell, not just investigate.'

'Sir.'

'And what about this Stoker woman?' Lawrence said.

There was the briefest hesitation. 'I thought you might be interested, Captain.'

'Yes, that's what you said on the bridge.'

Cadwell said, 'If Stoker's there, sir, then it must be for a reason. I can't see her wasting time on a low-grade planetoid like that moon unless there's something there for her.'

'That's what I thought. But it appears she might have bitten off more than even she can chew this time.'

'Sir?'

'Jyl Stoker wouldn't issue a mayday unless she absolutely had to, Cadwell. I know that for a fact. Pirates like her don't give claims up that easily.'

'Unless it is just a low-grade planetoid.'

Lawrence's eyes narrowed. 'Believe me, it won't be. Not if Stoker's there.'

There was a silence during which Lawrence realised his 2IC had more to say. 'Go on, Cadwell: out with it.'

'There is something else, sir.' Cadwell held out a data pod. 'I backtracked through the hypernet transmissions to and from the Akoshemon system. I found this simcord message on a narrow bandwidth spurt from Earth Central yesterday. It had been relayed through the Karula Koza comnet in an obvious attempt to avoid detection.'

Lawrence raised an eyebrow. This was above and beyond the call of duty. Impressed, and very slightly unnerved, Lawrence took the pod. 'OK, let's see what it is.'

He plugged it into the puter and played the recording. A bright 3D image of a human girl aged five or six coalesced on the desktop. Lawrence and Cadwell watched Rosie Cheung's message in its entirety before Cadwell hit the mute.

'Careless,' said Lawrence, stroking his chin thoughtfully.

Cadwell agreed. 'Could be useful. This Cheung person clearly misses his family. A weak spot in Stoker's armour, perhaps.'

Lawrence was about to say that Stoker didn't have any weak spots, but held his tongue. It wasn't true. 'We'll keep it in mind,' he said instead.

The cabin intercom blipped and Jenks's voice came through from the bridge. 'The *Adamantium* is entering orbit around the moon of Akoshemon, Captain. You asked to be informed.'

Lawrence aknowledged the call and turned back to Silas Cadwell with the faintest of smiles. 'The moment of truth, Cadwell. This could be our lucky day.'

A short-range comms scan picked out the precise location from which the subspace distress signal had been broadcast, and Jenks brought the *Adamantium* in to land on a narrow rock shelf adjacent to a natural cave system. The ship touched down less than fifteen minutes after breaking orbit, a cloud of sand dusting the hull silver-green as it came to rest on its landing fins.

Captain Lawrence congratulated Jenks and invited his helmsman to join him, Cadwell and three other crewmen in the initial excursion party. Lawrence authorised the issue of small firearms to himself and Cadwell only. He didn't want to look as though the Consortium was coming in with all guns blazing.

The caves were silent and apparently deserted. Lawrence maintained a brisk, businesslike attitude and hoped his men would emulate him. Cadwell appeared calm but alert, as always, and Lawrence envied the man's inscrutable manner. Privately Lawrence felt that there was something about this place that set the nerves on edge. Beneath his otherwise unflappable demeanour, the captain felt distinctly uneasy.

They met Stoker's party in the main cavern as agreed: there was a lot of cheap analysing equipment and samplers lying around, evidence of the rough-and-ready approach these rogues took to the job. If they had discovered anything of value on this rock with such rudimentary sensor tools then it wouldn't take the *Adamantium* long to find out what it was.

Stoker herself was not present at this first meeting; Lawrence didn't know whether he felt disappointed or not. It was Cadwell who pointed out that she could be injured or even dead. This was a possibility that had simply not crossed Lawrence's mind until that moment.

Representing Stoker was a giant of a man with brooding eyes and thick stubble.

'Cheung,' the big man growled. Lawrence exchanged a glance with Cadwell: they both knew this must be the father of the girl in the hologram message.

Cheung didn't extend his hand, simply glowered at the uniforms. He was evidently disappointed, but that was only to be expected. The arrival of a Consortium ship had to be the worst kind of help these people would want. But beggars can't be choosers, Lawrence reminded himself with satisfaction.

Lawrence introduced himself and Cadwell. Standing with Cheung were a strange couple: a very attractive young woman who didn't look dressed for mining operations of any kind, and a youngish, fair-haired man in light, casual clothes. Lawrence felt his attention drawn irresistibly to this man, who introduced himself as simply the Doctor.

'I didn't think your kind of operation had room for medical staff,' Lawrence said to Cheung.

'He's a specialist,' Cheung replied.

'If you say so,' Lawrence drawled. He forced a smile to his lips and said as blandly as he could manage, 'May I ask where Jyl Stoker may be found?'

No one expected the meeting to go well, but few could have guessed how spectacularly badly it would turn out. Bunny Cheung was treating Captain Lawrence with only a grudging respect. He was now obviously having second thoughts about the wisdom of calling in help. This made for a rather strained atmosphere, but nothing like the electric tension that filled the laboratory when Jyl Stoker first saw Captain Lawrence.

Lawrence walked confidently into the lab, ducking slightly as he stepped through the doorway.

Stoker looked up from where she sat, arms folded, lips tight. Her face drained of all colour and her eyes bugged with astonishment. The reaction was so unexpected that most people in the room did a double take from her to Lawrence, just to check that the Consortium officer hadn't grown another head.

'Good evening,' Lawrence said, his smile exposing perfect white teeth.

To her credit, Stoker recovered from her shock with record speed. She didn't say anything in reply immediately; she merely concentrated on lighting another cigar. It was a good performance but no one was fooled: she was playing for time.

Stoker blew out a stream of smoke and flicked her eyes up and down the captain. 'Uniform suits you,' she said, managing to make it sound like an insult.

Lawrence looked amused. 'I thought you'd be pleased to see me.'

'You never were much good at thinking,' Stoker shot back.

Bunny Cheung said, 'I can't believe you two know each other.'

'Our paths have crossed,' Lawrence admitted. He turned back to Stoker. 'Glad to see you're all right. I confess I was rather concerned when we received your mayday.'

'Wasn't my mayday,' grunted Stoker.

Lawrence ignored this. 'Care to tell me what's going on?'

'Go to hell,' Stoker told him, getting up to leave. She walked straight past Lawrence without a second glance but paused at the exit to speak to Bunny, 'He's all yours, *pal.*'

An uncomfortable silence settled over the remaining people in the laboratory. Lawrence said nothing, but there was something smouldering like a fuse in his eyes.

'Sorry,' muttered Bunny Cheung when it was clear no one else was going to speak. 'I had no idea…'

'Of course not,' Lawrence replied curtly. 'Why should you?'

Bunny closed his hands into giant fists. He clearly regretted sending the mayday now.

Satisfied that the conversation was over, Lawrence clapped his hands and rubbed them briskly together. 'Right then. Would someone else care to explain the precise nature of your little problem here?'

*

It was the Doctor who summarised what had happened so far. Tegan noticed that he was careful to remain neutral where the decision to issue the mayday was concerned. Tegan suspected that the others, like her, were secretly glad to see the arrival of uniformed officials on the scene. At least they no longer felt so isolated. But it was difficult to appreciate the way in which the Consortium was taking over: within moments, Captain Lawrence was issuing orders to his men with a cavalier disregard for any other authority.

'I'll have all my men armed with blaster pistols,' Lawrence informed the Doctor blithely. 'Organise them into patrols and search the cave system. We'll soon track this creature down and kill it for you.'

'And then?' the Doctor asked.

Lawrence almost hesitated. 'And then we'll see. The priority must be to neutralise the threat and render the cave system safe. Don't worry. My men are very experienced, they've dealt successfully with the occasional HLF before.'

'HLF?'

'Hostile life form.'

'I hope you're right,' the Doctor said.

Lawrence raised an eyebrow. 'You're not convinced?'

'Let's say I prefer to keep an open mind. Firepower is seldom a solution in itself. Besides which, there is more to our problem here than this creature. I have reason to believe that there may be some kind of extra-sensory field effect at work, generated by something located in or around this moon, which is causing perceptual variations.'

'Really?' Lawrence smiled condescendingly. 'Don't believe in phantoms, Doctor. If there's a hostile life form here then we can destroy it. End of story.'

'I doubt that.'

For a long moment the two men faced each other, neither willing to blink first. Eventually Lawrence pursed his lips and said, 'Perhaps you would like to accompany the hunting party? See for yourself when we shoot the damn thing down.'

'I can't say it would be a pleasure,' the Doctor replied smoothly, 'but it might be for the best.'

Nyssa sat with Ravus Oldeman for a while.

Neither of them spoke; Oldeman sat and frowned, his eyes sharp and bright with the effects of the neurolectrin, but Nyssa was consumed by her own anxieties. While the professor concentrated with his renewed clarity of mind, Nyssa was unable to pin down her own problem. Something prevented her from analysing her thoughts properly. Something like a mental block, yet more subtle and worrying than that: a lost memory, perhaps. It was all very confusing. She had not experienced such a sense of confusion and loss since her father had been murdered and Traken destroyed. Then, however, the Doctor had been there for her: he had taken her under his wing, offered her a home and a life and the opportunity to study. And to help others less… fortunate… than herself.

Her feelings for the Doctor had changed as well. She could not shake the feeling that he was avoiding her. He didn't seem to want to include her in his researches, almost as if he didn't trust her. How could that be? After all they had been through with each other? He only seemed to confide in Tegan now. Could the Doctor be that fickle?

'Charged particle-beam weapon,' said the Consortium officer, Crook, holding out a bulky energy pistol for all to see. 'Cuts through anything. I've seen one of these babies burn a hole in duralinium plate.'

'Yes, but have you actually used one before?' the Doctor asked.

'Don't get smart,' snapped Crook. 'I could vaporise an apple pip at five hundred metres with this.'

'You could vaporise a whole apple tree at five hundred metres with one of those.'

Crook glared. 'So it shouldn't have a problem with your Bloodhunter then, should it?'

'I just want you to be careful with it, that's all.'

'Bloodhunter?' Tegan echoed.

The Doctor looked uncomfortable. 'Yes, well, we had to call it something. Seemed appropriate at the time.'

'Call it what you want,' said Crook. 'It's already dead as far as I'm concerned.' The officer began handing out more blasters to a group of *Adamantium* crewmen.

The Doctor rolled his eyes. 'They never learn.'

Tegan smiled. 'Fed up with all the macho talk?'

'Guns always seem to bring that out in humans, I find.'

'You've got to admit we need some kind of protection, though.'

The Doctor nodded. 'Oh, we need protection, all right. But not necessarily from the Bloodhunter.'

'I don't understand.'

'Neither do I yet. At least not fully.' A light in the Doctor's eyes indicated that his mind was working ferociously. 'There's something else at work here, Tegan. I'm certain that the creature is not the real problem, but merely the symptom of a greater evil.'

'Have you got any theories?'

'As soon as I know anything useful, you will be the first to know.'

Tegan felt rather pleased with this. 'We can't do anything about that until we find this Bloodhunter thing, though, can we?'

'Apparently not.'

Tegan looked disappointed as she watched the last of the blasters being dished out. 'I thought they'd spare a couple for us.'

'Thank goodness for small mercies,' the Doctor said.

Lawrence walked into the comms area and found Stoker smoking a cigar.

'Thought I'd find you here,' he said. 'Followed the smoke.'

Stoker spared him a glance. 'Which smoke? The cigar smoke or the stuff coming out of my ears?'

He smiled. 'You always did have a temper.'

'You mean I always did have emotions,' she corrected him. 'Unlike you.'

He stepped in front of her and she had to look at him. His eyes were a perfect, commanding blue.

'I'm not a machine, Jyl.'

Stoker curled her lip. 'No, you're a lousy, double-crossing Consortium toady with a weakness for blondes. How could I have forgotten?'

'If it's any consolation at all,' Lawrence said carefully, 'I didn't know you'd be here. At least not at first. The mayday was intercepted by my 2IC, on one of his routine signal scans.'

'Fine.'

'I would still have come here, even if it hadn't been your name attached to the mayday.'

Stoker let out a harsh laugh. 'You still know how to make a woman feel special, don't you!'

'I didn't mean it like that.'

For a moment Lawrence had actually looked flustered, and Stoker took advantage. 'How is she, by the way? What was her name? Sacksomething. Sassy? Sasquatch?'

'Saskia.'

'Oh yeah.'

'Let's not go over all that again, please.'

Stoker stubbed out her cigar with enough force to snap it in two. 'This is the point where I should slap you in the face, isn't it? Well I won't, because you're ready for it now. When I do hit you, it will be low and hard and when you're least expecting it.'

'I see,' Lawrence said. 'Thank you for the warning. I'm surprised you still bear a grudge, although I suppose it shows you still have feelings for me.'

Stoker leapt to her feet, teeth bared. 'Go to hell, you bastard!'

'There you are,' Lawrence said triumphantly. 'I knew you still cared.'

Stoker pulled back her fist, but didn't deliver. She could see the amused look in his eyes. Those perfect blue eyes. 'It was never really about Saskia,' she said.

'I know. You just couldn't stand the thought that I wanted to join the Consortium. You thought I'd jump college with you and fly around the galaxy chasing fortune and glory. You were wrong. That's what you couldn't stand.'

'I couldn't stand the fact that you sold out to the Consortium!'

'Sold out? Don't be ridiculous. The Consortium paid for our education. We all owed it our loyalty. I decided to pay my debt, that's all.' Lawrence turned to leave the room, but paused. 'It's a pity you didn't do the same thing. Then you might not have ended up here, marooned on a piece of crap like this and begging for help.'

Stoker watched him leave and then sank back down into her chair. Her hand trembled as she raised another cigar to her lips.

'I insist on coming with you,' Tegan said. 'And I won't take no for an answer.'

'Tegan…' the Doctor began hopelessly, faltering the moment she turned those fiery brown eyes on him.

Bunny Cheung said, 'It could be very dangerous.'

Tegan looked at him witheringly. 'I've been in shootouts with Cybermen. Have you?'

'Er, well… no.'

Sensing victory, Tegan pressed on, 'Besides which, Doctor, you need me – to keep a clear head, remember? In case you start getting confused again.'

Bunny glanced nervously at the Doctor, who looked uncomfortable. 'All right, Tegan,' the Doctor sighed. 'Let's get on with it.'

The plan was brutally simple: track down the Bloodhunter and kill it. Crook wanted to conduct a systematic cave-by-cave search for the creature until the Doctor politely suggested a different approach.

'Does the *Adamantium* have bio-tracking sensors on board?'

Crook nodded as he turned the beam intensity control on his blaster up to maximum. 'State of the art sensor array. The best Consortium money can buy.'

Bunny growled, but the Doctor carried on. 'Recalibrate your scanners to detect an Akoshemon-human DNA combination like this,' he broke off to scribble something on a sheet of notepaper.

He passed the note to Crook. 'You should be able to pinpoint the creature's exact location. It might save us a little time.'

They found the creature within half an hour of the Doctor's instruction being relayed to the scan officer on board the *Adamantium*. It was almost too quick for Tegan's liking: her stomach started churning the moment the order to move out came through from Crook.

Tegan had done her best to wangle a gun from Crook, but he had refused, citing Consortium regulations as the reason. Tegan might have suspected it was a sex thing, certain that 400 years' progress since 1982 would have done little for gender equality among humans, but Crook wouldn't give Bunny a blaster either. The Doctor, of course, did not request a sidearm, although he positioned himself right at the front of the party with Crook. Tegan instinctively stuck close to the Doctor.

Following instructions radioed from the *Adamantium*, they found the Bloodhunter very quickly.

Or rather, the Bloodhunter found them.

Whether it was simply the creature's natural instinct to attack, or whether it was forced into fighting like a cornered rat, nobody could be certain. But it leapt out of the shadows at the end of the tunnel with shocking speed and fastened itself on to the nearest human being.

Tegan yelled as Bunny Cheung collapsed beneath the ugly, brutish form: then she heard its awful, sucking grunts as a number of thick white tubes sprouted from its face and latched on to Bunny's head and neck.

CHAPTER ELEVEN

No one could see clearly what was happening, but they could all hear the sounds of the beast as it tried to suck the life out of Bunny Cheung. That, and the cries of the men around him.

'What *is* it?'

'Do something –'

'Open fire!'

'No, you might hit Cheung!'

'Get back!'

There was a bright flash and then a horrible squeal as someone took a shot at the thing.

'Wait!' the Doctor yelled. 'You can't see properly –'

But his only reply was the sharp crackle of more blaster fire; Tegan saw Crook step forward, bringing his pistol up in a two-handed grip and taking careful aim. She saw past him, and realised that, for a moment, the creature's back was turned towards Crook, presenting a perfect target. His blaster shot sizzling lumps out of the Bloodhunter's flesh. It howled and squirmed away, but still maintained a hold on Cheung.

'Get this thing off me!' Bunny screamed. Somehow he had wrenched his head free of the thing's tentacles.

There were too many of them in the narrow tunnel. No one could get close enough for a clear shot. The Doctor had managed to slip forward and grab hold of Bunny's arms; Bunny gripped the Doctor's wrists for dear life. The Bloodhunter was in retreat, but it was determined to drag its prey with it.

'Help me!' Bunny yelled. His eyes were wide and full of terror, his face wet with blood.

The beast was now pulling both Bunny and the Doctor. It was phenomenally strong, dragging them across the floor. Even braced as he was, and with the rubber grips on his running shoes, the Doctor could not stop slipping inexorably forward.

'Can't you shoot it?' Tegan asked Crook desperately.

'I can't get a clear shot – I might hit the Doctor or Cheung!'

'It's going to get away!' Tegan shouted. 'It's making for that crevice!'

The Bloodhunter was backing into a narrow fissure in the rock wall. Bunny was already jammed against the entrance, his teeth bared in agony. 'It's got me! It's got me!'

The thing was extending more tubes, sinking them into Bunny's flesh, burrowing through his clothes. He started to shake violently.

'Come on!' bellowed the Doctor. 'Don't give up now! Try and brace yourself against the floor!' The Doctor's face was purple with the strain, veins standing out on his forehead.

Tegan grabbed the blaster pistol off a startled Crook and ran forward. Stepping over the Doctor, she pointed the gun into the crevice and blasted away at the monster. She was rewarded with a screech of pain and the smell of burning meat. She couldn't tell if she'd hit anything vital, but the creature lost some of its grip on Bunny and the Doctor started to haul him out of the crevice.

With a ravenous snarl the Bloodhunter leapt back, fastening itself on to Bunny's right arm. Bunny's shoulder was jammed painfully against the edge of the hole.

Tegan opened fire again, unsure if it was having any real effect but not knowing what else to do.

The Doctor switched his grip on Bunny, but the big man continued to be drawn into the crevice. 'It's going to rip my arm off!'

Suddenly the Doctor jumped to his feet and began to stamp hard on Bunny's shoulder.

'What're you doing?' Tegan gasped.

'Saving his life!' The Doctor was kicking down with his heel now, using all the strength he had to break the man's arm. The

Bloodhunter was squealing and grunting like a rabid pig. Suddenly, Bunny's arm broke free. Bunny lurched back out of the crevice as the Bloodhunter fell back, taking his arm with it.

The Doctor heaved Bunny aside as Crook took his chance, stepping into the gap and opening fire with another pistol. They all heard the Bloodhunter let out a blood-curdling cry and Tegan saw it reel back, lit for a moment by the flash of the blaster beams. Crook adjusted his aim in that fraction of a second and managed a head-shot. The creature recoiled, suddenly silenced.

'Got you, you bastard!'

Tegan caught her breath and knelt down next to Bunny. He was shaking, his face ashen and webbed with blood, his left hand clamped over the stump of his right shoulder. Tegan steeled herself to look, but where she expected to see bone and bloody tissue, saw only metal and wires.

'What —?'

'Sorry about the arm, Bunny,' said the Doctor. He caught Tegan's confused look and said, 'It's all right, his arm was a bionic replacement.'

Bunny smiled grimly. 'Lost my own in an explosives accident years ago.'

Tegan looked at the Doctor. 'You knew this?'

'A good guess, Tegan. It all added up: Bunny's prodigious strength, his supernormal dexterity…'

'You mean the juggling?'

'I'm afraid Bunny's juggling days are over for the time being.'

'What's happened to the Bloodhunter?' Bunny asked.

'I think I've killed it,' Crook told them. He was peering into the shadows, but there was a lot of smoke. 'I can't see much yet.'

A sudden cold seemed to fill the cave, as if the ghost of an icy wind had drifted down the tunnels. Everyone noticed it, and Tegan shivered. 'What was that?'

'Some kind of localised temperature drop,' the Doctor said.

Tegan hugged herself. 'What could cause that?'

'I don't know,' the Doctor replied, but he looked worried. He lowered his voice so that only she could hear him. 'I've got a feeling – a sensation, nothing more… the creature's dead, but something else is there, waiting, something intensely evil… and it's not very pleased. Shh!' the Doctor snapped a finger to his lips. 'I think I can hear it, too… Vega Jaal mentioned it not long before he died: he said he heard the distant screams of an entire planet destroyed by evil. Can you hear it?'

'Actually, no.' Tegan frowned. 'Are you all right, Doctor? You're not having another funny turn, are you?'

'It's shock,' Crook informed her. 'Happens to the best of us. Better get him out of here.'

The chilly atmosphere increased to the point where they could see their breath in the air. A damp, deadening breeze swept along the floor of the cave, dispersing the dregs of the smoke and then dying out further down the tunnel system with a soft moan.

'He's right,' the Doctor told Tegan. 'And Bunny needs medical attention, anyway. Come on, lend a hand!'

With a nervous glance back at the hole where the Bloodhunter had been, Tegan did her best to help the Doctor get Bunny to his feet. It wasn't an easy task, but Crook ordered a couple of his men to help. Bunny didn't want any fuss, assuring them all that he could walk unaided before collapsing to the floor in a dead faint.

In the laboratory complex, Nyssa had suddenly sat up straight with a little gasp. In fact she had flinched visibly several times during the last few minutes, and Ravus Oldeman had noticed.

'Are you all right?' he asked.

Nyssa's eyes were shut, her head tilted back slightly. 'I'm fine,' she told him finally. Her nostrils flared and a trickle of blood ran from her nose.

Nyssa opened her eyes and quickly wiped the blood away with a hand. She smiled at Oldeman. 'Really, I'm fine.'

She looked down at her hand. The blood on her fingers was as black as oil.

*

'What do you think you're doing?' asked Stoker. A couple of Consortium crewmen had come into the comms area and were starting to dismantle the communications unit.

'Orders,' said one of the men, without looking up. He produced a tool kit and set to work.

Stoker interposed herself between the man and the comms unit. 'Beg pardon?'

He looked up. He was young, sallow-faced and full of Consortium arrogance. 'Got orders to take this thing apart, miss.' He picked up a heavy tool and smacked it against the palm of his free hand. The implication was obvious: *don't get in my way*.

Stoker didn't move. 'Now look here. This is my equipment. If you so much as touch it, I'll –'

'It's Captain Lawrence's orders,' the crewman told her. 'You'll have to take it up with him if you've got a complaint.'

Silas Cadwell walked into the lab complex. He spared only the briefest glance at Oldeman and Nyssa, then went through to the next chamber to find Captain Lawrence. Lawrence was poking around in the scientific junk on one of the workbenches, obviously bored. He looked up and Cadwell acknowledged him with a curt nod of his shaven head. 'Crook's just reported in, sir. He thinks they've found and killed the creature.'

'Thinks?' repeated Lawrence.

'They haven't recovered the body yet. I'm sure it's only a matter of time.'

'Excellent, Cadwell. Fast work. Any casualties?'

'No sir. At least, none of our men.'

'Very good.'

At this point Jyl Stoker marched into the room looking furious. Both Lawrence and Cadwell looked up. If they noticed the fire in her eyes, neither reacted. 'This has gone far enough,' she told Lawrence angrily.

'I'm sorry?'

'You will be.' Stoker pointed back the way she had come. 'Your men are dismantling my comms unit up there!'

Cadwell nodded. 'You won't be needing it. We're in charge here now.'

'Like hell you are!'

'Wait a moment, Cadwell,' said Lawrence smoothly. He introduced his 2IC and Stoker curled her lip at him. 'Is there a problem, Jyl?'

She gaped. 'That's my comms unit! What d'you think you're doing?'

'My men have orders to tidy up,' Lawrence said, sounding almost apologetic. 'If it's inconvenient, then you're welcome to use the comms station on board the *Adamantium*. Do you need to contact someone?'

'A good lawyer, perhaps,' suggested Cadwell.

Stoker looked at him. 'I always knew the Consortium recruited slime, but it must have really been scraping the bottom of the barrel when it took you on.'

A humourless smile developed on Cadwell's skull-like face. 'Well, if *I'm* slime, Ms Stoker, what does that make you and your band of… riff-raff?'

Stoker looked from Cadwell to Lawrence. 'Is he allowed to talk to me like that?'

'You insulted him,' Lawrence said.

'I'll punch his lights out next time.'

This seemed to amuse Lawrence, although he was careful not to let his smile reach Cadwell's attention. 'I'm not here to indulge in your passion for brawling,' he said, 'and neither is my 2IC. For your information, Cadwell has just reported that your little problem here has been eliminated. Without, I might add, any further casualties.'

Stoker pressed her lips into a thin line. She was determined not to thank him.

Lawrence drew in a breath. 'All right, you can go, Cadwell. Keep me informed.'

'Sir.' Cadwell almost snapped to attention, and then left, knocking Stoker's shoulder slightly as he pushed past.

Lawrence watched him leave and then sighed. 'You really have to pity Cadwell, you know.'

Stoker said, 'Oh yeah. It can't be easy looking like a skeleton in a uniform.'

'He's very dedicated,' Lawrence explained.

'Perfect Consortium material.'

Lawrence pursed his lips, still looking thoughtfully at the door. 'Maybe.'

Stoker was intrigued, despite herself. She hadn't expected a chink in the Consortium armour. 'What do you mean?'

'I'm not really sure,' Lawrence admitted. 'Cadwell's everything one could want in a 2IC: very professional, extremely competent. Reliable, perhaps.'

'Perhaps?'

Lawrence shrugged. 'He's relatively new to the *Adamantium* crew. I haven't known him for very long. He was posted to the *Adamantium* for this trip, in fact. We've been surveying the outer rim for the last three months.'

Stoker considered what he had said very carefully. 'You don't trust him?'

The captain's head snapped round to look at her with cold blue eyes. 'I didn't say that.'

'You didn't have to.'

The door to the lab hummed open and the Doctor and Tegan bustled in with Bunny Cheung and a couple of *Adamantium* crewmen. Stoker's jaw dropped the moment she saw how awful Bunny looked. 'What the hell happened?'

'The Bloodhunter caught him,' Tegan said.

They all helped Bunny slump into a seat, where he looked up at Stoker with a weary smile. The blood had dried into dark crusts on his face and beard, making him look like some kind of caveman.

'Don't worry,' he said, 'I'm 'armless.' He twisted in his seat to show her the stump of electronics in his shoulder.

Stoker felt a wave of nausea in her gut. It wasn't the sight of bionics, which made some people feel queasy. This was the simple, thudding realisation that everything was really going wrong.

To look at, Bunny was a giant – big, tall and hairy. But he had none of the natural arrogance of the physically powerful. Stoker knew the real Bunny Cheung – the gentle, easy-going man trapped inside a thug's body. Bunny had worked for her all over the sector for many years, chasing fortune and glory, until a faulty micrex detonator tore his right arm off at the shoulder and landed him in intensive care for three long months on Earth. Stoker had saved his life and paid for top-of-the-range bionic surgery, but Bunny emerged from hospital a different man: quieter, almost subdued, and married to a nurse.

Bunny had stayed on Earth. It wasn't until the birth of his daughter, after many years' trying for a family, that something of the old Bunny showed up again: an exuberant, enveloping good humour that had been such a good foil for Stoker's grumpiness. But little Rosie was the light of Bunny's new life. He was truly happy. And utterly broke.

Stoker had called on him at just the wrong moment with just the right offer: the chance of one last grab for fortune and glory in the Akoshemon system. It had almost broken his heart to leave his wife and kid, but Bunny just couldn't afford not to go.

Stoker felt guilty as hell about it.

And what made it worse now wasn't just the sight of the machinery hanging out of his shoulder. That could be replaced. No, it was the new look in Bunny's eyes – something alien to the normal, jovial spark: a tiny flame of anger, flickering deep inside where he was scared.

Stoker swore. 'Hell's teeth, Bunny, that arm cost a fortune! What the hell happened?'

Bunny tried to hide the anxiety. 'That creature took it for a souvenir, didn't it?'

Lawrence was watching all this with an expression of real concern. Stoker sneered at him. 'No casualties?' she spat.

One of the Consortium crewmen had produced a first aid kit, and the Doctor was already busy with the contents. Bunny said, 'You'll need a set of spanners and a screwdriver, not antiseptic wipes.'

'Sit still and don't talk,' the Doctor said. 'The shock hasn't hit you yet, but this might soften the effects.' He pressed a dermal drug patch onto Bunny's forehead. 'The damage to your shoulder joint isn't too bad, but we might have to tidy up the control linkages and power lines.'

'Never mind that,' Stoker said as the Doctor started to fiddle with the machinery poking out of Bunny's torn sleeve. 'What about the arm? Where is it?'

'I dunno,' Bunny said. 'It's gone.'

'Gone?'

'It was either the arm or me, Jyl.'

'That's supposed to make me feel better?' Stoker glared at him. 'Trust you to get too close to the damn thing, you big ape.'

'Ouch!' cried the Doctor as something sparked. He blew on his fingers. 'I think I've located the power lines... Luckily the energy cell must still be in the arm, or you could've been fried.'

'Oh, blast,' said Bunny suddenly. 'My ring! The holograph ring – it was on the finger of my bionic hand!'

Tegan realised instantly what he meant. 'Your little girl's hologram.'

Bunny cursed loudly, and then more loudly as another circuit sparked in his stump. 'Sorry!' called the Doctor.

'Oh this is just *terrific*,' Bunny wailed. 'What have I done to deserve this?'

Stoker shot a murderous look at Captain Lawrence and then turned back to Bunny. Her eyes were full of fire. 'You tell me,' she said through gritted teeth.

Nyssa was sitting alone in the darkness when the Doctor found her a little later. He wandered into the lab with a puzzled frown. 'Nyssa? You've turned the lights down.'

'It's more comfortable like this,' she told him. 'The bright light was hurting my eyes. How is Professor Oldeman?'

'As well as can be expected,' replied the Doctor. 'The neurolectrin

142

treatment has to be carefully monitored. I've referred him to Captain Lawrence's medical officer for the time being.' He bent down to examine Nyssa more closely. 'Actually, you don't look very well yourself, Nyssa.'

'I'm fine,' she lied.

The Doctor sat down with a look of concern. 'Are you sure? Ever since Vega Jaal was killed, I've sensed an increase in mental pressure. I'm sure you must have, too.' He took her hand and felt gently for her pulse. His fingers were hot against her wrist.

She shook her head. 'I don't think so. But I… I've been thinking about Traken a great deal.'

The Doctor said, 'That's only to be expected, I suppose. It's your subconscious that will be under the greatest pressure here.'

'Why?'

'Well, that's what I'm trying to find out. There's something here, Nyssa, an enemy that we have to root out and deal with. I'll need you to help me with that.'

Nyssa frowned. 'I – I don't understand. Can't Tegan help you?'

'Oh, yes.' The Doctor gave a little smile. 'In her own way, of course. But you're more… sensitive… to what's going on here.'

Nyssa reflected on this for a long moment. She knew that the Doctor was right, but she didn't want him to be. She wanted him to take her far, far away from this place. She wanted to be back in the TARDIS, or better still, back on Traken. Safe and protected.

But *that* was impossible.

And the Doctor did need her help. She had to remain focused, to ignore the cold panic that was rising within her, lapping at her resolve and her intellect. Eroding her.

Your blood will run black with me

Nyssa couldn't tell the Doctor about the voice, of course. She was hoping that she had simply imagined that cold voice in the blackness, that it was merely part of some terrible dream or fever. The Doctor had, after all, postulated that some variety of psionic field was interfering with their thought processes. It seemed a little trite to Nyssa, but she had learned to trust the Doctor's wild theorising. The voice she had heard – *thought* she had heard – could just be a result of telepathic interference.

Besides which, on a purely practical level, if she admitted to the Doctor that she had heard the darkness speaking to her, then he might think she was becoming *too* affected, too *unbalanced* to be of any help at all. Also, and rather more chillingly, the very act of admitting that she had heard the voice of the darkness would make it somehow more real. And she did not want that.

Eventually, she said, 'Doctor, when the Consortium men killed the creature... I *sensed* it. I felt it when the creature died.'

He looked at her curiously. 'You're sure about that? That the creature was actually killed?'

'Without a doubt.' She looked up at him. 'How can that be? What connects me to that... *thing*?'

The Doctor took her hand again and this time simply held it. His skin felt incredibly warm. 'I don't know, Nyssa. I had hoped you might be able to tell me.'

'I can't,' she said. 'I'm sorry, but I can't.'

The Doctor thought for a long moment and then seemed to reach a decision. 'Would you be willing to let me try to... find... what that link might be? Where it might lead?'

'I don't understand.'

The Doctor produced his cricket ball and held it up. 'Look at this, Nyssa,' he told her. 'What do you see?'

'A ball. A *cricket* ball.'

'Very good. Keep looking at it. Watch it carefully...'

Nyssa stared at the ball. It was blood red; it was easy to imagine that it was a single droplet of blood, hugely magnified, somehow contained between the Doctor's finger and thumb.

'Watch the ball very carefully, Nyssa,' said the Doctor. His voice sounded a long way off.

In the gloom of the lab, the ball looked almost black. Nyssa imagined that it was an eclipse, a perfect disc of blackness casting its vast shadow over everything around her.

I know you are there, Time Lord

I'm coming for you
Soon

The Doctor reached out to touch Nyssa's face, reacting to a sudden compulsion he could not account for. There was something in the air around her, floating invisibly over her skin: as dark and intangible as thought. 'Where are you?' he asked quietly. '*What* are you?'

He heard it then: unmistakably, the horrifying shrieks and cries of a thousand million beings consumed by the blackness. It was very distant, made almost imperceptible by time but it pushed a cold blade of despair deep into his chest. The agony of all those tormented souls welled up inside him like a physical pain.

Then something crept into his mind, a moist tendril of blackness. It curled inside his subconscious like a finger, beckoning a memory. No, not a memory, he realised with a stab of apprehension: something from the future.

A stone plinth, or altar... or was it a tomb? There was a body lying on it, deathly still: a young man, dressed in the clothes of an Edwardian cricketer. His face was white, the lips blue. He was not breathing. His hands were clasped together over his chest, pallid and stiff with *rigor mortis*.

But then the body moved: it jerked, the face suddenly convulsing. Dead eyes snapped open and the man let out a terrible scream. Blood erupted from his mouth and then his face seemed to crack open like an egg, the skin falling away to reveal something else beneath: another face, larger, fleshier, with unruly blond curls. It emerged from the detritus and then it, too, let out a howl of mortal agony. The fresh skin split open and through the blood *another* face emerged, older, thinner... screaming and screaming until it burst open like a fruit and another face appeared, smeared in gore and screeching for mercy.

It went on and on, face giving birth to face after face, *death after death*, until the surface of the tomb was awash with blood.

*

Nyssa blinked; she had almost fallen asleep. The dark blur in front of her sharpened into a cricket ball, gripped lightly in the Doctor's hand.

'What happened?' she asked, feeling confused.

'What indeed,' the Doctor said quietly, a tremor in his voice. His face was pinched and white.

'Doctor?'

He looked up. His eyes, usually as blue as an Earth summer sky, were clouded with worry.

Nyssa said, 'The danger isn't over yet, is it? That awful creature may have been slain but everyone on this moon is still in peril.'

'I'm very much afraid so, yes.' The Doctor stood up abruptly, fumbling for his coat pockets, a sure sign of his agitation. 'It's time we took some positive action.'

'You need proper medical attention,' Tegan told Bunny Cheung. She'd tried to make him comfortable in the lab but Bunny was growing more and more impatient. The adrenalin rush was over, and now he was getting irritable. Tegan was cleaning up the cuts on his face but Bunny was not in the mood for fuss. He pushed away her hand and stood up.

'That's enough,' he growled.

'He was never going to win any beauty contests anyway,' said Stoker.

Bunny was trying to pull on his jacket one-handed.

'Where do you think you're going?' Stoker asked.

'To see Lawrence,' Bunny told her, still struggling with the jacket. 'Now the Bloodhunter's been dealt with, we can all go home on the *Adamantium*.'

'Best idea I've heard all day,' said the Doctor sternly as he entered the lab with Nyssa in tow. 'It's far too dangerous to stay here.'

'But the Bloodhunter's been killed,' Stoker argued. 'Problem solved.'

'You don't understand. I'm now certain that the Bloodhunter was only the tip of a very large and nasty iceberg.'

'You're exaggerating.'

'I don't think so. I have every reason to believe that the Bloodhunter was merely the representative, if you like, of a much greater evil.'

'Be specific.'

The Doctor glanced at Nyssa. 'I can't. Not yet. But I intend to speak to Captain Lawrence, and request that he arrange for everyone to be evacuated from this moon immediately.'

'And what about you?'

The Doctor hesitated. 'I shall stay here with Tegan and Nyssa.'

Stoker snorted. 'I thought so. How convenient.'

'I beg your pardon?'

'Well, that would leave you three here with nothing but a huge pile of lexium.'

The Doctor glared at her stonily. 'You know I don't care about the lexium.'

'I know you *say* you don't care about the lexium.'

'Must you be so insufferably stubborn?' the Doctor demanded, finally losing patience.

Stoker lit a cigar and winked at him. 'You said it.'

Bunny coughed. 'You've got to admit, Doctor, it sounds pretty lame. You're telling *us* we've got to leave, and I agree with you there wholeheartedly, but *you* intend to stay. If it's as dangerous here as you say, then why?'

It was Nyssa who answered. 'Because we must face the darkness. The enemy.'

'What does she mean?' Stoker asked.

'I'm not entirely sure – yet,' the Doctor admitted. 'But I intend to find out. I'm going to see Lawrence now. At the very least, he will have the medical facilities aboard his ship that both Bunny and Professor Oldeman need.'

'Don't count on it,' Stoker told him. 'Bunny and Oldeman aren't on the Consortium payroll. Yet.'

On board the *Adamantium*, Silas Cadwell approached Lawrence with a report. Lawrence took the plastic sheet and examined it quickly.

'Well,' he said quietly. 'That explains a lot.'

'Ninety-five per cent pure lexium,' Cadwell stated evenly. 'Unprecedented.'

Cadwell's cool grey eyes never betrayed emotion, but Lawrence fancied he could almost detect a note of excitement in his 2IC's voice. 'No wonder Stoker wanted to keep this to herself. She's found her fortune and glory here all right.'

'Has she, sir?' Cadwell asked.

Was that the trace of a smile on those thin, cruel lips? Lawrence wondered if he'd misjudged Cadwell. Perhaps he did know where his priorities lay after all. Despite his misgivings, Lawrence found himself grinning as he handed the scan report back. 'We'll just have to see, won't we?'

The door to the bridge hissed open and the Doctor walked straight in. Lawrence carefully concealed any hint of astonishment. 'Doctor. How nice to see you again, and your charming companions.'

Jyl Stoker and Bunny Cheung filed in behind Nyssa and Tegan.

Now Lawrence allowed himself to raise an eyebrow. 'Quite a deputation. How can I help you?'

'Captain Lawrence, I must ask you to evacuate this moon immediately,' the Doctor said.

'Must you?' Lawrence tried to sound amused.

'Out of the question,' said Silas Cadwell.

Lawrence shot a warning look at his 2IC and said, 'Actually, we haven't completed our survey yet.'

'*Your* survey?' said Stoker.

'Of course. Standard Consortium procedure in the circumstances.'

Stoker eyed him steadily. 'I would've thought that was the first thing you'd have done.'

'We've been a little busy,' Lawrence replied easily. 'In case you'd forgotten.'

'This is my moon,' Stoker blurted. 'My claim.'

'I'd dispute that this is *your* moon,' Lawrence smiled, 'but let's not argue. I'm afraid evacuation is impossible, Doctor. But if we can help in any other way… medical attention, perhaps? I'm sure Mr Cheung is in need of expert treatment. Consider my ship's facilities at your disposal.'

Before anyone could respond to the offer, the comms unit crackled into life. 'Captain Lawrence. We've got the Bloodhunter, sir!'

Lawrence nodded. 'Very good, Crook. I assume it is dead?'

'As a doornail, sir. It took too many blaster hits to survive for long, although it must've been one tough little bugger. Crawled away and died further into the tunnel system, but we've found it now.'

'And Mr Cheung's arm?' Lawrence asked.

'No sign of it, sir.' Crook hesitated. 'Captain, do you want the creature's body brought back to the ship?'

'I don't think that will be necessary, Crook.'

Silas Cadwell quickly interrupted, 'It might be a good opportunity to study the beast, sir.'

Lawrence looked unsure, but the Doctor agreed with Cadwell. 'A thorough examination would be invaluable, Captain.'

Lawrence shrugged. 'Very well. Bring it back, Crook, and put it in one of the cargo cells.' Something struck Lawrence and he narrowed his eyes at the Doctor. 'What's your interest in it?'

The Doctor smiled disarmingly. 'I can assure you my interest in that creature is purely professional.'

'Make a study of space monsters, do you?' Lawrence asked.

'I'm quite the expert.'

'Very well, we've got time I suppose.'

'I'd like to examine the creature as well,' Cadwell announced.

Lawrence didn't seem surprised. 'My 2IC won't be satisfied the thing's really dead until he's seen it for himself,' he told the others with good humour. 'You can go with Cadwell, Doctor.'

Crook had two of his men carry the Bloodhunter's corpse all the way back to the *Adamantium*. He had hoped Lawrence would simply have it destroyed; that seemed the most sensible option to Crook. Who'd want to study a repulsive little brute like this?

He opened the door to the cargo cell and stepped back so that the crewmen could throw the body inside. It hit the decking like a lump of old rubber.

It was roughly humanoid, hairless, with skin the colour of raw meat. There were blaster burns all over the body, many of them weeping a thick, clear jelly. It had long, powerful arms that ended in big, clawed hands. The fingers tapered to bony points. But its face… well, Crook doubted this thing had ever had a mother, but if it did then even its mother wouldn't have loved it. The head was little more than a fleshy stump on the round shoulders, with a cluster of eyes that had been burned away by blaster fire. Beneath the wound was some kind of organ, or group of organs, which looked to Crook like a nest of dead snakes.

'Ugly as sin,' commented one of the men.

'Hold on a mo',' said the other crewman. 'I thought I saw it move then.'

'Rubbish,' Crook said. 'Just a nervous twitch, probably.'

'How can you be sure?'

Crook shook his head. 'It's *dead*,' he said firmly. 'Watch.' Crook stepped across the holding cell and kicked the corpse, hard.

The Doctor followed Silas Cadwell down the *Adamantium*'s corridors, utterly failing to engage the man in any small talk. Compliments about the ship, the captain, even the neatness of Cadwell's own very smart uniform, all fell on deaf ears.

Eventually, Cadwell turned and cast a disparaging look at the Doctor. 'You don't fool me,' he told him.

'I haven't actually been trying to fool you,' the Doctor said. 'Sorry.'

'I know your kind,' Cadwell said with a sneer. 'Rogue trader. I have another name for you: pirate. Freebooter. *Parasite*.'

'Well I've always tried to be a good all-rounder.'

'If I were Captain Lawrence, I'd have you thrown off the ship.'

'It's so nice to feel welcome.'

Cadwell shot the Doctor an icy look and walked on. 'This way.'

They reached a low doorway marked CARGO CELL 2 and hit the button. The door slid away and the Doctor caught his breath. 'Oh no.'

Lying in the cell were three human corpses, all in Consortium uniform, all nothing more than withered, shrunken skeletons. The badge on one of the uniform tunics read LT CROOK.

Chapter Twelve

'Impossible!' thundered Lawrence.

'Evidently not,' Silas Cadwell responded. 'Sir.'

Lawrence gave him a black look. 'All *three* of them, dead? You're certain?'

Cadwell nodded, and the Doctor said, 'I'm afraid so. They never stood a chance.'

Lawrence suddenly looked a lot older than his forty-five years. Ashen-faced, he lowered himself into the captain's command chair. When he finally looked up at his 2IC and the Doctor, his eyes were haunted and he asked only one question: 'How?'

Cadwell said, 'The creature, the "Bloodhunter" as the Doctor called it, could not have been quite as dead as Crook and his men believed. They must have been mistaken in their analysis of the thing's ability to resist blaster fire. It's the only possible explanation.'

'No it isn't,' the Doctor contradicted him. 'It's perfectly feasible that the creature was dead. All that's happened is that it's come back to life.'

'That is nonsense,' Lawrence stated bluntly.

'Is it? You're forgetting that the Bloodhunter is a life form derived entirely from research into suspended-animation techniques. It was generated from material that can enter into a voluntary state of metabolic paralysis.' The Doctor met Lawrence's disbelieving stare. 'All right, perhaps it wasn't *technically* dead; perhaps it was merely in some kind of self-induced cellular stasis. But to all intents and purposes, it was no longer truly *alive*.'

'The exact reason for its resurrection is quite academic,' Cadwell said. 'The important question is: what should we do now?'

'Track it down and kill it,' Lawrence said. '*Properly*, this time.'

'That may not be possible,' the Doctor said.

'Why not? We've tracked it before, using the ship's sensors.'

'We've also killed it before. It's shown every sign of being indestructible.'

Lawrence rubbed a hand slowly down his face. 'I don't care, we've got to try. I owe it to Del Crook and his men to at least damn well try!'

'Sir,' said Cadwell, straightening. 'I'm ready to lead the hunting party, Captain, personally.'

Lawrence stood up. 'Very good, Cadwell. I'm glad to see I can rely on you.'

'I'd like to come with you, if I may,' the Doctor said.

Cadwell seemed on the point of refusing outright, but hesitated. He looked to Lawrence for his decision.

'Finding that creature is vital,' the Doctor added.

Lawrence noticed that the Doctor specifically omitted to say that *killing it* was also vital. Lawrence didn't like that, but the Doctor's attitude intrigued him. As a test, he said, 'I could just take your original advice and evacuate the moon. Leave the wretched creature to its own ghastly devices.'

'Then I would insist on staying here with it,' the Doctor told him.

'I'm not sure what your real interest in all this is, Doctor,' Lawrence said eventually, 'but frankly I'm past caring. I want that thing found and *destroyed*. What you do with it then is your own affair. I'll leave the decision to Cadwell.'

The Doctor looked immediately to Cadwell, who, after a short pause, nodded curtly.

'Thank you,' the Doctor said.

Lawrence left the bridge soon after that, unable to stomach any more. He went immediately to his personal cabin and locked the door behind him. Taking a small flask from his desk, he poured himself a stiff drink.

He had never before had to contend with the unexpected death of a single crewmember, let alone three at once. He felt miserable and lost. There was the lexium to consider as well: Lawrence knew where his duty to the Consortium lay, but somehow he had to deal with this incident first.

For the first time since taking command of the *Adamantium*, Lawrence felt a surge of fear: the fear of making the wrong decision.

After a minute, and another drink, there was a knock at the door. Lawrence told it to open and Jyl Stoker came in. 'Thought I'd find you here,' she said.

Lawrence looked at her. 'Why?'

'Because I followed you from the bridge, if you must know.'

If she was expecting him to smile, then she was mistaken. 'Three men!' he said fiercely. 'How could that happen? Three men, killed just *like that!*' He snapped his fingers angrily.

'I know it's not much consolation, and it certainly won't bring them back, but I do know how you feel.'

Lawrence shot her a sceptical look.

'No, really,' Stoker insisted. 'Don't forget I lost three of *my* men to that thing before you even arrived.'

'*Your* men?' Lawrence's blue eyes were like chips of ice. 'Will you have to contact their families and tell them the news?'

'Well, no,' Stoker admitted. 'But were Crook and his men *friends* of yours?'

Lawrence took a deep breath. 'All right, Jyl. You've earned yourself a drink.' He poured her a shot into a second glass and handed it to her.

'Kalazak brandy?' Stoker said as she sniffed the contents.

'Don't tell me it's too hard for you.'

'I hope it burns,' she replied, giving him the traditional Kalazak salute and downing the drink in one without taking her eyes off him.

'I hope it burns too,' he replied softly. For a few seconds they stood in silence, then Lawrence said, 'Look at us: back right where we started.'

'Not quite. We were kids then and neither of us knew anything.'

He smiled faintly. 'I meant we were rivals then, and we're still rivals now. Doing the same thing on opposite – sides of the dividing line.'

Stoker seemed puzzled. 'You admit we're doing the same things?'

'I admit there's a dividing line. But think about it: we're both opposites in many ways. You're fiery and unorthodox. I'm... conventional.'

'And cool.'

'Whatever. Ultimately, we're both loyal to our respective crews. Doesn't that make us... the same?'

She shook her head. 'It puts us in similar positions, that's all.'

'That's good enough for me,' Lawrence responded, but he felt a twinge of disappointment. Perhaps it was the Kalazak brandy, but Lawrence had forgotten how easily this woman could devastate his senses. Even with that broken nose, she was beautiful.

He cleared his throat and carefully put down his glass. Time to change the subject. 'What do you think Cadwell's up to?'

She raised an eyebrow, surprised by the change of subject. 'You think he's up to something?'

'I don't entirely trust him.'

'You said you could rely on him.'

'That's not the same thing.' Lawrence tried to clear his head; his fury over the killings and then the brandy was dulling his mind. He had to concentrate on something else. 'I'm not sure what it is about him,' he confessed, 'and perhaps I'm just a little paranoid, but I can't help thinking there's more to him than meets the eye.'

Tegan and Nyssa had accompanied Bunny Cheung to the *Adamantium*'s sickbay. He grumbled all the way, and pretended to be in pain when the ship's medic applied a number of Synthiskin plasters to his cuts. He reserved a special contempt for the poor man's efforts to deal with the wreckage of his bionic arm.

'I'm not really qualified in prosthetics,' the medic admitted.

'Then give your chief engineer a shout,' Bunny suggested tartly.

'He's only trying to help,' Tegan said. 'Stop complaining.'

'You're lucky to be here,' Nyssa added, a little more gently. 'These facilities are really quite advanced.'

'And usually reserved for Consortium personnel only,' the medic reminded them pointedly.

Bunny grunted and swung his legs off the treatment couch. 'Fair enough, if that's the way you want it. Consider me discharged.'

'Wait a minute,' Tegan said. 'Why don't you just sit back and relax? Let Captain Lawrence sort all this out. You could even ask him if he'll let you contact your daughter, I'm sure he'd agree.'

'You're forgetting, I'm not a Consortium employee. I'm a one-armed bandit in a very bad mood.' Bunny tore the diagnostic patch off his forehead and slapped it against the startled medic's chest. 'I don't need to tell you where to stick that, do I?'

'Where are you going?' asked Nyssa as Bunny headed for the exit. 'You're surely not thinking of going back down into the caves?'

Bunny looked back at them, his eyes blazing. 'Go back? You must be kidding. I'm going *home*.'

On the bridge, Cadwell was doing his best to ignore the Doctor.

'If I can be of any assistance…' the Doctor offered once again, positioning himself directly between Cadwell and the ship's sensor controls. 'You have only to ask.'

'I didn't ask,' said Cadwell.

'Nevertheless, I can help.'

'I doubt it. You were part of the original search party: it wasn't exactly an unqualified success.'

'You told Captain Lawrence I could help,' the Doctor protested.

Cadwell smiled coldly. 'I tell Captain Lawrence a lot of things. Now, if you would excuse me, *I* have a job to do.'

Bunny charged headlong through the *Adamantium* like a bear with a sore head *and* a mission. Tegan and Nyssa hurried after him, thinking that they ought to try to stop him but not really knowing how.

He halted abruptly when a Consortium man appeared around the corner. The crewman took one look at Bunny and drew his blaster. 'Hold it right there, chum.'

'Get lost,' said Bunny, grabbing the pistol and twisting it savagely from the man's grip. Before the crewman could even cry out, Bunny cannoned into him, shoulder down. The crewman's head thudded against the bulkhead and he slumped to the floor, unconscious.

'Bunny!' called Tegan. 'What do you think you're doing?'

Bunny adjusted the blaster control to maximum. 'Going home,' he said.

'Now that is interesting,' said Stoker. She was bent over Lawrence's puter terminal, the screen reflecting in her eyes as she stared. It had been her idea to access Silas Cadwell's company CV in the hope of finding something useful.

Lawrence studied the data on the screen and read out the line Stoker was pointing to. 'Last tour of duty was on board the *Titanium*. So what? He was transferred from that ship to the *Adamantium*. A routine request for change of assignment.'

Stoker shook her head. 'Routine request? Don't be too sure. Look where the *Titanium* was based: that's the star sector containing the planet Denox.'

'So?'

'Denox is where I picked up certain… information… regarding the mineral potential of this moon.'

Lawrence raised an eyebrow. 'An illegal tip-off?'

'Don't get all sniffy on me now. It's a bit of a coincidence, isn't it? Cadwell's in the Denox sector and suddenly he wants a transfer to *this* ship, which is running right past the Akoshemon system. Very convenient.'

'It's a bit tenuous,' argued Lawrence.

'You mean it's not obvious.'

Lawrence sat back in his seat. 'You know, when I think about it… it was Cadwell who intercepted your mayday. He could have been scanning the sector already.'

'I think you're right,' Stoker said. 'There is something going on here. Your ultra-loyal 2IC is following his own agenda.'

Lawrence's intercom beeped at that moment. 'Captain Lawrence, I think you'd better come to the bridge,' crackled a voice. Lawrence and Stoker glanced at each other: it was Cadwell's voice.

'What is it, Cadwell?'

There was a pause, and then Cadwell simply said, 'We have a... *situation.*'

It was, of course, an understatement. When Lawrence and Stoker arrived on the bridge an electric tension filled the air. They found Cadwell and the Doctor standing on one side of the room, facing, of all things, an armed take-over.

Bunny Cheung stood on the opposite side of the bridge, clutching a blaster pistol in his left hand. The gun was aimed at Silas Cadwell. Behind Bunny Cheung stood Tegan and Nyssa, looking suitably apprehensive.

'What is the meaning of this?' demanded Lawrence.

'Piracy,' sneered Cadwell. He glared murderously at Bunny Cheung. 'A one-armed take-over, it seems. All we could expect from these outlaws, I'm afraid, sir.'

'Bunny, what the hell are you doing?' asked Stoker.

Bunny's dark eyes never left Silas Cadwell. 'Trying to persuade this creep to take us all home.'

'With a gun, Bunny?' the Doctor asked, stepping cautiously in front of Cadwell. 'That's not like you.'

'It's all I've got, Doctor. There's no other way these people will listen. They're only interested in their own lives, you see.' Bunny stepped to the side in order to keep Cadwell in his sights.

'I'm sure Captain Lawrence will do his best to accommodate your request,' the Doctor went on. 'But not at gunpoint.'

'Don't try and talk me out of it, Doctor. I've gone too far to give in now.'

'Oh, don't be such a damn fool, Bunny!' said Stoker. 'Drop the gun and stop acting like an idiot.'

Bunny smiled. 'I see you've already fallen for the good captain's charm, Jyl. Again.'

Stoker's eyes narrowed. 'Cut it out, Bunny. It's not like that.'

'Never is for you, is it? You're *never* wrong. Well let's see what happens when Captain Lawrence finds out how much lexium he's sitting on here. I wonder if you'll still find him quite so charming then.'

There was a long, awkward gap before anyone spoke. It was Lawrence who broke the silence, 'I already know about the lexium. That's not an issue here now.'

Stoker glanced at Lawrence, clearly surprised.

Bunny adjusted his grip on the blaster. The Doctor had moved again, obscuring his view of Cadwell. 'Not another step, Doctor,' he warned. 'It's that Consortium creep I want.'

'Then you'll have to shoot me first, Bunny,' the Doctor told him calmly. 'Do you think you can do that?'

Bunny raised the blaster slightly. 'Don't *make* me.'

'I won't make you do anything. You'll have to pull that trigger yourself.' The Doctor took another step closer.

'Be careful, Doctor!' said Tegan. She turned to Lawrence. 'Can't you do anything?'

Lawrence said, 'This ship cannot blast off without my personal computer authorisation. I refuse to give it in these circumstances. You can shoot the Doctor, shoot Cadwell, shoot anyone you like – but I will not give in to blackmail.'

Bunny bared his teeth, taking careful aim at the Doctor.

'In the end,' Lawrence said, 'there will be no one else but me left to shoot. And then what will you do when you've shot me? Shoot yourself?'

Bunny started to speak, but he couldn't. A tear ran down into his beard.

'Think what you're doing, Bunny,' urged Tegan. 'That's the Doctor you're aiming at! What would your little girl think of you now? Carry on like this and you'll never see her again. Give up the gun, Bunny. Do it for Rosie.'

The Doctor stepped forward and slowly held out his hand. 'Let me have the blaster, Bunny. You have my personal guarantee that there will be no reprisals.'

Bunny said, 'I just want to go *home*. All I ever wanted was to go home.'

'You will.'

Bunny looked at Stoker. 'I never wanted to come in the first place. You knew that.'

'I know,' Stoker croaked.

The Doctor gently took the pistol out of Bunny's hand, and the big man seemed physically to shrink, almost on the point of collapse. Stoker rushed forward to help him, but Bunny shrugged her hand away. 'Just leave me alone,' he said harshly, and left the bridge with his head hanging low.

'Bunny, wait!' Stoker called, but Lawrence put his hand on her shoulder to stop her following him.

'Leave him,' he told her. 'He needs to be alone.'

'No he doesn't,' said Tegan hotly. 'I'm going after him!' She turned and ran out of the room.

The Doctor turned and handed the blaster to Cadwell. 'You'd better take care of that.'

'Pirate scum,' Cadwell said.

'That's enough, Cadwell!' barked Lawrence. 'Attend to your duties.'

'Sir!'

'That was awful,' Stoker said miserably. 'I don't know what's come over him.'

'Fear,' said the Doctor simply. 'He's terrified he'll never see his family again. And fear can be a powerful motivator.'

Gradually the normal atmosphere of the bridge returned. Lawrence sighed and ran a hand through his short, dark hair with a look of resignation. 'This is going from bad to worse,' he murmured. 'I'm going back to my cabin.'

'Sorry you came here?' Stoker asked, following him.

He looked at her. 'Aren't you?'

'That depends: you didn't tell me you knew about the lexium deposits here. Why not?'

'I hadn't had a chance. I've been more concerned with other things.'

'All right, I'll give you that,' Stoker conceded. 'But there is an issue here, despite what you said to Bunny.'

Lawrence stopped walking. 'An issue?'

'Mineral rights. I was here first, remember. It's my claim.'

Lawrence actually laughed. 'You're concerned about mineral rights after all that's happened?'

'Don't try and fudge the issue. It's important.'

Lawrence studied the determined light in her eyes. She looked like a lioness sizing up her prey. He took a deep breath and said, 'I'm sorry, Jyl. Truly I am. But I've come here as a representative of the Consortium, and I have standing orders that must be followed.'

'Meaning?'

'I have to put in a claim for the mineral rights to this moon on behalf of the Consortium.'

'You can't! I was here first dammit, the claim is *mine*.'

He shrugged. 'Then we are in direct competition.'

'I can't compete with you! The Consortium has the resources to force a claim through; I just haven't got that kind of clout and you know it.'

'Jyl, you're a rogue trader: you don't have any kind of clout at all.'

She went to hit him then, swinging her fist up in a lightning strike that would have broken teeth.

But Lawrence was too fast; he caught the fist and yanked it savagely down. She was pulled towards him, close enough to kiss. 'You said you'd aim low,' he reminded her.

'I know,' Stoker replied, bringing her knee up sharply into his groin.

Tegan raced after Bunny, wondering what he was going to do. He had gone straight for the airlock and left the ship. By the time Tegan caught up with him, he was halfway down the steps leading to the caves.

'Bunny, wait! Where are you going?'

'Nowhere,' he responded savagely.

She hurried down the steps and followed him into the main cavern. There was still a lot of Stoker's equipment scattered about, and Bunny kicked viciously at an empty crate. The plastic cracked and the box skidded away, the noise echoing all around the cavern.

'Just calm down,' Tegan told him. 'This isn't doing anyone any good.'

'Who cares?' Bunny snarled. 'God, what a mess. I've really screwed up this time. I was going to shoot someone! I was going to shoot the Doctor! What's the matter with me?'

'Don't be too hard on yourself,' Tegan advised. 'We're all under a lot of stress.'

'I don't see you holding anyone at gunpoint.'

'Given the right reasons, I might.'

'And what reasons would they be?'

'If I thought I'd never see my family again. If I thought it was the only chance I had. I don't know. We're all scared of different things.'

'What are you scared of?'

'Loads of things: snakes, for starters.' Tegan sat down on a crate and thought. 'Being alone. Not being any use to anyone. Letting my friends down. The usual stuff, I suppose.'

'I notice that you don't include gun-crazy lunatics with one arm.' Bunny sat down next to her. 'Thanks for coming after me.'

Cadwell turned from a monitor screen on board the *Adamantium* and said, 'I think you ought to know that your friend Cheung has left the ship, Doctor.'

'He was very upset,' the Doctor remarked.

'Like I care. But, typically, the fool's gone straight back into the cave system.'

The Doctor frowned. 'What do you mean?'

It was Nyssa who answered, sitting up suddenly erect in her chair. 'Doctor! The creature… it's hunting again!'

The Doctor glared at Nyssa, horrified by the implications. 'Tegan and Bunny – *it'll kill them both!*'

Nyssa closed her eyes as if in pain.

The Doctor had sprinted for the exit without another word. Cadwell followed him, collecting a blaster pistol on the way, a grim smile on his face.

Tegan simply wasn't ready for it. It wouldn't have mattered if she had been.

The impact hurled Tegan from the packing crate and flattened her. The beast squatted on her back, squeezing the breath out of her. Panicking, Tegan tried to twist and turn, but its grip was like steel. She could feel its fingers digging into the flesh of her arms like talons.

Then she felt it on her neck: something cold and moist, probing the skin of her throat and face. More things wound their way around her head, white tentacles crossing her vision like coiling snakes.

Her heart hammered like a fist in her chest as she felt the tubes digging harder, burrowing into the flesh, wriggling desperately. She could feel its wheezing breath in her ear. She fought like an animal to dislodge the thing from her back, but its slimy tentacles were winding tighter and tighter…

She never even had the chance to pass out.

The creature suddenly left her, with an abhorrent sucking noise, and she was free. Gasping, she crawled away, its foul wetness coating her face and throat. Her heart felt as though it was about to burst and the blood roared in her ears. A yard or two further and Tegan twisted shakily around to see where the beast had gone.

It hadn't gone far.

It was on Bunny Cheung now.

With a cry of horror Tegan realised what must have happened: Bunny had pulled the creature off her. Somehow, one-handed, he had managed to dislodge it. But now it had turned and attacked him.

Bunny was a giant compared to the Bloodhunter, but it didn't help. The thing clung to him, hands clawed around Bunny's head, its muscular white legs wrapped around his waist. Bunny staggered back and lost his balance, crashing to the rock floor with the creature still astride him.

Tegan let out a sob of fear and crawled towards them, desperate to help but terrified of getting too close. She wanted to scream for help but her mouth was bone dry – and who would hear her down here?

Bunny was struggling like a madman, but the Bloodhunter had opened its mouth, wide enough to swallow a melon, and a great mass of writhing tubes emerged. Sinuous, tongue-like extrusions were forced into Bunny's mouth and nostrils, driving down, further and further, inexorably searching for the greatest source of blood: the heart.

And all the while Bunny remained alive, his eyes bulging in agony. His whole body shuddered as the creature began to drain his blood. His skin shrank, visibly tightening over the bones, veins and arteries standing out like wires until they, too, collapsed as the blood disappeared from within them.

The creature drank hard and ferociously. Then, with a horrible sucking noise the thing slowly withdrew, and Bunny's withered corpse fell to the ground.

The creature turned back to face Tegan, its tentacles slippery with blood, its single red eye burning.

CHAPTER THIRTEEN

The Doctor entered the cavern at a fast run, leaping the last set of steps and skidding to a halt when he saw the Bloodhunter advancing on Tegan. He called out to distract it. The creature turned and snarled angrily.

For a moment nothing happened and nobody moved. Then the creature took a step towards the Doctor.

A brilliant flash of energy burned past the Doctor's ear and struck the Bloodhunter in the chest. It staggered back, then turned and fled, blaster beams chasing it as it disappeared down a side tunnel.

Cadwell jogged up brandishing his blaster. 'Lucky one of us came prepared.'

But the Doctor was already helping Tegan to her feet. She was shaking uncontrollably. He hugged her and let her cry: he had already seen the huddled, rag-doll remains of Bunny Cheung lying on the ground nearby.

Cadwell examined the crumpled body with distaste.

'No one deserves to die like that,' the Doctor said roughly.

The Consortium man shrugged.

A number of *Adamantium* crewmen appeared, all carrying blasters and looking worried. 'It went that way,' Cadwell informed them, indicating the tunnel.

'Don't bother going after it,' said the Doctor. 'There's no point: you won't find it, and besides, there have been too many needless deaths already.'

The men looked uncertainly to Cadwell for orders. Cadwell pursed his lips and said, 'Then what do you suggest, Doctor? An ambush, perhaps? We could all stand here and wait for it to return for dessert.'

'Is sarcasm all you have to offer?'

Cadwell smiled grimly. 'Let me know when you have anything useful to contribute, Doctor. In the meantime I shall begin another search for the creature. You can escort Miss Jovanka to the *Adamantium*, where she may remain safely out of the way.'

The Doctor glowered. 'You're not *thinking*, Cadwell! You're just reacting.'

Cadwell walked slowly over to where the Doctor stood and returned his stare easily. 'Point taken, Doctor. May I suggest that you return to the *Adamantium* with your friend and have your little think, and leave the reacting to us.'

'With pleasure.'

Stoker took the news of Bunny's death badly. The Doctor told her what had happened as gently as he could, but it was a deeply unpleasant task. Lawrence fully expected Stoker to lash out in frustration, but she merely sat down heavily in the armchair in his cabin and stared blankly at nothing.

Lawrence had never seen her so shaken. He poured her some Kalazak brandy but she ignored it. Lawrence settled for simply standing by her as the Doctor quietly withdrew.

'I can't believe he's gone,' Stoker said in a whisper. 'Not Bunny. *Not Bunny.*'

Lawrence bit his lip and held out his hand. He was slightly surprised when she took it, holding it in a tight, cold grip.

'I'm sorry,' Lawrence said.

She shook her head, unable to speak. She grasped his hand until her knuckles turned white.

The Doctor draped his frock-coat over Tegan's shoulders as she sat down. She barely noticed. Her head was buried in her hands, and when she looked up her face was streaked with tears. 'Why did it have to be him? Why?'

The Doctor stood awkwardly, not knowing what to say.

'He saved my life,' Tegan said. 'He dragged that thing off me, Doctor. And it *killed* him…'

'He was a very brave man,' the Doctor said. 'I liked him.'

Tegan wiped her face with a hand, smudging her make-up further. 'Oh, *rabbits*. What about his daughter? He's got a wife and a little girl on Earth waiting for him to come home, Doctor. She's only five or six…'

The Doctor looked pained. 'Tegan, I'm so sorry…'

Tegan cried out in anguish, her shoulders shaking as she wept. The Doctor watched her helplessly for a few moments, then turned to leave.

'Doctor?' Tegan sniffed.

He turned to look at her.

'Do whatever you've got to. Stop that thing. Stop it for ever.'

The Doctor found Nyssa in the *Adamantium*'s medical bay with Ravus Oldeman. He was lying on one of the treatment couches, wired to a nursing computer.

'I've just heard the news about Bunny,' Nyssa said solemnly. 'Is Tegan all right?'

The Doctor just nodded and stared disapprovingly at the diagnostic readout on Oldeman's computer. 'He's had another dose of neurolectrin! That's the third in as many hours.'

'It seems to be having less and less effect,' Nyssa observed. 'It's almost like an addiction.'

'It's exactly like an addiction,' the Doctor said. 'There's no need for it: the dosage must be strictly controlled or the patient will become utterly dependent on it for normal brain function.' He tore the connectors away from Oldeman's forehead with some impatience. 'I knew I should have overseen his treatment personally!'

'Not even you can be everywhere at once,' Nyssa said.

'I sometimes feel I should be.'

'Is there anything I can do to help?'

He looked at her bleakly. 'Perhaps. There's something troubling me about that creature, Nyssa.'

'You mean tracking it down again in the caves?'

'No, that isn't the problem.'

Nyssa was surprised. 'Then what?'

The Doctor tapped his chin thoughtfully for a moment and then said, 'Come with me.'

Stoker wiped her face and said, 'Look at me. Blubbing like a girl.'

'Don't be so hard on yourself,' Lawrence said. 'You've had a terrible shock.'

'So many people have died. I can't take it in. I just want to go now, I just want to leave this awful place.'

He squeezed her shoulders gently. 'What about your claim?'

She sniffed. 'Suddenly the mining rights don't seem so important. It's ironic: I argued like mad with Bunny to stay on here, to push the claim through, despite everything. All he wanted to do was go home. I can see his point of view now – only it's too late.'

The Doctor took Nyssa up to the bridge, arriving at the same time as Silas Cadwell. The Consortium man was in a terrible mood.

'Not a trace of that thing anywhere,' he told the Doctor angrily. 'We've scanned the entire cave system, even scoured the place on foot – *nothing*.'

'It can't have disappeared,' Nyssa said. 'I *know* it hasn't disappeared. It's there somewhere.'

'Where?' snapped Cadwell. 'And how would you know, anyway?'

'Never mind about that for the moment,' the Doctor said smoothly. 'If we're going to find the Bloodhunter, we have to *understand* it first. No one's stopped to think about what it's doing, what its purpose is.'

'It's killing everyone on sight, that's what it's doing.'

The Doctor ignored him. 'I've said all along that there's more to this creature than an insatiable thirst for blood. How did it survive for one hundred and sixty years while Ravus Oldeman was in suspended animation, with no food source? Unless, as I've already surmised, it is genetically predisposed to naturally suspend its own life functions when necessary.'

'That is certainly supported by the evidence so far,' Nyssa agreed.

'True, but we're still overlooking the most obvious question,' the Doctor said. 'The creature kills, certainly, and without compunction. But *how* does it kill its victims?'

'It sucks out all their blood and bile.'

'Why?'

Nyssa shrugged. 'Sustenance? Perhaps it's some kind of vampire?'

The Doctor shook his head. 'No, we already know it survived for one hundred and sixty years without any viable food source. Besides which, the rate of fluid consumption is simply too high: there are roughly eight pints of blood alone in the average human being. The creature isn't physically large, so where's all the blood going? It doesn't require it for its own survival. So why does it require it? What's its secret? To put it bluntly, what's it *doing* with all that blood?'

No one had an answer to that. The Doctor sat and gazed thoughtfully into space, turning the question over and over in his mind. 'If we can find that out,' he said, 'we will discover exactly what its purpose is.'

Cadwell said, 'Its purpose is to kill.'

'No. Its purpose is to collect blood. The question is – why?'

'This is wasting time,' Cadwell declared. He turned to address one of the crewmen working at a nearby console. 'Well, Jenks, what have you found?'

'Nothing, sir,' Jenks said. 'I've doubled-checked all the readings. I'm sorry, but there isn't a trace of the creature in the cave systems.'

Cadwell scowled and bent over the instruments. 'It *must* be in the cave system. You've made an error – try again.'

'He hasn't made any error,' the Doctor said.

Cadwell turned his scowl on the Doctor, clearly unhappy with the man's habit of contradicting him. The Doctor said, 'The sensors are functioning perfectly. If the creature was down there you'd have a reading.'

Jenks apologised again and the Doctor clapped him on the back. 'Not your fault. It's just gone into hiding, that's all.'

'Hiding?' Cadwell scoffed. 'Where?'

'Somewhere out of the range of your instruments,' the Doctor replied. 'Or somewhere that is shielded from the bio-sensor rays.'

'Such as?'

'Deeper into the cave system, I suspect. That's where the mineral deposits really build up. Bound to interfere with something as delicate as a passive bio-sensor beam.'

'It is possible,' Jenks confirmed.

'I know it's possible,' Cadwell snapped. 'So now what do we do?'

'Follow it into the deeper caves,' the Doctor said easily.

This was too much for Cadwell and a thick vein began to throb in his temple. Through gritted teeth he asked, 'And how, precisely, do you plan to do that?'

The Doctor smiled. 'Oh, I think I've got just the thing…'

'Are you sure this is wise, Doctor?' asked Tegan.

The Doctor shrugged on his coat and paused to adjust the sprig of celery on the lapel. But he didn't answer.

Tegan wasn't so easily put off. 'Is Nyssa happy with this?'

'Of course she is. Aren't you, Nyssa?'

'Well…' Nyssa began doubtfully.

'Jolly good,' interrupted the Doctor. 'Shall we get on with it?'

'I'm not sure I can help, Doctor,' Nyssa said. 'I mean, I think I can sense the Bloodhunter, but I don't think I can track it for you.'

'This is a terrible idea,' Tegan said. 'I just want you both to know that.'

'Thank you, Tegan, but we really don't have a lot of choice. It's imperative that we track the Bloodhunter down, and as soon as possible.'

'Why? Why can't we all stay on board the *Adamantium* where it's safe?'

'Because *nowhere* is safe,' the Doctor said with sudden impatience. 'Not while the thing that tried to enter the TARDIS is still here, still

170

trying to get free.'

Tegan was confused. 'But how do you know the Bloodhunter will take you to it?'

'I don't. But I've got a nasty suspicion forming in my mind.' The Doctor hesitated. 'Or at any rate, a nasty *something* forming in my mind.'

'You've lost me.'

'Then listen, both of you: a little while ago I induced Nyssa into a state of light hypnosis…'

'What?' both women exclaimed.

'It's really nothing to worry about, just a little technique I know to help lower the mind's natural defences.'

'I've heard about men like you before,' Tegan said drily.

'Tegan, please!'

'What does she mean?' Nyssa asked.

'Never mind,' the Doctor said. 'The important thing is, I established a link with… something, I don't know exactly what, but it was a definite sentience or force.'

'Inside my mind?' Nyssa said anxiously.

'Not necessarily inside, no. But a presence nonetheless. Your mind acted as a sort of link or conduit.'

'Were you able to communicate with it?'

'No. It did… speak… to me, though. After a fashion.'

'What did it say?' Tegan wondered.

The Doctor pulled a face. 'Nothing much. Enough to make me realise that it's *me* it wants.'

'You?'

'Well, try not to sound *so* surprised, Tegan. It did originally try to attack the TARDIS, remember. And the TARDIS and I are, well, very close. Perhaps the TARDIS was the only way to get to me.'

'And my mind was the only way for it to gain entry to the TARDIS,' Nyssa recalled. 'Doctor, what is it?'

'That's what I want to find out. Are you ready?'

Nyssa nodded after only a momentary pause. 'I'm willing to help you in any way I can, Doctor. You know that.'

The Doctor looked at her seriously. 'I know. But it could be very dangerous.'

Nyssa smiled faintly. 'I take that for granted, Doctor.'

'Yes, I know that too, but… well, the truth of the matter is this: this *force*, whatever it might be, can affect us all in very subtle ways. Ways of which we may not be aware at the time.'

Tegan said, 'You mean it's affecting our minds. Perceptual interference, you said.'

'Thought control?' Nyssa sounded worried.

'That's what Tegan said originally. But it's not thought control. It's subtler than that. Less easy to define or even notice.' The Doctor sighed. 'Nyssa, it's possible that you might be agreeing to this because *it* wants you to.'

'How would I know that?'

'You wouldn't. That's the difficulty. But it would mean that, if your decision is being influenced by the enemy, then that makes this whole undertaking even more dangerous.'

'Because it wants you to walk right into a trap.'

The Doctor nodded solemnly.

Nyssa sat upright and braced herself. 'It's a chance we will have to take, then.'

'No it is not!' Tegan declared hotly. She stared at the Doctor. He returned her look with haunted eyes, and she felt goosebumps rise up all over her skin. 'Is it?' she added weakly.

The Doctor's only answer was to produce his cricket ball.

He held the ball up before Nyssa, holding it lightly between finger and thumb. Nyssa instantly stiffened, her eyes taking on a horrible, unearthly look: not quite vacant, but totally expressionless. That she was in some kind of trance was obvious.

Tegan was appalled. 'Strewth, Doctor, that was quick work!'

'Post-hypnotic autosuggestion,' he said. 'Thought it might save time.'

'What now?' Tegan kept looking uncertainly at Nyssa.

'Now Nyssa will be able to find the creature. Take me to the enemy.' The Doctor turned to look at Tegan again. 'I've got a job for you too.'

She swallowed. This was it, Tegan thought, *put up or shut up time*. This was why she'd wanted to join up with the Doctor again in Amsterdam. Not just a chance to see the universe, but the chance to *help*. She looked him in the eye. 'Just say the word, Doctor.'

Unsurprisingly, Silas Cadwell refused to go with the Doctor and Nyssa, and nor would he sanction any member of the *Adamantium* crew to accompany them. It was, he said, 'an expedition of the utmost folly, and one that I will not condone in any way, shape or form.'

So, the Doctor and Nyssa went on their own. Tegan watched them leave on one of the ship's exterior monitors. The Doctor, ludicrously sporting his Panama, trudging across the dusty surface of the moon towards the cave entrance. Nyssa, small and frail, hurried to keep up with him. Tegan watched them disappear with a deep sense of foreboding. It was made all the worse by the fact that only the three of them really knew what kind of danger they could be heading into: and even then, they didn't *really* know what to expect at all.

Cadwell watched them leave as well, his cold grey eyes fixed on the viewer until the tiny white blob of the Doctor's hat disappeared from sight. A small muscle began to tic in his face as he leaned forward and switched off the monitor.

The Doctor led Nyssa down through the main cavern at a fair pace, keeping up a jaunty commentary about caves he had visited before – everything from the primitive dwelling places of prehistoric Earth to the mysterious, radiation-soaked subterranean world of Solos and the spectacular golden catacombs of Voga.

Nyssa knew that he was merely trying to take her mind off the purpose of their journey, and the possible dangers it might involve. She wasn't distracted for an instant; she heard the Doctor's voice but she did not listen to him. Instead, she was listening out for the other voice, the voice in her mind. The voice from her dreams.

I am here, last daughter of Traken

Nyssa closed her eyes, so that she could be in darkness. This was where the voice belonged.

I am always with you

Sleeping with you

'Nyssa?'

She snapped open her eyes, blinded by the brightness around her. For a second she felt completely disorientated.

They were back in Ravus Oldeman's laboratory complex already. The artificial lighting was almost overwhelming. In her confused state of mind, Nyssa saw a great sphere of red, like a planet of boiling blood and lava, floating in the glare.

'Are you all right?' the Doctor enquired.

'Yes,' she gasped. The glowing red planet resolved itself into a cricket ball. 'Yes, I'm fine.'

He regarded her dubiously. 'Don't let your mind wander.'

'Must you use that?' Nyssa asked.

The Doctor looked at his cricket ball. 'Doesn't it help?'

'Not really, no.'

He pocketed it. 'Then we'll carry on without it. If you're sure.'

'Yes,' she said firmly. She pointed across the secret door panel that made up part of the far wall. 'This way.'

She led him down into the lower chamber, where the stasis tanks were, and where Vega Jaal had been killed. With the exception of the equipment, the room was silent and empty.

'Over here.' Nyssa crossed to the back wall, between two of the stasis units.

The Doctor shone his torch down to floor level. The beam penetrated the shadows that clung to the rock and disappeared into a narrow black opening.

'So that's how it got out,' he murmured. 'That's how it was able to attack Vega Jaal when we were all up in the laboratory. It had its own little hidey-hole all along.'

'That's where it's gone,' Nyssa told him.

'Then that's where we go.'

The Doctor started forward, but Nyssa placed a hand on his arm.

'Doctor. Vega Jaal warned us about *the last door*, remember. He said we would not find the darkness beyond it – but the darkness would find us.'

'Yes, I know.' The Doctor smiled briefly. 'I assume he was talking figuratively, of course, but either way we'll have to meet the, er, *darkness* somewhere. We can always say we were just passing, can't we? And it would be terribly rude not to pop in and say hello.'

With a last, cheery grin, the Doctor lowered himself nimbly through the hole. Nyssa watched him disappear into the cold shadows and then, her heart pounding, followed.

CHAPTER FOURTEEN

Stoker had drunk enough Kalazak brandy to stun an Ogron. Lawrence put the cap back on the flask and returned it to his desk. He was still deep in thought about Silas Cadwell. The 2IC was busy co-ordinating the hunt for the creature, but didn't seem to be making much progress. Lawrence considered this unusual: Cadwell was normally very efficient.

'You're forgetting something,' said Stoker. She struggled to sit up, and Lawrence eyed her warily.

'I'd forgotten how much you could drink and still stay conscious,' he remarked.

'Helps me think,' she replied. 'But that's not what I meant. I've been wondering about your Silas Cadwell. Why don't you check his records again?'

'We already have. Remember?'

'No, I don't mean his service record. I mean his personal records.'

'I can't.'

'Crap.'

Lawrence stiffened. 'I beg your pardon?'

'I said crap! You're the captain round here, you can do whatever the hell you like.'

'I can't access Cadwell's personal records.'

'I'm not so smashed that I can't tell the difference between "can't" and "won't". Don't tell me you're letting some stupid moral code stand in your way? You're a thoroughbred Consortium bastard, remember? Scruples don't come into it.'

'I can't access his personal files,' Lawrence repeated patiently. 'It's completely against the Consortium's conduct and discipline rules.'

'I don't believe that for a second. You must have a security override.'

Lawrence hesitated. 'It's only for use in emergencies.'

'Right.' Stoker sat forward with a glint in her eye. 'And who around here is authorised to declare a state of emergency?'

For a long time Nyssa's only source of light was the Doctor's torch: its circle of illumination rippled over the craggy ground before them, scouting for unexpected hollows or crevices, leading them deeper and deeper into the freezing darkness.

Eventually the rock started to smooth out, the floor and walls of the tunnel becoming rounded and glossy, as if they were moving down a thick, glassy tube. The change was not lost on the Doctor, who quickly pointed out that the general effect was, 'almost organic, like the inside of an artery or vein'.

The image did nothing to comfort Nyssa, but the Doctor was intrigued. He pressed his torch against the curving surface and the beam sank into a dull green glow just beyond the surface. 'The translucence is fascinating, don't you agree? I've never seen anything quite like it.'

'I'm very cold, Doctor. Must we stop to admire the scenery?'

'Where's your scientific curiosity, Nyssa? Come on, this way.'

She followed him a little further until he stopped dead. 'What's the matter?'

The Doctor sent his torchlight roving further down the tunnel. 'I'm not sure. Time for a little experiment, I think.' And with that, he switched off the torch.

The darkness should have been absolute, but Nyssa was surprised to find that she could still see.

Further up ahead, there was a distinctly green glow. It seemed to be emanating from the rock itself, and after a few moments Nyssa could discern thick, wavering lines of emerald light buried in the stone. The lines wound their way into the distance, creating a wan luminescence that filled the tunnel.

The Doctor hurried forward, inspecting the rock closely.

'Fascinating! Look!'

Deep within the very rock of the tunnel wall were thick veins of light. The Doctor shone his torch into the rock and the nearest vein moved, as if it was recoiling inside its own narrow tube.

'What are they?'

'Some sort of life form, I imagine. Invertebrate, probably moving through the rock itself.'

'How?'

'Very slowly, I should think! Perhaps they use existing holes, with a bioluminescent mucous membrane acting as a lubricant to aid movement. Or the mucous could be corrosive, helping them to progress through solid rock.'

'I don't think I like the look of them.'

The Doctor was mildly perturbed. 'Nyssa! They're probably harmless: nothing more than very long worms. They probably move about an inch a year or so, and wouldn't survive outside of the rock itself. You've nothing to fear.'

'That's easy for you to say,' Nyssa murmured.

'Let's push on,' said the Doctor.

There was enough light now from the rock-worms to see quite clearly. Nyssa dutifully followed the Doctor's pale, green-hued shape along the tunnel; there was only one direction they could go in now and he seemed to have dispensed with her services as a guide. 'Doctor?'

'Hmm?'

'What do you fear?'

He stopped and turned to look at her, slightly bent in the narrow passage. 'Why do you ask?'

'You never seemed to be scared of anything.'

He smiled. 'Never judge by appearances!'

'I'm serious. What does scare you?'

The Doctor thought for a moment. 'Well, let's see: I've never much enjoyed the company of Daleks. Or Cybennen. I've crossed swords with the Master more times than I care to remember, and the Black Guardian is bound to catch up with me one day… but do I *fear* them? Not really: but I do fear the harm they intend, the misery and destruction they can cause.'

'And your greatest fear?'

'Ah, that's easy. Being out for a duck.'

Tegan watched Ravus Oldeman carefully: he was sleeping in the *Adamantium*'s medical bay, wired up to some kind of computer monitor. The Doctor had told her what signs to look out for and what to do when she saw them, but she hadn't anticipated the old man's delirious rambling.

He lay on the couch, covered with a single silver sheet, half-conscious and muttering incessantly. Tegan strained to hear what he was saying. It sounded like something to do with his time as a research technician in the underground lab: she thought he mentioned Professor Garondel a number of times, and other stuff about Akoshemon. In fact, every time he mentioned the planet, the monitor readings spiked alarmingly.

'What is it?' she asked him tentatively. 'What are you trying to say?'

His pale eyes opened a crack to look at her. 'Garondel's a meddlesome little fool,' he hissed. His eyes gleamed, diamond-hard, beneath the fleshy eyelids. 'He knows nothing! *Nothing!*'

The eyes closed and flickered. Oldeman twisted and turned a few times and Tegan glanced nervously at the life-signs monitor. What was this? Some kind of attack? A fit? A flashback?

'The Akoshemon DNA is perfect! Never seen anything like it!'

'It's all right,' Tegan said soothingly. 'Calm down.'

'It's not all right! That interfering little lab rat Garondel's got it all wrong, I tell you!'

Tegan was puzzled, but she jumped when Oldeman's eyes opened again and he reached out a cold, bony hand to grasp her wrist. 'Hey! Let go!'

'Neurolectrin!' he gasped. 'I need the neurolectrin!'

She shook her head. 'The Doctor says you can't have any more, not yet. You're going to become addicted.'

'Rubbish. Give me the neurolectrin, you silly little woman!'

Tegan twisted her arm free. 'Not likely!'

'I'm losing my mind!'

'The Doctor says it'll destroy your mind if you have any more too soon.'

Oldeman collapsed back onto the bed, chest heaving. The medical computer bleeped and something registered on the monitor. Oldeman's eyes flickered shut and he relaxed as the tranquilliser took effect.

'Should never… have… taken… him on…' he muttered.

'The Doctor?'

Oldeman shook his head feebly. 'Garondel…'

The passageway had narrowed dramatically, and the glow-worms had petered out: the Doctor and Nyssa were left inching their way along in perfect darkness once more. The Doctor brought his torch back into play, just as the tunnel widened out into a vast, low-ceilinged cavern.

At first Nyssa thought they had stumbled into some kind of weird, subterranean forest. The Doctor's torchlight fell on a number of thick, gnarled grey trunks sprouting from the cave floor like trees. They were densely packed, no two more than a metre apart, some as thick as a man and others slender enough for Nyssa to encircle with both hands. The torch beam was trapped and snared among the trunks, which seemed to continue in haphazard array for as far as they could see.

'How very odd,' the Doctor remarked. His voice reverberated unnaturally through the eerie forest.

'What are they?'

'Stalagmites,' he replied. 'And stalactites. The former growing up from the cave floor to meet the latter as they come down from the roof. Interesting phenomenon.'

The conversation echoed through the cave and disappeared in a ghostly moan. Nyssa shivered. 'It's horrible.'

'It's certainly going to make things a bit tricky,' the Doctor said. 'Stick close: we don't want to get separated in here.'

Nyssa followed him into the granite forest, one hand resting on his shoulder. They picked their way through the stalagmites, forced to take a winding path that she found utterly disorientating. After a couple of minutes they were completely surrounded by the ghostly grey columns. The Doctor flashed his light around them and they could see nothing but the stalagmites disappearing in every direction. Nyssa felt as thought they were closing in on her.

'Which way now?' she asked, terrified that the Doctor was going to admit he was lost.

'Down, I think.'

'Down?'

'The ground is sloping away, hadn't you noticed?'

She shook her head and followed him. The ground was indeed sloping downwards, and now the gradient was becoming quite marked. They slipped and stumbled through the rock trees, holding on to them for support when necessary. To the touch the stalagmites were as cold and hard as bone but coated with a thin slime.

Eventually the forest began to thin: the stalagmites grew slimmer and shorter, some of them failing to meet up with the stalactites hanging down from above. Soon there were none that came above knee-height, and the Doctor and Nyssa were able to duck beneath those that grew overhead. It felt uncomfortably as though they were clambering out through the serried teeth of a shark's jaws.

Beyond lay total darkness.

The Doctor pointed his flashlight into the void and they saw the beam reflect from a glistening rock wall cut with an arched tunnel entrance.

'That looks manufactured,' whispered Nyssa.

'It certainly isn't natural,' the Doctor agreed.

The mouth of the tunnel was bearded by silvery cobwebs. Hundreds of spiders clung to the web, but scattered as the Doctor brushed the strands aside. Beyond was a ragged, black hole. He stepped cautiously into the opening and his torchlight found the walls. They were slick and black, and cut with thousands of short, jagged marks in rows.

'Hello, what's this?'

'Those marks are deliberate,' Nyssa said, frowning.

'Looks like the writing's on the wall,' the Doctor said. 'These are ancient runes of some kind.'

'I don't like them,' Nyssa said quietly. 'They're a warning. I know they are.'

The Doctor glanced at her. 'We won't know for sure unless we can read them. They might be some form of greeting.'

'Do you honestly believe that?'

'No, not for a moment.' The Doctor smiled. 'But we live in hope.'

'You can read them?'

The Doctor shone his torch at the nearest set. 'Not yet. I've a gift for languages, though. Give me a few minutes and I might be able to cobble something together.'

'Doctor! Look!' Nyssa was pointing back towards the mouth of the tunnel. The spiders had already started to rebuild their cobwebs across the entrance, running busily to and fro.

'Closing the door behind us, as it were,' remarked the Doctor. 'Charming.'

'Here we are,' said Stoker. 'Pay dirt.'

She was slouched at Lawrence's computer terminal. Lawrence had just used his OC emergency override to break through the personal security codes on Silas Cadwell's private files.

'I'm not sure we should be doing this,' Lawrence said. He felt distinctly uncomfortable about the whole affair now, particularly the way in which Stoker was sprawling over his desk. She was still clearly under the influence of the Kalazak brandy and Lawrence felt that he, for one, should know better than to attempt something as morally dubious as this. But there was something about Stoker, even when she was drunk, that he found difficult to resist.

She was laughing at him now. 'Lighten up. That was always your problem, you know that? You always had to stick to the rule book.'

'Do the right thing, you mean.'

'I mean you had no imagination. If it wasn't in a textbook you didn't want to know.'

'But at least I did *know* what was in the textbook. Unlike some.'

'And another thing,' she said, leaning closer. 'You were always so *damned* good-looking.'

Lawrence took his eyes off the screen and met her stare. 'You're drunk.'

'Damn right. Kiss me.'

'Don't be ridiculous.'

'What's up? Isn't kissing in the rule book?'

'Let's just concentrate on the matter at hand, shall we?'

'OK. You're right, I'm drunk.' Her eyes twinkled amber at him. 'We'll play it by the rules.'

'I wish,' Lawrence grumbled ruefully.

Stoker's fingers tapped at the keys for a few seconds. The files that had shown up under Cadwell's name and codes were all disappointingly mundane, except for one.

'What's this then, Silas?' Stoker wondered aloud. 'It's pretty big, whatever it is.'

Lawrence frowned. 'It's some sort of data cache.'

'And it's firewalled,' Stoker realised. She slapped the keyboard in frustration. 'Old-fashioned but effective.'

'But why would Cadwell need to security-lock a file that was already security locked?'

'Isn't it obvious? Because the first security lock can be overridden – by you.'

Lawrence bit his lip. 'This is serious. Can you get through the firewall?'

'Hey, I didn't waste *all* my time at the Academy.' Stoker worked on the keyboard a little longer, but the files refused to open up whatever she tried. 'Enter your command override again,' she instructed Lawrence. 'Tell it whatever you have to: the planet's about to blow up, sun's going nova, you've lost your boot polish, *anything* to make the puter think it's a real emergency.'

'I've already done that.'

'Do it again,' she told him, 'with meaning this time.'

He entered the command code. 'This is hopeless,' he said.

'Wait,' Stoker said. 'Look at this: you've not accessed the file but you've cracked the file name.'

Lawrence leaned forward and stared at the screen. 'What the hell's that supposed to mean?' he muttered.

Stoker sat back in her seat, puzzled. Something cold crawled around her neck as she read the file name out aloud: *The Dark*.

The Doctor had made a rapid and intense study of the strange, unworldly hieroglyphics that covered the tunnel walls. His examination had led them further into the passageway. As they went deeper, the runes seemed to change, becoming less structured and rigid, and more free-flowing and expressive.

'I'm afraid these runes tell an unpleasant story,' said the Doctor.

'You surprise me.'

'I can't make out all the details, but it seems to concern the legend of an evil being that was once reduced to ashes and buried for ever.' The Doctor paused. 'At least I think that's what it says.'

'Buried here?' Nyssa queried.

'Probably.'

'Then this is a crypt, or a tomb, after all.'

'Yes. It's ironic, isn't it? Stoker's team claimed to be a team of archaeologists when we first arrived, looking for the remains of an ancient alien civilisation. All completely false, of course. Or so they thought!'

'Does it say what the being in the legend was? The one that was reduced to ashes and buried for ever?'

The Doctor scratched his head. 'Well, no, not in so many words. It all seems to get a little vague. As far as I can make out, a party of men came to the planet Akoshemon centuries ago – that's a guess – and battled with the evil that lived in the hearts and minds of…' his fingers traced the lines of an ugly pictogram, 'the monsters, I think it means, which inhabited it. The battle lasted for… well, for a very long time. Generations were sacrificed. Ultimately they triumphed, although at great cost.'

'But what was it they fought, exactly?'

'I don't know. It just keeps going on about darkness, or *the dark* at any rate.'

Nyssa shuddered. 'Then it *is* here.'

'Yes. But dead, remember. *Reduced to ashes and buried for ever.*'

'You once told me one shouldn't believe everything one reads.'

'Ah, yes. Quite true.' The Doctor rocked on his heels for a moment. 'There's only one thing for it,' he said. 'We'll have to check. Come on!'

'Must we?'

'This is what we came here to find, Nyssa,' the Doctor reminded her sternly.

'I know, but… I can't go on. The atmosphere down here is so thin and oppressive, Doctor. I have this feeling of terrible dread that… that something awful is going to happen.'

The Doctor peered into her eyes. 'I understand what you mean, Nyssa. I can feel it too, and it's been growing stronger every step of the way. It *wants* us to fear it. It's tampering with our perceptions, remember. But if it's trying to put us off, then there must be a good reason: perhaps it's weak now, vulnerable. This could be our best chance to find out exactly what it is and stop it.'

He took her hand in his and led her gently down the tunnel. The shadows seemed to be congealing around them, and Nyssa felt her heart straining in her chest. She knew the blood running in her veins was as thick and black as these shadows; she could feel the presence of her dream-voice close by, whispering to her just beyond the edge of hearing.

Presently they emerged into a large, circular chamber. The light in here was green and murky, emanating from a domed ceiling where hundreds of glow-worms snaked through the translucent rock like veins.

The floor of the chamber sloped sharply down to some kind of pit or well in the exact centre. The Doctor and Nyssa came to an unsteady halt at its edge. The Doctor hesitated for a second, staring into the dark hole, but could see nothing. It appeared to be completely black.

'What is it?' Nyssa asked with a shiver. There seemed to be a coldness surrounding the pit that she could feel deep inside her, as though her bones were slowly turning to ice.

'I can't tell, it's too dark.' The Doctor spoke softly but his voice echoed around the chamber. He aimed his torch directly into the black pit. 'It's full of some kind of tar or slime… I can't see it properly. It's absorbing the torchlight!'

Nyssa was shaking. The Doctor saw her and looked uneasy. 'What's the matter? Can you feel it? Is this it? The enemy?' He pointed at the black pit.

She nodded dumbly, hugging herself but unable to stop quivering.

I am here

She gasped. The voice was so close, right inside her head, behind her eyes.

I am so close to you

Waiting

Trapped

'Nyssa!' the Doctor said sharply. 'Snap out of it! Resist it, Nyssa!'

She closed her eyes and shuddered violently, feeling her legs weakening beneath her. Then she felt the Doctor's arms as he caught her awkwardly and they knelt together by the edge of the pit.

'It's here,' she said raggedly. 'Waiting…'

'What is it waiting for?'

'Its servant…'

The Doctor looked pained. 'You, Nyssa? Is it you?'

Nyssa opened her mouth to speak but nothing came. Her eyes were rolling up into her head. The Doctor grasped her face roughly with the fingers of one hand and made her look at him. 'Let me communicate with it, Nyssa. Let me talk to it!'

'I can't… it's not ready…'

The Doctor let out an exasperated hiss.

For a long, cold moment there was utter silence.

Then they both heard the noise at the same time: the soft rustle of something approaching from the rune-lined passage behind them.

Nyssa turned to look at the Doctor, horrified. 'The Bloodhunter!'

The Doctor quickly pulled Nyssa back from the edge of the pit and they crouched down by the wall, away from the tunnel entrance.

The creature entered the chamber and paused for a moment on the threshold, as if waiting or listening.

Then the Doctor and Nyssa watched it step forward, right to the very edge of the pit at the centre of the room. The Bloodhunter raised its hands, almost in an attitude of worship. The creature's liver-coloured head shone in the torchlight and then it knelt down as if in prayer.

Nyssa tore her gaze from the creature and looked at the Doctor, who was staring in wide-eyed fascination.

The creature was leaning forward, peering into the oily black depths of the pit. A shudder passed through its body and it coughed violently. Then, with a sudden convulsion, it threw its head forward and vomited a stream of dark liquid into the pit.

'What's happening?' Nyssa gasped in revulsion.

'It's regurgitating the blood,' the Doctor told her.

The creature retched and issued another flood of emetic, and then more, until a torrent of blood and bile had been ejected into the well. It paused for a moment and then the convulsions began again, followed by more blood.

The Doctor quietly moved for the exit, still keeping a firm hold on Nyssa's arm.

'We've seen enough,' he told her in the tunnel. 'Time we were going.'

Nyssa staggered after him. 'Why didn't it see us?'

'I don't know. It was pretty murky in there. And perhaps it was too concerned with its business to notice us.'

Nyssa wasn't prepared to argue, she was just thankful that it was over – for now. She had to get away from here, far away.

Because in her mind she could hear the voice talking to the creature, imploring it to continue, begging it to spew more and more of its evil elixir so that the darkness could drink, long and deeply, of life itself.

CHAPTER FIFTEEN

'What happened? What did you find? What's wrong with Nyssa?'

'She's just a bit tired, that's all,' the Doctor said. He lay Nyssa down on a spare bed. 'It's been quite an ordeal.' As quickly as he could, the Doctor recounted their adventure in the catacombs.

And the end of it, Tegan pulled a face. 'You mean it's like some kind of Pot Snack? Just add water and wait five minutes for a pool of delicious simmering evil?'

The Doctor winced. 'Well, it's true that it appears to require liquid reconstitution, yes. Only human blood and bile rather than plain hot water.'

'That's revolting.'

'It's certainly a good story,' agreed a voice from the doorway. Silas Cadwell entered the sickbay with his hands clasped behind his back and a sardonic expression on his face. 'Pity there's no one to corroborate it.'

'Nyssa saw everything,' the Doctor argued. 'When she wakes up –'

'I mean no one *reliable*.'

The Doctor looked at him wearily. 'Mr Cadwell, I offered you the chance to come with us. You refused.'

'Naturally.'

'Perhaps if you had come along, you wouldn't be so dismissive.'

Cadwell clicked his tongue. 'Ah, you mean that I might have found my blood suitably chilled by this bubbling pool of evil slime you found?' He smiled. 'I think you'll find I'm made of sterner stuff than that, Doctor.'

'Whatever is trapped in that pit is powerfully telepathic and monstrously evil,' the Doctor said firmly. 'And it's trying to get free.'

'Stop it, I'll have a heart attack,' Cadwell replied. He glanced at Nyssa's supine form on the medical couch. 'Or swoon right away, like your friend.'

'Am I to understand that you're not prepared to do anything about what we've found?'

'You've found nothing, Doctor! Do you seriously expect me to act on one fanciful story and a state of self-induced hysteria?'

'Then I shall have to speak to Captain Lawrence.'

Cadwell sneered. 'He won't be interested. The captain has only one concern: securing the mineral rights to this moon for the Consortium.'

'Then it will be left to me to deal with it,' the Doctor said. 'It usually is.'

'*Us* to deal with it, Doctor,' Tegan corrected.

Cadwell smiled condescendingly at the pair of them. 'Oh, I wish you both luck. Be sure to give my regards to the Pot Snack of Evil, won't you?'

He laughed and then turned on his heel, marching out of the medical bay without another word.

'Doctor…' said Tegan.

The Doctor slammed his hand down on a computer bank. 'Of all the arrogant, narrow-minded stupidity!'

'Oh never mind about him, Doc,' Tegan said. 'He's just a prat in a uniform. They're all over the place. But listen, I've got some news for you!'

'What news?'

'You told me to look after Oldeman, remember? Well, he starting talking in his sleep: he wanted more neurolectrin, and –'

'You didn't let him have it, did you?'

'Of course not. You told me not to. But he was getting pretty desperate, shouting his mouth off about all kinds of stuff to do with Professor Garondel.'

'The scientist who set up the secret research lab,' recalled the Doctor. 'The gentleman responsible for the creation of the Bloodhunter.'

'Right. Or so we thought.' Tegan looked excited. 'But I got the distinct impression from Oldeman that Garondel was little more than a lab technician. Oldeman said, "I should never have taken him on." It sounded to me like it was Garondel who was trying to stop Oldeman going ahead with the project, not the other way around.'

'Really!' The Doctor whirled around and glared at Ravus Oldeman. 'I think it's high time we had another little chat with our sleeping friend!'

Silas Cadwell returned to his own cabin and shut the door. Tight-lipped, he crossed to his personal computer terminal and switched it on. He worked at the machine for several minutes, studying the contents of various files in his private database very closely.

'I'll be damned,' said Stoker, sitting up suddenly in front of the puter display. 'He's just opened the file.'

Lawrence leant closer. 'That's a stroke of luck!'

'Don't knock it,' Stoker said. 'Luck happens.'

'What's he up to?'

'Wait a sec, we should be able to get a clear view of the whole file.'

Alone in his quarters, Silas Cadwell closed the puter down and stood up. He had an uncomfortable feeling that he was being watched. Nothing definite, just some kind of sixth sense. He wasn't unduly worried; it simply meant that the time had come to act.

Cadwell was a man with a mission. Actually, it was more than a mission: it was an inheritance, a fantastic duty that had been passed down to him and which would take his actions completely outside the remit of the Consortium.

He pressed a switch on his desk and the drawer buzzed open. He took out a plastic box and placed it carefully on the surface. The biometric lock was triggered by a specially coded DNA strand in Cadwell's saliva. He licked a fingertip, wiped it along the sensor, and the box flipped open.

Inside were the components for a squat metal projectile weapon.

He assembled it quickly and efficiently. The handgun was small, powerful, extremely expensive and strictly illegal for civilian or even Consortium use. It fired specks of super-dense matter, sometimes called Dwarf Star Alloy. In single-shot mode it could decapitate a man, and at close range a sustained stream could rip open a Dalek. It used a single cell of depleted ranidium for a power source and this was shielded against most shipboard sensors, rendering the weapon to all intents and purposes undetectable.

Cadwell carefully inserted the tiny but heavy magazine. It contained five DSA 'dot' rounds and that would be more than enough firepower for what he intended.

Next he took out four identical plastic canisters from his secure locker. He slipped them neatly into a pack and hung it over one shoulder. He was ready.

Comforted by the steely weight of the gun in his pocket, Cadwell left his cabin for the last time.

Ravus Oldeman returned to full consciousness very quickly. Tegan didn't know whether this was natural or a result of the medical computer's drugs cycle, but when the scientist opened his eyes they seemed to be bright and piercing.

They focused quickly on the first thing they saw: a small medical injector held between the Doctor's finger and thumb.

'Neurolectrin.' Oldeman reached up to snatch the ampoule, but it disappeared.

The Doctor spread his fingers. 'Now you see it… now you don't.'

'Give me the neurolectrin,' Oldeman rasped, trying to sit up. 'I need another dose.'

'I don't think so,' the Doctor told him coolly. 'Not yet at any rate.'

'I'll suffer permanent brain-damage without it!'

'I'm willing to let a few brain cells wither on the vine, if necessary.'

Oldeman gritted his teeth. 'I am due another dose. The medical computer will confirm it!'

'I know you're due another dose,' the Doctor said. 'All I said was – *not yet*.'

Oldeman sank back onto the couch, his ribs heaving. He licked his lips. 'What do you think you're playing at, man? Call yourself a doctor?'

'*The* Doctor, if you don't mind. I'm very particular about that: I've always been a stickler for accuracy.'

Oldeman shook his head, confused. 'What do you want?'

'The truth!'

'What?'

The Doctor leaned over the scientist, dangling the neurolectrin injector, which had magically reappeared in his hand, right in front of him. 'I want the truth, Oldeman. Or should I say *Professor* Oldeman?'

'What do you mean?'

'I mean that you've been lying to us, *Professor*. It wasn't Garondel who set up the secret research base here on Akoshemon's moon. It was you. It wasn't Garondel who insisted on including Akoshemon DNA in the genetic mix, it was *you*. It wasn't Garondel who rode roughshod over everyone else's instinct for caution when trying to generate a life form based on a human-Akoshemon combination. *It was you.*'

Oldeman stared at the Doctor in panic, finally glancing at Tegan, who stood with her arms folded by the Doctor's side.

'Hard luck, Oldeman,' she said. 'You talk in your sleep.'

'Not very original,' the Doctor said. 'But quite revealing.'

'You don't understand the whole truth,' Oldeman spat.

'Then why don't you tell us the whole truth?'

'Give me the neurolectrin first.'

The Doctor shook his head. 'Not until you tell us everything, Oldeman. And I mean *everything*.'

'For pity's sake! Give me the neurolectrin!' Oldeman's eyes bulged. 'The potential damage to my brain would be irrevocable!'

'Irrevocable damage to your brain? I'll take that risk. Will you?'

Oldeman gasped.

'You may have the idea that I'm all fair play and scruples, Professor,' the Doctor went on, 'but I'm a very worried man and my concern for your continued good health comes quite low on my list of priorities at the moment. Now start talking.'

'All right, so the research project *was* mine. Garondel was just a technician – bright enough in his own field but idealistic. I didn't have any time for him. He tried to sabotage my work at every stage.'

'It's a pity he didn't succeed,' said Tegan sourly.

'He was a young fool! I was on the cusp of a real breakthrough! The creature was created from a genetic blueprint we calculated using Akoshemon DNA. I truly believed that the study of this specimen would bring tremendous benefits to the field of suspended animation and gene manipulation. But almost as soon as we had generated the creature, I realised it was something *special*! I had created a new, completely unique life form!'

'And so you set it free,' said the Doctor.

'I had to see what it could do, what its instincts would be. Don't you understand?'

'I understand that you are an egotistical fool, Professor Oldeman,' the Doctor said. 'There was never any sign of the creature having broken out of its generation chamber. It must have been released.'

'Why did you lie to us?' asked Tegan.

Oldeman looked desperate. 'What else could I do? The creature was uncontrollable – a savage. It killed everyone else. I barely escaped it, and then only by hurling myself into an experimental stasis tank for goodness knows how long. One hundred and sixty years, as it turned out – and that wasn't long enough!'

'But why didn't you tell us who you really were when we woke you up?' Tegan asked.

'Would you have done?' Oldeman sagged. 'I knew there was a good chance whoever found me in the stasis tank would have checked the computer files first. I took the precaution of altering the scientist ranking in the hope of escaping the blame when I was found.'

'Meanwhile the creature has followed the genetic instincts you were so keen to observe,' said the Doctor. 'Instincts that were coded right into its very unique DNA.'

'I don't understand,' Oldeman said.

'No, you wouldn't,' the Doctor responded. 'Professor Oldeman, your blind arrogance has released a creature whose only instinct is to obtain human blood and bile for the *thing* it serves.'

'Thing? What thing? I don't understand!'

'The creature drained its victims of their blood for use in the revitalisation of an ancient evil, buried at the centre of this moon.'

'What? How do you know all this?'

The Doctor straightened up and pushed his hands into his pockets. 'I really don't have the time to explain it all to you, Professor,' he said. 'Come along, Tegan, we'll have to see Captain Lawrence.'

'Wait a minute,' Oldeman said, sitting up. 'What about my neurolectrin?'

The Doctor stopped on his way to the exit and tossed the injector to Oldeman, who caught it. 'But it's empty!'

'I know,' the Doctor said. 'I gave you the dose just before you woke up.'

Silas Cadwell watched the Doctor and Tegan leave the medical bay. They didn't see him lurking in one of the recessed doorways further along the corridor. Cadwell waited until they had disappeared from view and then entered the sickbay unseen.

'What do you want?' snapped Oldeman, sitting up and glaring fearfully at the 2IC.

'Go back to sleep,' Cadwell told him, following the instruction with a ferocious blow to the man's head with the butt of his gun. Oldeman fell back onto the bed, stunned and bleeding.

Cadwell then walked over to the couch where Nyssa lay. He pressed the cold metal of the gun barrel against her temple. 'And you,' he said. 'Wake up.'

'This is unbelievable,' said Lawrence as he studied the data screen. It was full of information concerning the demonic history of the planet Akoshemon. 'Cadwell's working to his own personal agenda. He's a Consortium man in name only.'

'In some ways, then, you have to admire him,' Stoker said.

'Don't be facetious. Why has Cadwell brought an entire historical tract on the planet Akoshemon with him?'

'That's a very interesting question,' said the Doctor, walking into the cabin behind them.

Lawrence whirled around. 'What the devil! How did you get in here?'

'What's going on?' Stoker asked.

'That's what we're trying to find out,' Tegan told her.

'What have you found here?' asked the Doctor.

Stoker said, 'Silas Cadwell's a rogue Consortium officer, would you believe it. He's engineered this entire trip: according to his personal files, he's something of an expert on Akoshemon.'

The Doctor frowned. 'Is he really?'

'It's all in here,' Stoker said, tapping the puter. 'He keeps everything locked away in a file called *The Dark*.'

'The Dark?' The Doctor looked eagerly from Stoker to Lawrence and back. 'Are you sure?'

'According to this, Cadwell is an expert on Akoshemon mythology,' Lawrence explained. 'This file concerned the legend of a terrible creature from that planet's vile history called "the Dark".'

'So Vega Jaal was right all along,' Tegan said. 'He said that was what was waiting for us – the Dark!'

'Do go on, Captain,' urged the Doctor. 'This is fascinating!'

'It seems this Dark thing was destroyed and burnt to ashes thousands of years ago by a band of early space travellers.'

'Yes, I've recently read a similar account of the story,' the Doctor said. 'Written as a warning on the entrance to its burial crypt, right at the heart of this very moon.'

Lawrence and Stoker both stared at him, and the Doctor quickly explained where he and Nyssa had been and what they had found.

When he had finished, Lawrence in particular looked horror-struck. 'It seems I was wrong to doubt you, Doctor. And doubly wrong to trust my 2IC.'

'But what exactly is Cadwell up to?' Tegan asked.

'The best person to ask would be Cadwell himself,' the Doctor said.

'I'll call him in,' Lawrence said, reaching for the ship's intercom.

'No, wait,' Stoker said quickly. 'If he gets suspicious you'll only scare him off. Find out where he is and then *we* can go and see *him*.'

Nyssa stared at the muzzle of Cadwell's gun. 'What do you want?' she asked weakly.

'Get up,' Cadwell said. 'We're going on a little trip.'

'I don't understand. Where do you want to go?'

'I want you to take me to the same place you took the Doctor.'

Nyssa shook her head. 'Oh no. I'm not going back there.'

'Yes you are.' Cadwell cocked the pistol loudly. 'This is a DSA gun. It's not registered to my name and it won't show up on any of the ship's onboard scanners, because they are calibrated to detect phased energy weapons only. No one knows I'm here and if I shoot you no one will suspect me. *Now do as I say.*'

'I'm too ill…'

'Like I care.'

'I can hardly walk!'

'Let's put that to the test, shall we?' Cadwell jammed the barrel painfully into Nyssa's throat.

She took a series of deep breaths to steady her nerves, and then said, 'If you shoot me I won't be able to take you anywhere.'

Cadwell smiled. 'I don't have to shoot to kill.' Slowly he lowered the gun down her neck, over her chest and then across to her right arm. The flesh on her upper arm quivered as the cold metal brushed against it. 'In fact I'd rather not shoot at all. But if you make me I will not hesitate.'

'All right,' Nyssa said carefully. 'Let me stand up.'

She clambered down from the medical couch and straightened up with as much dignity as she could muster. Cadwell slipped behind her and rested the gun against her hip. Nyssa knew that any projectile fired from this range would cut right through the flesh and probably chip her pelvic bone, but it would not disable her.

Swallowing with difficulty, she said, 'You wish me to take you to the pit?'

'Yes.'

'Then you're more of a fool than even the Doctor thinks you are. You can't possibly understand what's waiting there.'

'You'd be surprised.'

'You're mad.'

'Maybe, maybe not,' Cadwell said with shrug. 'But I *am* in a hurry – so move!' He reached up with his free hand and caught a fistful of Nyssa's hair, twisting it until he had her bent backwards and gasping in pain. Then, still holding the gun against her waist, he pushed her roughly towards the exit.

'There's no sign of him in his cabin,' said Lawrence.

They were standing in one of the *Adamantium*'s passageways, wondering where to look next. Stoker had suggested tracking Cadwell down on foot, worried that he might intercept any attempt to use the ship's computer to locate him.

'Well if he's not on the bridge and not in his cabin,' said Tegan, 'where could he be?'

The Doctor was looking worried. 'What about the medical bay?'

'The medical –?' Lawrence frowned. 'Why?'

The Doctor turned and marched off, calling back over his shoulder, 'We now know Cadwell has more than a passing interest in the secret history of Akoshemon and the Dark. We also know that he heard me telling Tegan all about my trip to the underground crypt where this Dark thing is supposed to be buried. At the time he didn't seem the slightest bit interested. In fact he was almost dismissive.'

'But that doesn't make sense, given what he know about him now!' complained Tegan.

'Exactly,' the Doctor said. 'The thing is: who accompanied me on that trip?'

'Oh, rabbits!' Tegan said. 'Nyssa!'

'Come on!' shouted the Doctor.

*

As soon as Nyssa's feet touched the dusty surface of the moon at the foot of the ship's embarkation ramp, she knew she had to fight. Up until now she had let Cadwell push her through the ship to this airlock without struggling. But now she moved suddenly, catching Cadwell off guard. She twisted her hips towards the gun, knocking it to one side and spoiling his aim. But his grip on her hair was too strong. With a grunt of annoyance Cadwell yanked his hand down and Nyssa felt her head jerked with it.

'Don't try any stupid tricks,' he snarled, dragging her round by her hair.

She lashed out with her foot, connecting hard, but his boots protected his shins. He kicked back and swept her legs from under her. She hit the ground and he kicked again, burying the toe of his boot into the small of her back.

'I'm not in the mood for any heroics,' he hissed.

She lay there gasping in the dust, and then yelped as he kicked her once more. 'On your feet!'

She struggled to stand up, and he hauled her to her feet by her hair. Tears ran down her face and she bit her lip against the pain. Then she felt the gun being pressed hard into the nape of her neck, and Cadwell used it to propel her towards the cave entrance.

'I quite enjoy a little walk, don't you?' he said.

When they reached the medical bay it was empty, except for Ravus Oldeman.

Stoker pointed at the bloody gash on his skull. 'Looks like he's been knocked unconscious.'

'But where's Nyssa?' Tegan demanded.

The Doctor crossed over to Oldeman and said, 'Professor! Wake up!'

'He's out cold, Doctor,' Stoker told him.

'We'll see about that.' The Doctor quickly tapped in a series of instructions to the medical computer. 'These things are really very handy. You just dial up the drug you want and it does the rest for you. Right now we need a little something to help our friend here to

198

come to his senses. All it takes is the right kind of stimulus.'

The computer clicked and bleeped and administered a chemical stimulant. Instantly Oldeman's eyes fluttered open and he looked blearily at the Doctor. 'Not you again!'

'What happened, Oldeman? Where's Nyssa?'

'Cadwell,' said Oldeman faintly. 'Came in… He had a gun… hit me… don't remember anything else…'

'Cadwell must have taken Nyssa,' the Doctor said, thumping the medical computer angrily. 'He wants her to lead him to the Dark.'

'But why?' Lawrence asked.

'Isn't it obvious? This is why Cadwell's come to Akoshemon: he knows the Dark's buried here on the moon. That's why he was so interested in the Bloodhunter. That's why he didn't want me with him when he went to examine it: he's come to finish its job. *He's come to help resurrect the Dark.*'

Chapter Sixteen

Nyssa spun around and jabbed her fingers straight into Cadwell's eyes. He couldn't help but flinch, and as he twisted around, the gun went off. There was a deafening report that echoed and reverberated through the caves but Nyssa was beyond caring. She followed up her attack with a kick aimed straight for the man's groin: if it had connected it would have finished him.

If it had connected.

Cadwell was simply too fast. He lashed out with the gun, catching Nyssa across the face.

She fell back, pain opening up all over her head. Her skull hummed with the impact, and Nyssa dropped to her knees.

Cadwell took two strides towards Nyssa and brought the gun down again, from right over his head this time; a hard, calculated blow to the side of her neck. She groaned and sagged as all feeling disappeared from her left arm. She lay on the rocky floor and sobbed, unable to move, suddenly frightened that he had done her some permanent harm: damaged the nerves in her neck, perhaps. Maybe she was even paralysed.

'I ought to kill you now,' she heard him say. His voice sounded ragged. 'You nearly blinded me.'

'That was the idea.' Nyssa could taste blood: the gun must have split her cheek.

Cadwell pulled her roughly to her feet. Her shoulders and arms were buzzing with pins-and-needles. 'I didn't think you had it in you, to be honest,' he told her.

'Neither did I.'

'All I want is for you to take me to the Dark,' Cadwell said. 'I don't care if you have to crawl on your hands and knees. I don't care if you're no longer pretty when we get there, or if your teeth are all smashed in, or if you've lost an eye. Am I making myself clear?'

She nodded. 'I hate you, Cadwell.'

'I'm heartbroken. Get going.'

'The man's a traitor,' said Lawrence.

'To the Consortium, maybe,' said Stoker. 'To everyone else he's just a lunatic.'

'And to think I trusted him,' Lawrence went on miserably. 'At first.'

'Well, he was efficient, ruthless and without a trace of anything like common decency,' Stoker said. 'The perfect Consortium employee.'

'I wish you'd stop joking about this.'

'Who's joking? I haven't forgotten how he talked to Bunny Cheung.'

Lawrence stood up angrily. 'All right! I don't suppose there's any point in going on about it. I just hope the Doctor can find him and stop him in time.'

'The Doctor knows where this Dark thing is hidden. He'll find Cadwell if that's where he's gone.'

'Which leaves us here alone.'

'If you're thinking what I think you're thinking then forget it,' Stoker said. 'I'm sober.'

Lawrence managed a weak smile. 'No, I was actually referring to our business here.'

It took Stoker a moment to understand what he had actually said. 'Wait a sec: *our* business?'

'The mineral rights to this moon,' Lawrence explained. 'Your claim versus my claim.'

Stoker watched him carefully, but Lawrence's blue eyes were giving nothing away. She took out a cigar and lit it slowly. 'You know I can't beat the Consortium.'

'Yes, I know. Which is why I'm willing to let you in on the claim.'

Stoker took out the cigar from between her teeth. 'Let me in?'

'There's more than enough lexium on this moon for all of us.'

'Meaning what, exactly?'

'I'm on a percentage, Jyl. The bonus I receive from putting through a claim on behalf of the Consortium will be substantial. *Very* substantial. I'd like to share it with you.'

'I don't believe it.'

Lawrence said, 'I mean every word. I would never have come here if it weren't for your mayday.'

'It wasn't *my* mayday.'

'You know what I meant.'

Stoker's eyes flashed gold. 'It was Bunny Cheung's mayday and he's *dead*.'

'I know, and I'm deeply sorry about that. But when all is said and done, when Cadwell's brought to book, the lexium will still be here. Waiting for someone to claim it.'

Stoker stood up. 'I'm not interested any more. It's gone beyond all that for me. The lexium can stay here until the crack of doom for all I care.'

'I never thought I'd hear you say that.'

'I never thought I'd hear myself say that.'

'Jyl, you may think like this now, but when the dust has settled…'

She shook her head. 'I don't think so. Bunny was a good friend. An old friend. We argued and we fell out but we never let each other down.'

'Except when he sent that mayday.'

'Everyone's entitled to one stupid mistake.'

Lawrence took a step towards her. 'So Bunny makes a stupid mistake. But *I* let you down.'

She stared him out. 'I meant everyone's entitled to one stupid mistake, except you.'

'Damn it, why do you have to make everything so difficult?'

Stoker took a drag on her cigar and smiled thinly. 'No pain, no gain.'

'And just how much pain do you intend to go through here,' asked Lawrence hotly, 'without any gain at all?'

'Set your weapons to stun,' said the Doctor. He turned to Tegan. 'I've always wanted to say that.'

Tegan watched the company of *Adamantium* crewmen dutifully adjust their blasters and marvelled once again at the Doctor's knack for working his way into a position of trust and authority.

'What exactly are you expecting to find down here?' asked Ravus Oldeman. He sounded irritable and Tegan couldn't blame him; the Doctor had insisted that he came along but had not yet given a reason.

'At best, Silas Cadwell and my companion Nyssa – unharmed,' the Doctor replied. 'At worst, a being of total evil and devastating power already risen from the grave. Does that answer your question?'

Oldeman bridled. 'I still don't see why I have to come. I'm an old man!'

'It's my hope that by the time we've finished here, you will understand exactly why I wanted you to come,' the Doctor told him stonily. 'And for your information, Professor, you may be pushing three hundred years old, but you're not the only one here who doesn't look their age.' The Doctor glared at Oldeman for a long moment and then turned back to address the *Adamantium* men. 'Follow me, stay close and don't get lost. We'll be going through a labyrinth of underground tunnels and falling behind could prove fatal. We're going after Silas Cadwell, but don't forget that there is still the Bloodhunter to contend with. Keep your eyes peeled and stick together.'

'Sir,' said one of the crewmen, a thickset young tough called Vinson. 'Is Cadwell armed?'

'It would appear so, yes,' the Doctor answered. 'But according to Captain Lawrence, he's probably carrying a projectile weapon of some sort: simple but highly effective at close range.'

'You mean lethal, sir,' said Vinson.

'Er, yes. And please, call me Doctor.'

'Well then, Doctor,' Vinson went on, 'can you tell me why we're only shooting to stun? If Cadwell intends to take a pop at me with a bullet, it doesn't seem fair.'

There was a murmur of agreement from the other crewmen.

The Doctor stepped forward and took Vinson's blaster. With a sharp twist the Doctor reset the pistol and aimed it at the crewman's forehead. 'This gun is now set to kill. When I pull the trigger, it will bum a hole right through the middle of your head. The energy pulse will fry your brain into a charred lump and exit via the back of your skull. It will then burn its way right through the heads of the men standing behind you.'

The men standing behind Vinson shuffled back nervously.

'If there's going to be any shooting, then it will be in an enclosed space, in darkness, and very quick. I don't want you all shooting lumps out of one another.' The Doctor smiled grimly and handed the gun back to Vinson. 'We'll have to leave that side of things to Mr Cadwell.'

Fingers shaking, Vinson returned the blaster to stun.

His point made, the Doctor offered them all a cheery smile. 'All right, follow me,' he said, moving off. Tegan fell in behind him with Oldeman, and the *Adamantium* men formed a line behind them.

They passed quickly through the underground lab complex; Tegan was surprised to find it strangely familiar now. Beyond the laboratories were the deeper, darker caves that were certainly not familiar to her and decidedly unwelcoming.

The Doctor pointed out significant landmarks on the way: most interesting of these were the glowing snakes buried in the translucent rock. They pulsed with a weird green light that made everyone look ill and fear-stricken.

'Look,' whispered the Doctor, coming to a halt. His fingers brushed a section of the rock that had clearly been chipped away. There was a deep gouge in the tunnel wall and fragments of the glassy stone scattered over the ground.

'What is it?' Tegan asked.

'Bullet damage. Some kind of high-density projectile at any rate.'

'Cadwell?'

The Doctor nodded solemnly. 'There's no sign of any blood, so presumably Nyssa's unharmed.'

'But for how long? We'd better get a move on!'

'I wonder what happened?' the Doctor muttered.

'Does it matter? Nyssa must have tried to make a break for it.'

'Hm.'

'Do you have to analyse everything?' hissed Tegan. 'We must be running out of time!'

'Yes, I am aware of that. It's just that… well, something must have prompted Cadwell to shoot.'

'Like I said, Nyssa probably tried to escape.'

'Yes, but… well, fighting? It's just not Nyssa, is it?'

'You're forgetting something,' said Oldeman. 'Cadwell may not have been shooting at your friend. He may have seen the Bloodhunter.'

'Hm,' said the Doctor again.

'Either way Nyssa's in trouble,' Tegan said impatiently. 'Let's go!'

'Is this it?' Cadwell asked.

Nyssa shivered and nodded. 'It's through there,' she told him, indicating the tunnel entrance. She could see the ugly little runes lining the passage walls, telling their evil, sordid story. And beyond that, she could even make out the faint green glow of the crypt.

She could also feel the heavy, black presence of the thing in the pit: a brooding, impatient sensation bubbling in her stomach like bile.

Cadwell prodded her with his gun. 'Go on, then.'

'Please don't make me go in there!'

'Don't be stupid.'

'You don't understand,' Nyssa said quietly. 'I *can't* go in. It knows I'm here.'

Cadwell frowned. 'The Dark?'

'If that's what you call it.'

'You're shaking.'

'It's in my mind already. And my blood!'

'You're talking rubbish,' Cadwell told her, but he sounded unsure.

The thick, black blood stirred in Nyssa's veins, pushing its way through her body faster and faster with every laboured heartbeat. 'It hates me. It hates everyone. Everything.'

Cadwell peered down the tunnel. 'Is that so?'

'Please, Cadwell. Listen to me: don't go in there. You don't know what you're dealing with.'

'I've a shrewd idea, actually. It's a pit full of ashes – the remains of an entity so ancient and evil none of us can truly comprehend its power. It's being revitalised, though. Slowly. Using the blood and bile and snot and what-have-you, sucked out of living beings by its servant and spat back into the ashes.'

Nyssa trembled. 'How do you know all this?'

'Privileged information.'

'Why have you come here?'

'To keep an appointment,' Cadwell said simply. 'One for which I do not intend being late, so please, carry on.' He gestured graciously to the tunnel entrance with his gun. 'After you.'

The Doctor led Tegan, Oldeman and the crewmen into a cavern full of stalagmites and stalactites that looked to Tegan like ghostly, fossilised trees. Their footsteps echoed strangely through the unnerving black silence of the forest. Tegan clutched her blaster tightly as they crept forwards, aware that they seemed to be heading down, as if they were descending the slope of a natural amphitheatre, overgrown with grey, petrified trees.

'Wait, I thought I saw something,' said Oldeman, reaching out to touch Tegan on the arm. 'Something moving, over there.'

They halted and peered into the gloom around them. It was impossible to see much through the stalactites and stalagmites.

'I can't see anything,' Tegan said.

'What did it look like?' asked the Doctor.

Oldeman was rattled. 'I don't know, I only caught a glimpse, and my eyesight isn't what it used to be!'

206

'Could it have been Nyssa?' wondered Tegan. 'Or Cadwell?'

'Or the Bloodhunter,' Oldeman said anxiously.

'There it is!' cried one of the Consortium men, pointing to a thick patch of stalactite-trees.

Immediately Vinson swung his blaster up, but the Doctor's hand flashed out and caught his wrist. 'Don't shoot,' he hissed. 'The flash will alert whatever's there to the fact that we're *here*!'

Vinson glared at the Doctor, his gun hand trembling. His finger was white on the trigger.

'Stun guns won't be effective on the Bloodhunter,' the Doctor warned him quietly. 'You fire that thing now and it could very well be the last thing you ever do.'

Vinson glanced nervously back into the stony forest. Gradually the Doctor let go of his wrist and Vinson lowered the blaster. 'Thanks.'

'What now?' asked Tegan.

The Doctor took a deep breath. 'We go on. It's not far from here.' The message was passed back along the line of Consortium men.

'Nyssa and Cadwell must have reached that crypt thing by now,' Tegan said as they moved on and the stalactites began to shrink.

The Doctor agreed. 'We'll have to go into the actual crypt. I was hoping to avoid this. Tegan, you don't have to come. In fact, I would advise that you didn't.'

Tegan looked at him in the gloom and recognised the honest concern in his eyes. She had seldom seen the Doctor look so full of trepidation. 'I'm not leaving you or Nyssa,' she told him bluntly.

He nodded but didn't say anything. He clearly hadn't expected any other response, and Tegan felt glad.

'I'll stay out here then,' said Oldeman, 'if it's all the same with you.'

'No you won't,' said the Doctor. 'I want you to witness the full extent of your folly.'

'But I don't feel very well.'

'Nonsense. You're extremely fit for two hundred and sixty-five.'

But Oldeman was sweating and beginning to shake.

'What's up with him?' Tegan asked, sensing something was wrong.

Oldeman shook violently and collapsed into the Doctor's arms. The Doctor lowered him to the ground, where he began to suffer severe convulsions.

'He's fitting,' groaned the Doctor. 'I should've realised!'

'What?'

'It's a nervous reaction to the neurolectrin addiction.'

'He needs another fix?'

The Doctor nodded and fumbled through his pockets. 'I think I've brought a spare injector.'

'I thought you said he couldn't have any more?'

'We can't leave him like this. Hold him steady.' The Doctor produced a neurolectrin injector and applied it swiftly to Oldeman's neck. Within moments the professor began to calm down, the spasms subsiding to a slight tremor. The Doctor shook his head and discarded the empty injector. 'I shouldn't have brought him with us.'

'It's too late for second thoughts, Doctor,' Tegan said.

Nyssa walked into the domed chamber and staggered against the wall, weak at the knees. The sight of the great pit at the centre of the room, full of its dreadful black ooze, filled her with terror. The throbbing green glow from the snakes lining the ceiling made her feel nauseous. Her stomach churned.

Cadwell stepped into the chamber. He was looking less confident now. His eyes were wide with fear and his skin looked waxy in the putrid luminescence.

'It's here,' he said in a hoarse whisper, staring at the black pit.

Nyssa tried to press herself into the rock wall, keeping as far away from the deadly well as possible. The dark slime it contained was now bubbling, the sound echoing around the chamber like distant laughter.

Cadwell wiped a hand down his face, as if trying to gather his wits. Suddenly he pulled the bag from his shoulder and opened it. He pulled out a large plastic container and set it down on the floor beside the pit.

'What are you doing?' Nyssa asked.

Cadwell glanced up at her and smirked. 'Fulfilling a promise,' he said. He unscrewed the lid of the jar.

Nyssa felt as though she was about to burst: the black tar in the pit was calling out to the dark blood oozing through her veins. Somewhere inside her she felt as though the black slime was rising in her gut, bubbling thickly and making her gag.

'That's far enough, Cadwell,' said the Doctor, stepping into the chamber behind him.

Cadwell jerked around in surprise. 'You!'

Nyssa stared mutely at the Doctor. He stood framed in the entrance, Tegan and Ravus Oldeman just behind him.

'Stop what you're doing and stand up slowly,' the Doctor instructed Cadwell.

Cadwell climbed to his feet with a murderous look in his eyes. 'You blundering fool, Doctor! Why don't you just leave now, while you still can?'

'I was about to say exactly that to you,' the Doctor said. 'Come over here, Nyssa.'

Nyssa started forward, and Cadwell took that opportunity to strike: he snatched her arm as she passed him and jammed his gun into the side of her head.

'Don't be stupid!' cried the Doctor.

Cadwell leered at him and gave a harsh laugh. 'I was about to say exactly that to *you*, Doctor! Now get back or I'll blow Nyssa's brains out. I don't need her any more.'

But Nyssa squirmed in his grip and bit down on his hand with enough force to draw blood. Cadwell howled and the gun went off, missing Nyssa's head by a fraction and blasting out a chunk of rock from the wall.

The Doctor leapt forward, tackling Cadwell and bringing him down heavily. They hit the inclined floor and rolled towards the black pit. Cadwell's gun clattered away and Tegan snatched it up.

Cadwell stuck his elbow into the Doctor's throat and heaved. The Doctor spun away and the two of them scrambled to their feet. But the Consortium man was evidently trained in unarmed combat: a barrage of tightly controlled kicks and punches soon had the Doctor reeling, every blow connecting despite his best efforts to block and parry. Finally Cadwell kicked out and the Doctor lurched back towards the pit, his nose and lips bleeding.

'Stop it!' shouted Tegan, aiming the automatic. 'I'll shoot!'

Cadwell ignored her. He took one long stride towards the Doctor and grabbed him by the lapels of his frock-coat. Cadwell's face was a mask of fierce concentration as he prepared to finish the job.

'I said stop it!' Tegan shrieked.

Oblivious, Cadwell slammed his forehead into the Doctor's face and then hurled him towards Tegan, spoiling her aim.

Nyssa grabbed Cadwell and pulled him backwards. There were black tears running from her eyes as she threw Cadwell heavily against the wall. His legs gave out and he slid to the floor.

For a second everything seemed to stop.

'I've just been beaten up,' the Doctor mumbled in disbelief, climbing shakily to his feet. He gently touched his split lip and winced.

'Never mind that,' Tegan said. 'Nyssa's just saved your life.'

The Doctor blinked. 'Nyssa?'

Tegan pointed to where their friend was standing by the pit. Silas Cadwell lay at her feet, groaning senselessly. Nyssa looked up from his inert body and glared at the Doctor and Tegan. Her eyes were black spots swimming in blood.

'Nyssa?' said the Doctor quietly, stepping towards her.

'What's wrong with her?' Tegan asked, suddenly panic-stricken. She still held Cadwell's gun but she didn't know where to aim it.

Nyssa was just standing there, right at the edge of the pit. Behind her the dark slime welled up and burst with huge, thick bubbles. A revolting stench filled the air.

'Nyssa, listen to me,' the Doctor said. His voice was full of desperation. 'It doesn't have to be like this. You can fight it!'

'I can't,' she croaked.

Tegan gripped the Doctor's sleeve. 'What's the matter with her?'

'It's the Dark. It's securing its bridgehead in her mind. Taking over.'

'We've got to stop it!'

'Yes. I'm open to suggestions.'

'Not… yet… complete…' gurgled Nyssa helplessly. She swayed on the edge of the pit, and looked as if she could topple backwards into it at any moment. 'Help… me…'

'Doctor, do something!' Tegan urged. 'She's begging for help!'

'Is she?' the Doctor said. 'Or is it the Dark, begging through her?'

Tegan looked again at Nyssa. Her eyes had rolled up into her head, the tears forming two black streaks down her face. Her mouth fell open but no words came out.

Suddenly Ravus Oldeman let out a sharp cry. They all turned to see him stagger forward as something grabbed him from behind. Something the colour of fresh meat.

'Get back!' ordered the Doctor, pushing Tegan and Vinson away as the Bloodhunter lifted Oldeman into the fetid air and carried him bodily towards the pit. Oldeman squirmed in its grip and tried to scream, but it was too late. The Bloodhunter had dug its powerful, clawed fingers deep into the man's throat, cutting off his air supply. Then, with one sudden motion, the creature ripped open Oldeman's neck and a fountain of blood emerged with his last, convulsive breath.

The blood spattered across the floor and immediately began to trickle down towards the pit.

The creature dropped Oldeman's body without ceremony. Oldeman lay where he fell, emitting terrible gasps and gurgles as his life-blood gushed from him. With wide, pain-filled eyes he watched the scarlet river running away from him, down the slope and into the pit. The blood streamed over the edge and disappeared into the blackness.

Nyssa let out a sigh of relief.

A final tremor passed through Ravus Oldeman's body and he lay still. The light faded from his eyes.

The Doctor stared at Oldeman's corpse, utterly aghast.

'I am complete,' whispered Nyssa.

Immediately the chamber darkened and everyone instinctively

looked up at the ceiling, where the green snakes were growing dimmer by the second.

'They're dying,' realised Tegan.

The light began to fade. The Doctor appeared to be paralysed, his eyes wide and glassy as the appalling truth hit home. 'The Dark's being reborn,' he said. 'We've got to get away from here!'

Tegan said, 'Wait, Doctor! What about Nyssa?'

They looked back at her: Nyssa with her head thrown back, a terrible gurgle building in her throat. Suddenly thick black liquid streamed from her mouth and nose and she staggered forward. She collapsed onto her hands and knees, shaking. The dark bile spread out beneath her, seemingly with a life of its own, then began to run back down the slope towards the pit.

The Doctor was ashen-faced. He gripped Tegan's arms, trying to push her towards the exit, but she refused to move. 'We can't just leave her!' she shouted.

Then something huge and dark erupted from the centre of the pit. It blotted out the sickly remains of the light and filled the chamber with a freezing, impenetrable blackness.

CHAPTER SEVENTEEN

Tegan felt herself pushed out into the light. Hands grabbed her and pulled her forwards. She was outside the crypt again, at the edge of the stalactite forest, with the *Adamantium* crewmen. Vinson was standing over her with a powerful torch.

'What's going on?' he asked.

'We've got to get out of here!' Tegan told him.

'Someone else is coming,' said one of the *Adamantium* men. They turned their flashlights towards the tunnel entrance and Silas Cadwell staggered out, his face drawn and white.

Vinson's blaster snapped up to cover him. 'Hold it right there, sir!'

'Get out!' Cadwell screamed at him. 'Get back! Run!'

Vinson lowered his gun but stayed put. Cadwell clearly wasn't armed. In fact, he seemed to be terrified.

'I'd do as he says if I were you,' said another voice. Tegan turned to see the Doctor emerging from the crypt entrance, Nyssa slung over one shoulder in a fireman's lift. 'Run for your lives!' he gasped, almost stumbling to the ground with Nyssa.

The instruction carried the weight of genuine fear: every Consortium man turned and sprinted for the grey forest, with the exception of Vinson. 'Here, let me help,' he said, tossing his flashlight to Tegan and heaving Nyssa to her feet. He slung one limp arm over his shoulders, and, with the combined effort of the Doctor, carried Nyssa away from the crypt.

'What happened in there?' Vinson asked.

'Explain later!' grunted the Doctor. 'Keep going!'

They half-ran, half-stumbled onwards, Nyssa hanging between them. Tegan ran on ahead with the torch, but the stone trunks of the stalagmites were growing dimmer already. 'What's happening to the light?' Vinson asked.

'It's being absorbed,' the Doctor panted. They pushed on into the forest, forced to slow down because of the density of the stalagmites. 'The Dark has come back to life, and it's draining the light away.'

'How?'

'I don't… know!' The Doctor shifted his weight and stepped past another stalactite. 'Some kind of… photon assimilation I should think.'

'Let's do the science bit later,' Tegan suggested. 'We have to hurry, Doctor. The torch is failing!'

The flash's beam was weakening. What had at first been a brilliant circle of white light was now a dim pool of yellow. 'I don't know how much longer it'll last!'

The Doctor gritted his teeth and pushed on with Vinson's help. They kept grazing their knuckles and cracking their shoulders against the stalagmites, but refused to slow down any more. They could all feel the coldness at their backs, and it was getting colder.

At one point Tegan looked back, to find the forest behind them was lost in darkness. It was a malignant darkness, almost like a vertical wall of black ink spreading through the stalagmites, engulfing them one by one, faster and faster. And it was gaining on them.

'It's coming!' she yelled.

'I can't see where we're going!' called Vinson. 'It's getting too dark!'

Suddenly they heard the crackling whine of blaster fire: somewhere in the gloom a number of bright energy bolts leapt through the trees.

'My men,' Vinson realised, pausing. 'They're shooting at it.'

The Doctor caught his breath. 'They're wasting their time,' he panted. 'It absorbs light!'

In amongst the trees, lit by the sudden flash and zap of the blaster beams, were a number of the *Adamantium* crewmen. They had stopped and turned to fight the encroaching wall of blackness with the only weapons they had. The blaster bolts plunged into the darkness and faded from view. The swelling shadow didn't even falter in its progress.

'We must keep going,' Tegan urged.

'Fall back!' cried Vinson, desperately signalling to his men.

'They've split up,' the Doctor said. 'They're going to get lost.'

The Dark approached one of the men, who continued to blaze away at it uselessly. The burning glare of his blaster silhouetted him briefly against the blackness and then he disappeared from view. A terrible scream tore through the freezing air.

The other men turned and ran, but it was impossible to gain any speed in the forest. None of them could see clearly enough to dodge past the trees, and within moments they had been overtaken by the blackness. Each let out a horrifying shriek of agony as the darkness swallowed them up.

'Come on!' the Doctor said, picking Nyssa up again. He began to move up the slope, Tegan doing her best with the torch's feeble beam to show the way. Vinson, swearing mightily, brought up the rear.

'It's gaining on us!' Vinson cried.

'It's getting darker!' Tegan sobbed.

The Doctor lifted Nyssa onto his shoulder again and scrambled on. 'Don't stop!'

Suddenly they were out of the stalagmites and into the caves again; the light from the rock-snakes seemed an incongruously bright and cheerful green. There were some more crewmen up ahead, calling for them to hurry. Tegan sprinted towards them, her shoes slipping and sliding on the glassy rock. The Doctor staggered after her, almost bent double under Nyssa's prone form.

Behind them, Vinson turned and stood in the entrance to the tunnel. He watched the blackness fill the forest cavern and race towards him.

'Vinson!' Tegan screamed as she looked back. 'Hurry! You'll be killed!'

The Doctor collapsed and lay Nyssa on the tunnel floor. Some of the *Adamantium* men came back to help him pick her up. The Doctor turned around when he heard Tegan shouting.

Vinson, lit green by the glow-snakes and framed against the Dark, stood up straight and aimed his blaster in a double-handed grip.

'This is set to burn, you bastard,' he said, and pulled the trigger.

Brilliant red light burst from the gun and vanished into the blackness. The terrible shadow suddenly filled the tunnel entrance and swept over Vinson where he stood. Wraiths of darkness swirled and dashed around him, lifting him off his feet and shaking him like a rat. As he faded from view, Tegan almost thought she saw him turn transparent, as if she had glimpsed his bones and internal organs for just the briefest moment. Then there was nothing but the darkness and a blood-curdling shriek that seemed to linger in her head for far longer than she actually heard it.

'Quickly,' she heard the Doctor shout, feeling him grab her arm and pull her back. But she kept her eyes on the Dark: it seemed as though pieces of it were breaking away, solid shadows that rushed on ahead of the main body of the blackness, chasing after them. A dreadful, blood-freezing howl built up in the tunnel and a great blast of cold air heralded the approach of the shadow wraiths. Tegan turned and ran for her life.

The Doctor held on to Tegan's hand, pulling her after him. Together they dashed back up the tunnel. Tegan had no idea how far away the entrance to the laboratory complex was, but she knew she couldn't run much further. Her heart was grinding painfully in her chest and she could feel herself weakening.

'Come on!' the Doctor insisted, yanking her after him, harder, faster. His voice was ragged with the exertion. *Keep going!*

She could feel the icy breath of the Dark on her skin, hear the scream of its wraiths as they swept up the tunnel behind them. The darkness began to close in, the cave walls growing dimmer with every step.

Suddenly there was a bright light ahead of them: the door to the stasis-tank chamber. With a final, lung-bursting heave they shot through the doorway and sprinted up the steps that led to the main lab. There they collided with a small group of *Adamantium* crewmen.

'Close the door!' cried the Doctor from the floor.

Someone hit the switch and the big metal door hissed shut. Something massive struck the other side with a huge clang and the door shook in its frame. Everyone in the lab flinched.

Tegan lay on her back, breathing so hard she thought she would faint. The Doctor clambered to his feet and moved back to the door. As he approached it, there was another huge *clang* as something pounded against the other side.

The Doctor stepped back. 'Well, it seems to be sealed… for the moment.'

The door was struck again with a terrible *boom*.

'Can it get through?' one of the crewmen asked shakily.

'Given time, undoubtedly,' the Doctor replied. He was still breathing heavily.

'How much time?'

The door boomed again and vibrated with the impact.

The Doctor licked his dry lips. 'I don't know. A couple of hours? A few minutes? It's impossible to tell.'

'What is it?' asked another man.

'If it gets through that door, it'll be the end of us all,' the Doctor told him bleakly. 'We have to get away from here and quickly.' He headed for the exit. 'If we can get back to the *Adamantium* in time, we may be able to get you all off this moon.'

The door shook again, and dust dropped from the ceiling. Then it shook again. And again. Each impact reverberated around the lab with a heart-stopping *clang*.

Boom! Suddenly a dent appeared in the metal. *Boom!* Then another dent.

'It appears we haven't a moment to lose,' said the Doctor. 'Let's go.' He helped Tegan to her feet and began to usher the *Adamantium* crewmen from the room. Behind them, the door shook again and distorted visibly. As they left the lab complex, they all heard the repetitive clang of something hurling itself against the metal with terrible ferocity, harder and harder, and faster and faster.

Those that survived returned to the *Adamantium* in a state of shock and despair. Many of the men had lost friends and comrades, and few of them really understood how.

The Doctor and Tegan quickly caught up with the crewmen who had taken Nyssa back to the ship.

'How is she?' Tegan asked.

Nyssa looked deathly pale. There was no trace of the black bile they had seen in the crypt, however.

The Doctor examined her quickly on the medical couch. He checked her pulse and lifted each eyelid. 'She's all right,' he said at last, although his voice sounded quiet and strained. 'But she's lucky to be alive.'

He leant forward on the bed and hung his head. All his strength and vitality seemed to have been drained away. 'If anything had happened down there...' he began. 'If she'd... If I'd let anything *happen* to her...'

Tegan reached out and touched his hand. It was cold. 'It's all right, Doctor. She's going to be OK. You saved her.'

He looked up at her. His eyes looked as blue as snow shadow. 'No I didn't. I left her to the Dark and when it had finished with her, when it had *discarded* her... I took back what was left.'

'You're punishing yourself. The important thing is that she's all right, that she's free of it now.'

'But at what cost? The Dark is free. I risked her life for nothing!' He was breathing heavily. 'The Dark was in control all the time, Tegan. It used her and I knew it was using her. But I was powerless to stop it.'

'That's not your fault.'

'But the fact is that the Dark managed to do all that even *before* it was fully resurrected, Tegan. Don't you see what that means? It's been brought back to life: it's even more powerful now. How am I going to stop it?'

'You'll think of something.'

The Doctor shook his head. 'We have to see Lawrence. He has to blast off now, while he still can. At least that way we might save the lives of those that still remain.'

The Doctor and Tegan headed straight for the bridge, where they found Captain Lawrence and Jyl Stoker. One look at the Doctor's sombre expression told Lawrence all he needed to know.

'We were too late,' the Doctor told him, and quickly gave an account of what had happened. 'You have to prepare for take-off immediately, Captain. It's your only chance.'

Lawrence looked impassive. 'I see. What about Cadwell?'

'I don't know.' The Doctor slumped into a vacant chair and gingerly felt the blood that had dried around his nose. 'He got out of the crypt, I think. I didn't see him after that. Presumably the Dark got him.'

'And good riddance, if you ask me,' Tegan said bitterly. 'It was all Cadwell's fault anyway: somehow he managed to resurrect the Dark.'

There was a dry chuckle from the entrance to the bridge. 'Is that what you think?'

Silas Cadwell stood in the doorway. He was pale but there was a familiar sneer on his lips.

Lawrence stared at him. 'You'd better have a good explanation for this!'

The Doctor jumped to his feet. 'I hope you're satisfied, Cadwell! Have you even the slightest conception of what you've done?'

The smirk slid from Cadwell's face to be replaced by a look of cold fury. 'I didn't *do* anything, Doctor. That's the tragedy. It is you, I think, who doesn't have the slightest conception of what *you* have done.'

'Explain yourself, Cadwell,' Lawrence ordered.

'You've got me all wrong,' Cadwell said. He gazed at each of them in turn, fixing them with his pale stare. 'I didn't come here to resurrect the Dark. I came here to *destroy* it.'

When Nyssa woke up she felt a lot better: apart from the slightest headache and a sore throat, she felt more like her old self. She hadn't felt like this, in fact, since before the first nightmare visitation of the Dark in the TARDIS.

That, she was surprised to find, had only been a couple of days ago; to her it felt like half a lifetime. Exhausted but relieved, she swung herself from the medical couch just as Tegan came into the sickbay.

'Hey! You're looking a lot better!'

'Thank you,' Nyssa smiled.

'Let me help you up.'

'Thanks, I'm still a bit weak. But I feel so much better. Everything's a blur in my mind, Tegan. What have I missed?'

'Quite a lot,' Tegan told her. 'In fact, more than you'd think. It's a good job you're up, anyway: the Doctor says if you're up to it, you should come and hear what Silas Cadwell's got to say.'

Nyssa looked troubled. 'Cadwell?'

The meeting was convened in Lawrence's private cabin. Lawrence sat at his desk with Stoker at his side, facing Cadwell. The Doctor, Tegan and Nyssa sat slightly apart.

'What's she doing here?' Cadwell asked when he saw Nyssa.

'Nyssa has played an important role in all this,' the Doctor explained. 'She has a right to a full and proper explanation.'

'Which you will now provide.' Lawrence informed Cadwell firmly. 'The Doctor has recommended that I order the *Adamantium* to blast off without delay, but I will not give that order until I am in possession of the full facts.'

Cadwell returned the unfriendly stares with a cool indifference and a small sigh. 'Very well, Captain. I'll keep this as brief as possible.'

'Please do,' the Doctor said, with an impatient glance at Lawrence. 'We haven't much time.'

Cadwell smiled humourlessly and said, 'You might be forgiven for thinking that the story of the Dark begins on the planet Akoshemon: a world synonymous with wickedness and depravity throughout this part of the cosmos for many thousands of years. But you'd be mistaken. The planet is nothing more than a toxic wasteland now, it choked on its own poison and decay. Such an end was inevitable, when one considers its beginning: because the Dark was present at Akoshemon's birth, a terrible force for evil already ancient and cursed when Akoshemon was in its primeval infancy.'

'So where did this Dark come from?' Lawrence asked.

'I don't think anyone can answer that question,' Cadwell replied.

'But some have tried. Some believe that it was spawned alongside the universe, that it is as old as creation. Some believe that, before our own universe even existed, there were strange forces at large: gods, if you like – from before time began.'

The Doctor shifted uncomfortably in his seat. Cadwell looked at him and met his stare. 'You believe me, don't you?' he asked.

The Doctor cleared his throat. 'I've heard the theories. Legends of powerful forces for good and evil that survived the Big Bang.'

Cadwell nodded. 'The Dark is none of those. The Dark is all that remains of the void that existed before the Big Bang, the cavity in Time and Space, if you like, where those forces were first spawned. The Dark was shredded by the forces that created our universe, but it was not destroyed. For billions of years it lay spread across the universe, like the very faintest of shadows. Over the aeons it managed to reform itself, and finally coalesced amid the primal matter that became the planet Akoshemon.'

'A rather unfortunate start for a world,' the Doctor commented grimly.

'The worst! Akoshemon became a planet where evil flourished and grew, where every civilisation was locked into a downward spiral of corruption and destruction, war after war, atrocity on atrocity. Over the millennia, the wretched people of Akoshemon systematically injured, slew and desecrated every last one of their own kind. Eventually all that was terrible about the planet was distilled into a single, living being: the Dark personified.'

'Excuse me,' said Stoker, 'but how, exactly, did you find this out?'

Cadwell had lost his habitual sneer; in its place was a look of the gravest concern. He had spoken quietly but passionately, and there was no mistaking the intensity in his eyes. 'The culmination of Akoshemon's vile history was a physical form for the Dark: the first it had ever known. A thousand years ago, a band of space explorers discovered the planet Akoshemon at the very depths of its journey into Hell, and fell into conflict with the deadly evil at its core.

'At first my ancestors were caught in a simple fight for survival as they became prey to the malignant forces Akoshemon had spawned in the name of darkness. Gradually they became aware that this planet of destruction was a sad and terrible victim of something far worse, something rotten and vengeful that lurked in the darkness like a demon.

'At first they could not find it, because it had no lair: its tumescent evil existed outside the natural physical laws of the universe, like an abscess on reality. But its effects were all too apparent: greed, hunger, strife, violence, betrayal… everything that is awful and evil to us. Eventually they tracked it down, and found it in the shadows. The being they sought concealed itself there, living at one with the darkness. They called it simply *the Dark*.

'The Dark knew our universe only through the complete absence of light. In time my ancestors cornered the beast and burned it. The flames were entirely beyond its ability to withstand.'

'A very old remedy for a very old illness,' commented the Doctor.

Cadwell gave one of his thin smiles. 'Destroyed in our physical universe, the Dark left physical remains: its ashes. These were taken and buried deeply in the moon of the benighted world the Dark had poisoned to death. Stupid, really.' Cadwell's eyes hardened into the colour of flint. 'Because it wasn't enough: the Dark's physical form was destroyed, without question, but its *mind* lived on. Trapped within the ashes, of course. But it knew there was still a chance of life, of freedom. All it required was the blood of its enemies. The blood of human beings to act as a glue to join together the burnt remnants and its vile mind.'

'And Professor Oldeman provided it with a means to acquire that blood,' the Doctor said. 'He used genetic material from Akoshemon and combined it with human DNA to produce a creature that could extract the blood and take it to the crypt.'

'The Bloodhunter,' confirmed Cadwell. 'A direct descendant of the mutant abominations that had bred themselves to extinction on the Dark's host world.'

'But why would Oldeman do that?' asked Nyssa. 'Surely he wasn't in league with the Dark? I thought he came here to research into suspended-animation techniques.'

'It's doubtful Oldeman really knew what he was doing,' the Doctor said. 'I suspect he was being influenced by the Dark.' The Doctor lowered his head. 'I was foolish not to have seen that. I made Oldeman go to the crypt to see the result of what I thought was his crass stupidity. And the Bloodhunter killed him.'

'You can't hold yourself responsible for that!' Tegan protested. 'It could have been any one of us.'

'Is that supposed to make me feel better?'

'His blood was the final ingredient the Dark required,' said Cadwell. 'Don't talk about Oldeman's stupidity! You, Doctor, are a fool among fools! And your foolishness did not end there.'

The Doctor looked up bleakly at Cadwell but said nothing. Cadwell's eyes were stony but they still held a gleam of real fear.

'I said earlier that I was here to stop the Dark from being reborn,' Cadwell continued. 'I knew soon after my arrival here that the beast must be perilously close to full resurrection: as the blood congealed in the ashes, it would both bind the Dark's physical remains and give them new life. It was my intention to locate the crypt and administer a powerful anticoagulant to the contents of the pit.'

'Preventing the blood from congealing any further,' Nyssa realised.

Cadwell began to pace the room and the Doctor lowered his gaze once more.

'It might not have destroyed it,' Cadwell admitted, 'but it would have given me time to consider what to do next. It might even have saved some more lives, although in truth that was not my immediate concern.'

'Then it should have been,' said Tegan hotly. 'A lot of good men died down there unnecessarily.'

Cadwell gestured toward the Doctor. 'Look to him for an apology, my dear. I was interested only in halting the Dark's evil resurrection. *He* prevented that.'

The Doctor sprang to his feet. 'You should have said so before! Why didn't you tell us what you were here for in the first place? What you already knew? What you were intending to do!'

Cadwell shook his head. 'You are all blind fools under the power of the Dark. Only I can see what had to be done. How could I trust any single one of you with the details of my task?'

'It's not like that,' the Doctor said sharply.

'It is,' replied Cadwell. 'You know it is. You know the Dark has been trying to affect your own mind, Doctor, don't you?'

The Doctor didn't reply.

Cadwell said, 'It held your friend Nyssa in its thrall. Not even I realised just how much she was being influenced by its black presence in her mind. Perhaps I should have realised, when she kept on attacking me and trying to prevent me from reaching the crypt. The Dark knew what I intended, recognised me as a threat, and used Nyssa to try and stop me just as I was using her to help me.'

Nyssa lowered her head in shame. The Doctor grew more and more angry, striding across the room to stand before Cadwell. 'Nyssa and I are more attuned to the telepathic qualities of the Dark, it's true…'

'You mean more susceptible,' said Cadwell.

'But Tegan isn't so affected – nor is Captain Lawrence or Stoker.'

'Perhaps not. But they are all loyal to *you*, Doctor. Don't you understand? How could I trust anyone who might be loyal either to you… *or* to the Dark?'

Breathing heavily the Doctor stepped back. He seemed to have to make an effort to control his temper before speaking again. 'Be that as it may, Cadwell, we still have a duty to stop the Dark.'

'It's too late!' Cadwell protested. 'The Dark is free. There is nothing we can do. In time it will break into the laboratory complex and the upper cave system. If we are still here when it does, then every single one of us will be consumed by its evil will. We will be utterly destroyed.' Cadwell turned slowly, meeting the gaze of every single person in the room. 'Our only chance for survival is to leave, *now*.'

CHAPTER EIGHTEEN

Cadwell turned to Lawrence. 'Captain, you must prepare the *Adamantium* for immediate blast-off.'

Lawrence climbed slowly to his feet, almost wearily, and when he was standing he gazed narrowly at Cadwell before saying, 'You've never given the orders on my ship, Cadwell. You certainly won't be starting now.'

Cadwell smiled knowingly. 'I thought you'd take that attitude, Lawrence. You always were a boring stick-in-the-mud who couldn't see beyond the last line of his rule book.' He aimed a blaster pistol steadily at Lawrence's chest. 'Now, *Captain*. I'm afraid I must insist: the order, if you please, to take off.'

Lawrence growled. 'What's this, Cadwell? *Piracy?*'

The irony was not lost on Cadwell; a muscle twitched along his jaw and he raised the pistol. 'Survival,' he said.

The Doctor leapt forward, his hand slashing down on Cadwell's gun arm. The blaster discharged, punching a hole right through the deck. With a sudden twist, the Doctor forced Cadwell to drop the weapon.

Lawrence picked it up, calmly adjusted the setting, and shot Cadwell with a stun bolt as he struggled with the Doctor. With a gasp Cadwell sagged to the floor and collapsed, unconscious.

'Thank you,' the Doctor said.

'I wish I could've killed him,' said Lawrence, 'but it's against Consortium rules.'

'You're very quiet,' Tegan said as she sat down next to Jyl Stoker a little later.

Stoker looked tired and bewildered. There were dark rings under her eyes, which were still raw with tears. 'I can't think of anything worth saying,' she said. 'What's the point?'

'I think Captain Lawrence could do with a bit of help,' Tegan told her, not unkindly.

'Don't be daft,' Stoker said. 'He knows what he's doing.'

'None of this is in his rule book, surely!'

Stoker smiled sadly. 'No, but the most important thing is: secure the Consortium's mining rights to this moon.'

'You still want to contest the claim?'

'No. I don't care about the lexium any more. He's welcome to it as far as I'm concerned.'

'Then what?'

Stoker shifted uncomfortably in her seat. 'I just wish Lawrence felt the same. But I know he wants the lex more than anything, or *anyone*, else.'

'You don't know that.'

'Of course I do. Lawrence's a Consortium man. He's trained to put the Consortium first.' Stoker smiled bitterly. 'He always did. He always will.'

'Then what are you frightened of?'

'Who says I'm frightened?'

'You still love him, don't you?'

Stoker eyed Tegan carefully for a long moment. 'I fell asleep before. Not for long, but I was exhausted. And I had a dream. You'd think I'd have had a nightmare after all this, wouldn't you? But no; I had a rather pleasant dream.' Stoker paused long enough to light one of her cigars. 'It was one of those stupid dreams where you meet the person you love. Really love. You know: it's perfect. It feels so natural and right and good that there's no mistaking it. True love. Sounds kind of corny, I suppose.'

Tegan shook her head. 'And this person in your dream would be...?'

'Lawrence, of course,' Stoker said sadly. 'It always is. You see, I've had the dream before.'

'Sounds like a good dream.'

'It isn't. Because when I wake up, the dream fades.' Stoker blew out a cloud of smoke and watched it slowly dissipate. 'All I'm left with is cold, hard reality.'

'Does Lawrence know how you feel?'

'How can he when not even I know how I feel?' Stoker stubbed out her cigar angrily. 'This isn't the right time to find out, anyway.'

'Now is exactly the right time,' Tegan said. 'And I mean for both of you. At the moment, I think what you really need more than anything else… is each other.'

Lawrence coughed quietly to attract the Doctor's attention. 'Don't be so hard on yourself, man. You weren't to know what Cadwell was up to. None of us could have guessed.'

The Doctor, who had been sitting staring at the floor for the last ten minutes, looked up gloomily. 'I knew more than most: I knew the Dark was here, waiting to be freed. I knew Nyssa was under its malign influence.'

Nyssa touched his hand gently. 'You couldn't have known what would happen to Ravus Oldeman. Stop blaming yourself.'

'But perhaps I *did* know what would happen,' argued the Doctor. 'Perhaps I, too, was being influenced by the Dark.'

'Then how can you blame yourself?'

'Because anything else is just too convenient,' said the Doctor steadily. 'I refuse to let the Dark assume responsibility for my actions.' Abruptly he stood up and faced Lawrence. 'Captain, have you reached your decision?'

Lawrence nodded briefly. 'Yes. I intend to follow your advice, Doctor, and prepare for take-off. The sooner we're away from this blasted moon the better.'

'Thank you.'

'I have to say that it irks me to think that in doing so I'm also following Cadwell's advice, though,' Lawrence added ruefully.

'Indeed,' said the Doctor. 'It is the one thing we're all agreed upon, at least.'

Lawrence paused at the door of his cabin. 'I assume that you will be accompanying us, Doctor. No damn fool heroic idea of staying behind? I seem to recall that was your original plan.'

The Doctor hesitated before replying, aware of a searching look from Nyssa. 'No, Captain. It's not a risk I'm prepared to take any longer. I certainly can't allow Tegan and Nyssa to be exposed to such extreme danger. Even if I did elect to stay behind, I'm afraid they would insist on staying with me.'

Nyssa smiled sadly at him. 'You know us too well, Doctor.'

'Then it's settled,' the Doctor said. 'We stay with the *Adamantium*.'

It was with a palpable sense of relief, passing through the vessel like the hum of its engines as they started to warm up, that everyone on board the *Adamantium* prepared to leave the moon of Akoshemon.

Nyssa found Tegan sitting in the mess. 'What's the matter?'

'I'm not sure. I just feel a bit down.' Tegan rubbed her eyes. 'Maybe I'm just tired.'

'It's this place,' Nyssa told her with a shiver. 'The moon, I mean. The Dark must be affecting everyone in some way.'

'That's what the Doctor said.'

'Perhaps it's for the best that we're leaving.'

'Yeah. I just hope we can get the TARDIS back.'

'The Doctor says that won't be a problem: he's got some sort of remote-control device with him, and he can bring the TARDIS to us when we're safely away from the moon.'

'I won't feel safe again until we're a million miles from here – and about a million years.'

Nyssa chewed her lip thoughtfully. 'It's a bit odd, don't you think?'

'What?'

'The Doctor, backing off. I've never seen him like this: it's almost as if he's frightened.'

'Probably with good reason.' Tegan shrugged. 'I suppose even Time Lords get the heebie-jeebies.'

'It doesn't make any sense. The Doctor said we'd never be free of the Dark until it was destroyed, remember? That it could always find the TARDIS again in the space-time vortex. So what's the use of running away? It's not like him.'

Tegan frowned. 'You're right, it isn't. And I've never heard of any remote-control gadget for the TARDIS before, either.'

'Do you think he's lying to us?'

Tegan stood up. 'We'd better find him!'

Stoker stepped onto the bridge and felt her stomach twitch the moment she saw Lawrence. He was standing with his back to her, looking tall and ramrod straight, shoulders squared. She felt a huge rush of affection for him.

When he turned around his eyes glittered and he smiled that perfect, white smile. She noticed, too, that he had somehow found the time to shave before arriving on the bridge. 'Hello there,' he said. His voice was low and soft. 'We're nearly up to speed: blast-off in ten minutes.'

'Ah,' Stoker said. 'Just enough time.'

He was still smiling. The decision to leave had been the right one. 'Just enough time for what?'

'This.' She walked over to him and kissed him. 'I bet that's not part of the normal take-off procedure.'

'It isn't,' he said. 'But it damn well ought to be.'

Various control consoles around the bridge were humming into life, displays lighting and flickering. The power build-up from the ship's engines could be felt through the soles of their feet. The computers whirred happily as the *Adamantium* gradually came back to life.

'I've missed you,' Lawrence said. He clasped Stoker's shoulders in his large, powerful hands. 'You're everything to me.'

Stoker felt her heart beating faster and faster as the whine of the ship's motors began to increase. 'What about the lexium?'

He flashed a feral smile that she had never seen before. 'What about it? Let it rot on this godforsaken hole with the Dark.'

'You say the nicest things.'

He pulled her to him and kissed her again. Stoker was surprised at how cold his lips felt on hers.

The Doctor stopped in front of the cabin door and tripped the lock. The door hissed open and he went in. Silas Cadwell sat on the small, narrow bunk opposite and eyed him blearily.

'It's polite to knock first,' he said.

'I was rather hoping you'd still be unconscious,' replied the Doctor.

Cadwell smiled. 'I told you – I'm made of pretty stern stuff, Doctor. It takes more than a stun beam to keep me down. And my congratulations, by the way: you caught me off guard for a second there on the bridge. Well done. Never knew you had it in you.'

'You'll find I'm full of surprises.'

'I'll take it this is a social call, then.'

'Sorry,' said the Doctor. 'I'm particular about the company I keep.'

'Ah, pity. Only I'm confined to quarters so there's little else for me to do but entertain visitors.'

'I'm afraid we've run out of time for a chat, Cadwell. The ship is almost ready for blast-off.'

'Judging by the sound of the engines, we could be leaving any minute,' Cadwell said. 'What do you want?'

'I want to know how to stop the Dark.'

Cadwell laughed out loud. 'You can't! I've already told you that. Are you deaf as well as wet?'

'It's been stopped before,' argued the Doctor. 'Your ancestors defeated it on Akoshemon, or so you say. They used fire.'

'Oh, yes! "A very old remedy for a very old illness", I think you said. Very poetic!'

'We could stop it again. I'll help you.'

A grey cloud gathered in Cadwell's eyes. 'You? Help me? It's a bit late for that, Doctor!'

The Doctor grabbed Cadwell's arm and pulled him to his feet. 'There isn't any time for recriminations, Cadwell! The Dark *has* to be stopped.'

'Using fire?' Cadwell yanked his arm free and sneered. 'Don't be ridiculous. The Dark is cunning and hungry for life. It won't be caught the same way twice.'

'But if it could be weakened in some way first…'

'That was what *I* was trying to do, if you care to remember.' Cadwell shook his head. 'It's *unstoppable*, Doctor. It's more than just a force of nature; it's *unnatural*. That's the whole point. It's not even from our universe. It isn't bound by the same laws of physics that we are. There's nothing we can do that can affect it. The best we can hope for is to escape with our lives, which is what we're doing now.'

The sound of the *Adamantium*'s primary engines had reached maximum pitch; the deck plates were vibrating beneath their feet. Cadwell lay back down on his bunk and put his hands behind his head. 'I'm not proud of what I've done here, Doctor. My mission has been a failure and I've betrayed the trust of my ancestors in allowing the Dark to live again.' He stared blankly at the ceiling. 'I could have stopped it, but it's too late now.'

The Doctor turned on his heel and left without another word.

Tegan and Nyssa went to the bridge to witness the blast-off. Tegan smiled at Stoker when she saw her standing close to Lawrence. Stoker gave her a thumbs-up and grinned back.

'Prepare launch sequence,' said Lawrence calmly. The computer bleeped in response and a number of indicator lights flashed. Lawrence turned to the others. 'You're just in time: we lift off in sixty seconds.'

Everyone on deck could feel the anticipatory throb of the ship's engines. 'I wonder where the Doctor's got to?' said Tegan.

'He'll be here soon,' said Lawrence.

Tegan turned to Nyssa. 'I don't like the thought of him being on his own right now. From what you've told me he seemed pretty stressed.'

'I'm sure he's fine,' Lawrence insisted. 'Stop worrying. I'd take a seat if I were you.'

They lowered themselves into the padded chairs, uncomfortably aware that they belonged to dead men.

Stoker slipped into Silas Cadwell's seat with a nervous smile. 'Can't wait to get away from this place.'

Lawrence smiled at her but remained standing. The deck shuddered as the primary engines directed power to the take-off thrusters and the *Adamantium* rose into the air.

'I don't like this,' Nyssa whispered to Tegan, reaching out to her.

Tegan squeezed her hand gently. 'No worries. Take-off's all right. I love this bit!'

The ship thrummed with power and floated gently upwards, with none of the sudden acceleration and heart-stopping lurching into the air that Tegan vividly remembered from her airline days.

On the viewport they could all see the jagged, glassy surface of the moon lowering beneath a plume of green dust. The engines rumbled and slowly the *Adamantium* began to turn. The horizon disappeared from view to be replaced by empty space; empty save for the bright specks of distant stars.

'Twenty degrees to starboard,' ordered Lawrence confidently. Akoshemon swung into view as the ship turned, glowing red and black like a lump of burning coal. Nyssa closed her eyes.

The planet rolled smoothly out of sight as the ship continued to turn. Eventually the *Adamantium* faced nothing but the open blackness of intergalactic space: the abyss, Tegan recalled, between star systems. The sight of the endless darkness made her shiver.

Lawrence was staring at the viewport, his blue eyes intense. It was almost as if he could see something out there in the void.

'Something's wrong,' Tegan announced.

The Doctor stepped cautiously into the laboratory complex. Even here, deep beneath the surface of the moon, he could sense the heavy beat of the *Adamantium's* thrusters on the rock above.

The equipment around the lab rattled as the vessel took flight, and a tiny shower of dust rained down on the Doctor's shoulders. For a few moments he thought that he could actually hear the ship's powerful engines, but he knew that was impossible down here.

The Doctor let out a sigh of relief when he was sure the

Adamantium had blasted off safely. At least he could be certain that Tegan and Nyssa were now out of danger. This was not for them: *this* was something he had to face alone. Adric's death was still the sharpest thorn in his memory: he could not bear the thought of having to endure a loss so tragic and foolish again. Nearly losing Nyssa here had filled him with the deep, heavy dread of a pain from which he knew he would never recover.

Alone, he could take the risks that might prove necessary. He did not want to die here, but he was ready to, now, if it finally came to that. The terror he had felt when he had connected with the Dark through Nyssa, the apparitions of his own mortal life being ripped out time after time, death upon death, had been so powerful that it still felt like a physical injury in his brain. The scar was fresh in his mind, still tender to the touch. But if Vega Jaal's chillingly accurate vision of his *death after death* was to be his destiny, then the Doctor could face it in the knowledge that he would, at least, not be taking anyone else with him.

Apart from his possible future selves of course. Best not to think about *that*.

The lab complex was still brightly lit, and it was quiet. The Doctor was glad that the generator was still functioning, but he wondered what the Dark was up to. It appeared to have given up hurling itself against the lab door, but it was unlikely to have gone into retreat. More likely it was planning something else.

The Doctor crossed over to the door that led to the caverns. It was buckled and dented but still sealed. He reached out to touch it, resting only the tips of his fingers against the metal. It was cold, as cold as the rock he had felt outside the crypt: a deep, internal chill that made him shiver.

He pressed the flat of his hand against the door. Somewhere on the other side of that a monster waited for him. Well, I'm here now, he thought. I've made my walk from the shelter of the pavilion and I'm standing at the crease, bat in hand. Let's see what you can throw at me.

'Where's the Doctor?' demanded Tegan, rising from her seat. 'He should be here, with us.'

'I haven't seen him for a while,' confessed Stoker, turning to Lawrence. 'Do you know where he is?'

Lawrence didn't reply, he was still concentrating on the blank rectangle of the viewport. Stoker reached out and touched his hand, but his skin was as cold as stone.

Stoker got to her feet. 'Hey, what's up?'

Lawrence ignored her. He stepped down from the command deck to the helm and began to operate the controls. He was frowning now, fiercely, and they could see the sweat standing out on his forehead.

'What's he doing?' Tegan asked.

Lawrence hit a switch and a metallic voice said, 'Computer off-line.'

Nyssa stood up. 'He's disengaging the autopilot!'

Lawrence twisted his head around and scowled at the women. His lips were coated in spit. 'You simple-minded wretches! Did you think you'd get away from *me*?'

He turned back and ran his hands across the navigation board. Bright warning lights flashed beneath his fingers and he clawed at the controls and the ship gave a sudden, sickening lurch.

Tegan, Nyssa and Stoker sprawled as the vessel listed dramatically. The engines howled as the *Adamantium* dipped its heavy nose back down towards the moon.

Stoker crawled back towards Lawrence. 'What are you doing? You'll kill us all!'

He lashed out with his boot and kicked her away. Tegan helped to catch her and together they watched the jagged surface of Akoshemon's moon fill the viewport.

Lawrence pulled out a blaster and aimed it at the women. He was laughing.

'What's happened to him?' wailed Stoker.

'It must be the Dark!' cried Nyssa. 'Controlling him!'

'Lawrence,' screamed Tegan. 'Stop this! Fight it! You must!'

Stoker crawled back towards him, holding out her hand. 'Please!

Please, Lawrence! Don't do this! Not now!'

The surface of the moon began to rise up towards them on the viewport. The ship's engines seemed to be snarling with anger as they pushed the vessel downwards.

Stoker held on to the helm control panel, pulling herself up. 'Lawrence, don't do this! It's the Dark! It's in your head!'

Lawrence sneered at her. 'You pathetic little cow.'

Then he turned and fired his blaster pistol point-blank into the helm controls. There was a blinding flash and an eruption of flame. The *Adamantium* gave a groan of agony and tipped further forward, almost standing on its nose as it fell towards the ground below.

Tegan and Nyssa grabbed hold of each other just before it hit.

PART THREE
EXIT WOUNDS

What's gone, and what's past help
should be past grief
William Shakespeare

CHAPTER NINETEEN

The Doctor ducked instinctively when he heard the crash. The lab complex heaved as if struck by an earthquake. The floor bucked beneath his feet and equipment scattered off the work surfaces.

The laboratory continued to shudder for several seconds as something huge scraped along the rock above: a few small stones fell through the cracks in the roof and a cloud of dust filled the room.

The Doctor held on to the nearest solid object: the door. He felt, rather than heard, a massive explosion and the lab shook again. A number of ceiling tiles fell down with a clatter around him and then there was silence.

He listened to his own breathing for a few seconds. Something akin to real panic was making his hearts race; breathing slowly and deeply he fought to control the hammering double-beat. He then peered warily at the ceiling, but there was no way to assess the damage. All he could do was hope that it, and the thousands of tons of rock above it, would hold up.

The whole moon seemed to let out a groan of despair.

The Doctor closed his eyes, trying not to imagine what had actually happened, trying not to visualise the wreckage or consider the implications. Tegan. Nyssa.

He couldn't move. He was paralysed, frozen against the door. He was leaning on it, like a drunk or a man at sea in a storm, unable to stand upright. He could feel the deep, insidious cold seeping through his clothes, crawling under his skin, chilling his blood. His hands were stuck to the doorframe.

There was a loud, metallic crack and something gave fractionally beneath him.

He looked down. Around the edge of the door, there was a shadow. It was oozing through the crack, a thin glimmer of absolute darkness.

It was coming for him.

The Doctor tore himself from the door and hurled himself across the lab, skidding on the debris. He reached the exit and charged back up the steps.

Tegan coughed and spat out blood, found it tasted of smoke and nearly retched.

She was on all fours, trying to keep a grip on the floor. The deck was leaning up at a crazy angle. If she let go she would slide right down to who knew what. Behind her she could hear the snap and crackle of flames, smell the fumes from burning electric cables and plastic whatever. All around her she could see a haze of black fog. She knew that if she didn't move soon the smoke would kill her.

And the heat.

Rabbits! This place was on *fire*.

'Nyssa?'

'Over here!' Nyssa appeared through the smoke, her face smudged black, her eyes wide with shock.

With Nyssa's help Tegan climbed off the inclined deck and slid over to one of the control seats. It was bent back on itself, parallel with the floor. Leaning over it was Stoker, blood running freely down her face from her nose.

'We've got to get out of here,' Tegan said. 'The whole place might blow up any second.'

'It's a miracle we survived,' Nyssa said.

'Not a miracle,' gasped Stoker. She raised a hand and pointed across the twisted remains of the bridge. A body was slumped over the helm controls: Lawrence. 'He tried to pull us out of the dive at the last second. I saw him!'

'Is he hurt?' asked Tegan.

'He's dead,' said Stoker flatly.

Tegan moved towards the helm to check, but the deck shifted

suddenly beneath her. A metallic grinding noise filled the smoky air as the bows started to collapse. The whole port side of the bridge suddenly fell away, sheered clean off the ship by the crash. Electrical cables and power lines snapped and gushed sparks everywhere. Tegan jumped back, crouching low. Smoke rolled out towards the empty space and for a second they all had a glimpse of dark, sharp rock jutting through the metal and plastic of the hull. A cold wind blew in.

Something exploded on the far side of the bridge, flames spurting along the floor. The entire ship lurched and sank against the rock with a terrible noise. Lawrence's body slipped off the helm console and rolled lifelessly onto the deck. The breeze threw a sheet of flames over him.

'No!' Stoker cried out, falling to her knees.

Tegan grabbed hold of her. 'Come on. If we don't move we'll all burn to death.'

Tegan and Nyssa helped Stoker up and together they tried to cross to the rear of the bridge where the exit was. An angry fire was chewing its way through the plastic of the frame, and the airlock itself was bent right out of shape.

'Exit's blocked,' Tegan called over the noise of the flames.

'We'll have to get out that way,' Nyssa said, pointing to the huge rent on the port side.

They staggered across the deck, leaning against the tilt. Halfway across, Tegan slipped on something and they all fell in a painful heap. The fire roared behind them, reaching out with scalding hands, trying to catch hold of anything flammable.

Nyssa crawled on with Stoker, coughing and choking on the fumes. Tegan found that she had slipped in something wet and red: a stream of blood that ran from beneath Lawrence's body. The blood sizzled as the flames lapped it up.

She caught up with Nyssa and Stoker. 'How are we going to get out?' she demanded. They could all see the rock, but they could also see the razor-sharp, metal teeth of the *Adamantium* where it had bitten into the moon's surface.

The three of them let out a loud squeak of surprise as the deck suddenly moved again, slipping down the rock. Sparks flew from the metal as it grazed against the stone.

'We've got to move soon!' Nyssa shouted. The metallic scrape of the hull against the rock outside was now constant and control consoles were bursting into flames all over the bridge. The ship was determined to die; it was writhing in agony, but all the time pushing itself harder against the spears of rock upon which it was impaled.

Tegan guided Stoker towards the jagged metal precipice. 'We'll lower you down.'

Another explosion rocked the ship and it pitched sideways, hurling the three of them towards the hole. Tegan felt her head hit something hard and then had a confused glimpse of the rocks. She scrabbled for a grip and felt her wrist grasped by a strong, warm hand.

'Don't worry, I've got you.'

'Doctor!' she yelled, opening her eyes. The Doctor was holding her, pulling her out onto the rock. His white trainers stood out starkly against the slippery black stone as he braced himself to take her weight.

'Thought you might need a hand,' he told her.

'Where the hell were you?' Tegan climbed onto the rock and yanked her arm free. 'Where's Nyssa and Stoker?'

'They're all right,' the Doctor said. 'They've already made it down to the ground: it's not far.'

Tegan heard Nyssa call out, saw her standing on the moon's surface a couple of metres away. Stoker was kneeling on the ground next to her.

'If you're going to jump,' said the Doctor in her ear, 'I'd advise you to do so sooner rather than later. I don't know how much longer this wreckage is going to stay put.'

As if to underline his concern, the *Adamantium* gave another terrible death-rattle. Tegan jumped down from the rock and joined the others, the Doctor following. 'I suggest we get away from here,' he urged them. 'Where's Captain Lawrence?'

'Dead,' said Tegan. 'It was Lawrence who crashed the ship.'

'Was it indeed?'

'No,' said Stoker defiantly. 'It wasn't him! It was the Dark.'

The Doctor nodded thoughtfully. 'I'm very sorry.'

Stoker lowered her head. 'Just get me away from here.'

'What about Cadwell?' asked the Doctor.

'I don't know,' said Tegan. 'He wasn't on the bridge when we crashed.'

'He was confined to his quarters,' the Doctor reminded them. 'He might still be there.'

'He's probably been killed!'

'I'll have to check,' the Doctor said. He turned and climbed back up the rock towards the tangled wreck of the *Adamantium*'s bridge.

'Don't be stupid!' Tegan called after him.

'It's too dangerous!' Nyssa argued.

The Doctor paused on the threshold of the wreckage. 'He could be trapped, or hurt. We can't leave him.'

Tegan said, 'Yes we can! Doctor, this thing could blow up at any moment!'

'I'll be back in a jiffy,' he called, disappearing inside the bridge. Smoke rolled out of the torn hull and the metal groaned again.

'He's mad,' Stoker said dully. 'It's suicide.'

'The Doctor specialises in suicide attempts,' Tegan said.

An explosion rocked the front end of the ship and flames blew out of the open wound in the hull. The three of them turned and ran as the bows of the ship disintegrated in a ball of orange flames.

The *Adamantium* was on its side, nose buried in the rocky surface of the moon, snorting flames. The tail fins stood proudly from its aft end, the thrusters still glowing, but the main hull was ruptured and charred. Fire was spreading quickly throughout the vessel: flames could be seen through the portholes.

'He'll never get out,' Tegan said miserably. Another conflagration erupted around the ship's bows and the bridge collapsed into a tangle of burning metal. The rest of the ship sank with a final, metallic rending and smaller, brighter explosions ripped along the length of the hull like gunfire.

'We've got to get right away from here,' Stoker said. 'Down into the caves, it's our only chance.'

'What about the Doctor?' cried Nyssa.

'Done for. Come on!'

'Wait!' shouted Tegan, pointing. The side of the *Adamantium* closest to the ground was torn wide open and the ship's guts were hanging out: loose cabling and chunks of smouldering machinery. Flames were bleeding from the wound, but there was something moving through the smoke: a pale figure stumbling beneath a heavy burden.

'I don't believe it,' said Stoker.

The Doctor came running, crouched low, a figure hanging limply over his shoulders. Through clenched teeth, he yelled at them all to get down. Just as he threw Silas Cadwell's body to the ground, the *Adamantium* finally blew up with a massive, deafening howl of protest. Bright yellow fire leapt for the night sky, trailing debris. A wave of hot, pressurised air scalded them where they lay, face down in the dust.

'Sorry about that,' panted the Doctor as the noise of the explosion died away. 'Took a bit longer than I intended.'

'It's time we pooled our resources,' the Doctor told Silas Cadwell a little later. They were in the main cavern again: Cadwell was sitting sullenly against the rock wall while the Doctor paced back and forth.

Cadwell was nursing an ugly head wound. The pad of material he was using to staunch the flow of blood was entirely red. 'Don't be ridiculous,' he said faintly.

'We haven't any choice,' said the Doctor.

'That's what I mean,' Cadwell replied. He dabbed at the cut on his scalp and winced. 'The Dark's going to kill us: we don't have any choice in the matter.'

The Doctor turned abruptly on his heel, hands deep in his trouser pockets. 'I'm sure your ancestors would be proud of you. They fought the Dark for centuries, so you said.'

'We haven't got centuries. If we're lucky, we've only a few hours.'

'Lucky?'

'I'm trapped here with the Dark,' Cadwell explained carefully, as if the Doctor was stupid. 'Death can't come soon enough.'

'Now you're just being melodramatic.'

'Don't try and goad me into helping you, Doctor,' Cadwell said.

'I refuse to give up hope.'

'You're pathetic.'

'At least I'm prepared to do something.'

'Oh, don't get me wrong: I fully intend to *do* something.' Cadwell tossed the blood-soaked bandage away and smiled at the Doctor. 'I'll blow my own brains out before I let the Dark get to me. I could have died quite happily on the *Adamantium*, if it hadn't been for you. Once again, your Space Cadet heroics have only made matters worse.'

The Doctor squatted down in front of him. 'I need your help, Cadwell. I don't want Tegan and Nyssa involved in this.'

'They already are, you fool.' Cadwell shook his head sadly. 'If I were you, I'd put a bullet through their heads before the Dark catches them: it's by far the kindest thing to do.'

The Doctor stood up with a hiss of exasperation. 'All right, Cadwell. If you won't help me, I'll do it myself.'

Cadwell lay back against the rock wall and gazed mockingly at the Doctor. 'What are you planning?'

For a long time the Doctor said nothing. Then, taking a deep breath, he said, 'Tegan and Nyssa are helping Stoker search the *Adamantium* wreckage for a zenesium flare.'

'A zenesium flare?'

'Incredibly powerful light source, used as a beacon during planetary surveys.'

'Yes, I know what it is!'

The Doctor looked intently at Cadwell. 'If I can detonate one close enough to the Dark, there might be enough light energy to… to…'

'To *what*, exactly?'

'Well, I'm not sure: destroy it, hopefully. Stun it, even. Something. Anything.'

'That's pretty desperate!'

'It's all I've got!' the Doctor thundered. 'Have you a better idea, Mr Cadwell, because if you have then I'd be very glad to hear it!'

Cadwell simply looked at the Doctor as if he was insane.

'At the very least,' the Doctor added quietly, 'it's something to do while I'm waiting for the Dark to come and destroy us all.'

'What's the Doctor up to?' Tegan asked. 'Why does he want this flare thing anyway?'

Tegan, Nyssa and Stoker were working their way through the wreckage of the *Adamantium*. The fires had all but died out now, and the ship's smouldering remains appeared to have settled. A good part of the starboard side of the ship was still intact and undamaged by the fire. It was in this section of the ship that the practical survey equipment had been stored.

'I suppose he thinks it might be useful against the Dark,' Nyssa said. 'He must be working on the theory that it will avoid light, or perhaps even find it harmful.'

'Sounds pretty desperate if you ask me,' Stoker muttered, ducking beneath a partially collapsed section of the corridor ceiling.

Every so often the ship would give out a metallic groan or a series of heavy, distant clangs as it settled; as far as they could tell it was reasonably safe for the moment but Tegan found the trip very unnerving. She expressed this feeling via a stream of constant complaints.

'We've got to try something,' Nyssa argued. 'We can't run away from the Dark. We can't reason with it. We have to stand and fight.'

'But it's going to be like standing and fighting an elephant with a pea-shooter!'

'What's a pea-shooter?'

'It's a small tube kids use to blow peas out of.'

'Peas?'

'Yeah. Little round vegetables. About this big.'

'I see,' Nyssa said. 'What's an elephant?'

'Oh, never mind!'

*

The Doctor threw down the comlink in disgust. 'Antiquated junk!'

'That's Consortium property,' Cadwell warned. 'You break it, you pay for it.'

'I'm trying to get in touch with Nyssa and Tegan: they're taking too long.'

'What's the hurry?'

The Doctor was still pacing up and down the cave. He stopped and glowered at Cadwell. 'Look around you.'

Cadwell looked around him. 'What?'

'What can you see?'

'The cave. Some of Stoker's crappy equipment. You. Not much else.'

'Why not much else?'

Cadwell shrugged. 'It's too dark.'

The Doctor nodded slowly. 'And it's getting darker. It has been getting darker ever since we came down here.'

Cadwell sat up, suddenly tense.

The Doctor squatted down close to him again. 'When the *Adamantium* crash landed, the impact fractured the door seal in the laboratory complex. There was a fractional gap. It was still very bright in the lab itself, and I think that held it at bay for a little while, but the Dark started to seep through. Even now it's forcing its way out of the catacombs, into the lab complex. And then up here, into the caverns. It's gathering up here, preparing to strike. That's why it's getting darker. It's coming for us.'

'Here's the stores section,' said Stoker. The deck was twisted out of shape, and it was difficult to stand upright. She edged forward and shone her torch through the buckled doorway: the door itself was a bent piece of metal lying on the floor. 'There's a fair bit of stuff in here: space suits, survival equipment, portable sensor suites. All the latest mod cons. The Consortium always had good kit.'

She climbed through the doorway and the deck immediately groaned.

'Look out!' Tegan cried, clutching at the corridor wall. Something clanged deeper inside the wreck, a sonorous tolling that rattled everyone's nerves.

'I think this might be riskier than we first thought,' admitted Stoker. She moved forward and the deck complained loudly once more.

'Be careful,' said Nyssa.

'I'm OK.' Stoker shone the torch around the storeroom. 'I think the zenesium flares are over here.'

'Can you reach them?'

'I'll try: it looks like part of the wall's gone, though... it's smashed the lockers wide open.'

'Is it safe?' Tegan pointed her own torch through the doorway. 'I can't see much.'

Stoker slowly knelt down. 'Some of the flares have been crushed. But there's one here which still looks functional.' She leant forward to pick it up and the whole deck suddenly tilted. 'Whoa!'

'Keep still!' Nyssa instructed. It was then that they all heard the comlink bleep again. Nyssa pulled the handset from her trouser pocket. 'Doctor? Is that you?'

There was a crackle from the device followed by the Doctor's voice, small and tinny: '...terference. We haven't... deal of time... etting dark...'

'You're breaking up,' Nyssa informed him.

'Can't hear... very well,' the Doctor replied. 'You're breaking...'

Tegan leant over and took the mike. 'Doctor! We've found the flares! We'll be right back!'

More crackling. '... you, Tegan? There's no need to shout.'

'Tell him I've got it,' Stoker called, and then she screamed.

Part of the deck had suddenly given way, falling through with a shriek of torn metal. Stoker hurled herself forward, scrabbling for the door. Tegan grabbed her and pulled her to safety as the whole storeroom caved in behind her.

'The flare!' cried Stoker.

'I've got it!' Nyssa said, leaning into the jagged black hole. 'It's just here...'

The ship lurched and Nyssa pitched forward into the empty space. As she fell, she flung the zenesium canister back into the corridor.

'Nyssa!'

Tegan leant forward but the ship moved again and she felt herself pulled back from the edge. 'Leave it!' ordered Stoker. 'Or you'll go with her!'

'I can't leave her!' Tegan turned back. 'Nyssa! Are you OK?'

There was no answer, save the cracking and groaning of the starship's hull bending under its own weight.

'What's happening?' the Doctor's voice crackled over the radio. 'Have you got… flare?'

'Doctor!' Tegan yelled into the mike. 'The ship's collapsing and Nyssa's fallen somewhere inside. She's not answering me!'

'…orry, didn't quite… that. Say again.'

'I said –'

'Never mind… isn't any time to… ust have the zenesium fl… soon.'

Tegan shook the little radio furiously. 'But you don't understand!'

'Getting darker…' the Doctor's voice sounded strained. 'Please hurry…'

Stoker said, 'I'll go: I've got the flare. You stay here and see if you can help Nyssa.'

Tegan nodded dumbly, tears in her eyes.

'Don't do anything stupid,' Stoker told her. 'This place could fall apart any second.'

Tegan watched Stoker go. 'My whole life is spent doing stupid things,' she complained.

Stoker clambered back through the *Adamantium* and emerged from a large hole amidships, jumping down to the sandy ground below. She picked her way through the debris surrounding the crash site and headed back for the cave entrance. She didn't understand what was happening, but the Doctor really needed the zenesium flare and it had sounded urgent. And it gave her something to do, something to fill her mind so she didn't have to think any more. She didn't have to think about Bunny Cheung. She didn't have to think about Lawrence.

Her footsteps slowed as she made her way across the surface of the moon. It was very cold out here, colder than she remembered it. The chill seemed to have passed straight through her clothes and skin, and penetrated every bone in her body. She shivered and then became aware of something else: the silence.

It had always been quiet on the surface, but now the quiet seemed unnatural, as if every sound had been deadened. It was the crisp, abnormal silence that followed a deep snowfall: the only noise she could detect were her own footsteps, strangely loud as they crunched into the sand.

Now she could hear her own breath, getting faster and faster.

Something made her look up at the stars.

Only there were no stars. The heavens had been dimmed along with all that she could no longer hear. To one side was the impenetrable blackness of the intergalactic void: but where there had once been the bright haze of the nearest star systems there was now only a dull, grey fog. Akoshemon, a hard scab on the night sky, was now barely visible.

Stoker clutched the zenesium flare tighter and sprinted for the cave entrance.

Inside the spaceship, Tegan leaned as far as she dared into the black space that had been the stores section. The hull was badly torn and the decking had given away, but she couldn't see a thing: she couldn't even tell how far Nyssa had fallen. She hadn't answered Tegan's calls. She could have been knocked unconscious or worse.

Tegan angled the beam of her torch down into the well of blackness again. She could see nothing but a tangled mass of metal and electric cabling and an awful lot of shadow.

'Nyssa?' she called again. 'Are you OK?'

Nyssa was hanging upside down, her legs caught in a mass of wires and power conduits. Luckily there seemed to be no power running through them. After a short struggle she managed to extricate her feet from the web of cables and tumbled to the ground.

It took a few seconds for her to realise that she was lying in sand. She must have fallen right through the base of the ship, where the outer hull had been torn away. She shuffled around in the dark until she was able to determine that she was now trapped beneath the wreckage, enclosed on all sides by tangled metal and plastic.

But there was a breeze coming from somewhere; she could feel its cool breath on her face. Or was that actually someone breathing? Startled, Nyssa moved quickly away.

Then she glimpsed a light: a wavering spot of yellow, sliding over the sand and the fallen decking. Her heart leaped: it was the beam of a torch, probably belonging to Tegan or Stoker. They were looking for her.

Then she heard Tegan's voice calling her. She sounded a long way off. How far had she fallen? Nyssa picked her way through the debris, heading back to the spot where she had originally landed. But just as she was about call back, a large hand was clamped over her mouth.

She struggled violently but her assailant had the advantage of surprise. Nyssa felt herself forced down into the sand. The hand over her mouth smelled of cooked meat.

As her fear-widened eyes grew accustomed to the darkness, she was able to see the shape of a man bending over her. A stray light, probably from Tegan's torch, momentarily picked out his features: a charred, blackened head, teeth bared where the flesh of his jaws had been completely burned away. Bloodshot eyes gleaming red before disappearing into shadow as the torchlight passed.

But Nyssa had seen enough.

She had recognised those pain-wracked eyes. And recognised the uniform.

It was the raw and blistered remains of Captain Lawrence.

CHAPTER TWENTY

The burnt figure leaned closer. It was Lawrence, Nyssa reminded herself. Captain Lawrence. How could he have possibly survived?

Nyssa could feel his breath on her skin; it smelled of ashes. She heard the blackened lips parting, heard him trying to speak, but he couldn't summon a voice that was anything more than a dry, incoherent rasp.

Eventually his hand fell away from her mouth and Nyssa gagged. She could see him more clearly now, even in the dark. His burns were awful, the injuries incredible. His face was caked in blood, which had been boiled into a mask over the flesh beneath. There was very little skin left. His eyes were red and full of agony.

Tegan swore. She'd shone her torch as far as she could but found nothing. At one point she had thought she saw something moving, but she'd lost it. She'd called and called but Nyssa wasn't responding. She must have been stunned by the fall.

Just stunned.

Hands trembling, Tegan tried the radio again. 'D-Doctor? Can you hear me? Come in! Come in, please!'

Static.

She shook the radio. 'Doctor! Answer me!'

'… very faint. Speak up, Tegan!'

'Doctor! You've got to come and help! Nyssa's fallen somewhere and I can't find her.'

'Sorry. Didn't quite catch that. Say again.'

'Nyssa's in trouble!'

'Have you got the zenesium flare?'

'Oh, rabbits! Stoker's got the rotten flare, she's on her way back…'

'The wrong flare?'

Tegan tried describing it another way, to be met with a barrage of static and the remains of the Doctor's response, '…need for that kind of language, Tegan…'

Tegan was close to tears. 'But Nyssa's fallen. She's hurt. I'm going down to look for her.'

The Doctor stared at the radio in his hand.

'Well?' Cadwell asked.

'I'm not sure,' the Doctor said. He sat down next to Cadwell against the cave wall. 'There was a lot of interference. There's been some kind of problem.'

'Have they got the flare?'

'I don't know.'

'So Plan B bites the dust, eh?' Cadwell rested his head back against the rock and closed his eyes. 'Followed, no doubt, by us.'

The Doctor stared into the gathering gloom. The cave was much darker now; he almost believed that he could see the deep shadows moving, thickening, creeping closer. He pulled his feet in. 'Do you have to be so defeatist?'

'Sorry. What I meant to say was, "Not to worry, I'm sure the Seventh Galactic Fleet will touch down any moment now and rescue us in the nick of time." Is that better?'

'Sarcasm has never appealed to me, Cadwell.'

'Like I care.'

The Doctor tried the radio link again, but all he got was static. The shadows were edging closer. He turned to look at Cadwell, and was surprised to find him barely visible in the gloom. 'How long do you think we've got?'

'How should I know?'

'You're better informed about the Dark than anyone else, Cadwell. You must know something.' The Doctor took out his pencil torch and switched it on. The narrow finger of light prodded the nearest shadows back a few feet.

'Like I said, Doctor, it's impossible to know: the Dark isn't of our universe. It's not even subject to the same scientific principles.'

The Doctor chewed his lip thoughtfully. 'But in trying to exist in our universe, it *has* to find some common ground. It must adhere to some of our physical laws, or it couldn't react to anything.'

'My understanding is that it exists on many different planes at the same time,' Cadwell said.

'Yes,' the Doctor agreed. 'It's telepathic, so it has a mental presence. And I know for a fact that its mental presence can reach beyond the normal boundaries of space and time. But it also has a physical existence, because we've seen the ashes and the blood that went into making it. A *physical* presence.'

'We're talking about the Dark,' argued Cadwell. 'Darkness. Shadow. That's not something you can put a bullet in or throw off a cliff.'

'Or burn,' said the Doctor.

Cadwell frowned. 'What do you mean?'

'It was burned once, by your ancestors. To ashes. We've seen those ashes; we know it to be true. So it *did* have a physical existence, once.'

'If you're going to come to a point with all this, Doctor, then please do so quickly.'

'It wants a physical existence again, don't you see?'

'And, it's got it, largely thanks to you as I recall.'

'Not quite,' the Doctor said. 'Not *yet*.'

'I heard it trying to break the lab door down earlier. I'd say that was pretty physical.'

'Yes, but only there; only on the other side of the door. Out here, it's still formless, existing only as shadow.' The Doctor sat forward, energised by his own train of thought. 'Why?'

'It's getting darker,' Cadwell said. 'I can hardly see a thing. Switch your torch on again.'

'It *is* on.' The Doctor held the pen torch up. Its tip glowed faintly. 'But it's fading… Wait! That's it! Cadwell, I think you've got it!'

'I have?'

'The Dark can only achieve physical existence in *complete* darkness. That's why it was able to hurl itself against the lab door – it was *completely* dark on the other side. But out here it's still light.'

'But not for much longer.'

The Doctor glared at the failing pen light. 'Worrying, isn't it?'

Tegan eased herself down through the jagged gap, found a narrow foothold with the tip of her shoe, and then fell the rest of the way. She landed in a heap in the sand.

Her torch rolled a few feet away, the business end buried in the dust. For a long moment Tegan was in total darkness, spitting out the alien grit and exercising her swear words.

It was *so* dark.

She had a flash of memory, right back to her early childhood: not wanting to go upstairs to the bathroom on her own. Not straying out of her bedroom in the middle of the night unless her dad came for her, answering her call.

She had an urge to call out for him again, now.

Her fingers closed on the torch and pulled it from its grave. The light shone weakly, picking out bits of metal she couldn't identify. 'Nyssa? Are you there?'

No answer. She swept the light around but there was nothing here but bits of spacecraft wreckage. They stuck out of the sand like old tombstones, throwing up big shadows.

But no Nyssa.

She thought of checking the sand for footprints, but it was useless. Everything was mixed up and swirled around; the tracks could have meant anything.

But there was no doubt about it: Nyssa was gone.

The shadows *were* moving. They were deepest in the far corners of the cave, and up in the dim recesses of the cavern's roof, but the Doctor could see the shadows thickening there. The blackness was somehow more intense, almost intrusive, as if it was *too* black for this universe.

The darkness gathered itself, crept closer, stronger, colder.

Cadwell sat hunched against the rock, sweating with fear. His face was drawn. 'That torch won't last much longer.'

The Doctor gave the pen torch a shake. It was pointless. The light was feeble. 'Where are they with that flare?' he muttered.

'Dead, probably. We could be the last ones left alive, and now it's coming for us.'

The Doctor had to aim the torch right at Cadwell to see him now. His bald head glistened in the shadow. He was taking something from the pockets of his uniform jacket; several metallic components that he began to fit together with a series of sharp clicks. 'What's that?' asked the Doctor, pointing the torch at Cadwell's shaking fingers. The light glinted off a small handgun. 'What're you doing?'

'Like I said, I'm not waiting around for the Dark to finish me. I'll do it myself, first.'

'Don't be stupid.'

'Stupid? It's the only intelligent thing left to do, Doctor. If I'm going to die, it'll be on my terms.' Cadwell slotted a magazine into the butt of the gun. He looked up at the Doctor. 'You might want to die screaming like an infant. I do not.'

The Doctor grabbed hold of his wrist. 'I can't let you do that.'

'You can't stop me. If necessary I'll shoot you first and then do myself. Clear?' Cadwell stared at the Doctor. They were very close and Cadwell only had to whisper. 'Believe me, I'll be doing you a favour.'

'Be quiet.'

Cadwell raised the pistol and pressed it against his own head. 'Goodbye, Doctor. It's been –'

'I said be *quiet*.'

Intrigued despite himself, Cadwell hesitated. 'What?'

'Look,' the Doctor instructed. 'And listen.'

The darkness had clotted in the centre of the cave: there was no ignoring it, no denying it. A mass of blackness, too much blackness, bulging out of the shadows like a tumour on reality. It hurt the eyes to look at it, as if all the available light was being painfully sucked into nothing.

They could hear it, too. A faint rushing noise at first, like the hiss of a distant waterfall, but growing louder all the time. Soon it sounded like the roar of a crowd, a thousand voices raised in exultation – or torment. A million voices, crying out for mercy: screaming in agony and despair.

'The people of Akoshemon,' said Cadwell, his voice barely a breath in the Doctor's ears. 'Or the things they became…'

The Doctor gritted his teeth, unable to block out the searing river of anguish as it poured down the centuries. 'We're too late. It's here.'

With a rising howl, like a million souls tortured beyond the point of madness, the Dark solidified. Shadows rushed towards it like children to their mother. It grew darker, and deeper, with every passing second and each additional shadow.

Something huge cast its shade into the universe.

The pen torch's tiny bulb died. The Doctor and Cadwell were embraced by the darkness.

It heaved and sucked and clawed its way from nowhere, right in front of them. They couldn't see it. But they could hear its first guttural breath, feel the rancid air on their fear-pricked skin. The blackness pressed against their eyes, filled their ears, probed every orifice with a clammy urgency.

Something moved in the dark, heavy and wet as a bath full of worms.

A cold, moist finger touched the Doctor's face.

Up until that point the Doctor had kept his eyes resolutely, pointlessly open. Now, as he felt its first touch, he shut them tight. The finger moved slowly over his nose and lips; the gentle caress of a drowned lover. The Doctor began to shake.

I've come for you, Time Lord…

The light, when it came, was sudden and brilliant and intense.

The Doctor's first thought was: I'm dead!

Then he realised he was glad he had shut his eyes. *Lucky* he had shut his eyes, because even through the lids he could see the light: a hazy, painful red that made him flinch so hard he struck his head against the rock behind him.

He clamped his hands over his face and twisted away. The light was scalding, blinding, penetrating.

He could hear something: a whoosh of air that was like a scream of agony or a shout for help, he couldn't tell which. He realised the light had faded when the scarlet fog was gradually replaced by a fuzzy darkness.

He opened his eyes. They were watering, but he could see. The cave, empty of darkness, lit by the dying light of a minuscule sun at its centre. There was someone lying there, face down, a woman with dirty blonde hair tied in a ponytail. She was clutching something in one hand.

The Doctor crawled quickly over. 'Stoker?'

She lifted her head and looked at him. Her eyes were darting. 'Doctor? That you?'

'Relax.' His voice was thick with relief. 'You're all right.'

'I can't see!' Stoker said, panicking. 'I'm blind!'

'It's all right. It's temporary. The zenesium flare has stunned your optic nerves, but they'll recover.'

She fumbled her way into his arms.

The Doctor said, 'You saved my life.'

She let out a sob. 'I didn't save Lawrence.'

'It wasn't in your power to save him.'

Stoker's eyes were clearing, beginning to focus. She winced. 'Hell, but you look awful.'

The Doctor pulled gently free. There was a sore spot on his cheek and he fingered it tentatively. 'I think the Dark touched me. Just before you arrived with the zenesium flare.'

'I didn't know if it would work,' Stoker said after a while, nodding at the forgotten flare. 'When I got here I couldn't see anything, it was so dark… dark like I've never seen before.'

'You arrived just in time.'

'Is it dead? The Dark, I mean?'

'I don't know.' The Doctor stood up stiffly and turned to Cadwell. 'What do you think, Cadwell?'

Cadwell was still sitting propped up against the rock wall, staring at nothing.

'Cadwell?' The Doctor knelt down next to him. Cadwell didn't move. His eyes were blank, his lips slightly parted. He looked shockingly pale, almost completely white: the veins beneath his skin stood out like roads on a map.

Stoker rubbed her eyes. 'What's happened to him?'

'The Dark must have got him,' said the Doctor quietly. He gently shut Cadwell's eyes, but the pupils were still visible through the eyelids.

'He's almost transparent,' said Stoker.

The Doctor jumped as Cadwell's hand suddenly grasped his arm. Cadwell's head turned towards him, his eyes staring out through the closed lids. The white lips opened to reveal glassy teeth and a colourless tongue.

'Take it easy,' the Doctor advised, holding on to him. 'Don't try to speak.'

'Not dead yet,' Cadwell gasped.

'I know, I know. You'll be all right.'

'Not me… you fool… the Dark.'

The Doctor frowned and leaned closer. Cadwell's voice was as thin as his flesh. 'Flare… scared… it away… for now.'

'Shh,' the Doctor said, supporting him as he began to wilt. He had never seen anyone look so fragile. 'Don't talk. Save your strength.'

'Too late… again… Doctor.' Tears eased their way from Cadwell's watery eyes. Every word seemed to be painful. 'Not got… long to go… now. But… the Dark… will be back. It's hurt… angry… but… you've got some time… now.'

The Doctor gripped Cadwell harder, but he could feel his fingers sinking into the transparent flesh of his arm. His bones felt as though they would crumble to the touch.

'Take… this…' Cadwell held up his gun. 'You might need it.'

Because he couldn't think of anything else to do, the Doctor took the gun. Cadwell's fingers felt as cold and brittle as glass.

'Do the… decent thing, for once,' Cadwell croaked. 'Kill yourself… and your friends… while you still can.'

Then he slumped down, breaking apart in the Doctor's arms as his bones shattered and his skin tore like tissue. Blood gushed out like water over the cave floor.

The Doctor stood up and watched the liquid run off his hands. Then he turned to Stoker. 'It seems we have a reprieve, at least.'

Stoker couldn't stop looking at Cadwell's remains. 'For how long?'

'I don't know. Long enough to think of something else, perhaps.'

Stoker switched her gaze to the Doctor. Even he looked sceptical. He was still fingering the dark bruise on his face, but he stopped when he noticed her looking. 'Now then,' he said. 'Where did you say Nyssa and Tegan were?'

Tegan had crawled out from beneath a large section of hull plate and found herself in the shadow of the *Adamantium*'s steel carcass. At least, she had thought it was shadow; when she stood up and walked out into what she thought was the light of Akoshemon, she discovered that the whole moon seemed to be bathed in an eerie dusk. Akoshemon itself was a dark blot against the darker sky above. It reminded her of the strange twilight that accompanied a solar eclipse.

She heard the radio bleep and snatched it up to her lips. 'Doctor?'

'Tegan?' The Doctor's voice was loud and clear. 'Are you all right?'

'No! I've lost Nyssa. She fell inside the ship and I can't find her anywhere.'

There was a pause before the Doctor replied. 'You'd better get back here.'

'Not until I've found Nyssa.'

'Tegan, we need to regroup.' The Doctor gave a terse account of what had happened in the cave. 'I think we've given the Dark a bloody nose but it'll be back for more very soon.'

Tegan stiffened. 'I'm not doing anything until I've found Nyssa. And that's final.'

'Well, where do you think she could be?' A note of exasperation entered the Doctor's voice. 'We may not have a lot of time, Tegan.'

'So you're saying I should just forget about her?'

'No! But we need to stick together. Come down to the main cavern and we'll think what to do.'

'No, Doctor. *You* come up here.'

The Doctor gritted his teeth and switched off the comlink.

'Problem?' asked Stoker.

'There always is,' he spat venomously, 'with *her*. She's been a problem ever since she first blundered into my TARDIS!'

'Take it easy,' Stoker said. 'You're getting overwrought. Doesn't suit you.'

The Doctor seemed to realise what he had said and sagged against the cave wall, abashed. He was pale and there was a haunted look in his eyes. He rubbed at the bruise on his face. It was a strange-looking mark: dark grey, but deep beneath the skin. Stoker took a step closer so that she could see it more clearly.

'What's the matter?' asked the Doctor, suspicious.

'That's no bruise.'

'What?' The Doctor touched the mark again. 'It feels so... cold.'

The skin was transparent. The black mark looked like a shadow on the bone beneath.

'You say the Dark touched you there?'

The Doctor nodded. 'It wanted me. It nearly got me. It was too close.'

'You're shivering.'

'It's just a reaction.' The Doctor turned away so that Stoker couldn't see the black mark.

'It did that to Cadwell,' said Stoker, pointing at the Consortium man's body, 'then it started on you. Only I interrupted it.'

'Possibly. But it could have destroyed me in an instant.'

'Then why didn't it?'

Tegan was circling the *Adamantium*, hoping to see some sign of Nyssa. She kept calling out to her but there was no response. It was difficult to see anything very clearly in the gloom, anyway. And her torch looked like it was giving up the ghost.

She had almost walked around the entire ship. She was beginning to think that it really was hopeless, and that she had better find the Doctor. Maybe he could think of something. But Tegan wasn't happy with the idea: the Doctor had sounded strange on the radio, almost distracted. It wasn't like him not to worry about Nyssa.

It occurred to her that he might have been affected by the Dark. He had said that it had tried to manifest itself or something in the cave. And after all, it had been playing with his perceptions and his reactions ever since they had arrived on this wretched moon.

Maybe the Dark was trying to influence his thoughts again.

And if that were the case, then he would be in need of her help.

She activated the comlink. 'Doctor? Are you receiving me? Over.'

Nothing but static.

'He's switched it off,' she realised. And then she started to run, heading for the caves.

'You need to rest,' Stoker said, putting her hand on the Doctor's shoulder.

He flinched. 'Can't rest,' he said. 'Got to fight it.'

Stoker was disconcerted. She hadn't seen the Doctor so badly upset since Nyssa's heart attack. He looked to be on the verge of panic. 'Well, OK. Is there anything I can do to help?'

He smiled faintly at her. 'I'm afraid not; the Dark has been chipping away at my mental barriers since I arrived. It's nearly through. But I can't let it in. I mustn't!'

Abruptly he fell to his knees with a sharp gasp. 'It's trying again,' he said. He reached out and grabbed her hands, squeezing them. 'Got to resist it!'

'Right!' Stoker agreed. She felt like panicking herself. What the hell was she supposed to do now? 'What the hell am I supposed to do now?'

'Stay with me,' the Doctor told her. Sweat stood out on his face. 'Where are Tegan and Nyssa? I need them here as well.'

'I, erm…'

The Doctor screwed his eyes shut, remembering. 'Nyssa's lost.

Fallen. The Dark will take her again.' His eyes snapped open, and he looked stricken. 'It'll get Tegan next. She's… coming down here. It's a trap. She thinks I'm not in my right mind…'

'Well,' Stoker said, 'you're not, are you?'

He pulled her dose. 'Of course I'm not! The Dark's tried to get me one way… now it's trying to get under my skin. Using my friends against me!'

'They'll be fine. I'm sure they will.'

The Doctor stared intently at her. 'They are *not* fine. Look around you.' A black haze was slowly filling the cavern again. 'It's getting darker. It's coming back!'

CHAPTER TWENTY-ONE

Tegan ran into the main cavern and found herself lost in a black fog. Her torchlight was swept aside like a wisp of pale silk in the night.

Steeling herself, she pushed deeper into the gloom. 'Doctor? Stoker? Are you there?'

There was no reply. It was so cold she couldn't breathe properly and she felt her heart racing. She turned around and realised that she couldn't even see the cavern exit any more.

She tried the radio.' Doctor? Where are you? Are you receiving me?'

The comlink gave a buzz and the Doctor's voice responded, 'Tegan! We've had to go deeper into the caves. We're heading for the lab.'

'It's really dark in here,' Tegan said plaintively. 'I'm scared, Doctor!'

'I know,' the Doctor said, and Tegan was surprised at how strained his voice sounded. Almost as if he, too, was scared: but that was impossible. Wasn't it? When the Doctor spoke again, it seemed to be with some effort. 'The Dark is attempting to coalesce. It can only achieve complete, corporeal existence in total darkness. It's absorbing all the light energy from the cavern to try and create the right environment for it to enter this dimension.'

'Doctor, I don't know what you're talking about. Just tell me what to do!'

'Try and get back out of the cave. If you can't do that, then follow us down here. But be quick!'

'But what about Nyssa?'

The radio crackled and went dead. Tegan looked nervously all around her. She couldn't see a thing. But she could hear a distant, anguished wail building slowly behind her, like the cry of a thousand grieving parents.

The Dark was coming for her.

'What are you looking for, for grief's sake?' Stoker demanded.

She was watching the Doctor yank open locker after locker in Ravus Oldeman's lab, scrabbling through the contents of each with increasing exasperation.

'Something. Anything. I don't know,' he said. He opened another locker and swept the contents out onto the floor. Medical supplies scattered across the tiles. He instantly dropped to his knees and started to hunt through them.

'Why didn't you answer Tegan? What about Nyssa?'

The Doctor continued with his frenetic search. 'There isn't time to think about anyone else at the moment.'

Stoker felt a chill run through her bones. That didn't sound like the Doctor at all.

'Got it!' the Doctor said triumphantly, holding up a small medical injector.

Stoker knelt cautiously down by him. 'Neurolectrin?'

The Doctor's eyes gleamed. 'Just the ticket.'

'What for? I thought it was only used for treating people coming round from suspended animation.'

'It is!'

'And you need it because…?'

The Doctor opened his mouth to reply and then stopped. He looked uncertainly at the injector and then at Stoker. His eyes had the look of a small boy struggling to find the right answer to a simple question. 'I need it because… I need it because…' He faltered. 'I don't know why I need it. Do I need it?'

'Get a grip, Doctor. The Dark must be messing with your head again.'

He nodded. 'Yes, that must be it: the Dark. I was thinking about Professor Oldeman. About how he died.' The Doctor sank into a sitting position and hugged his knees. He looked so helpless, and that was scaring Stoker more than anything. 'All his blood, just running away like that. His whole life…'

'Don't dwell on it, Doctor,' Stoker told him firmly. 'It wasn't your fault.'

'No, but still…' The Doctor stared into space. 'All that blood.'

'Many people have died here. All of them nastily. But now is not the time to start brooding about it!'

'Are you sure?' The Doctor gazed intently at her. There was something odd in those blue eyes. 'Think about it: what happens when someone dies? What actually *happens* to them? To the *person*. Where do they go?'

'No one knows the answer to that one, Doctor.'

'They should.' His voice was small and frightened. 'Someone should find out. Then we'd all know.'

'You're getting irrational, Doctor. More than that, you're starting to get on my nerves.'

He looked at her again, and his eyes seemed to gain focus for a moment. 'Hit me,' he said.

'What?'

He scrambled to his feet. 'Hard as you can. Quickly!' He barked the last word like an order and Stoker jumped up. Then she slapped him across the face.

'Harder!'

She slapped him again, and it felt rather satisfying.

'Again!'

This time his head jerked to one side with the force of the blow.

'Better!'

'Mind telling me what this is supposed to achieve?' Stoker asked, hitting him again. 'I mean, besides making me feel a whole lot better.'

'I'm trying to use pain to weaken the Dark's mental grip; give me something else to think about.'

'Right,' said Stoker. She made a fist and punched the Doctor hard enough to send him sprawling across the lab. He smashed into a workstation and flipped over the desk, landing heavily on the other side. 'That do the trick?'

It took a couple of minutes to bring him back to consciousness. When his eyes finally opened Stoker said, 'Sorry. Didn't mean to hit you *quite* so hard.'

He sat up and rubbed his jaw. 'Did you ever meet John L Sullivan?'

'No, but I was the bar-room brawl queen at college,' she said. 'How d'you think I got this?' She pointed to her crooked nose and the Doctor looked a trifle alarmed. 'Don't worry, your boyish good looks are unmarked. Relatively. At least you sound a lot better.'

He got up, with a little help, and leant against the desk. 'I *am* a lot better. For now. But it's getting more and more difficult to resist the Dark's mental pressure. It's getting stronger and I'm getting weaker.' He sat down heavily in a chair. 'I don't know how I'm going to stop it.'

'You'll think of something.'

'I wish I shared your confidence in me.' He looked absently at the little injector of neurolectrin that was still lying on the table in front of him. 'I wonder...'

'What?'

'Neurolectrin helps reverse synaptic decay. It acts like a sort of lubricant for rusty brains.' He picked up the injector. 'What if I were to take this dose? Would it help me resist the Dark?'

Stoker said, 'I've no idea. But I've never liked drug abuse. Apart from alcohol. And tobacco. And caffeine. And...'

The Doctor prepared the injector and rested it against the skin of his throat. 'It's worth a try,' he said.

He sat there with his finger on the activator, unmoving.

Stoker watched him and waited. 'Then why don't you try it?'

'Because I've just had second thoughts: what if it has just the opposite effect? The neurolectrin might make it *easier* for the Dark to control me.' He pulled the injector away and stared at it as if it was a live scorpion. 'It's doing it again!' he cried. 'Trying to trick me! Giving me ideas that aren't my own!'

Stoker suddenly stiffened and glanced around her. 'The light's fading.'

The Doctor leapt to his feet, looking around the lab. 'Photon absorption. The Dark's trying to get in here.'

The shadows lengthened around the laboratory like expectant shrouds. 'What now?' Stoker asked.

'We run!'

Tegan ran down the steps from the main cavern and found the lab complex in darkness: cold fear gripped her stomach tightly as she stepped inside. She could see the tell-tale lights on the computers and workstations, glaring like little red eyes from the shadows, but that was all.

The Doctor and Stoker had gone.

She crossed through to the main section, breathing heavily. Darkness behind her, darkness ahead: she knew she was being surrounded. Cut off.

She could feel its malevolence in the turgid air all around her, like a swelling under the skin of reality.

In front of her a shadow bulged, growing out of the blackness, full of hate and spite. It hissed and writhed into a formless shape, filling the lab and almost blocking the way ahead. With a rush of desperate courage, Tegan flung herself past it and through the doorway beyond. She felt its cold, moist kiss as she slipped past and shuddered.

She stumbled down the short flight of steps into the stasis-tank chamber. The room was dark and empty. Where the hell was the Doctor? Tegan yanked the radio out of her pocket. 'Doctor! Where the hell are you?'

The comlink bleeped and the Doctor skidded to a halt. He fumbled through his coat pockets and eventually produced the radio. 'Hello? Who is it?'

'It's me! Tegan!' crackled a voice. 'Where are you?'

The Doctor hesitated. 'Er, well, I'm here. Where are you?'

There was an angry squawk from the comlink and the Doctor glanced helplessly at Stoker.

Stoker grabbed the radio. 'This is Stoker. We've had to get out of the lab complex because the Dark's trying to manifest itself there.'

'You're telling me!' Tegan's voice was distorted with fear. 'It's right behind me! What's wrong with the Doctor? Why can't I speak to him?'

'The Doctor's not, ah, feeling very well. At the moment.' Stoker's mind was racing. 'I think the Dark's affecting his mind.'

Tegan's voice dropped to an anguished whisper, 'What am I going to do?'

Suddenly the Doctor's hand closed around Stoker's and he pulled the comlink to his lips. 'Tegan! listen to me: I won't have time to repeat this.' The Doctor's face was as pale as smoke in the gloom. His eyes were shut tight with concentration. 'Get into the stasis tank. Close the lid and seal it. It's your only chance of hiding from the Dark.'

There was a stutter of protest from the radio. 'W-what? Are you sure?'

'No,' the Doctor told her. 'But it's all I can think of. Do it, Tegan, quickly!'

Tegan switched off the comlink and wiped her eyes roughly. The seething mass of darkness was pressing close behind her. Almost before she had thought about it Tegan was running her hands clumsily over the nearest stasis tank, searching for the opening mechanism. The tank looked like a big steel bathtub with a lid, but raised on some kind of dais. There were little lights blinking on the control panels and they made her wonder if the thing might accidentally activate itself while she was in it: would she try and hide in there only to wake up again in two hundred years?

The darkness intensified and she heard the outrage of a planet that had lost itself to evil over a million years before. The anguish settled like a physical weight on her shoulders and she felt faint. Then she found the latches and slid back the heavy metal lid of the tank and clambered inside.

It was cold and hard and smelled of iron and rubber. She felt like she was lowering herself into a submarine's torpedo tube. Cursing the Doctor, she lay back down and, with a struggle, slid the lid back up and over her face. It shut with surprising ease and a solid thud. It was sound proof: all she could hear now was her own rapid breathing and the hollow beat of her heart.

Right above her was a small rectangle of thick perspex. She could see the darkness outside, right above the stasis tank. She almost thought she could see the deeper, more evil shadow of the Dark itself rearing up over the tank, ready to strike.

Like a snake, she thought.

No. *Not* like a snake.

Like soil and dust, ready to fall down into the freshly dug grave and scatter across the lid of her coffin. More and more, thicker and thicker, until she couldn't see anything.

She realised then that the torch was still on. The beam shone right up under her chin, illuminating her face for all to see through the little window. She remembered her first glimpse of Ravus Oldeman's face through the little hatch, viewed from the other side. She fumbled around, her arms restricted in the confined space, and eventually squeezed the flashlight's button. The beam vanished and darkness filled the coffin.

She was holding her breath.

She could see something in the blackness above her: a face, staring down at her through the window. It was blood red, with mad, wide eyes full of terror and loathing.

Her heart stopped for a long moment.

Then she blinked and realised the crimson face was her own reflection. There were a number of little red control lights inside the tank, level with her head; the faint glow picked out her features with just enough clarity to be reflected right back at her in the dark glass above.

She started to breathe again, trying to control the urge to take great, loud gulping drags of the air. It was already hot and stuffy in here and she felt faint again. She shut her eyes and tried to breathe deeply and evenly.

Something pressed itself against the outside of the tank. She actually felt the tank move slightly, and she could sense a great weight bearing down on the lid and something, something smearing itself across the little window. It was pitch black inside the tank and pitch black outside, but there was *something* there: it was oozing across the glass like a giant slug.

Any second now that glass or plastic or whatever it was would crack, the weight would be too much, it would break and the glass would fall in and her face would be covered with an avalanche of worms and bugs, filling the coffin, all wriggling and burrowing into every little crevice they could find…

Tegan swallowed something wet and cold at the back of her throat and almost retched before she realised it was just phlegm.

She had to speak to the Doctor. She had to speak to someone, anyone.

Then she realised she'd left the radio outside on the edge of the tank.

The Doctor stopped and leant against the rock wall. He patted his face with his handkerchief and then, with great deliberation, tied a knot in one corner.

'What's that for?' asked Stoker wearily.

'Tegan,' he said. 'I won't forget her now, will I?'

Stoker stared as the Doctor carefully folded the handkerchief with its knot. 'What about Nyssa?'

'Who?'

'Your other companion. Nyssa.'

'Oh,' the Doctor said with a smile. 'Yes. Another knot, I think.' He unfolded the hanky.

'Doctor, do you want me to thump you again?'

The Doctor looked startled. 'No!'

'You're sure?' Stoker balled her fist. 'It might not help but it'd make me feel better because you're really starting to spook me out. You've got to fight the Dark, Doctor! Don't let it in! Don't forget your friends!'

The Doctor straightened up. 'Of course I won't forget them. I've tied two knots in my handkerchief, that should do the trick. Now, what were we doing?'

'This is impossible. I might as well give up now and take my chances with the Dark. You're useless.'

'It's all right,' he said. 'I know what I'm doing. I'm just trying to simplify my thought-processes, conceal what I can from the Dark's mental probing. But it may mean I only have occasional moments of lucidity.'

'If that's supposed to reassure me in any way, then it isn't working.'

The Doctor looked hurt. 'Really? I'm doing my best.'

'Maybe your best isn't good enough!'

'That's a possibility. But it's all I've got. That, and the fact that the Dark is still after me…'

'What? You're talking crazy again, Doctor.'

'No, listen: the Dark could have killed me in the cavern when it killed Cadwell. It's chasing me – and by that I mean us, of course – right now. It's trying to reach into my mind to control it, to influence it, but not actually destroy it.'

'Why?'

'I don't know. But at least it means we've got a chance of keeping one step ahead of it.'

'Until?'

The Doctor shrugged. 'Well, until it catches us of course.'

'And *then* it kills us, right?'

'Well, I'm not so sure it will kill me straight away. But it will almost certainly kill you without hesitation.'

'Great.'

'Don't worry,' the Doctor looked Stoker in the eye, and the effect was strangely unnerving. 'I won't let it come to that.'

Stoker ran a hand through her hair, which was damp with perspiration despite the cold. 'All right,' she said after a breath. 'But what about Tegan?'

The Doctor looked blank. 'Who?'

*

Tegan had no idea how long she lay in that stasis tank, petrified like some stone effigy on a tomb. It could have been minutes, but it felt like hours: staring at the blackness just above her, seeing things moving through the obsidian glass like the phantoms from someone else's nightmare. She couldn't make out any shape or detail, or even movement, but there was a sense of *something* being there, something palpable pressing against the lid of the tank: dark, heavy, wet, with tentacles that picked nimbly at the latches and probed the casing for the tiniest aperture or weak spot.

She remembered lying in her bed as a child, staring at the dull grey rectangle that was her bedroom window at night. She could see someone standing outside her window, a thin, gnarled figure, bent like a witch, gently tapping on the glass. She could hear the ta-ta-tap all night long. The witch never left the window; she just stood there, and occasionally tapped to let Tegan know she was there, watching her, waiting for her to fall asleep.

Her dad had told her it was just one of the branches of the big tree in the yard, and the wind was making it tap against the glass. The witch's hand was a stump of wood and her fingers were just twigs.

Tegan knew that there was a tree right outside her bedroom window, of course she did.

But she also knew there was a witch there at night time, a witch who lived in the tree, who was part of the tree, with skin like rough black bark and eyes like little dried berries.

She could still hear the witch now, ta-ta-tapping against the window.

And she could see her, too: the gnarled features were peering at her through the glass, eyes shrunken and crusty, sharp yellow teeth bared in a cackling laugh.

With a moan of dread, Tegan realised that there *was* a face visible through the tank's inspection hatch: a hideous, dark skull with empty eyes.

As she watched, a skeletal hand, clad in bark-like skin, started to tap against the glass.

*

273

'Tegan!' Stoker yelled into the comlink. 'Can you hear me? Tegan?'

'Maybe we're down too deep in the caves,' suggested the Doctor anxiously. 'Perhaps the signal's too weak.'

Stoker shook her head irritably. 'These things are Consortium issue.' She pressed the transmit switch again. 'Tegan! Come in, Tegan! State your position.'

The radio crackled.

'What was that?' asked the Doctor, sitting forward.

'It sounded like, I don't know, something tapping,' said Stoker. They listened again as the radio hissed with static and then, distinctly, they heard a definite tapping noise. Something metal being struck repeatedly.

'The stasis tank,' said the Doctor.

'It's found her,' said Stoker quietly.

There was a clank and a loud hiss from the comlink. The Doctor and Stoke both hunched closer to the radio, straining to decipher the noise. 'That's the lid being released,' said the Doctor. 'It's opening the stasis tank.'

Stoker swallowed and then shut her eyes as a terrified scream tore through the radio, distorting into a squeal of static and then silence.

'Oh, Tegan...' said the Doctor, collapsing against the rock wall in despair. 'Oh no... not you as well...'

Stoker, aghast, shook the comlink and kept depressing the transceiver. 'Tegan! Tegan!' She glared at the radio in horror. 'Dead.'

The Doctor had covered his eyes with a hand. His head was tilted back to rest against the rock wall. He sat there, unmoving and silent; in his other hand he clutched his handkerchief tightly.

CHAPTER TWENTY-TWO

The Doctor remained motionless for several minutes, a glassy, brittle look in his eyes.

It was, Stoker thought, the look of a man forced to confront his worst fear; and then finding that he simply wasn't ready for it.

Or perhaps it was the Dark, forcing its way into his head like a syringe needle and sucking out his most precious thoughts, his compassion and love and friendship and resolve. In a moment, all that would be left was the husk, his eyes remaining cold and empty.

Stoker grabbed his hands, which were continuously massaging the knotted handkerchief. She forced the fingers to remain still and looked into those cold, empty eyes.

'Don't let them die for nothing, Doctor,' she told him. 'Not Bunny, or Lawrence, or Tegan. *Fight* for them.'

Slowly his eyes regained focus. 'Fight? I'm sorry, I'm not terribly good at fighting.'

'Don't give the Dark the satisfaction,' Stoker hissed. 'It's trying to destroy you from the inside out, don't you see? It's wiping out everything that means anything to you.'

His eyes narrowed. 'I can feel it, you know, touching my mind. No, it isn't touching... it's scraping, scratching away at my thoughts. It's so evil. It's so evil it can't think straight. And now neither can I.' He pressed his fists into his eyes and grimaced. 'It's twisting my mind... confusing me... making me doubt myself. I can see what it's doing but I can't stop it.'

'You must!' Stoker was surprised and dismayed at how desperate she sounded, her voice cracking as she implored him. 'You *must!*'

The Doctor let out a long, shuddering breath and looked at her again. His eyes were full of pain. 'How? And what would be the point? All that death and destruction: Vega Jaal, Bunny, Lawrence, Tegan and Nyssa and even Cadwell and all the others… gone for ever. And what good have I done? Who have I saved?'

'Well, *we're* still here,' Stoker tried to hide the hopelessness she now felt. An ice-cold despondency was rising up inside her. She tried to think of something useful, something uplifting to say. *'We are still alive.'*

The Doctor seemed to sag with defeat. 'But for how much longer?'

It had grown very dark, very quickly, as they talked. With a fresh tremor of fear, Stoker realised that the Dark was gathering once again, thickening like black, arterial blood all around them. She could hear the distant screams of ancient Akoshemon, and the sucking, moist sound of the planet's evil nemesis trying to make a physical shape in the shadows.

She took out her cigarette lighter and flicked it on. The flame leapt up and lit the Doctor's face: the tiny point of light danced mockingly in his eyes as they dilated. The grey shadow on his cheek had spread across half his face.

Tegan couldn't stop shaking. She didn't know if it was just a reaction to the stasis tank or plain fear, but she couldn't stop. She knew how to control panic attacks, how to quell anxiety, it had all been part of her training as an air hostess, but this was different. There was something in the air, something evil, something you couldn't get away from.

And then there was that *thing*.

He was in the shadows now, slumped against the laboratory wall, breathing with a harsh, rasping noise that did nothing for her nerves. He was burned raw, the last vestiges of his uniform little more than charred rags. His features were unrecognisable, the skin blistered and blackened.

It was, apparently, Captain Lawrence.

'H-how did he survive?' Tegan asked. She couldn't take her eyes off him.

'I've no idea,' said Nyssa simply. 'By rights he should be dead. I don't know how much longer he'll last.'

Lawrence shivered and croaked. It had been his face looking down at Tegan through the stasis tank's window. She had screamed just as the seals on the lid were broken and the tank opened. Then, unbelievably, Nyssa had been there, holding her, hugging her. Tegan had cried, a mixture of utter relief and terrible fear boiling inside her.

'Maybe he is dead,' Tegan said quietly, still glaring at Lawrence. 'Maybe it's the Dark, controlling him still. Using his body.'

Nyssa shook her head. 'I don't think so.'

Lawrence's head turned blindly towards them, hearing their voices. His eyes were little more than scraps of blackened flesh. 'H-help… me…' he gasped. His voice was a dry croak.

'We don't know what to do,' Nyssa explained to him carefully. 'We have no medical equipment.'

'Help… me…'

Tegan wiped her eyes. 'We need to find the Doctor. Maybe he can do something.'

'S-Stoker…' whispered Lawrence.

Nyssa turned to Tegan. 'We found Silas Cadwell's body in the main cavern. Or what was left of it. I don't know what happened, but there was no sign of Stoker.'

'She's still alive, as far as I know. She's with the Doctor.'

Lawrence's lips moved with painful slowness. 'T-take… me… to… S-Stoker…'

Tegan bit her lip. She wasn't sure Stoker would want to see Lawrence like this. To Nyssa she said, 'The Dark's been trying to form itself into something, I don't know what, something that can live in our universe I think. It killed Cadwell but the Doctor and Stoker managed to get away.'

'Which way did they go?'

'Down into the caves,' Tegan said. 'But the Dark keeps trying to materialise. The Doctor says it can only do that in complete darkness. I was hiding from it when you found me.'

Nyssa looked worried. 'The Dark must be after the Doctor. It had gone when we found you in here. Presumably it's followed the Doctor and Stoker into the deep caves.'

'We've got to go after them,' Tegan realised. The prospect made her feel almost breathless with fear.

'I know.'

Tegan glanced at Lawrence. 'What about him?'

Lawrence moved, straining to hear them speak. His ears had been burnt away, leaving little more than crisp, puckered holes on the sides of his head. 'Please... take... me... to... Stoker...' he implored.

The Doctor took the lighter from Stoker and turned up the flame. The sudden increase in illumination was horribly revealing: in the darkness all around them they glimpsed thousands of moist, wriggling black shapes which recoiled from the blaze of light. The dark, slime-covered coils withdrew into the deeper shadows with a sucking hiss of displeasure.

'Eew,' said Stoker.

'Interesting,' the Doctor murmured. 'It still can't quite manage to overcome the light.' He thrust out the lighter at arm's length, and they caught another brief sight of the Dark: an oleaginous mass of blackness, like a peek into a seething nest of worms. It fled from the brightness and the shadows swallowed the crawling mass whole.

'It's so close,' whispered Stoker, terrified.

The Doctor waved the lighter. 'But no cigar.'

She looked at him. 'You feeling better now?'

'Not at all,' he said. 'But I can't help being curious...'

'I can think of other words.'

'Then try this one: hungry.'

'Hungry?' Stoker blinked. She stole a quick, fearful look into the darkness, and was glad that she couldn't see it. But she could hear it moving wetly in the shadows. 'No, sorry. I am definitely not hungry.'

'The Dark's hungry,' said the Doctor quietly.

'What for? Us?'

'No. Something else. I'm not sure what.'

'Breakfast?'

The Doctor shook his head. 'It's not food it wants. I wonder what it is?'

The Dark shifted in the shadows, a mass of something that now had them surrounded but dared not penetrate the circle of light. The noise it made sounded to Stoker like the mouth of some great beast preparing to eat.

The Doctor bit his lip. 'It wants *me*,' he said, as if thinking aloud. 'More than anything else. It wants my TARDIS.' At the edge of the light, the Dark seethed in agreement. 'It sensed the TARDIS in the Vortex. Sensed *me*. Brought us here… and then destroyed everything and everyone to get to this moment. The moment where it has me completely at its mercy.'

'But it doesn't have any mercy,' whispered Stoker fearfully.

'I know.' The Doctor looked at the cigarette lighter, and the little tongue of flickering light. 'Oh, my small, bright friend: are you all I have left?'

Tegan and Nyssa helped Lawrence through the tunnels. He could barely stand and their progress was painfully slow. Worse than that, he smelled of roast meat and it was making Tegan feel sick.

'What's that?' asked Nyssa suddenly. 'I thought I heard something.'

They stopped and listened, which wasn't easy because they had to support Lawrence and his breathing was hard and noisy.

But Tegan soon heard it: a voice, light, almost childlike, echoing down the passageway. It was too dark to see anything up ahead, except for a faint, watery glow.

'What is it?'

'It could be a trap,' said Nyssa. 'The Dark…'

'No,' said Tegan. 'I think I recognise the voice.'

They pressed on, rounding a corner in the tunnel. The glow became a little brighter. They stopped dead when they saw the ghost of a little girl floating in the shadows ahead. She was no more than a silvery shape against the dark rock wall, white-faced and incredibly beautiful. Tegan felt the hairs moving on the back of her neck as the child spoke again.

'Is it silly to be scared of dreams?'

The ghost stared plaintively at them. Tegan almost opened her mouth to reply, but the child continued, 'Mummy lets me sleep in her bed at night but it's still dark. I don't like it when it's dark.'

Tegan said, 'It's Rosie. Bunny Cheung's little girl!'

'Some kind of three-dimensional image,' Nyssa speculated.

'Mummy says you work in caves where it's dark all the time and you're not scared one bit,' said Rosie. 'Is that right? How come you're not scared?'

'Hologram,' said Tegan positively. 'Bunny kept his hologram recordings of her in his ring.'

'Please come home soon, Daddy. I don't like it when you're away. Neither does Kooka. His arm's come loose again. Mummy says it's going to drop right off soon, so you'd better come back home and fix it real quick.'

'But why is it here?' Nyssa wanted to know.

'Oh, but Daddy, be careful you don't fall off the edge of the gaxaly. We miss you. Bye.'

'Wait a sec,' Tegan said. She moved forward and bent down, picking something up off the cave floor. The image of Rosie swung wildly around in the darkness. 'Look what I've found.'

She held up a human arm for Nyssa to see. Wires and machinery poked out of the shoulder and biceps where it had been torn away.

'Bionic arm,' Tegan announced. 'With Bunny's hologram ring still working. The Bloodhunter must've dropped it here when it found it couldn't eat it or something.'

'It has an integral power source,' said Nyssa.

The image of Rosie flickered and died as the recording came to an end. 'Poor Rosie,' said Tegan. 'She's got no way of knowing what's happened to her dad…'

Nyssa's lips tightened. 'He was murdered by something evil. Perhaps it's best that she doesn't ever know.'

*

The flame was shrinking. The lighter was running out of fuel. The Doctor looked at Stoker, and she knew he didn't have to spell it out: when the flame died, so would they. The Dark would be on them in a second, closing around them like a cold, wet fist in the night.

'How much longer do you think we've got?' Stoker asked.

'I don't know.' The Doctor passed the lighter to her and she took it in trembling fingers. 'Don't drop it!' he warned.

'What are you doing?' Trapped inside the little bubble of flickering yellow light, Stoker had never felt so close to anyone she hadn't actually made love to. She could feel the heat of the Doctor's body. She could sense him fumbling through his coat pockets. 'What are you looking for?'

'This,' the Doctor said, producing a small metal pistol. It was the gun Silas Cadwell had bequeathed him. He cocked the weapon with a loud metallic click.

Stoker gaped. 'W-what are you going to do? Shoot the Dark?'

He shook his head. 'No. That would be pointless. I'm going to shoot you.'

For a second Stoker was speechless. And then it all seemed to fall into place. A great weight of despair settled on her shoulders and neck, crushing her almost to the floor. After everything that had happened, after all she'd been through, wasn't this the most obvious and sensible result? After discovering the lexium and then losing it; after arguing with Bunny and losing him... after finding Lawrence again, only to see him die under the control of the Dark... What else was there for Jyl Stoker? Even if she survived, *what would be the point?* All this seemed to swell up inside her head like a vast grey balloon of misery until she was able to stare straight into the barrel of the gun without the slightest flinch.

But she still, perhaps automatically, said, 'What?'

The Doctor held the gun steadily and aimed right at the centre of her forehead. 'We've reached the end of the line, I'm afraid. The choice is simple: stay alive for the last few minutes' worth of lighter fuel that remains, and then die horribly and terribly at the hands of the Dark... or take matters into our own hands now. Kill ourselves before the Dark can get to us. Quick and painless. I'll shoot you and then shoot myself.'

Stoker blinked. The Doctor sounded under strain but reasonable. 'This is a trick, isn't it?' she whispered.

'No,' he said. 'We can do it the other way around, if you prefer. You shoot me and then shoot yourself. It doesn't really matter, does it, so long as we're both dead before the Dark has a chance to get to us.'

Just beyond the edge of the light, the Dark seemed to writhe impatiently, as if aware that its prey was about to escape.

Stoker's gaze focused on the muzzle of the gun again. She was amazed that it didn't tremble or waver.

'Is this the only way?' she asked in a small, child's voice. She wanted assurance, comfort, from someone who knew better. Someone she could trust to look after her.

The Doctor nodded. 'I'm sorry.'

A tear rolled down Stoker's cheek. It was, she realised, going to be the last tear she ever shed. 'Please,' she croaked. 'You'll have to do it. I don't think I could… do that to anyone.'

'It's all right,' he told her gently. Was that a tear glimmering in the corner of his eye as well? 'I understand. I… just wish there could have been another way. But what the Dark wants… what it's hungry for… I cannot let it have. I'm sorry.'

The flame of the lighter was almost gone. If Stoker's hand shook any more it would disappear completely. The thing hiding just beyond the fringe of the light hissed and moved closer, eager for the chance to strike.

The lighter flame faltered and shrank to a tiny nub of light. The Doctor's finger tightened on the trigger.

'Guess what,' said a little girl's voice out of the darkness. 'A cat poo'd in our garden yesterday and Mummy had to pick it up with a stick.'

The little girl appeared from nowhere, as bright and silvery as an angel: the Doctor looked quickly away and Stoker blinked. The Dark snarled and recoiled as if stung, the light of the angel throwing into sharp relief the rough rock walls of the cave. The Dark itself, black and glutinous, bled away into the shadows.

Tegan and Nyssa rushed over to the Doctor, who looked at them with complete shock.

'You're supposed to be dead,' he said, almost sounding hurt.

'No way, Doc,' said Tegan. 'Haven't you heard: we're indestructible!'

Nyssa was holding Bunny Cheung's bionic arm, the heavy ring on its finger still projecting its startling hologram.

The Doctor scrambled to his feet, too amazed, it seemed, to even smile with relief. Instead, he looked rather quizzical. 'Are you sure you're not dead?'

Tegan grinned. 'One hundred per cent.'

The Doctor stared at them both, open-mouthed, and then looked down at the gun he was still holding in his hand. He glanced at Stoker.

'Get rid of it,' she sobbed.

The Doctor, dazed, looked back to Tegan and Nyssa.

'What were you two up to?' Tegan asked. 'Why the gun?'

'Kooka's arm needs fixing again,' said the hologram of the little girl brightly. 'It's come right off this time.'

'Who's that?' asked the Doctor.

'That's Rosie Cheung,' Tegan said. 'Our guardian angel against the Dark.'

'No, I meant, who's *that*?' The Doctor pointed past the hologram, to a figure standing bent and huddled in the entrance to the cave.

The figure shuffled forward.

Stoker let out a choked cry. 'Lawrence!'

She stood up just as the burnt figure staggered forward and collapsed into her arms. She held him tightly and he groaned. His lips brushed her ear. 'Wanted… to be with you…'

Stoker sobbed. 'I'm here, I'm here! I've got you. Don't worry!'

The Doctor stared at them. They held their embrace in the silvery light of the little girl's hologram. Rosie Cheung said, 'I've got to go now, Daddy, the puter says my time's all used up. So bye.'

The Doctor looked down again at the gun in his hand. An expression of revulsion twisted his features and he hurled the weapon viciously away from him. It landed with a clatter next to Stoker.

Lawrence was leaning against Stoker, and she had to take nearly all of his weight. But she kept him close, kept whispering to him, kept pushing her fingers through the brittle remains of his hair. 'I love you,' she told him. 'Thank God you're here. I love you.'

Lawrence returned the embrace with as much strength as he could muster, weeping into the soft skin of her throat.

The Doctor turned back to Tegan and Nyssa. After a moment's hesitation, he said, 'I really thought I'd lost you both. The Dark has been eating away at my resolve ever since. But I can't tell you how pleased I am to see you, because we simply don't have the time. You've sent the Dark skulking back into its shadow dimension but it will be back very soon.'

'What should we do?' Nyssa asked.

The Doctor looked across to where Stoker and Lawrence were still holding each other. 'Fight,' he said.

CHAPTER TWENTY-THREE

The Doctor looked up at Stoker and shook his head sadly. 'I don't know how much longer he can last,' he told her quietly. 'I'm very sorry.'

Tears streamed down Stoker's face as she cradled Lawrence in her arms. His breathing was shallow and noisy and he was clearly in great pain.

'I don't even have any medical equipment with me,' the Doctor said. 'We might've made him comfortable with basic analgesics, but I'm afraid his burns are life-threatening.'

Stoker pulled Lawrence closer to her. His blackened fingers gripped her arm tightly.

The Doctor stood up. They were in the stalactite forest again, trying to put as much distance as they could between themselves and the Dark before it attempted another assault.

Tegan was holding a makeshift torch very gingerly: the Doctor had improvised using a metal rod and an oil-soaked handkerchief, lit with the last vestige of fuel from Stoker's cigarette lighter. The flame cracked and spat at the end of the stick, throwing out greasy smoke. Its flickering orange light was their only source of illumination, but it made the shadows move around them in unsettling ways.

The handle of the torch was getting hotter by the minute, and droplets of flaming oil kept falling from the hanky.

'This is useless,' Tegan told the Doctor bluntly as she struggled to hold the brazier. 'We're trapped. There's nowhere to run, Doctor.'

'I know. We can't afford to sit and wait for the Dark to come and get us, Tegan. We have to do something.'

285

'And going back *there* is your best idea?' Tegan nodded down the slope towards the dark entrance to the crypt.

'You said it yourself, there's nowhere else for us to go.'

They helped Stoker carry Lawrence through the stalactites until they reached the crypt. Inside, the empty pit was in darkness. The glow snakes that had lived in the ceiling were no more than lifeless grey stripes in the rock. In the flickering light of Tegan's torch they were little more than a mottled discoloration in the glossy black stone.

They rested Lawrence against the wall and Stoker cradled his head in her arms. His breathing was faint and shallow, and he felt deathly cold to the touch.

'Doctor,' said Stoker in a small, alarmed voice. 'I… I think he's dying.'

Lawrence raised a skeletal hand to Stoker's face, but his strength was failing. The hand drooped and then lay on the floor, curled up like a dead spider.

'Take it easy,' whispered Stoker.

His mouth moved silently, desperately.

'Shh.' Stoker clutched him tighter. 'Please… Please, don't go. Don't leave me.'

'I… love you…' Lawrence said quietly, in a voice that was barely more than a whisper but somehow carried to everyone in the chamber. 'I will… always… love you.' With tremendous effort he raised his hand again towards Stoker's cheek. 'Don't waste… tears on me. Save them for when… you might need them.'

'Oh God,' Stoker sobbed, pulling him closer. She grasped his fingers with one hand and held them to her lips, kissing the scorched flesh, tasting her own tears. 'Don't die. Don't die. *Don't die.*'

'Got to go now…'

Her mouth fell open in a rictus of despair. 'I won't let you die!'

'No good… getting very cold now.'

'I won't let you…' insisted Stoker. 'I won't let you!'

Lawrence was trembling. 'C-can't feel anything. Can't feel… you any more.'

286

She dug her fingers deep into his arms. 'I'm here!'

Lawrence said nothing.

'I'm here!' Stoker cried. 'I'm here! Don't go!'

Still Lawrence said nothing. He lay, stiff and unmoving, in her arms. She kissed him again, awkwardly and hurriedly, but there was no breath between his lips.

The Doctor had knelt down quietly beside Stoker. He rested a hand on Lawrence's head and looked gravely at Stoker. 'He's gone. His pain is over.'

In a low, wretched voice Stoker ground out, 'The Dark did this!' She held grimly on to Lawrence's empty body. 'The Dark did this!' Her voice fell into a wail of despair. 'It *was* the Dark, wasn't it?'

'Yes,' said the Doctor.

Stoker looked up, her eyes glittering. 'Then promise me something: promise me you will destroy the Dark. Stop it, kill it, do whatever you have to but *get rid of it for ever.*'

Stoker's words echoed vehemently around the chamber. The Doctor said, 'I promise.' But he would not look her in the eye when he said it.

Abruptly he stood up and turned away, one hand rubbing absently at the grey mark on his face. He looked distraught.

Tegan moved away from where Stoker lay with Lawrence's body, thinking that she might want some privacy. Besides which, Tegan didn't feel she could cope with another dead body now. She took the flickering torch across the chamber, only to find another corpse at her feet.

Ravus Oldeman's cadaver lay on the floor where it had been discarded. Tegan moved the torchlight quickly over his remains, not wanting to linger. They had come to a place of death. There was no way out. This was where they would have to make their final stand, like children against a ravenous tiger.

'Why have we come back here?' she complained, her voice echoing stridently.

'There's nowhere else to go,' Nyssa said.

'Don't you start!'

The Doctor was making a circuit of the pit, staring into the empty well. 'Bring the torch over here,' he instructed.

Tegan held the flame over the pit and they peered down into the shadows. There was something moving in the glimmering light: something the colour of raw meat, with a nest of tentacles for a face.

'It's the Bloodhunter!' Tegan exclaimed, drawing back.

The light from her torch wavered drastically as she withdrew from the edge of the pit, and the Doctor quickly shushed her. 'Don't frighten it,' he said.

But this was the least of Tegan's concerns. 'Don't frighten it? Doctor, we've got to get *out* of here…' She began to back towards the exit.

'Wait,' the Doctor ordered. 'It's not attacking us. Look.'

Nyssa joined Tegan and together they watched as the Doctor took a careful step closer. The Bloodhunter crouched low in the pit, glaring back up at them from the shadows. The flickering light glinted in its cluster of eyes. Its gaze fixed on the Doctor, who was now leaning over the edge to examine the creature.

'Be careful, Doctor.'

'It's all right, Nyssa,' the Doctor said quietly. He kept his voice low and soothing. 'I think it knows its usefulness is over. It served the Dark, but now it has no further purpose. It's rather sad, actually.'

'That thing killed Bunny Cheung,' spat Tegan, 'and a good many other people besides. Don't ask me to feel sorry for it.'

The Bloodhunter let out a low growl, its face-tentacles stirring. It was still staring at the Doctor, but there was a lusting gleam in its eyes.

'On the other hand,' said the Doctor, 'it might be safer to keep our distance.'

Tegan's torch flickered wildly and the shadows leapt around the chamber in a frenzy.

'Please,' Nyssa implored, 'don't let the light go out!'

'I didn't do anything!' Tegan retorted. The flame was jumping and snapping on the end of its stick like a flag in a high wind. But Tegan was holding it steady. 'It's gone crazy, that's all.'

'It must be caught in a draught,' Nyssa persisted.

'There's no draught,' the Doctor said.

They watched as the flame now began twisting and turning like a wild animal trying to escape from a trap.

'It's the Dark,' said the Doctor. 'It's found us.'

Tegan whirled and held the torch out towards the chamber entrance. 'Get back!' she shrieked. A now familiar moan began to swell up from the distant past as the shadows dragged memories of ancient torment with them. Tegan waved the spitting flame about with primeval desperation.

'We're trapped,' wailed Nyssa. 'The Dark's out there and the Bloodhunter's in here!'

The Doctor looked quickly around the chamber for his friends: Stoker cradling Lawrence's body on the far side, Nyssa clutching his sleeve, Tegan standing her ground with the torch. Its flame was nearly free, tugging at the oily rag which gave it life with desperate vigour. A spark leapt from its tip into the gloom, but it was a futile gesture: the shadows simply turned on the brave little light and crushed it.

The tip of the torch glowed for a moment longer and then began to fade.

'No!' shouted Tegan.

The Dark hissed eagerly, drawing closer, filling the chamber.

The Doctor crossed the room in two quick strides and held Tegan firmly by the wrist. 'Let it go,' he said.

'What?' Tegan peered at his face in the semi-darkness. The dying torch cast a sickly umber light across his features, turning them muddy in the gloom. Like a ghost, he hardly seemed to be there at all. 'Doctor?'

'There's nothing more we can do,' he said. His voice sounded resigned but firm. 'It's time to stand and face the Dark.'

And with that, the last embers finally died, turning to grey ash for a second before the blackness claimed them.

The chamber was plunged into more than darkness: something massive and blacker than anything else surged into the air around them. Tegan found herself discarding the spent torch and grasping hold of the Doctor; not for comfort, just for something or someone to anchor her space in the void.

'Is it here?' she heard Nyssa whisper.

'Very nearly,' replied the Doctor. 'It needs total darkness to achieve a physical presence.'

'Then we've lost.'

'Was there ever any doubt that we would?' asked Tegan.

'Never give up hope,' ordered the Doctor. 'Remember, the Dark craves a physical existence in our universe: once it's fully manifested it can't go back to its own dimension.'

A thick, glutinous shadow poured into the chamber, distorting everything around it. The space was moving, full of things they could not see crawling and seething, closer and closer. It felt cold and wet, like something that lived beneath a stone. Then, impossibly, they *could* see it: a formless mass, blacker than the pitch darkness, swelling out of nowhere. The Dark arrived like something being retched from the back of reality's throat.

It filled the chamber like a giant black squid, tentacles of shadow thrashing around the room. A cavernous maw split open and spurted a scream of exultation. Then the writhing mass turned in on itself, stretching and contracting, reforming into another shape. An even more unsettling shape.

'At last,' said a voice that sounded like worms frying. 'I live! I live! *I live!*'

It was tall, barely discernible in the gloom, but shaped like a man. Tegan thought she could make out long, lank hair hanging like rat-tails on its shoulders.

'Hello,' the Doctor was saying. 'So glad you could make it.'

The black figure turned to face him. There were small, sinuous things crawling all over its flesh: so many that the skin seemed to be in constant motion. Tegan thought that she could just make out ragged coat tails hanging level with its knees. The material of the coat was rotten and caked in filth, but with a start Tegan realised that the Dark presented the same silhouette as the Doctor.

The Doctor had not failed to notice this. 'They say imitation is the sincerest form of flattery.'

Something opened in the shadowy face with a wet, hollow noise. A single word escaped from the orifice, born on dead breath, 'Doctor…'

'That's right. I hope you won't mind if we don't shake hands.'

'You meaningless fragment of dirt,' whispered the Dark. 'I will make you suffer before you die!'

'Ah, straight into the insults and threats,' the Doctor said. 'What a relief. Saves time in the long run, don't you think?'

'Time,' growled the shadow as if savouring the word. 'Yes… I can feel it now, the very progress of the universe around me.'

The Doctor was intrigued. 'You mean you couldn't feel it before?'

The eyes glittered like coal in the shadowy face as they regarded the Doctor. 'Yes, what would you know of the endless, empty void that bore me? At last I can sense the soft, stealthy passage of time itself.'

'Well, perhaps congratulations are in order: they say there's a first time for everything. Even feeling the passing of time, I suppose.'

The Dark hissed. 'You don't understand, Doctor. How could you? I have drifted, formless and outside of time, for uncountable millennia. I have been forced to watch from the sidelines of a half-dimension, unable to interfere. But not any more!'

'Ah yes, now about that: there seems to be a misunderstanding. Correct me if I'm wrong, but you appear to believe that, through me, you will now be able to gain access to the rest of time and space…' The Doctor thrust his hands into his trouser pockets and rocked nonchalantly on his heels. 'Well, I'm sorry but I'm afraid that is completely out of the question.'

'For all eternity I have waited for the chance, the means, to live fully and completely in your universe.'

'But you haven't been idle, have you? Your mind has existed within the planet Akoshemon since its formation… lain waste to a thousand million years of that world's evolution, doomed by *your* will. You have stirred civilisations into an endless cycle of self-destruction, and the worst kinds of corruption.'

'Hardly something to boast about,' added Tegan.

The Dark shrugged. 'That time… is over.'

'Ah, yes. Now you're alive and kicking and ready to spread your malign influence across every world and every civilisation in the universe. Courtesy of my TARDIS.'

'My consciousness sensed your little time craft in the Vortex. It required only a moment's thought to breach its meagre defences.'

'You mean me,' said Nyssa shakily.

The Dark let out its breathless laughter. 'The last little orphan of a pitifully weak planet torn out of creation and flung, forgotten, into nowhere.'

'You violated my memory of Traken,' Nyssa said. She took the smallest step forward, bravely turning her face up towards the towering figure of night. 'Why?'

'Ah, last daughter of Traken… You were simply the most receptive to my influence. The way had already been cleared for me. There was an empty space in your mind where Traken had once been; I simply filled that void.'

The Doctor rested a hand gently on Nyssa's shoulder. She stared back at the Dark and then lowered her gaze.

Tegan felt curiously as if something in her own mind was relaxing, uncoiling, satisfied that a threat had vanished. It left her feeling perplexed, almost introspective. She automatically looked to the Doctor for an explanation, but he was already speaking to the Dark again.

'An intriguing plan, but you've overlooked something: my TARDIS isn't for hire. It's not an intergalactic taxi waiting to ferry you around the cosmos, spreading doom and disaster!'

'I have finally achieved the transition into your physical universe,' said the Dark. 'I can do anything.'

The Doctor sighed loudly. 'Your point being?'

'I now have absolute power over you all.'

'I beg to differ.'

'No, Doctor. Not yet. I will tell you when to beg.'

'You know, it's amazing,' the Doctor said. 'The way your kind always has to throw its weight around. Why don't you just kill me and be done with it?'

'But you have something I want, Doctor.'

'The TARDIS? I've already told you, you can't have it. Is there anything else I could interest you in? I have a cricket bat signed by Mike Gatting, if you'd like that. Worth a fair bit, now, I'd say.'

'On your knees!' the Dark roared.

'I'd rather stand, thank you very much.' The Doctor suddenly let out a gasp of pain and dropped heavily to his knees.

'That's better,' said the Dark.

'Psychokinesis,' grunted the Doctor, now on all fours. 'A cheap trick.'

'But effective. I've already touched you, Doctor: you bear my mark! If I wanted to, I could make you act like the dog you are, Time Lord. Running around on all fours, panting, with your tongue hanging out like that of the lowest mongrel.'

The Doctor groaned as his mouth opened painfully and his tongue lolled out. With an effort he regained control. 'You can only pull strings,' he gasped. 'I won't do anything for you of my own free will.'

'Such presumption!' The Dark moved closer. 'I don't think you quite understand, Doctor. I could *make* you behave like a frightened puppy, it's true. But I'd rather you did it voluntarily.'

The Doctor raised a hand and tentatively touched the shadowy mark on his face again. It was ice cold, right through to the bone. He could feel its evil. The Doctor suddenly shook his head. 'I think you'll find I fight for my principles.'

'Worm,' said the Dark.

The Doctor gagged and sank to the floor, as if pressed down flat by a giant hand. Forced to prostrate himself, the Doctor came face to face with the corpse of Ravus Oldeman.

Oldeman's eyes were still open, dry and blind but still full of pain. His expression was frozen into one of anger and torment. The

Doctor lay transfixed, almost unable to breathe. The dead man's eyes bore into him and the Doctor experienced a sudden sense of importance, as if the man was trying to tell him something from the grave.

The Doctor blinked. He was starting to hallucinate, surely. Oldeman just lay there, unmoving, empty and lifeless.

The Dark cackled. 'Do you doubt my power, Time Lord, even now?'

'Not at all,' the Doctor panted, struggling to his knees with as much dignity as he could muster. 'I admit manifesting yourself out of nothing but darkness like that is a pretty good trick. But telekinetic torture… well, I've seen it before.'

The Dark moved closer. 'But I can sense your terror, Doctor. Your juvenile prattling is the thinnest of disguises.'

'Is it really so obvious?'

'You seek to shore up your companions' meagre courage with humour. It won't work.' The Dark gave a throaty chuckle. 'Your mind is overflowing with dread. Your hearts are pulsing, faster and faster, as the blood races around your frail body in blind red panic. I can even *hear* your hearts, Doctor, rushing through their last remaining beats in such a terrible hurry. You're going to die soon – you know that, don't you?'

'Be that as it may,' said the Doctor stonily, 'I won't let you have the TARDIS.'

'Death after death,' the Dark reminded him. 'You've seen the future, Doctor. You know it isn't good.'

The Doctor climbed slowly to his feet. A terrible weight seem to have descended on his shoulders. 'I haven't seen the future. You're just trying to scare me with the prospect of death.'

'Death is your weakness!' spat the Dark. 'All of you!'

The Doctor gave him a sad smile. 'But for us, death is inevitable: a *condition of our existence*. We live, we die. Nothing can alter that.'

'You had better listen to him, you filth,' said a voice from the other side of the chamber. It was Stoker. She spoke from where she lay, still holding Lawrence's corpse. 'You've had all you're going to get from us: Vega Jaal, Bunny, Jim, all my friends and all the other people. *And the man I love!* You can do what the hell you like now because *you just can't hurt us any more!*'

The Doctor looked across at Stoker and she caught his eye. He nodded.

'A facile argument!' roared the Dark. 'But even if there is no fear in death… then there is fear in *life*. Humans fear me; they fear the dark! They learn to fear it from infancy – what they cannot see, or know, or understand.'

'Exactly!' the Doctor said. 'Because fear of the dark is really just a fear of the *unknown*. What can't be *seen*. Like the future. But I don't fight the future… I fight *for* the future. And I protect it from the things that thrive on the unknown. Fear. Hostility. Cruelty. Injustice.'

'All the things I represent,' admitted the Dark. 'But I too will fight for my principles.'

'Then it's you against me,' replied the Doctor. He left the statement to drift for a long moment before adding, almost as an afterthought, 'So how come you haven't killed me yet?'

Something bubbled inside the Dark and it took a step towards the Doctor.

The Doctor stood his ground. 'Shall I tell everyone,' he asked lightly, 'or would you prefer to?'

The Dark moved towards him again, lips drawing back from sharp black teeth.

The Doctor looked at his companions and said, 'You see, I've just realised I have something the Dark wants very badly. And I don't just mean the TARDIS.'

The Dark's mouth hung open, oily saliva hanging from its lips.

The Doctor turned back and stared it in the eye. 'There's something else you want, isn't there? Something you hadn't anticipated in your great, greedy plan for universal domination. Which, I have to say, is quite the most ludicrous of schemes! Only a mind warped by an eternity spent bringing terror and cruelty to one single planet could have thought of it. And, of course, one that had been warped by something else perhaps…'

The Dark hissed explosively, spraying blackness through the heavy air. 'Give me want I want, Time Lord, and you alone shall live.'

The Doctor smiled sadly and turned again to Tegan and Nyssa. 'You see, having taken on a physical form based on the human blood it absorbed, the Dark is now subject to the same physical needs of its donors – including the late Professor Ravus Oldeman.'

'Give me what I need!' roared the Dark. 'Give me it!'

'What?' said the Doctor. 'This?' He drew his hand from his pocket and held up an injector.

'What is it?' asked Tegan.

'Neurolectrin,' said the Doctor. 'The Dark has inherited Ravus Oldeman's condition… *and* his addiction to the neurolectrin. I should have realised when it made me search the laboratory for the drug before. I *did* realise it just now, when I saw Ravus Oldeman's body again. The Dark wants the TARDIS, certainly, but at the moment it wants *this* more.'

The Dark lunged for the injector and the Doctor skipped back out of reach. 'Sorry. But I don't think you deserve it.'

'Imbecile,' snarled the Dark.

The Doctor took another step back, but suddenly found himself trapped by the Bloodhunter. He hadn't noticed it behind him in the darkness.

'My loyal servant,' sneered the Dark. 'You have gone far enough, Doctor.'

The Doctor convulsed, letting out a sharp cry of pain and dropping to one knee.

'I can control your every movement,' the Dark said. 'Don't tell me you have forgotten my *cheap trick* so soon?'

The Doctor groaned as the mental pressure forced him to raise the hand holding the neurolectrin.

'No witty riposte, Time Lord?' the Dark enquired as it moved closer. It leaned over the Doctor, pushing its diseased, black face into his. 'No clever deception?'

The hand holding the neurolectrin began to shake as the Doctor fought for control. The fingers and knuckles turned white around the injector as the hand began to turn. The Doctor's teeth ground together as his face paled with the exertion.

'I have an idea,' whispered the Dark. 'Why don't *you* take the neurolectrin?'

The Doctor's eyes widened fractionally. His hand, controlled by the Dark, moved slowly towards his own throat, twisting the injector into position. The tip trembled against his skin, ready to deliver the dose. 'It won't harm me,' the Doctor protested.

'I know…' The Dark leant closer, close enough for the Doctor to see the tiny black worms wriggling on its tongue and lips. 'But I could squeeze it back out of you like blood from an open wound.'

'An easy victory,' gasped the Doctor. 'Wouldn't you say?'

'I'd be disappointed,' replied the Dark, 'if I had expected anything else.'

'Then take away the mark,' the Doctor panted. 'You touched my face and left your mark. You're using it to control me somehow. Remove it and let me do it myself!'

'You would inject the drug into yourself of your own free will?' The Dark sounded sceptical.

But the Doctor nodded. 'On one condition.'

The Dark snorted. 'Go on.'

'Do what you will with me but spare my friends.'

'Do you really believe that I would honour such a bargain?'

The Doctor, trembling as he fought the psychokinesis, let out a desperate sob. 'I don't know. B-but it's all I have left!'

The Dark seemed to consider this as the Doctor sagged against the Bloodhunter.

Clearly weakening, the Doctor said, 'Please!'

'Ah! *Now* you beg!'

'I c-can't fight you m-much longer…'

'I know.' The Dark leant closer, staring into the Doctor's pain-wracked face. 'So much for principles. But you wish to make your last act in life your own… Very well.'

The grey mark on the side of the Doctor's face gathered into a black pustule and burst through the skin. The poisoned blood oozed down his face and dripped away into the shadows.

'Thank you,' he gasped.

Then the Doctor whipped around and stabbed the injector straight into the Bloodhunter.

The Dark bellowed with rage and surged forward, suddenly relinquishing its human shape in a flailing mass of tentacles and snapping jaws. It fell on the Bloodhunter as the creature staggered backwards, the neurolectrin injector sticking out of its chest like a tiny arrow.

The Doctor had thrown himself to one side and rolled clear. Tegan and Nyssa helped him to his feet as the air was filled with a terrible, bone-freezing scream.

The Dark had returned to a roughly human shape, a black shadow bearing down on the Bloodhunter. The Bloodhunter responded automatically, latching on to the Dark and forcing its own tentacles and probes deep inside the blackness.

And there it found the blood: the same blood that had been used to reconstitute the ashes of the original Dark.

'What's happening?' yelled Tegan.

'The Dark wants the neurolectrin,' shouted the Doctor. 'The Bloodhunter wants blood.'

The Bloodhunter opened up like a side of meat under a cleaver as the Dark tore into it. The screams were unmerciful.

'They're feeding on each other,' realised Nyssa.

The two beasts writhed and screeched. Although maddened, the Bloodhunter began to succumb to its own wounds. Sensing its weakness, the Dark went into a frenzy and suddenly the Bloodhunter was torn apart. The Dark literally wrenched it in half and threw the quivering flesh across the chamber.

For a moment there was a stunned silence.

Then the Dark turned and advanced on the Doctor. 'Pitiful thing,' it snarled. 'A presumptuous trick, doomed to failure! You cannot destroy me! I *am* death!'

The Dark's black hands fastened around the Doctor's neck. The

Doctor gasped and crumpled, his face screwed into a mask of pain. But still he managed to speak through gritted teeth, 'It's not over yet!'

'It is now,' said Stoker.

The Dark twisted its head towards Stoker. She was standing right next to them, holding a gun. Through a scarlet haze the Doctor recognised it as Cadwell's DSA automatic. The muzzle flashed and the Dark's head jerked sideways. Instantly its grip on the Doctor weakened, allowing him to tear free.

He crawled away and turned, just in time to see Stoker fire the next shot.

The Dark rocked back, a jet of black ichor flying from its skull. The Dark shuddered and gagged, unable to comprehend what was happening.

'I'm glad you came to life,' said Stoker, advancing on the monster. 'It means you can die.'

The Dark grabbed Stoker and pulled her close, one giant hand grasping her head and twisting. But even as her neck snapped, Stoker squeezed the trigger on Cadwell's gun and the last round was discharged. The barrel of the gun was stuck deep into the Dark's throat. The back of its neck exploded, flinging black blood and gristle across the chamber.

For a long time the two figures remained together in a macabre hug. Eventually Stoker's lifeless body slipped from the embrace and fell to the floor.

The Dark staggered backwards, choking on its own blood. A look of incredulous horror filled its gleaming black eyes.

'Is it dying?' Nyssa asked.

The Doctor stared impassively at the stumbling figure. 'I don't know. But having taken on a physical form in our universe, the Dark is finally subject to the same physical rules as we are. It *can* die. That, remember, is a condition of our existence.'

A pool of thick, black blood had opened out beneath the struggling monster, oozing slowly down into the empty pit at the centre of the chamber.

The Dark wavered on the very edge of the pit. 'So…' The voice was now a wet rasp of hate. 'Your own cheap trick, Doctor.'

The Doctor shook his head. 'Killing is no trick. It's all too easy.'

The Dark spat out a brittle laugh. 'The irony… is not lost on me.'

'I don't rejoice in death. I don't believe in violence or cruelty. Where I can, I try to save life.'

The Dark swayed, and seemed to wither before them. Its midnight blood gushed from the wounds in its head and neck and spread across the floor. The voice had now fallen to a whisper. 'Then prove it: *save me!*'

The Doctor started forward, but Tegan held him back. 'Don't go near it!'

He shrugged her hand away and stepped around the wide expanse of blood.

'I've already failed here,' the Doctor said, and pushed the Dark back into the open pit. It fell with a heavy crunch into the shadows.

Immediately, there was a sudden, thrashing mass of blackness that defied identification: something reared up from the morass, a head perhaps, with a pair of small, almost human eyes wide with agony and despair. Beneath the eyes was a sagging mouth full of jagged black fangs and membranous spittle.

The eyes fixed the Doctor with a terrible, imploring glare. '*Save me!*' it screamed.

'I can't,' the Doctor said.

'*Help me!*'

The Doctor moved closer, clearly anguished. 'I can't,' he repeated. 'I can't.'

'*Help me!*' the dark mass screeched, spraying the air with blood and filth.

Thin strands of blackness leapt from the pit, lashing at the Doctor with desperate ferocity. He fell back, watching the sinuous cords whip back and forth in an effort to locate him. The strands groped at the air like the legs of a huge, dying spider; leaving a trail of blood wherever they touched. The blood boiled and sizzled and then ran back down into the pit.

Then, impossibly, the thing inside the pit began to pull itself back out, heaving its shrunken torso up on the spindly legs extruded across the chamber.

'It won't die!' Tegan yelled.

Several eyes snapped open inside the writhing mass and glared madly about the chamber.

'It's got to burn,' realised the Doctor suddenly. 'Of course!'

The Dark lashed out towards him and he dived over to where Stoker lay. She still hadn't moved. The Doctor quickly went through the pockets of her vest until he found the cigarette lighter. It felt uncomfortably empty.

The Dark was out of the pit, trailing black slime. It started to crawl towards the Doctor like a giant, oil-soaked spider.

'Doctor!' cried Nyssa. She was throwing something to him. Bunny Cheung's bionic arm skidded to a halt by his feet. The Doctor snatched it up and tore at the synthetic skin until he had exposed the machinery beneath. Then he lit the cigarette lighter and jammed it underneath the arm's power cell. Something inside the arm must have been flammable because fire burst out immediately and singed the Doctor's hand.

He swung the burning limb awkwardly into the path of the Dark. The flames disappeared into its oily gut as, squealing and spitting, the Dark raised itself for a final lunge.

Then the power cell in Bunny's arn exploded.

Bright fingers of flame rose up and grasped the Dark, igniting the film of black ooze that covered it. It shrieked and howled and threw itself backwards. The flames followed it into the pit. With a terrible cry, the thing rose shakily in one final grab for freedom. But the burning tendrils of blackness that formed its limbs could not support it and it sank, with a snapping crunch, back into the well. The fire took hold and it began to quiver uncontrollably, spitting and sizzling.

It took a full minute before the thing stopped moving altogether. Eventually, even its nervous twitching ceased and the monster lay still in death. The flames ate noisily through its remains.

The Doctor turned away from the decrepit spectacle, his face grim. He rested his hands on his companions' shoulders, as if offering reassurance, but also taking comfort from their presence.

'Horrible,' said Tegan with a sob.

The Doctor moved to where Stoker had fallen. She lay with the unnatural slackness of death, her head at an ugly angle. But in the exposed flesh of her neck, a tiny pulse could be seen. The Doctor knelt down and touched her face. 'She's breathing,' he announced with some astonishment. 'It's faint, but she's alive…'

Tegan and Nyssa knelt down by Stoker as her eyelids fluttered open. Her eyes were like little pools of melting honey. They gazed up at the Doctor but did not focus on him.

Her jaw worked as she tried to speak. 'Has… it… gone?'

'Yes,' the Doctor said.

Stoker's eyes closed softly. 'Then I can go now…' Then she smoothly, silently, relaxed into oblivion. The pulse in her throat slowly faded.

'Death after death,' the Doctor said quietly.

Epilogue

The Doctor pulled the lever that controlled the TARDIS doors. They whirred shut behind him and sealed out the rest of the universe. For a few seconds he simply stared at the control console, lost in thought.

'I can't believe we're back in the TARDIS,' said Tegan gratefully. 'Safe at last.'

'Is that true, Doctor?' Nyssa asked. 'Are we safe, now?'

The Doctor nodded. 'The Dark's consciousness died with its physical form. It can't reach us now.'

'How can you be sure?' Nyssa pressed. 'It was destroyed once before, remember.'

'Not like this.'

'What actually happened back there, Doctor?' Tegan wondered. 'I thought the Dark couldn't be stopped.'

'It couldn't. Not in its original form anyway – an immortal, evil intelligence left over from the remnants of the universe that existed before this one. It hung around the cosmos like a ghost searching for a way to exist properly. It nearly managed it on Akoshemon. But when it finally succeeded in taking on life, it sacrificed its immortality.'

'I thought you'd got it when you did that trick with the neurolectrin.'

'Ah, well. That was a pretty desperate ploy, I admit. But I'd seen Stoker, with Silas Cadwell's gun. She was waiting for her chance. In the end that's all I could do.'

'Did you realise... I mean, did you think that she would be killed as well?'

The Doctor glared at Tegan. 'How could I?'

Tegan glanced at Nyssa. Both felt a little troubled by the Doctor's solemn attitude. It wasn't like him to be so taciturn. 'At the end... when the Dark was dying in the pit, asking you to help it...'

'Begging me to help it, Tegan.'

'Whatever. Were you going to?'

The Doctor sighed and leant forward on the console. 'No. It was merely trying to lure me closer. One last chance to kill me.'

'It would never have got the TARDIS if it had killed you,' said Nyssa.

The Doctor began to operate the TARDIS controls. 'No, but it was motivated by the need for revenge, for destruction and death. That is all it had ever known, all it had ever believed in.'

'Then good riddance to it,' said Tegan. 'Why be so glum about it?'

'I was just thinking about all the people who died,' the Doctor said, as he flipped switches and twisted dials with great deliberation. 'And those that very nearly perished.'

'You mean us,' said Nyssa.

'We were the only ones to survive,' said Tegan heavily.

'None of us is indestructible.' The Doctor looked grave. 'I thought I'd lost both of you at least once on this trip.'

Nyssa touched his arm. 'But we're still here.'

'More by luck than design, I fear.'

'Stop blaming yourself, Doctor,' Tegan said. 'You took the risks as well as us. The important thing is that we survived, at least.'

'Yes, we should be thankful for that, I suppose.' The Doctor remained lost in thought, perhaps contemplating the moment when he had thought he had reached the end of the line, too, had been forced to look death in the face. He shivered. 'But there were many, many lives that were lost and destroyed because of the Dark.'

'You mean Vega Jaal, and Bunny and the others,' said Nyssa.

'And Captain Lawrence and Stoker,' said Tegan.

'Yes, all of them,' the Doctor agreed. 'But also the people of Akoshemon. An innocent world corrupted and brutalised by the Dark's presence from its very beginnings. All the people we met in the last couple of days, and who lost their lives, amount to little more than *that* –' the Doctor clicked his fingers – 'compared to the billions of lives twisted and ruined by evil on that planet.'

The Doctor's cold tone provoked an uncomfortable pause. For a few seconds his companions watched the Time Lord resetting the TARDIS co-ordinates. 'What are you thinking?' asked Nyssa.

'That I could use the TARDIS to travel back in time, far enough back in time to prevent the Dark merging with Akoshemon during its creation. Avert the death and suffering of an otherwise doomed world. And thus, perhaps, eventually save the lives of Stoker and her mining team and Captain Lawrence and his crew.'

Tegan said, 'You know you can't do that. It's impossible.'

The Doctor tapped the console irritably. 'I know. I know. But sometimes it's very hard to understand *why*. There are so many things that can be altered, put right. Made better.'

'You're thinking of Adric again,' Nyssa said.

The Doctor looked up sharply but didn't reply. He didn't need to say anything, because the answer was plain to see in his troubled gaze: *I'm always thinking of Adric.*

'What's done is done, Doctor,' said Tegan. 'That's what my Aunt Vanessa always used to say. Just because we can materialise before or after "what's done" doesn't make any difference.'

The Doctor frowned slightly as he thought this through and then managed a faint smile. 'Do you know, Tegan, I think you've just managed to summarise all the Laws of Time put together.'

Nyssa couldn't let this pass. Rather more primly than she intended, she said, 'Surely it's not really as simple as all that!'

'No,' agreed the Doctor. 'But it will do us for now, don't you think?'

He dematerialised the TARDIS and the glass column at the centre of the console began its soothing motion. And, almost as if the ship's transition into the space-time vortex erased all that had gone before, the Doctor's face cleared and his tone lightened. He clapped his hands together decisively. 'Now, I was thinking: it's high time both of you learnt to read some of the TARDIS star charts…'

'Not just yet, Doctor,' protested Tegan. 'I don't know about Nyssa, but I'm beat. I've got to get some sleep.'

'Yes,' agreed Nyssa. 'I think we could all do with a rest.'

The Doctor looked disappointed. 'Well, all right then. In the morning, perhaps.'

They nodded gratefully and left the console room. The Doctor stayed behind, leaning on the console and staring into the bright lights of the time rotor, where the past and future mixed to form endless possible presents.

Exhausted, Tegan and Nyssa retired to their quarters and fell into a dreamless slumber.

Both slept with the lights on.

ACKNOWLEDGEMENTS

Thanks to:

Martine – the only person who could endure the dreaded First Draft.

Justin – trusted editor and a gentleman to boot!

Pete – patiently waiting!

Vicki – agreeing to all my cover requests!